THE SCARLET
TREFOIL

BOOK 3

THE SCARLET TREFOIL

A NOVEL

L. A. KELLY

Revell
Grand Rapids, Michigan

Published by Fleming H. Revell
a division of Baker Publishing Group
P.O. Box 6287, Grand Rapids, MI 49516-6287
www.revellbooks.com

Printed in the United States of America

Library of Congress Cataloging-in-Publication Data
Kelly, L. A.
    The scarlet trefoil : a novel / L. A. Kelly.
        p.   cm.
    ISBN 10: 0-8007-3156-5 (pbk.)
    ISBN 978-0-8007-3156-4 (pbk.)
    1. Dorn, Tahn (Fictitious character)—Fiction. 2. Good and evil—
Fiction. 3. Middle Ages—Fiction. I. Title.
PS3611.E4496S28 2007
813'.6—dc22   2006031913

To my church family at Glory Worship Center in Clayton, with whom I have found a marvelous inheritance. And to Mom and Dad, my grandparents, Smyrna Primitive Baptist Church, and Melvin and Bonnie Fiscus, who each had a part in starting me early on the path of grace.

PROLOGUE

Dearest Lord and Lady,

Your fellow countryman, Lord Bennamin Trilett, with great pleasure announces to you the marriage of his daughter, Lady Netta Trilett, to the honorable Tahn Dorn, whose brave deeds have earned him the highest regard of worthy men. Your presence and that of your sons and daughters shall be welcomed as we celebrate this joyous occasion at eventide on the fourteenth day of the sixth month in this most blessed year of our Lord.
A party open to your noble ladies shall be held in honor of the bride on the prior evening at the home of Lord and Lady Nassur Eadon. Accommodations for all shall be made available there or at the Trilett estate for the celebration. God grant his mercies in travel that you may rejoice with us in this union destined of heaven. Our Lord's blessings be extended to you. Amen.

As the ink dried on his handwritten parchments, Benn Trilett rolled each one and applied a ribbon and his seal. They would be sent by the hand of messengers to the head of every noble house in the land. Save one.

"I still think you should invite him, Uncle," Jarel Trilett said with a sly smile. "I should like to see his face turn three shades of gray as you honor Tahn before the nobles."

"I honor the groom more with his exclusion," Benn answered sharply. "An invitation would require that Lionell at least send a messenger or a representative. He could be brash enough to arrive with a full entourage. And you know very well that Tahn would not be at ease with Trent men about. I wish it to be a day of peace and rejoicing for all of us."

"Lionell *would* add a bit of a sour note, you're right about that."

"He's more than sour, Jarel. He's obsessed. And I, too, shall be relieved to have him absent."

I

The day before the wedding, Tahn Dorn stood on the stone steps of the Trilett house, watching a shiny golden carriage glide up the lane and come to a stop almost in front of him. The silver-haired coachman gave him a merry smile and a nod, but instead of responding, Tahn turned his eyes toward the stable and guardhouse. Where was Josef? He and the other men should be standing at the ready to escort Lady Netta. If she must go to this party, at least she should go with a full guard.

As though he had heard the thought, Josef led his horse from the stable at that very moment, followed almost immediately by four of the other men. Then the last three came riding from behind the guardhouse. *Good*, Tahn thought. *They're armed and ready.* He turned his eyes to the carriage once more and finally gave the old gentleman at the reins the courteous nod that was due him.

"Are you the Dorn, sir?" the coachman asked him.

"Indeed."

"Congratulations to you," the man said pleasantly. "May God bless your union."

"Thank you."

None of this seemed real. Finally, the day had nearly come. Tahn looked down for a moment at the stone stairs. Why wasn't he sharing the joy that floated around him like water in this place? Everything was fine. The children were all well, and excited. He was happy. There'd been no trouble since leaving Alastair almost nine months before. This was the grandest time he'd ever known, and he knew he was blessed. But an old fear still lingered inside him, dark and numbing, as though everything that mattered could still be snatched away.

Behind him, the estate house door opened swiftly, and Tahn spun around. But it was only Netta's cousin Jarel coming out to meet him on the steps.

"What's the matter?" Jarel laughed. "Did you think Netta would try sneaking up on you?"

Tahn turned his eyes again across the courtyard to the approaching guardsmen. "I *am* waiting to see her off. But it would please me better if she were minded to stay."

"What bride is there to shun her own bridal party?" Jarel exclaimed. "Relax. There's nothing to fear from the House of Eadon. The party shall be all women, and Netta's father has approved the guest list. There's no cause for concern. Besides, it appears you're sending the lady with a small army—"

"Her party should have been held here."

Jarel shook his head. "Netta has no sisters. So the Eadon girls have a right to be hostesses for her. They're among her oldest friends. Besides, *your* party will be here. We couldn't possibly have both—"

"I wanted no party."

"I realize that," Jarel replied patiently. "But if you're going to marry Lord Trilett's daughter, you'll have to accept some attention and ceremony now and then. It will be fun for you tonight, I hope. You have friends coming."

"My friends are no more used to noble parties than I am."

"I'm aware of that too. Deeply. And it does pose quite a challenge. *I* may be the one to feel out of place."

Tahn studied Jarel's expression but said nothing in reply. Josef, still leading his mount, strode to the side of the ornate carriage and made a quick bow toward Tahn and Jarel on the steps.

"Ride two to the front and two to the back of the carriage as you go," Tahn instructed him. "Two to each side as the road allows."

"Yes, sir."

"Tahn—" Jarel interrupted. "You needn't act as captain of our guard during your wedding time—"

"If I thought less about her safety now, I could not claim to love her." Tahn turned his attention quickly back to Josef. "Please stay in waiting at the door once you escort the lady inside, and do your best that you're not late bringing her home."

Jarel shook his head. "One who didn't understand could think you had a jealous streak, Tahn. Lord Trilett has been careful. If he thought there was any danger tonight, he would not have agreed to this."

"I expect he is right," Tahn answered. "This should be an occasion for my lady to enjoy. But I would still thank you to be watchful, Josef." He glanced again at Jarel. "Perhaps I'll be called a worrier without cause. I hope so. Or jealous. I don't care. I've been called far worse."

"You'll certainly never be called lighthearted."

Tahn didn't answer Jarel. His eyes moved beyond the carriage in front of them, toward the gate where he'd heard a distant noise.

Jarel put a hand on his shoulder. "I don't mean to belittle your caution or your heart to duty, Tahn. I do understand. Though I wish you could be at ease."

"Someone else has arrived."

Jarel smiled. "So we can expect, with the noble guests beginning to grace us. But perhaps it's some of your friends. I hope they have such excellent timing, to take your thoughts from Netta's absence. Shall we go and see?"

Tahn didn't have time to answer before the gilded door behind him swung open again. With a sudden leap of his heart, he turned, knowing what he would see. Netta stood at the top of the stairs in a green satin gown and pearls, her auburn hair done up with ribbons and fresh flowers yet still cascading down in waves in the back. She was such a glorious vision that he had to catch his breath. And he wasn't the only one. He heard what sounded like admiring sighs from the old

11

gentleman at the carriage behind him and from at least one of the guards.

"Netta—" he started to say, but her merry eyes met his immediately, and he stopped. A bright smile spread across her face, and she came skipping down the steps in her embroidered slippers to snatch him into her arms.

Jarel cleared his throat. "I believe I'll go and greet whoever it is at the gate for you, Tahn. No need to trouble yourself."

"Tonight will be splendid!" Netta exclaimed as though no one else was even there. "And I can scarcely wait for tomorrow!"

She kissed Tahn, and he spread his arms around her and returned the kiss, drinking in all he could of her. Everything about her, everything, was marvelous. More than the satiny gown and the intoxicating perfume. She was more than beautiful. Godly, loving, trusting, and kind. *Lord, help me,* Tahn prayed. *It is almost too much. Too good to be true.*

"Netta, I wish you would stay here with me," he told her.

She kissed him again. "I would like you to be where I am as well. But you'll have your own guests tonight. I don't belong in the middle of that, and the bride's party is no place for the groom. We have to let everyone have their fun tonight. Beginning tomorrow we can be together always."

"I didn't want a party. I'd rather be with your guard."

"I know. But Father and Jarel do well to honor you. And you should have a good time with your friends. I want you to."

"I only wish to be alone with you," he told her, feeling suddenly small. "I've been thinking again about Lionell Trent—"

Gently she put her finger to his lips. "Don't. He's a fool not to let himself know you. To decide you must be all the dog he is, before ever meeting you to learn for himself! I don't want to hear his name now. I don't want you to think of him. This is our time, and he cannot touch us here."

Tahn couldn't answer. His eyes were drawn to the clear

peace shining out of hers, and he was hungry for it, hungry to believe that the troubled days were finally over.

"Everything will be all right," she assured him as she took both his hands in hers. "These are capable men you're sending with me. More than necessary for a blessed occasion so close to home. I'm sure they'll be dreadfully bored with their evening." She smiled again, radiantly, and in the warm breeze one long wispy curl moved from its place to kiss her forehead.

With a sigh, Tahn drew her close to him again. "Perhaps you're right. But I'm glad your father was willing to oblige me with the double guard for you. I'll rest easier at your cousin's table tonight. It's hard for me not to worry."

Netta stroked his hair softly. He felt a wonderful warmth spread through him. He didn't want this moment to end.

"You seemed so at ease only weeks ago," she whispered. "And there has been no sign of trouble. But now that the wedding draws near . . . Tahn, perhaps you're only nervous. It wouldn't be strange for you to worry along with the nervousness, or mistake such feelings for a cause to fear, considering all you've endured . . ."

He'd thought such things himself, that the pain, the horrors of his past, had prepared him only for wariness and not for the joy she so much wanted to see in him right now. "Maybe you're right," he agreed softly. "But we don't know that Lionell's heart has changed. Though his words of late have been peace, it would be wrong for me to forget him."

With gentle understanding in her eyes, she kissed him again. "We trust. We rest in God's hands. I love you, my friend."

"I love you too." *Thank you, God, for such a thing as love.* He looked into her eyes, wanting to ask her not to stay late at the Eadon house, but before he had the chance, she spoke again.

"I won't linger long into the night. I promise you we'll leave before the chime of ten. You can rest assured of that. So forget me and enjoy your party."

13

"You are impossible to forget, my lady."

She smiled. "As much as you are. But you know what I mean." She touched the old scar across his left cheek and then gently kissed him again. "I should be going. The sooner the night is done, the sooner we'll have tomorrow."

He nodded.

"I wish your sister was coming with me," Netta said with a glance across the yard. "She should. She has every right."

Tahn sighed. "She feels far more comfortable here with the children. She's planned games for them. They're having their own party."

"Good. But you know I tried to include her."

"Maybe she's a bit like me."

"Yes. A bit." Netta lingered for a moment after a glance at the waiting carriage.

Tahn lifted her hand and gently kissed it. "Don't let me darken your thoughts, my lady. Have a pleasant evening. Please."

"Oh, Tahn. You'll be in my thoughts, but not to darken them. I dream of the future and all God has in store for us."

Softly she kissed his cheek and brushed her hand against his hair, and then she turned. The aroma of her perfume lingered with him even as she stepped away. The coachman climbed from his seat to open the carriage door for her, and accepting his hand, she stepped inside.

Josef mounted his horse and rode to the front of the carriage with a salute toward Tahn. "Upon my life, sir, she'll not leave my sight."

"Thank you."

Netta wore her infectious smile as the carriage began to move. With a wave she called to Tahn again. "Enjoy your party."

"And you the same," he answered with his heart suddenly in his throat.

The carriage disappeared quickly down the lane toward the gate, and Tahn found himself feeling strangely empty.

"My," a voice behind him was suddenly saying. "She looks *real* nice tonight."

Tahn hadn't heard anyone else come near, but he turned to find his young friend Vari on the steps behind him. "I thought you had eyes only for Leah Wittley, the farmer's daughter," Tahn chided him gently.

"Well, that's true. But I'd have to be blind not to notice the lady dressed so fine as that. It's like a dream—the life we got now. Like a dream come true."

"Yes."

The one word seemed all Tahn could say. He patted Vari's shoulder and lifted his eyes again toward the gate. Vari was only fifteen but had always seemed much older. He was one of Tahn's closest friends, the eldest of the captured street children Tahn had rescued. But that all seemed so long ago now. Almost forgotten in this blessed place. Even the nightmares were faded away. He should be able to be happy now, the way Netta wanted him to be.

"Is something bothering you, Tahn?" Vari asked.

"No," he answered softly, thinking of Netta's words. "We rest in God's hands."

Jarel was crossing the courtyard with three men who had come from the gate. Tahn recognized the Toddin brothers immediately, they were both so tall. And the other man who traveled with them could be none other than Lucas, now a priest's aide in Alastair, and Tahn's earliest friend.

It seemed strange to greet them here, strange to see their smiles and receive Lucas's brotherly embrace when he drew close enough. It seemed not so long ago that they were all in danger because of him, because of enemies he'd never asked for and pieces of the past he couldn't help.

"Tomorrow's the day!" Marc Toddin exclaimed merrily. "Are you nervous, Dorn? I certainly was when *I* married." But he stopped and gave Tahn a quizzical look. "Do you ever *get* nervous?"

"He gets pensive, that's what I'd say," Jarel put in. "Lorne is already here. And Marcus, of course. Tobas and Amos Lowe should be arriving soon. That's not many for a party,

I know. But your Dorn here wouldn't let me invite anyone else. The estate may be full of noble guests, but they'll be entertained separately for most of the evening at your friend's insistence."

"You required me to tell you who I'd be comfortable with," Tahn answered the charge. "There isn't anyone else. Except the Wittleys, and they'll be here tomorrow."

"I couldn't get any agreement over good entertainment either," Jarel continued, turning to the Toddins. "Would you like to eat first?"

"A bite after the journey would be welcome," Marc answered.

"We'll have food aplenty," Jarel was quick to assure them. "But besides that, it won't be your typical party."

"We couldn't expect a party for Tahn Dorn, even a groom's party, to be typical," Marc answered with a slight smile.

"No dancing girls, I suppose," his brother Lem lamented.

"Why would he want them?" Lucas asked sincerely. "When he's got Lady Netta in his dreams?"

"A blessed man," Lem Toddin agreed. "But tonight should be full of revelry. Every sort. Last chance, after all."

Tahn shook his head at him. "Last chance for what? To think of myself alone? I want no entertainment I'd be ashamed for Netta or her father to see."

Lem frowned and said no more. But Marc Toddin offered a quick suggestion. "Maybe all the children you've taken in have some lighthearted antics they'd share before the evening's gone. My own children love pretending, and that can make for a silly show. I know what I'd like most tonight, and that is to see the Dorn laugh."

Tahn looked at him. Why would it matter to Marc Toddin, or anyone else, if he laughed? He had. He was sure of it, though he couldn't think of a time just then. And Lucas and Jarel were both looking at him far too seriously.

"I can't even picture it," Jarel said. "Not that it's your fault, Tahn. There's been nothing very funny—"

"Stop," Tahn told him before he could say more. "There

are funny things enough around here now. Not the least of which is the way you try to treat me as though I were a rare bird. Enough of that. Let's go eat. These men have ridden a long way. And I'm sure Hildy's prepared a feast."

A feast it was, and Tobas and Amos arrived from Onath in time to share in some of the grandest dishes Tahn had yet seen, even after all the time he'd spent with the Triletts. There seemed no end to the food, and Tahn tried his best to enjoy it. He tried to turn his mind from worries and act as lighthearted and comfortable as the men around him. They were all good men, men he could trust. Lucas, with whom he'd shared so many dark days of the past. Lorne, Vari, and Marcus, all barely more than boys, who'd been part of the same captive world that he and Lucas had known. Thank God they were free.

Tobas was a longtime friend of the Triletts who'd been quick to befriend Tahn when first he came here. Amos Lowe was a skilled healer who'd been needed more than once. Marc Toddin, who had once dutifully tracked Tahn for hire, was now a friend who, along with his brother, had not hesitated to put himself at risk in Alastair for Tahn's sake.

Jarel was the only Trilett among them tonight because his uncle, Netta's father, would be dining with his noble guests and hosting the separate entertainment on their behalf. Jarel had been more distrusting of Tahn than anyone at first. But his acceptance now was so strong that he'd been anxious for this wedding even before Tahn had been able to manage asking for Netta's hand.

Tahn was glad they would all gather and sit around this table for him. It seemed a miracle of God that each of these men would come here and call him friend.

"Jarel and I spoke earlier today," young Marcus was suddenly saying around a bite of Hildy's pudding. "We agreed that a little activity would be in order after the meal this eve. It takes more than fine food to be merry."

Tahn raised an eyebrow. "I've heard few suggestions. What did you have in mind?"

"Something a former warrior should appreciate. I want to demonstrate my bow to you, Tahn. And then challenge the lot of you to try it."

Tahn smiled. "Your bow? I've heard about that. You bagged the pond the other day, and in only one shot."

"I'm getting better. Really, Tahn. I think the bow could be useful to us. I know you weren't trained at it, and Benn Trilett has never employed bowmen, but think of the range in a battle—"

"If you want to show your new skill, I'll be glad to see it," Tahn agreed. "And to try my hand if that's what you want. You can set us up a target. Perhaps I'll put you to training some of the men before long. You're right to consider it. A good barrier that would make, with bowmen at the wall."

"I had a lighthearted target play in mind when we discussed this," Jarel confessed with a sigh. "Not more talk of battles and defenses."

"Once a warrior, always a warrior," Marc Toddin told him. "You can't stop the way they think, your lordship."

"Perhaps not, and we've had reason to be grateful for it a time or two," Jarel conceded. "Still, I wanted nothing tonight but a little friendly contest—"

"A contest it will be, then," Tahn challenged obligingly. "If *you* are shooting."

Jarel laughed. "I'll be shooting. And happy to find something where we can begin on even ground. I've no more touched a bow than you have."

The words conjured a bitter memory suddenly, but Tahn would not show the force of it. True that he'd never touched a bow. But arrows had felled him to the dirt once. He realized that Marc Toddin's eyes were on him and wondered if he were thinking of the same painful day.

"Anyone for pie?" Vari asked suddenly.

"I'll have a mite of it," Lem spoke up.

He wasn't the only one. Pie was passed around the table

till it disappeared, though Tahn could not stomach anything more.

"You might actually gain some meat on your frame with food like this around you every day," Marc Toddin commented.

"He'd have to eat a lot more of it first," Vari said. "I think I out-eat him three to one."

"You're still growing," Tahn replied soberly.

"Is everything all right, brother?" Lucas asked him with a solemn expression.

"Yes," Tahn answered simply.

Lucas studied him a moment. "Perhaps a prayer is in order before the party progresses. Let us bless the coming union and your life together."

"Amen," Tobas agreed quickly. "You're good as a priest, Mr. Corsat. Continue. Please."

Tahn nodded his head. "With my thanks, yes."

Quietly, Lucas began his simple prayer, for blessing upon the ceremony and both the bride and the groom. "Be a covering by your Holy Spirit, Almighty God," he continued. "That they may live free from fear and be a blessing to others as they have already been. Prosper their lives together that they may have joy, safety, and peace."

"Amen," Lorne echoed when Lucas was finished. For a moment, no one else said anything.

"Thank you," Tahn finally said.

And as though that were a dismissal to something else, Jarel stood to his feet. "Well, shall we enjoy young Marcus's bow skill while the evening is young?" He plucked an apple from the table's centerpiece. "A toast to the first man to plant an arrow through the center of this."

Soon everyone was outside, and Marcus passed around his hand-carved recurve bow for everyone to admire. Behind the house, they could hear the voices of children. Tahn's sister, Tiarra, was apparently leading them in a merry game beside the stream. Lorne's eyes drifted in that direction, and Tahn thought surely he would rather be in Tiarra's company. It was no secret how the two felt about each other, which pleased

Tahn greatly. Life was good here. They'd been blessed in so many ways.

Vari assured the group that Marcus had become quite a good shot after plenty of practice, but in front of everyone he couldn't seem to hit the target at all. His first arrow sailed wide of his chosen tree by nearly two feet, his second by not much less.

"Ah, well," Tobas joked. "At least we're safe from your aim here alongside you."

"Focus," Tahn told Marcus, leaning back in the grass with his legs crossed. "You don't care who's with you. That's a bandit with a broadax. If you miss again, he'll have your head."

Jarel gave Tahn a strange look, but Marcus nodded and turned his eyes solemnly to the tree again. He was quiet for a moment, staring, slowly raising his bow. And then he let loose with his arrow and hit the tree trunk almost dead center.

"Yea!" the young man exulted. "Got him!"

"So falls the bandit with the broadax," Jarel said with a sigh. "Are you ready to try your hand, Tahn?"

"After you."

Marcus turned and offered Jarel the bow.

"You all want a good laugh at the noble son first, eh?" Jarel joked. "I don't think so. It's your party, Tahn. You go first."

Tahn rose to his feet, willing to play along with the occasion. "You've as good a chance as I have," he said. "Let's try one shot each at our bandit tree, and then see who can fell that apple."

He took the smooth wood in his hands and turned it over to admire the workmanship. "Who made this?"

"Abias Cain, brother to the new guardsman, Olath."

"Oh yes. When you see him, tell him I said well done."

"I will." Marcus smiled and handed him a short-shaft arrow. "He makes these too. I'll have to get more. I've lost one and broken one."

Tahn fitted the arrow to the bow the way Marcus showed him and glanced across the courtyard at their "bandit" tree.

"Focus," Marcus prompted.

Tahn smiled in reply, but when he turned his eyes to the tree again, he thought suddenly of Burle, once a fellow warrior, never a friend, now a bandit whose men had twice attacked his sister in Alastair. Lorne, Lucas, Vari, Marcus—all of them were hated by the man because they were Tahn's friends. Burle was huge, big as a tree, with a swift and deadly sword. Almost before Tahn realized it, he let his arrow fly. It was swift and true and hit the trunk just above Marcus's. Right at the neck, Tahn thought, and then shook that thought away.

"Well done!" Marc Toddin exclaimed.

Without a word, Tahn handed the bow to him and sat in his place again. Marc's shot was very low. Vari's was almost with Marcus's, and Jarel, Tobas, and Lem Toddin missed the tree altogether. It was Lorne who made the best shot over all, and Tahn found himself wondering if he'd pictured the very same villain.

No one could hit the apple from forty paces, though Marcus swore he wouldn't truly rest until he managed the trick. But clouds had covered the darkening sky, and Jarel invited everyone back inside. The children had gone in just before them, and the first raindrops fell as Tahn reached the pillared porch.

"You have a beautiful home here," Lem Toddin remarked.

"It's not finished," Jarel answered. "Not for Tahn and Netta. Building is well under way for their own house on the eastern side of the estate. It'll be as big as this one. It'll have to be. I imagine the children will be running through it every day the same as they do here. And there may even be more, soon enough." He turned his eyes to Tahn with a gently teasing smile. "May you beget for Benn Trilett grandchildren. Many of them. A dozen or two. Or more."

"I'll leave that to the Almighty," Tahn answered. "And to Netta."

"I daresay you'd have to have some kind of a hand in it,"

21

Lem Toddin added with a laugh. "Have you ever known a woman before?"

Tahn looked at him with a frown. "I'm not sure what use could be made of that information if you had it."

"None at all," Lem admitted. "Just simple curiosity. The city of Alastair found you frightening, but I'm sure that was temptation to more than one woman. My own wife just got one glimpse of you out her window, and she said you were the sort to draw anyone's interest."

"As a gazing-stock," Tahn replied. "Especially in Alastair. A curiosity. Until the double-edged reputation can be deciphered."

Lem laughed. "True enough spoken. I've heard squabbles in Alastair still over whether you are a murderer or a saint."

Lucas spoke up quickly. "Let the promised toast be unto God, giver of grace."

"Well enough, since none of us won the apple," Jarel agreed immediately, ushering everyone inside for refreshment.

Tiarra brought the children to greet the group and sing a song that Netta had taught them. And then when she took her leave, Lorne disappeared for awhile with her.

"They'll be the next ones," Marcus remarked.

A group of musicians had come out from Onath to perform for them, and Tahn listened patiently to the sounds he supposed were very good but that held little interest to him. He couldn't fathom at all the juggler who came next. Why would anyone wish to spend his time perfecting such a pointless skill? But some of the other men seemed to enjoy watching, and Tahn supposed that idle noblemen might pay enough for the man to make his living at it.

As the evening wore on, Tahn's thoughts turned to Netta again. Without trying, he found himself very aware of the hour and calculating in his mind the time she should return. Jarel, Tobas, and Amos Lowe did their best at teaching the rest of the men the game of chess. Lucas was the only other one of them who had ever played, after being introduced to the game by his mentor, Alastair's priest.

"Is there a virtue to this?" Lorne asked after awhile. "Some benefit to the thinking?"

"So it is said," Amos told him. "It can teach you to watch and think at the same time, and to out-plan even a skilled opponent."

"Any fight will do that if you let it," Marcus complained. "I don't think I'll ever have the knack for this."

"It's far better than fighting to my mind," Vari observed. "And it's not too hard. Just remember that knights and bishops never take a normal line, and the queen exceeds all in power."

"What do you think, Tahn?" Lucas asked.

"The carriage should be back soon," he remarked absently. "Perhaps I'll ride out to meet it."

"Don't," Jarel protested. "Netta will think I bored you completely. And I promised her you'd have a good time."

"It has been good. I'll be sure to tell her."

"Give it some time, please," Jarel continued. "She may choose to linger longer with her friends. It's a special night. Let her have her fill of it."

"Be white to my black, Tahn," Marc Toddin challenged. "I'll run you a merry chase across the game board."

Reluctantly, he let himself be delayed. She wasn't late, not yet. Surely Jarel was right. Netta might stay to the last moment, enjoying her party and her old friends more than he was able to. Netta knew something about parties, after all. She'd been raised by Bennamin Trilett in a household that once gave them and attended them often enough. It must feel wonderful to enjoy that life again.

Perhaps she'd been missing such things since the tragedies that had brought them together. Tonight's was the first party any Trilett had given for anyone since seven Triletts were murdered almost two years ago. Sometimes it seemed longer. Tahn wondered how often Jarel thought of it, if he still mourned his parents, his brothers, and the others who were lost. Jarel, Netta, and Benn Trilett were strong people to carry on at all.

He sighed and moved a knight in answer to Marc's ad-

23

vance of a pawn. *I don't think I'll ever get used to this*, he thought. *I hope Netta does get her fill of the noble festivities, because I will make her a miserable party companion.*

Though chess was about focus just as much as aiming an arrow could be, Tahn's mind wandered to the night he'd stolen Netta from her bedroom in that other Trilett house, now destroyed by wicked hands. He'd meant to save her life, though she'd hated and feared him for it at first because she didn't understand. And it was still a regret that he'd not been able to find a way to spare more of the Triletts alive.

"Ho! You've got to watch, Tahn. I've got you in check already."

He moved a bishop to block Marc's zealous maneuver and smiled, thinking about Netta's boldness in the cave where he'd hidden her with the fugitive children. She'd stood up to him, despite her fear, for the children's sakes, and that was something he could greatly respect even then.

"You're far away," Marc said as he captured a pawn.

"It's like a dream," he answered, "to play a battle that isn't real."

"It must seem so to you," Marc agreed. "I've thought much about such things. I don't think there are many men who could make this kind of change."

"It's God's gift, Marc. Not something I've done for myself."

"Takes some of both, don't you think? You've made strong choices and gone from killer to saint in a very short time. But not a killer true. Not with a killer's heart, and I'm sorry to use the term."

"Perhaps not a saint true, either," Tahn answered soberly. "Lucas toasts well the grace of God. There's nothing in me without it."

Marc smiled and captured a knight. "Perhaps you should pray for your game."

"I doubt the heart of God cares any more than I do who wins or loses at this. It's an exercise for me, I guess. In the occupation of peace."

"May you become very good at it."

Tahn stared down at the board for a moment. "Samis would have laughed me to scorn for such play as this."

"Samis was demon spawn and not worthy of remembrance."

Lucas turned his head to look at them. Tahn took a deep breath. "I think it is a good thing to remember. The gift of God. Our freedom. A new life." He glanced at Lucas, Lorne, Marcus, and then Vari. "In remembering Samis, we can't fail to see the miracle of God that brought us out of there. And the blessings we have now."

"That's just the thing to tell myself," Marcus said with a sigh. "The next time he invades my dreams."

Lorne bowed his head for a moment and then looked up at Tahn with a solemn expression. "Forgive me, but it isn't only Samis in my dreams anymore. The baron walks even into my waking thoughts and makes me wonder if I'll have to kill again one day. For your sister's sake, Tahn. And yours."

Jarel rose to his feet and clapped his hands. "Let's have those musicians again for a merry tune! The baron has no place at all in this party."

As the musicians regaled them again, Tahn tried to turn his mind from such thoughts the way Jarel wanted him to. But Lorne's admission was far too true for him to be able to accomplish that. Perhaps all of tonight was one big game. Playing at peace when he knew as well as Lorne did that the matter was not settled. The baron. Lionell Trent. For all his months of silence, his noble talk, his feigned peace, he was still minded the same. Tahn knew it, and there was no use thinking otherwise. Lionell would have heard of the wedding by now. And he would be fuming, fretting, beside himself trying to find a way to see Tahn dead.

Tahn stood to his feet, too uncomfortable even to pretend to enjoy the music. "Netta's on her way home by now," he announced. "The tenth bell has struck. I'm going to ride out to meet them."

"Tahn," Jarel called. "You sent her with eight men, plus the coachman. More than enough escort on her way."

He took a deep breath, unwilling to betray his thoughts to them. "She'll not mind seeing me come to greet her. Nor any of you, if you wish to ride along."

"We can't be sure she's even left yet," Tobas countered. "It's not that late, and women love the chance to talk without the ears of men. She may still be enjoying her party, and hoping you're doing the same."

"Then I would find that out if we see no carriage until we reach the Eadon house."

"It wouldn't be good form to show up there," Jarel cautioned. "The groom has no invitation."

"She'll have left when she told me. I don't expect to go halfway." Tahn went through the door to the hallway that led to the front entry. Vari jumped to his feet and hurried after him. Without a word spoken, Lucas followed them, and then Lorne.

"*Now* what shall we do?" Jarel asked the others.

Tobas heaved a sigh. "There can be no more groom's party without the groom. Perhaps we should follow."

Jarel nodded. "All right, then. Go and let my uncle know our party is riding to meet Netta. And tell Hildy. We should all be back shortly, and tea might be in order then."

"You will go too, sir?" Tobas asked with surprise.

"I was charged to host Tahn's party. I think I'd better stay with him."

"All right, sir. I'll meet you at the gate."

Amos sighed. "Perhaps you'll all forgive me if I wait for you here. I'm not the horseman some of you are, and I don't take to riding at night. I'd rather wait for the opportunity to greet the lady here if I might."

Jarel nodded. "Make yourself comfortable. Enjoy the music. I'll not require anyone else to come along."

"Seems the party's going riding, though," Marc said. "Come on, Lem. Let's join them."

"Might as well," Lem said with a sigh. "A ride in the

night air may be the most entertaining thing we've done so far."

<hr/>

As Tahn reached the front entry hall, his sister, Tiarra, was halfway down the curving staircase.

"The little ones are all abed," she told him. "Is Lorne still busy?"

Her tiny smile hid just a bit of excitement, and he understood very well her feelings for his friend. "No. I'm sure he'd be happy to sit with you."

"Where are you going?"

"To meet the carriage."

Tiarra hurried the rest of the way down the stairs. "She's not late, is she?"

"She's due. Soon."

"Oh, Tahn. Perhaps Netta would like to walk in and find you in the midst of your party, smiling and happy. That's what she wants for you. There's nothing to worry about. Is there?"

Her eyes were so clear, so hopeful. He didn't want to upset her. "I don't think she'd object that I couldn't wait any longer to see her. And I've learned by now to do what I feel I should. Perhaps she's been hoping for me to meet them."

Tiarra stood quiet for a moment, as if studying him. She drew a deep breath. "There's more than what you're saying. The baron would not dare extend his hand here. Would he? Surely not! It's Trilett lands—"

"I said nothing to alarm you—"

She put her hand on his shoulder. "But . . . but I see it in your eyes, Tahn."

He pulled away. "I'm just riding to meet her."

"With plenty of company," Lucas said suddenly as he and the others joined them from the hallway.

"Lorne," Tahn called. "Please stay with Tiarra. She was

just seeking your company. Marcus, you stay with them too. That would be the proper thing."

"What need that I sit with them?" Marcus protested. "Amos Lowe is still in the parlor."

"Good. He can teach my sister that game of his, and you can go and get her some pie, if Hildy has any more."

"Tahn . . ." Tiarra began, but he had already opened the door and was on his way out.

"He seems rather driven," Marcus remarked with a sigh. "I suppose it'll hurt nothing to do what he says."

"I think he had all the party he could stand," Lem added as he and his brother stepped outside. "It's a good time for a ride."

The night was warm, but rain began to fall as they crossed the yard to the stable. Tahn said nothing to the others as he saddled Smoke and led him out into the weather. He knew the other men probably thought him ridiculous for doing this. There was nothing wrong with the shelter of the house, no certain reason to leave it. But this was a compulsion he wouldn't ignore. When the rain increased as they left the stable, he expected most of the others to turn back. To his surprise, none of them did.

"Wet or not, we may as well have a merry ride," Marc Toddin said with a smile. "I believe our coming will surprise them."

"They may have cause to appreciate our arrival if a carriage wheel bogs in the mud," Lem suggested.

"They have enough men for such a mishap," Jarel told them. "More likely for Josef to think I've gotten you all drunk. Or that you've gotten *me* drunk."

"Perhaps we should be drunk," Lem added with a lopsided grin.

"Night air with good company is far better for the soul," Tobas informed them.

Tahn drove his horse forward without a word to them.

And Lucas rode first behind him with the Lord's Prayer on his lips.

Tiarra's words churned in Tahn's mind as they passed the gate. *The baron would not dare extend his hand here. Would he?* These were Trilett lands, far from the baron's strongholds to the north. Lionell would be a fool to come here. Lord Trilett had assurance from every noble house in the land that they would take arms against the baron if he attacked them. It would be madness for Lionell even to try. That was why everyone was so confident.

Low thunder rumbled in the distant west. Why could it not be clear tonight? With full moonlight?

"When are they due, my brother?" Lucas raised his voice enough to ask him.

"Any moment. She promised me she would leave before the tenth bell, and I expect she might have gone before, for my sake."

"There's a chance she'll forget to note the time."

"She'll note it. Or she would not have promised."

Lucas stayed as near to Tahn on the roadway as he could. From his look, Tahn knew he understood better than the others the unrest he was feeling.

"I'm sorry," Tahn told him just loudly enough to be heard in the rain.

"For what?" Lucas asked.

"This trouble tonight. I'm sure you came for merriment."

"A ride in the rain is no trouble. And I pray there's nothing to your concerns beyond that."

"I pray the same."

They rode in silence for more than two miles, following the road south and west of Onath. The rain did not let up. Tahn knew that at least part of his group had hoped and perhaps expected to meet the carriage well before this.

A sense of dread plagued him as he drove his trusted horse, Smoke, farther from the Trilett estate. His friends were quiet. He could imagine their discontent with him to be growing.

Why had he agreed to these separate parties before the

wedding? Why hadn't he found a way to convince Benn Trilett of the foolishness in it?

He hurried Smoke along, expecting some of the others to turn back to shelter. But they were loyal friends. Good friends. Better than he'd ever known to expect. Perhaps better than he deserved.

"*It's not your fault, Tahn.*" Netta's long-ago words echoed in him strangely, and he didn't understand why such things should be entering his head now. But Benn Trilett had made it a point more than once to tell him the same thing. "*You bear no fault for the folly of Lionell Trent, Tahn. You've not even met the man. It is madness, his rage against you.*"

Madness, almost certainly. But that was far from a comfort.

He took a deep breath and strained to see as far down the road as he could manage. Why must he keep thinking such thoughts? Why couldn't he trust as Netta did, that everything would be all right? They'd had no indication of trouble from the baron since leaving Alastair. And they'd been careful. Very careful. He hoped Josef would laugh when he saw them coming. He hoped Netta would sweetly rebuke him for his lack of patience. But as they rode on, and the night advanced around them, he knew he wasn't wrong to wonder. It'd been too long now. They'd gone much farther than they should have needed to.

After a time, the rain quit and the moon broke through clouds. Tahn stopped his horse to allow the others to catch up as they approached a bend in the road.

"Let us hope they're just ahead," Jarel said quickly when he was close enough. "Josef will likely think we've taken leave of our senses."

Let us hope, Tahn echoed in his mind, feeling too heavy to answer the words aloud. He prompted his horse forward, and Smoke obeyed him as always, but as they neared the bend ahead, the horse gave a toss of his head in protest. Tahn knew Smoke well enough to understand what that meant. With his heart pounding mercilessly, he advanced with caution, knowing something was wrong. Just ahead where the road bent into the trees, he began to see a dark shape lying in the mud. And just beyond that, he thought he saw movement. Tahn threw up his hand to signal the others to stop.

No one said anything. The large thing moving in the trees seemed to retreat, but the shape in the mud did not move. Tahn drew the dagger he'd worn at his waist and moved forward on foot. It took but a few steps before he realized that the lump on the ground was a body. Beyond it, at the edge of the trees, was another, and behind that was the creature Tahn had seen moving, a riderless horse standing restlessly, as if waiting for one of the dead men to rise and tell it what to do.

Tahn bent cautiously over the first body to see if life remained, though he was almost certain what he would find. It seemed plain already that nothing was left of this soul but a dark and crumpled heap on the roadway. But when he touched the lifeless man, he thought he recognized the collar of his cloak, the curl of his hair. With his heart in his throat, Tahn rolled the body enough to be sure. Josef.

Tahn couldn't speak. He couldn't call to the others. He ran forward to the second body. Eduard, another of the men he'd so carefully sent with Netta. *God, no! Where is the carriage?*

"Tahn!" Tobas called behind him. "What is it?"

He heard footsteps, and he knew the others did not wait for his answer. He couldn't answer.

Jarel cried out behind him. He'd recognized Josef, of course.

"He's got the marks of swordplay," Marc Toddin pronounced. "But his own weapons are gone. Even his boots. It looks like the work of bandits."

"Bandits would take the horse," Vari pointed out, his voice sounding pinched and grave.

"This horse is wounded," Lucas's voice answered him.

Tahn couldn't focus on their words. A short distance away, on the road ahead, lay two more bodies. Another man, nearer the trees, showed weak evidence of life. Tahn knelt beside the struggling man and took his hand. "Where is the carriage?" he pleaded. But the man could not answer him.

"Tobas!" Tahn called, feeling the press of dread deeper than he'd known for so long. "Tobas!"

The big man ran to Tahn's side.

"Evan lives. Please. Tend him." He could say no more. He turned away.

"Tahn?" Tobas addressed him softly, but he rushed away in his search.

Another man lay facedown in a ditch, head nearly severed from his body. If the attackers were bandits, they were vicious indeed. Skilled, to fare so well against armed men. Six were here fallen. But there had been two more guards, plus the coachman. And Netta. The rich carriage would have made a fanciful sight trotting down the road with its attendants, but there were no bandits known here. And if they'd happened here by chance, why would they dare attack so many?

"Here!" Vari suddenly called, and Tahn rushed to find the young man kneeling beside another survivor.

"Bandits," the fallen man croaked out, his voice sounding as though forced with great effort.

"How many, Jarith?" Tahn pressed him. "Who were they?"

But the man could not answer him.

"Which way? Did they take Netta with them?"

The fallen man turned his head only slightly, toward the woods. The old coachman lay dead just a few feet in that direction, and near him the remaining guard was stretched lifeless at the base of a tree. Down a slope in the mud lay Netta Trilett's gilded carriage, on its side, the horses gone. Tahn ran to it, frantic, and wrenched the carriage door near off its hinges. But it was empty. Lady Netta was gone.

32

2

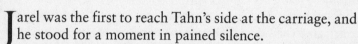

Jarel was the first to reach Tahn's side at the carriage, and he stood for a moment in pained silence.

"She may be hiding," Tahn tried to assure him quickly. "She may have run from them."

But the young nobleman sank to his knees. "It was ruthless men, Tahn. And she is such a fair one—they would take her, wouldn't they? If they could?"

The words were like poison to Tahn's spirit. The trees seemed to whirl about him, and he could scarcely breathe. "Indeed." It was all he could say.

"Why? After all we've suffered! These good men dead! And Netta gone!"

Tahn couldn't bear the words. He grabbed Jarel by the arm and pulled him to his feet. "We haven't time to mourn," he insisted. "Not now. You must take those who live back to Amos at the estate. Take Tobas and Vari to help you. Go."

Jarel seemed dazed. "You will search?"

"Yes. Give word to Lord Trilett. Ready more men for us. If we can find the villains, we will have need of help."

"I can stay with you."

"Evan and Jarith may die if we wait," Tahn insisted. "You must take them *now*."

Stiffly, Jarel nodded his agreement.

Soon Tahn, Lucas, and the Toddins stood alone with the dead in the darkness. This was supposed to be a night of

33

joy, of celebrating the blessing of marriage to come. But a nightmare had descended. Tahn drew a heavy breath. *Dear God, may Evan and Jarith live. May Netta live. Help us find her!*

Marc Toddin bent low to the ground and then turned his eyes upward. "Would God I could show you some sign, Tahn, but it may be futile in the darkness after such a rain. What tracks I find are almost certainly our own."

Tahn nodded to him in silence. He had no way of knowing how long ago this attack had occurred, nor for how long the rain had been washing the bandits', and Netta's, tracks into oblivion. Halfway he expected Marc or Lucas to suggest that they wait until morning to search when some sense could be made of things in the dawnlight, but neither of them did. They stood beside him when he called Netta's name into the blackness. And as they began their search in the trees, he could hear Lucas's quiet prayers.

"Hallowed Father, maker of heaven and earth, God of all that is good, guide our steps. Preserve our sister . . ."

Tahn could not have said anything more if he'd tried. Breaths came harder, as though he'd been kicked in the chest or lost his wind in a fall.

"All the pain is over," Netta had told him just days ago. "You can have peace. The past is done."

But she'd been wrong.

It was bandits that did this, Marc had said. And Jarith had seemed to confirm it. Tahn's mind raced over what they knew. Seven men gruesomely dead. Two more gravely wounded. All of them had been robbed of their weapons and possessions. And all of the horses had been taken except the injured one. Many men had done this, Tahn was sure of that. Skilled men who had probably lain in wait. He could not accept the occurrence as mere chance. Not on such a night as this.

Tomorrow he would have held Netta in his arms as his

wife, but now she was most likely in the hands of killers. Too well Tahn knew the things that could happen, might already have happened, and he felt like he was dying inside. He never should have let her leave his sight.

They called and searched, but the moon hid from them again, and it all seemed to no avail. No sign could be found in the dreary darkness. And they had left the party without full weapons, something Tahn upbraided himself for now. Reluctantly, he went back with the others to the Trilett estate for their swords and for more men. The guard at the gate met them with news that the surviving men yet lived but neither had been able to waken and tell them anything more. Tahn expected to go only to the guardhouse to gather what he needed. But before he got there, Lord Trilett sent for him. And the thought of facing Netta's father right now made his stomach feel like lead.

"I'll go with you," Lucas immediately volunteered.

But Tahn could not allow the gesture. He ran alone across the courtyard, not wanting to lose any more time than he had to. The familiar steps at the front of the grand house were difficult, as though his feet were somehow weighted, and he couldn't help thinking of Netta standing here only hours earlier, smiling, holding him in her arms. But he shook the picture away and the tug of emotion it had brought with it. Benn Trilett had called for him. He'd surely been expecting a boisterous bunch of revelers returning to his estate, and this news instead must be awful to bear.

Tahn wasn't sure what to expect from Netta's father. He wasn't even sure how he himself would react inside the marbled room where the nobleman conducted most of his business. Everything seemed to be closing in on him all at once. But he took a deep breath and forced himself through the paneled doors. Benn Trilett stood at his desk waiting, with one hand against the back of his great oak chair.

"My Lord Trilett, sir," Tahn cried immediately, bowing his head away from the pain in the nobleman's eyes. "I'm so sorry—"

"Tahn—"

"We've found nothing . . . and I'll not linger here . . . with your permission." He reached behind him to the door again.

"Tahn, stop. I would speak with you. Please."

Benn hurried forward, and Tahn noticed Jarel against the wall on one side of the room. But he wanted to rush away from them, back to the searching. There was nothing he could tell them. Nothing more than he'd already said.

"I'm sorry, my lord," he said again, aware this time how his voice came out shaken, strained, so much that he hardly sounded like himself.

"Tahn, no one is blaming you. You could not have helped—"

"Yes! I could have! If I'd listened to what I've known all along!"

"It is my fault more than yours, son. You cautioned me. You cautioned all of us."

"I sent men to their deaths."

"Trying to protect her! You did the best you knew. And it was more than any of us thought necessary. You cannot blame yourself."

"It was my responsibility . . ." Tahn tried to turn away, his head still down. "My lord, I need to go."

Benn took hold of his arm. "I know you do. I wouldn't expect anything else. But I want you to stop first, please. Think about this. What might be done to help? You saw what was done. Tell us what you would have our men do."

With a deep breath, Tahn tried to calm his heart enough to respond. "Send someone to the Eadon house, my lord. Perhaps it would avail us nothing, but if we knew when Netta left her party, at least we would have some idea how long, how far . . ."

"Yes, I understand." Benn raised one arm gently around Tahn's shoulders, and the gesture was such a shock that Tahn could not speak in answer. "Was there any indication who these men might have been?" Benn continued. "Or in which direction they've gone?"

"No, sir."

"You're shaking, son."

"It is nothing."

"Could you tell how many?"

"Only that our men were surely outnumbered. And taken by surprise. Whoever the men, they were skilled, and they took their own wounded or dead, if there were any."

"Is there any reason to suspect Lionell?"

The words were like a sick weight pressing against Tahn's stomach. "There is every reason. But no sign. No evidence at all."

"It may be rogue bandits. But I wish to tell the other nobles all I can. What would you have me say?"

Tahn nodded. "Every searcher is welcome. Every man they would give us. When the villains are found, there will be a fight."

"I have already received pledges of help among the guests. And anything else that's needed, son, you'll have it. If a ransom is required, I'll pay whatever the amount. We'll find her, Tahn. By faith, and with God's help."

Tahn nodded again and turned to the door, too overcome to speak.

"Godspeed," Lord Trilett told him, but the voice was that of a wounded man trying to sound strong.

Tahn hurried away down the hallway and back outside. Vari met him at the base of the steps, but neither of them said anything as they crossed the courtyard.

In his guardhouse room, Tahn strapped on his sword and took up the extra knives that he had once always worn in his clothes.

Too good to be true, that's what all of this had been. He'd been kidding himself, thinking all the battle was done. He should have gone away, far away from here, so that Netta would have had no more part in it.

Father God, she is an innocent lady with a gentle heart! Bring her home to her father's arms again!

For a moment he wondered at his prayer, that he didn't ask for Netta to be returned to his own arms. But maybe it wasn't meant to be. And with the entrance of that thought came a blackness like the dread in his past, turning his mind from the happiness he'd dared to hope for.

Some of the men urged him to rest until the daylight, but he couldn't. Not when Netta could be out there somewhere suffering the unspeakable. He set out again, with torches this time, and men armed and ready for whatever they might find. But there was no way to know where to look.

3

Netta struggled against the ropes at her wrists as the horse beneath her kept pace with the mounted men. Loathsome villains, filthy murderers, wicked thieves. The sight of them, the smell of them, was horrid. She wished she could scream as they hurried her along into now-unfamiliar territory. But a tight cloth gagged her, and with her bound hands secured to the horn of the saddle, she could do nothing.

Her head was throbbing since the spill she'd taken when the carriage overturned, but worse than that had been the wrenching sight of her guardsmen lying dead or dying. What could be the purpose of such an attack? The dreadful men had told her nothing, not a word, just bound her, set her on a horse, and began their flight away from everything she held dear.

"She's a prize, this one," a man at her left was snickering. "All dolled up an' everything. Be a pleasure to get to the Ganders' and have a little fun."

"Don't be an idiot," a larger man answered him. "Business before pleasure. You know that. We get our gold first."

They rode on briskly, six of them, with the horse they'd put her on tied by a length of rope to the two on either side. There had been more men. Netta wasn't sure how many. Two groups had split away from them shortly after the attack was done. And they'd been far too many. Too skilled and too quick. They'd felled three of her guardsmen before they had a chance to know what hit them, with knives thrown from their hiding places alongside the road.

And then they'd come leaping out from all directions with their swords.

She drew in a breath and trembled to think of these harsh men's words. There was no good in what they had planned. Who would pay the gold they spoke of? Her father? Might they already have asked a ransom?

With barely another word, the men rode what seemed like endless miles. Netta tried to determine where they were or which direction they were going, but they'd left the road behind, and she just couldn't be sure. She was terribly thirsty, weary and sore when the first glow of dawn began to show through the trees ahead of them and to the right. At least now she knew which way was east.

By now her father must be frantic. By now Tahn would be searching, maybe following, with his sword at his side. He'd find them eventually, she was confident that he would, but what would happen then? *Lord, why? This is our wedding time! Could it be your will that instead of knowing joy, we suffer this way?*

Finally in the growing light she saw a small stone dwelling in the woods ahead of them. Another structure, probably a barn or a stable, stood behind it. It seemed that this must be their destination, at least for now. As soon as they'd drawn near, the rough men around her stopped and dismounted. One tall and thin fellow took several of the horses for the others and led them around the back of the house. She was surprised to see a candle's glow in the window. Was someone here? Waiting for them?

One of the men, with a scraggly black beard, stood looking at her. "Lordy, she's a fine one. Forget about business. I say we lift her skirt—"

"Not yet, fool!" came an angry voice behind Netta. "That'll be soon enough. If all goes well."

"I tell you it ain't reasonable to expect us to wait around just lookin' at her!" the black-bearded man whined. "If he takes her off someplace we could miss our chance—"

"Shut up, Cole. You get the chance when I say you do, and not before then."

Netta's heart thundered within her, knowing all too well the subject of their argument. And the forceful voice behind her was somehow familiar.

"How's he gonna know?" The first man continued his complaint. "What difference would it make—"

"The difference is he's paying us extra to get at 'er first! Double! And I wanna see that gold. He'll know if you touch her, mark my words, and I'll take any loss out of your hide."

Suddenly the huge man who had been speaking stepped alongside the horse and cut the rope away from the saddlehorn. He grabbed at Netta's waist, and she struggled all she could, but there was no way she could get away from his grasp. He lifted her and threw her over one shoulder as if she were a sack of grain.

"You be good," he told her with an icy chuckle. "Pretend I'm the Dorn."

Netta tried her best to scream despite the gag, kicking at the man as hard as she could.

"Does he like you feisty?" the man laughed. "You're gonna be fun, all right, when the time comes."

Oh, God! She pleaded. *Help!*

She thought he would carry her to the house, but instead he went alongside it toward what looked like nothing but a mound of earth several yards distant. Not until he'd gotten very close did she realize that there were steps beside it leading downward to a doorway. It was a simple root cave, probably dug by peasant farmers years ago. Apparently, it was to be her prison now. She tried to fight the man again, tried to struggle as he carried her down the steps, but it did her no good. He simply hauled her through the doorway into the tiny dismal room, plunked her onto the hard floor, and held her down with his foot as he pulled her arms free of the loosened ropes and re-tied them behind her back.

"There now. Be a little harder to wrench yourself loose. Don't need no shenanigans out of you, lady."

Struggling to catch her breath, Netta looked up into his loathsome gaze.

41

"Ain't no doubtin' what he sees in you," the rough man told her, still looking her over. "Question is, what in all blazes do you see in him?"

Spiteful words. And such a familiar, horrible face. Suddenly Netta knew who this was standing over her. Burle. The despicable man who had taunted Tahn so horridly last autumn when they left Alastair with a newfound sister and the answer to some of the puzzles of Tahn's past. Burle was a leader of bandits who hated Tahn enough to try to kill him, but the presence of Trilett men had backed him down in Alastair. What was different now? Why had he traveled all this way, to do this evil? The double gold he spoke of? What monster would make him such an offer?

"Think your Dorn'll come for you, Lady?" Burle suddenly asked with a snort. "He'll know soon enough what this is about."

She closed her eyes for a moment, trying to put together all the things she'd heard. She was a prize to be used viciously, she could not doubt that. But what about Tahn? Burle seemed to want him to come searching. Maybe that was the whole point of this. Of course Tahn would come, if he had any inkling how to find her. But surely he would bring a troop of men with him to rescue her and apprehend these men, or slaughter them if need be. He would do what had to be done.

But Burle laughed as though he had heard her thoughts. "You think somehow he'll win out, don't you? People say he's charmed. But he's weak, Lady. He's always been weak. That's why it's so easy to bait him."

She shook her head, on the verge of tears as her captor gave another snort and turned to the door.

"I let you get by with kicking me while I carried you in here," he told her. "But if you give me any more trouble, you'll get the back of my hand. Do you understand that? Highbrow lady or not, you can be brought down to size."

He slammed the door behind himself then, and she could hear the heavy sound of a bolt being set across the wood outside.

Only tiny cracks of the dawnlight were visible to her now, but she could hear Burle's rough voice shouting as he climbed the stone steps. "Jud! Bring me my horse! And see that nobody opens that door till I'm back."

He must have left soon after that, and not alone. Netta heard the sound of horses. But other men remained. She heard them once or twice outside, their voices too muffled to make out what they were saying.

In the oppressive darkness, she tried to muster her strength, but there was no way she could loosen her hands even a little from the ropes that held them so tightly. She thought of the tragedies her family had known, and all that Tahn had suffered and survived for so long. That was more than enough death, and sorrow, and pain. It was supposed to be behind them now. She was supposed to be blissfully wed. This very day.

Like a dam breaking, tears rushed over her, and there was no holding them back. She and Tahn were supposed to be able to live happily now! Safely! *Oh, God, why this? Why now? It's not fair!*

Helpless and weary, sore from the saddle and the mistreatment, thirstier than she ever remembered being in her life, Netta tried to remember some Scripture from the Holy Writ to give herself peace.

"He that endureth to the end, the same shall be saved."

The passage drifted into her mind like a breeze. And then another.

"Why art thou downcast, O my soul? Hope in God . . ."

You are my hope, she prayed in the stillness of the cave-like room. *And you are Tahn's hope. We are in your hands.*

4

Tiarra paced about in the Trilett drawing room, unable to stay still. "This isn't right. We should be helping in the search."

Lorne took her arm and spoke softly. "Your brother commanded that I stay with you."

"You could ride beside me as we go!" she protested. "We could join them together!" Furious, frightened, she pulled her arm away from his grasp.

Lorne shook his head sadly. "You mustn't go outside the gate. Tahn charged me especially. He told me to stay—he wanted an extra guard in the house."

"Does he think we are all under siege?"

"He knows the danger," Lorne answered her with a sigh. "Think about it."

"We don't even know who has done this evil!"

"If it is the baron, you could also be in danger. If it is rogue bandits, killing men and snatching women, you are a feast to the eyes the same as Netta. Your brother would not risk you leaving this estate, Tiarra. Nor would I."

She turned from him, her heart pounding, her fists clenched tightly. How she wished there was something she could do to let off the explosive fury inside her. "How could they? To slaughter a peaceful company. A thousand curses on Lionell Trent! And all men of his ilk! I long to meet him one day!"

"I pray that you don't. I pray it every day."

He sounded so broken that she stopped. She turned to him again, and his head was bowed.

"Perhaps my own fears have brought this," Lorne continued. "For days I've been tormented with thoughts that he would not just leave Tahn to this happiness . . ."

A lump rose in Tiarra's throat, and she found it suddenly difficult to answer him. "Would he . . . would he kill Netta, just to hurt my brother?"

Lorne drew her into his arms. "I don't know. If Lionell has abandoned reason enough to do such a thing as this, he might do anything."

Tiarra's heart ached. "Then almost I wish I could have set a guard over Tahn, to keep him safe here as well."

But Lorne shook his head. "You know him too well for that. We could sooner have stopped the sun from shining."

Tiarra leaned into him as he cradled her in his arms, but she could feel no real comfort. Kidnappers, murderers, held Netta in their grasp. Who could know what might already have happened to her? And she could not help the feeling that Tahn's enemies were at the center of the matter. Seven men dead. And Netta gone. It could all be designed to tear at her brother, to set him out searching. They would be waiting somewhere. She could almost picture it. She wished she could warn him, but she knew he would not stop his search for Netta regardless of any danger to himself.

"They will try again to kill him," she whispered gravely to Lorne. "I wish there was something I could do."

"I think he would want us to pray."

She nodded, leaning her head against his shoulder. Lorne took her hand and began his prayer with solemn voice. "God in heaven, in the name of Christ, send your angels . . ."

━━━

Miles away in the village of Jura, a man named Saud leaned his back against a building on Market Street and waited, glad to be away from the unpleasantly necessary company of bandits for a few moments. It should not take long to find what he needed here. He would borrow a tactic from Samis, the now-dead master of villainy, and snatch a boy off the streets.

He could appreciate the irony of using a child to help snare someone who seemed to care so much for children. Tahn Dorn was a puzzle he'd grown weary of thinking about. He would be glad when the man was finally dead. Dorn was a snake, trained by Samis in the brutal art of killing, a ruthless fiend who pretended to be a hero in order to win his way into Trilett graces. That much he did not question.

But Dorn was also a fool who'd risked himself to rescue Samis's captives. He'd walked into a trap for the sake of a girl he didn't even know. He'd let himself be whipped in Alastair to spare his sister's back. And now the bandits were confident that he'd give himself up to them for Netta Trilett's sake. Everything depended on it, though it made no sense whatsoever.

Saud looked out over Jura's streets as more and more people stirred from their houses. Dorn's own foolishness would kill him. As it should. A truly worthy schemer could find a way to protect his own hide and still maintain Benn Trilett's favor.

But the Dorn wasn't interested in protecting his own hide. That's what some men said. Nor did he need to be, if he was charmed as the rumors had it.

Saud could almost laugh at that notion. It was nothing more than ridiculous to think that angels or demons might protect any man, but especially the Dorn, from the mortality that should have overtaken him long ago. Dorn was lucky, no denying that. He was still breathing. But he would die soon enough, and that should quiet the superstitious. Saud wished it could be his own hand to do the deed. But perhaps it would be satisfaction enough just to see it finally done after all this time.

A poorly dressed boy with dark wavy hair ran from a nearby building, and Saud tensed. This child was bigger than the Dorn had been when Saud had first hunted him, but there was a strange resemblance just the same. The boy

46

looked afraid already. He was hurrying down the street on quick little legs as though he were seeking someone.

Hastily, Saud followed, thinking of the time he'd searched through a long night for the Dorn when he was a boy no bigger than a water urn. The scrawny little whelp had escaped him. He seemed to be always escaping. But no more. Now it was time to put the pieces of this new plan together and end such unfinished business once and for all.

The boy who ran Jura's streets carried a small package in one tightly clenched fist. Saud didn't know what it was, but if it had value to the boy that would only work to advantage. He drew ever nearer to him until they'd left the sparse crowd of Market Street and he saw his chance. Where a muddy side street turned away between two buildings, Saud caught up to the boy and jerked him quickly into the shadows, clamping one hand tightly over his mouth. With his other hand he drew a dagger and held it against the child's throat.

"You'll do as I say, boy. Everything. Or I'll kill you. Do you understand?"

Shakily, the boy managed a terrified nod, never once loosing his hold on whatever it was he held in his hand.

"You'll come with me," Saud told him icily. "And if you cry out, I'll leave you to drown in your own blood. Is that clear?"

Again, the little boy nodded, and Saud felt a rush of satisfaction. He would love to hold the Dorn's life in his hands this way. But if he could not personally have Dorn's neck, then perhaps he could find a worthy substitute when the time came. Perhaps Netta Trilett or this dark-haired boy. Or better yet, Dorn's own sister or one of the street urchins he'd labored so hard to save. Any of them might make a pleasurable kill, a fitting finale for all this effort.

Victory by blood. The revered words suddenly filled his mind. He'd seen them so many times, carved onto a doorpost in one of his lordship's great houses, woven into the tapestry that hung in the council chamber. They were words

47

he'd come to appreciate so much that he'd had them graven into the hilt of his own sword.

Victory by blood. The Trent motto for generations. And he could not imagine one that suited him, or this present circumstance, any better. So let it be, indeed.

5

With a heavy heart, Marc Toddin continued his hunt for any kind of track that could lead to the attackers. Searchers had gone in all directions from where the carriage had been found, and Marc hoped at any moment to hear a signal horn from one of them, to tell that they'd found something. But there were no signals sent.

With Lucas and Tahn still near him, Marc concentrated his attention on the winding stream that meandered only two horse-lengths from the road in some places. The rain had been a curse. It had washed away any available sign near the carriage. But the villains could not have known how the rain would work for them. Surely they would have planned their route in advance, thinking they had to be careful. And the stream was an obvious choice.

Marc followed the stream first one way and then the other, but he knew he could not be sure that any sign he saw now belonged to those they sought. All of this seemed to be a frustrating exercise in futility.

"There's no use, Tahn," he finally said. "I had no track to start with. And with more guests arriving and the searchers out, there's no way I can confirm one I see now. We can't tell which way they went, or in how many ways. I'm sorry. If only the rain had not been so bad—"

"There will be a way."

That was all Tahn would tell him, and Lucas said nothing at all. The search continued, futile or not, and Marc prayed for a scrap of fabric to be found, a bit of one of the carriage horse's bridles, or anything that Tahn could recognize and that could give them a direction. But there was nothing. Marc began to doubt that the men they sought could be simple bandits after all. Would men like that bother to be careful? He had first thought this whole thing to be random violence against Trilett wealth—just eager men happy to line their pockets with whatever they'd happened upon. He should have known better. With Tahn Dorn involved, nothing was ever quite what it appeared.

Marc glanced in Tahn's direction, afraid for the things that might happen next. There was nothing Tahn would not do to help someone in danger, especially someone he loved. That had been proven without doubt. And he seemed driven now, possessed almost, with a fiery intensity, because he loved Netta like no other. Marc felt such heaviness that he had to pray for his solemn friend.

"This burdens my heart, Lord," he whispered, careful that no one else could hear him. "I fear it will all end badly. But let it not be! God, is it not time that the Dorn knew peace?"

Hours passed in the fruitless searching, and Tahn's frustration grew. There must have been many men and horses. And they had escaped with even more horses stolen from the Trilett guards and carriage. Had it been daylight, such a group would surely have been seen. He had sent men to the town and even to the scattered farms to ask if anything had been noticed in the night, but there was nothing reported. He wasn't sure what else to do.

With heavy heart he continued to search the woods for any sign that might be discovered. Finally he heard a horn blast to the east, and for a moment his heart quickened. But it was only three short tones. A message. Not something found. With a sigh, Tahn lifted the signal horn tied to his belt and answered the call. Lucas and Marc both drew near, and soon a rider from the Trilett estate met them.

"Lord Trilett sent me to the Eadon house and told me to

report to you," the man explained. "They say Lady Netta left there earlier than expected last night. Before the ninth bell. They are saddened by what has happened and wish to help in any way they can. Irzam and Caden Sprade rode back with me from there to help in the search. They are with Tobas now."

"Thank you," Tahn told the man heavily. "It seems the assassins may have had plenty of time to gain distance before the worst of the rain even started."

"Master Jarel also wished me to tell you that Jarith is awake again. He thought you might have questions for him."

Tahn nodded. "Thank you."

"A message in return?"

He looked down at the soggy ground. "No."

"I have drink with me, sir, sent from the estate. And bread, if you need it."

"No. Thank you." He gestured toward Marc. "Give to my friends if they wish it, and the men beyond the ridge to the west of us there."

Tahn turned away from them then. He had no more heart for the company of their words. He mounted Smoke in silence and rode into the trees. But someone followed, and he knew without looking that it would be Lucas.

"Stay here," Tahn asked of him. "Continue for me. I need to ride alone awhile. I'll go to the estate and try to speak with Jarith. Perhaps there's something else he could tell us."

"Let me come with you," Lucas's solemn voice answered.

"I wouldn't pull a man from the search."

"But it's part of searching to help you learn what we can," his friend countered. "I don't want you to ride alone. You're exhausted, and this is too much to bear."

Tahn turned to him, barely able to conceal a sudden fire. "You would worry about *me*? When Netta lies missing or in villainous hands? Don't, brother."

"Tahn—"

"I said don't."

51

"It only makes sense that you should have someone with you," Lucas persisted. "In case you should encounter something on the way."

"You think there will be men between here and the estate?" Tahn snapped at him. "They are long gone!"

Tahn kicked Smoke abruptly into a trot, but behind him he could hear that Lucas followed. He was angry about it, though he wasn't sure why. Lucas was the friend who understood him best, who'd been through the most with him, and Tahn knew his heart without question. But Lucas's love and concern seemed a mockery right now. *What good is it? Why should he misplace his worry so? I don't deserve a pittance of it! Netta's the one in need!*

Not even in Alastair had Tahn felt such a weight of hopelessness press against him. *God! This is my fault! It should never have happened! But there must be some way now! You will make a way. Netta loves you. She prays. She trusts. God, I know you'll not leave her. I know you're with her. Bring her home, Father! Keep her safe.*

The prayer was strangely painful, and Tahn struggled against a mist in his eyes as he rode. Keep her safe? How could he begin to hope she could be that? She was a lovely, innocent noblewoman, far too beautiful for her own good, and dressed in the finery of a party besides. He knew what a temptation that would be to vile men. He had known many who would not hesitate to hurt a woman, to take from her what they wanted and then destroy her when they finished. He could almost picture Netta's ravished body lying in a ditch somewhere, but he shook the image forcefully away.

No! Father, lead me. I will do whatever I must, that her life may be spared. Forgive me! I should have known not to stay with the Triletts, not to let her love draw me in. I'm only a danger to her. It was selfish of me to think otherwise.

The sun struggled to break free from clouds as Tahn urged Smoke toward the Trilett manor. These were familiar woods as he grew nearer, beautiful hills where he'd often gone riding with the children or with Netta's cousin Jarel.

Those had been pleasant times. But now heaviness hung over everything like a fog.

Lucas drew nearer again, but Tahn said nothing to him for the rest of the ride. He knew as they approached the estate that Lucas's concern was growing, but he couldn't address that again without something raw rising up inside him.

Soon the Trilett wall was in view, and then the gate. Not far from it, sitting against the weathered stone, a dark-headed little boy lifted his head as they came closer. He looked like he'd been crying. For a moment, Tahn thought it was one of the boys he'd rescued, that Lord Trilett had adopted. But this boy he'd never seen before.

Any other day, he might have spoken to the child, but at that moment the guard at the gate opened to them. "You bring news?"

"No," Tahn confessed sadly. "I bring questions. For Jarith if he can answer them. I am told he wakes."

The guardsman nodded. "If it can be any comfort, sir, my family is in prayer."

"Thank you. Please, tell them thank you." Tahn turned his eyes again toward the little boy, who'd risen to his feet and stared at them.

"A beggar, sir," the guard explained. "I told him that today you are all occupied with weighty matters."

Tahn closed his eyes for a moment and then nodded. "Nonetheless, please do what you can to meet his need."

He rode through the gate with his heart pounding. Something about that boy and the look in his eye was like a wound. It wasn't unusual for beggars to come here. Not anymore, when so many had heard what Benn Trilett had done for the street orphans.

But he had to turn his mind again to the problem that faced him. With Lucas at his side, he went to find the healer. On the way in, he could feel himself trembling inside, still struggling with his concerns for Netta and his sorrow for those who had died. Most had left families. Every one of them had been good men whom Tahn had selected person-ally for the duty. The burden of that was heavy.

Evan and Jarith lay on adjacent beds in a large room in the east wing of the estate house, neither yet able to rise. Amos Lowe was still with them, and Jarel came quickly into the room from another door. Evan was pale and unconscious. His torn shirt was open, and Tahn knew well enough about sword wounds to wonder if Evan would yet leave them. His breaths were shallow.

Jarith was stronger, trying to sip from a cup the healer held to his lips. Tahn moved beside them.

"Is there any news?" Jarel asked immediately.

"No," Tahn answered somberly. "I'm sorry."

Jarel nodded. "I had only hoped there might be something found—"

"Nothing." Tahn's eyes turned to Jarith, who looked up at him and struggled to speak.

"I . . . I'm sorry, sir."

Tahn clasped his hand. "Can you tell us how many men?"

"I . . . I don't know. Many. Behind the trees. I couldn't tell—"

"Behind the trees?"

"I was . . . I was hit before I saw anyone. A knife. Thrown from the trees. Then men rushed at us with swords . . ."

"Did you get a good look at any of them?"

"Too . . . dark. Too fast."

Tahn nodded, though his heart felt like lead. "It's all right. It's not your fault. Did they say anything? Any names, anything at all?"

"Not at first. But . . . but one asked if they had the lady. They went away . . . I . . . I couldn't stop them . . ."

Looking down at the man's wounds, Tahn knew it was a wonder he was even talking to them. He'd had a knife in his side. Sword wounds to the chest and arms. Tahn took a deep breath. It was a struggle to ask him more. "Did they take the lady?"

The man was shaking, his eyes raw with pain and regret. "I didn't see . . . I think I blacked out . . ."

"Do you know how the carriage was overturned?" Tahn

persisted with his heart pounding. "How came it to be off the road?"

"The coachman . . . he . . . he tried to get the lady away. I tried to follow them, tried to fight. But the bandits were rushing us. I . . . I fell from the horse. I don't know what happened. I'm sorry . . ."

Tahn sighed. "It's all right, Jarith. You did what you could to fight them. You couldn't have done more."

"The lady is not found?"

"No," Tahn answered, closing his eyes for a moment. "She is not found."

Lucas offered prayer then, for the wounded men and for Netta. But Tahn found it hard to linger and listen. Any other time, he would have appreciated the prayers, and he did now, but he wanted to rush out and put his hands to something practical. Lucas was a man of God, and Tahn deeply respected his bravery and commitment ministering to the street children of Alastair. But right now it seemed they should rush out with their swords. There must be some way, somehow, for them to do something.

"Thank you," Tahn told Lucas softly when his prayer was finished. Lucas didn't answer, only looked long at him as they started back outside.

It's been hours, Tahn was thinking. *Without a sign. Already into the afternoon. And Netta and I were to be married this very eve. That can be no coincidence. The devil does not choose his timing at random.*

Tahn would have gone to his horse again and left quickly, but as they crossed the courtyard, the guard from the gate hurried toward them. "Dorn, sir," the tall young man called. "I hate to trouble you—"

"What is it?"

"The lad outside. You charged me to meet his need. And I tried. I offered him money. But he insists he must speak to you. I tried to tell him that you told me to give to him and send him on, but he won't leave. He said you're the one he came to see."

"Did he give his reason?"

"No, sir, he wouldn't tell it. I tried to explain that this is a terrible time. Shall I try again to send him away?"

Tahn bowed his head for a moment, almost unable to answer. He'd been asked for at the gate before this. Trilett kindness was widely known. But it was not unusual for someone to come and ask for the Dorn now. He supposed it was because of the tales that had been circulating since he left Alastair. Some even called him Tahn the Merciful, though he'd never venture to claim such a name for himself. Almost surely, the lad was an orphan. It was difficult to turn his mind in such a direction, but this timing too might be no coincidence.

"Let me speak to the lad for you," Lucas offered. "Under the circumstances, if you don't wish—"

"No," Tahn answered wearily. "Go get yourself something to eat. Rest a moment. I'll see the lad before we go back."

"Are you sure?"

"We can't just turn him away when he's come to us for solace."

Lucas nodded, though his eyes seemed uncertain.

Stop, Lucas, Tahn wished he could tell him. *I am not the one to be troubled over.*

But he did not try to speak his thoughts. Instead, he turned to the gate.

The boy was almost in the same place he'd been before. He wasn't very big, maybe only nine or ten years old. His clothes were torn and dirty. His cheeks were wet with tears. He looked up and then jumped to his feet as Tahn approached him. The fear in his eyes shone strong and unmistakable, but he didn't run away.

"I've come to speak to you as you asked, lad. Do not fear."

"You—you're the Dorn?"

"Yes. Why do you seek me?" Slowly Tahn stepped closer,

well aware of the child's near panic. "I'll not hurt you. Please. Tell me what it is that troubles you so."

The boy's eyes darted to the guard at the gate behind Tahn. "Please, sir. I—I must speak to you alone."

The words struck like a hammer blow to Tahn's gut. Secrets were too often born of evil. And this boy clearly feared the thing he had to say, or the response he might get. Tahn began to doubt that he had come of his own accord to beg bread or shelter or anything else. He turned to the guardsman behind him. "Stay with your post. We will walk into the trees."

He motioned to the boy to follow him. "Come. You have my word I'll not hurt you. Tell me what you must."

Trembling, the child followed him. Tahn walked into the nearest stand of trees until the Trilett gate was no longer in sight. He sat upon a fallen log beneath a great oak and motioned for the boy to join him.

"What can I do for you, lad? You've nothing to fear from me."

"Y-you've lost a treasure b-better than gold," the boy recited, dropping suddenly to his knees. "Do everything you're told or she . . . she will die by morning."

"Who sent you?" Tahn asked immediately, anger like a dark cloud rushing over him.

New tears coursed the child's cheeks. "Oh, sir . . . please . . . I don't know his name! You have to let me go . . . please . . . my mother might die!"

Quickly Tahn moved to his own knees in front of the boy. "Tell me what you mean. I'll not keep you. What am I to do? Where is your mother?"

"In Jura."

"She is in danger from someone?"

"She's sick. And I'm scared she'll get worse! I went to get medicine. But a man, he—he grabbed me and took it. He said I had to do what he said!"

"And he brought you here?"

The boy nodded. "He said if I didn't give you his message they'd kill a lady and it would be my fault. And I'd never get my mother's medicine back."

"Please, then. Tell me this message."

With fearful eyes watching warily, the boy pulled a crumpled, rolled paper from his shirt and placed it in Tahn's hands. It was tied with a satiny green strip of cloth that almost made Tahn's hand tremble. A piece of the waist ribbon of Netta's gown. He knew it because it seemed like only moments ago he was holding her in his arms. Hastily, he slid the ribbon from its place and unrolled the stiff paper. The few words didn't take long to read.

Brader's Point. Alone. By sunup. Tell no one. Let no one follow. Or the lady will die.

The little boy took a deep breath. "I'm sorry. I didn't want to do this."

"I understand, child."

"He—he said you'd be angry. He said you might hurt me."

Tahn bowed his head. "No. This is not your fault. Did you ever see the man before?"

The boy shook his head.

"What did he look like?"

"He was big. And ugly. With a dagger and a long sword and a brown horse. He said he'd kill me if I didn't come with him. I couldn't help it! But I thought . . . I thought *you* might kill me too."

"I'll not hurt you, child. Where did he leave you when he brought you here?"

"At the edge of that town—Onath. He pointed the way for me to go toward the wall. And he watched to make sure I didn't try to run away."

Tahn looked about them in the trees. "But there is no one near us now. He's not watching. Why didn't you run before I got here?"

The boy swallowed hard. "I didn't want him to kill a lady because of me. And I need to get the medicine back. I wasn't sure he wasn't watching."

"I think whoever he is, he'd not stay and risk that I find

him." A cloud of anger stirred in Tahn's heart. This was so much like something Samis would have done, to snatch up a child and terrorize him, to use him for his own ends. And someone had dared coming very close in order to do this. But neither he nor the guards had seen or heard any indication of anyone. "Did he tell you anything else, lad?"

The boy's lip trembled.

"I must know. Please. You've nothing to fear."

The boy struggled to continue. "He called it a trade. If you come alone. They'll let her go because it's you they want. Sacred honor." He stared, the fear still plain in his eyes. "I'm sorry, sir. I'm real sorry."

Slowly, Tahn nodded. He could not be surprised, except at the boldness of the words. Sacred honor? That was a spoken pledge worth more than life, or so it was said.

"You mustn't tell anyone," the boy prompted, the tears still on his cheeks. "Or that lady, whoever she is, is going to die."

"I understand, lad."

"Are *you* going to die, sir, if you go?"

He took a deep breath. "If they can manage it."

"I wish I knew how to stop them," the boy said, crinkling up his brow. "You're not like that man told me. You're not near so scary as he is. I've heard your name before. Are you really a killer?"

Tahn sighed. "I've done things I thought I had to do. When I was afraid and knew no other way. Perhaps you can understand that."

The boy nodded.

"Thank you. For bringing me this word."

The boy stood to his feet suddenly. "I hope that lady's all right. I hope they can't kill you. I have to go now."

"Wait. Jura's too far for you on foot, child. You'd not reach there by nightfall. Let me send you with a ride. I owe you much. Let me help you—"

"But if the man sees somebody with me, he'll be angry! Maybe he won't give me Mama's medicine! He told me he'd wait in Jura—behind the church—and I could have it back if I . . . if I did everything he said."

"He won't be there, lad. He wouldn't take that chance."

"But the medicine!" The boy's eyes filled with tears again. "I have to have it!"

"He's only used you, child. And used a lie to hold you, surely, when he saw your heart. Such a man wouldn't risk himself to stay and wait. That medicine is gone."

"But we don't have any more money! And my mother—she might die!"

Tahn stood to his feet. "Come with me. Onath's healer is here within the gate. He may have the medicine you need or know where to get it."

"But I can't pay him."

"I'll pay for it. And I'll see that you have a way home, as I said."

The boy looked worried. "What if that man is watching for me?"

"I doubt you'll ever see him again. Likely he'll be waiting for me now, at the place he said. But come." Tahn turned back to the gate and motioned for the boy to follow.

"I thought you'd be angry. Why would you help me?"

"Because you helped me. You're a brave boy who loves his mother's life as much as his own. It's only right that you have what you need. I pray your mother recovers swiftly. Have you a father?"

"No, sir," the boy said, looking up at Tahn with wonder. "Not anymore."

"Then I would give you something." Tahn reached and lifted a thin gold chain that hung around his neck. "Keep this hidden, at least for now. It was a gift from my lady. Her father will recognize it. If you have more need, you or your mother, come back here if you can. Show this to Lord Trilett and tell him I gave it to you because you did me service for the lady's sake."

The boy only stood and stared at him.

"What is your name, lad?"

"Char."

"Well, Char. Let us find the healer. But don't tell him or anyone what you've told me. Not a word of it—I know you understand—or we risk my lady's life."

"Yes, sir."

"Let them believe only that you've come to me because of your mother's need."

The little boy nodded soberly as they walked. "You love that lady very much, don't you?"

"Yes. I do."

"It isn't right that you should die." The boy looked up at him with sadness in his eyes. "Why do they want to catch you?"

Tahn sighed. "It would make no better sense with the telling."

Solemnly, the child moved his hand into Tahn's. The simple gesture gave Tahn a feeling of sadness he couldn't understand, as though the boy's small hand represented all the children here that he loved, all the times he'd hoped to share, and even the longing inside him to make a family with Netta. All must be laid down now, all the future he'd wanted. He could not even take the chance to tell anyone good-bye.

This boy could be trusted not to betray what he knew, Tahn felt sure of that. And Amos Lowe would not question them too greatly. But as they walked to the estate house, Tahn realized that Lucas would never be willing to let him ride off alone, especially with evening drawing nearer. Lucas would try to follow him, even if he knew nothing of the ominous demands. So he must send Lucas away, and quickly.

Amos Lowe had the medicine the boy's mother needed. Tahn tried to pay him, but he refused the money, so Tahn gave the coins to the child for the healer in Jura, should there be need to call on him.

"Lucas, I need you to see the boy back to his home for me," Tahn told his friend, though he knew there would be a protest.

"Another would serve as well as myself," Lucas answered as quickly as expected. "Tahn, I don't want to leave you in your search for Netta. I want to be here to help."

"There are many searchers, brother," Tahn assured him steadily. "But you're the only one among us almost the same as a priest. Please. Go and pray for the woman. Stay with her through the night so we may see how she fares and that the boy is not left alone."

"But, Tahn—"

"Please, Lucas," Tahn begged him resolutely. "The hurt we feel cannot cloud our minds against the needs of others."

Lucas studied him with a grave expression, and for a moment Tahn wondered if he could read the awful truth through his eyes. But finally Lucas nodded. "All right. Because it's important to you. But my prayers remain here with you as well. And I'll be back as soon as I can."

"Thank you," Tahn told him with relief. "For your prayers above all."

⚇

It was hard to watch them ride away. Tahn felt like a door was closing, but there was nothing he could do. He wanted to clasp Lucas's hand, to embrace him, so close had been their friendship, but he held himself against it. No one must suspect anything now. With heaviness, he visited the wounded men again and then knelt for prayer in his room at the side of the guardhouse.

Brader's Point was a rocky place he'd only known the name of for less than a year. An easy lookout to be sure; no one could approach an encampment there without being seen, and the slopes held crannies and dips enough to confuse an unprepared traveler. Netta's captors had chosen their spot well. But it was miles across the forest from the Trilett estate. Had they taken Netta there? Or was she hidden at a different location? There was no way he could know, and that bothered him about the whole matter. There were no assurances of anything.

He wondered about telling Jarel Trilett, or even Lord Bennamin, about the boy's message. But he couldn't be sure how they'd react. They might be glad for Tahn to be willing to go alone as ordered. Or they might insist it was wiser to have help on such a quest, even hidden at a distance. But if anyone were seen to be following, Netta's throat might be cut before they could reach her. Tahn could take no such chance.

"Father God," he prayed. "Be with me as you were when I rescued Vari from the wheel. And when you led me to my sister in time to save her from Burle and his men. You've been good to those I care about. You've answered prayers above what I ever thought could be. Help me in this too."

Tahn remembered the time Samis had him tracked for miles through the wilderness north of Merinth. He'd been caught then only by a blatant trap. He'd known there would be men lying in wait. Just like there would be now. Samis had understood how to bait him, and now someone knew an even surer way. Could Lionell have conceived of this alone? Or only someone who had been with Samis, and trained by Samis?

Perhaps it didn't matter. Netta must not be left to suffer and die over what was his to face. Even delay could cost her life if he did not arrive by sunup. *"It's you they want,"* the boy had said. Very well, then. He could see no other option.

6

Netta would not have thought it possible to doze even for an instant lying on the hard floor where Burle had left her, and yet she must have. A sudden noise jolted her awake. Her bound hands felt cold, prickly numb. She struggled to sit up, looking fearfully toward the door. She thought she'd heard someone on the stone stairs outside.

Despite her own fear, a nightmarish image from what must have been a dream still lingered over her mind. Tahn was in a cage, the way she'd seen him in Merinth. Beaten and shot with arrows, chained and condemned, but the look in his eyes had still been only concern for her, not for himself.

She heard the movement of the bolt on the door, and it suddenly swung open. She tried to straighten herself to face whoever it was that had come. Her shoulders and her head were aching. Her thirst was horrendous. And she fully expected one of those vile men to grab her, to force her on their way again, or something worse.

A tall, thin man with hungry eyes stared down at her. He said nothing at all, only studied her for a moment and then pulled a knife from the sheath at his belt. She could not read his expression, whether he intended to cut her bonds or do her harm. But she did not turn her eyes away, did not shrink back.

He caught a fistful of her hair, ribbons and pins and all, in his grimy hand, and with one quick cut had a handful to shove in his pocket. Not content with that alone, he cut a piece of her satiny dress ribbon to go with the shorn locks.

Then with a sickening grin, he put up his knife, turned around to the door, and disappeared.

That affront was the second time a piece had been cut from her clothes. It left Netta shaken, feeling violated, though she knew that helpless as she was, he could have done much worse. *Help me, God*, she sobbed as she heard the man secure the door and leave. Voices were barely discernible somewhere outside.

Where was this place, anyway? She longed to get up and look through the crack at the door, but the way she ached she wasn't sure that she could. She was so thirsty that she felt faint, with no way to call out or beg for water with the cloth still tied across her mouth. She didn't know how many hours it had been, or if these men would ever care at all to think of such needs. She was only a plaything to them. Bait. That horrible man Burle had made his intentions very plain. He was glad to be paid, yes, but all of this seemed very personal too.

She remembered what Tahn had told her, that he'd had to cut Burle in Alastair, in a fight he'd never asked for, in order to save his sister. Was the man so set on revenge for that wound? What could he have expected—for Tahn to let his sister be ravished? How could a man be blamed for doing what he had to do?

The voices outside increased in fervor for a moment and then died back again until she could scarcely hear them. Carefully, with all the effort she could muster, Netta began to scoot across the packed earth floor toward the doorway. She wasn't sure she'd be able to pull herself to her feet, but perhaps she could get some small glimpse outside through the crack at the door. Perhaps a look could be helpful if she could find any chance to escape.

With every inch of progress she made across the floor, she thought of the many things that had happened since Tahn had appeared in her room like a phantom and kidnapped her to keep her from Samis's hands. Less than two years ago, but it seemed like so much longer. He'd been terrifying then, but only because she didn't understand the life he was trapped in.

Tahn had been so fierce. So hopeless. Yet still trying to do her good. And he would try now, she knew he would, even to his own hurt.

But now at least, he had her father's men behind him. Because Tahn was chief of their guard, even her father would listen to his counsel and do the things he suggested. If they could find her, they would come with more than enough men to overwhelm this bandit band and whoever was paying them.

But that seemed to be just what Burle wanted. At least for Tahn to come searching. How could they be so foolish? Burle knew Tahn to be a formidable fighter! How could these villains hope to best him and all the men he would have with him? Were they ignorant enough to open themselves to a bloody battle?

She thought back to the things Burle had said. *"Think he'll come for you, Lady? He's weak. He's always been weak. That's why it's so easy to bait him."*

The thought almost choked her. Burle was counting on snaring only one man, not a whole troop. He expected Tahn to come alone.

What would they tell him? Had they already sent a message? Netta tried to imagine what her father might be thinking. Surely he wouldn't sacrifice Tahn. He couldn't in good conscience send him alone. He couldn't let it be!

But Tahn could. He would trade himself for a hope of sparing her, she knew it with all that was in her. Was it too late already? Even if she could escape, was he already on his way? Vari wouldn't let it be so, nor Lucas, nor Lorne, nor even Marc Toddin. But they would all listen to him in a circumstance like this. He could tell them whatever he needed to, and then slip away.

Uncomfortable heat spread down her spine. That filthy, horrid Burle and his friends would use a man's love against him, make it his weakness, and draw him to his death. And for what? Gold? Vengeance? Spite?

With breathless determination she struggled the rest of the way to the door, but the sliver of light at its side afforded her a very limited view indeed. If only she had a knife somewhere in her clothes, perhaps she could cut herself free. Tahn had told her once that she should carry one. She hadn't listened to him about that. She hadn't thought she could bring herself to use it and had hoped to never need to. But she knew now that if she had any opportunity she wouldn't hesitate to fight at Burle for her freedom, or for a chance at Tahn's.

Leaning against the door with a tease of daylight against her skirt, Netta found it hard not to despair of everything. There was nothing she could do. In that awful cage in Merinth, Tahn had pleaded with her to go away, to save herself and let him die. She wished she could make the same plea back to him now. *Don't come. Don't love me to folly, to your own death.*

She heard a noise again outside. Someone else drawing near. They might be angry if they found her against the door this way. She told herself she didn't care, but she could imagine a cruel shove if she were found in the doorway, so she edged along the rough stone wall away from it for her own protection. The bolt moved, and the door creaked. The gag suddenly seemed to be choking her, and she struggled for a long breath, trying to steel herself against the fear she felt.

She recognized the man who stepped in as the one who had ridden at her left over all the distance getting here. He left the door open behind him, and she was glad for the burst of sunlight into the room. He stood for a moment, just looking her over. He held what looked like a waterskin in his hand.

"Eger didn't hurt you none, I see that. Burle wouldn't like me letting him in, but he don't never do much damage. It's just a lot easier dealing with him if you let him have what he wants, you know what I mean? Got a saddlebag full of baubles and bits and locks of hair. Not something I understand, but it keeps him sane to ride with."

He took a step toward Netta, and she tensed.

"You're a pretty one. No denying that. Won't be so pretty after they get done though, I don't suppose. No need shrinking from me. I don't take to forcing my way on women so much as some."

She looked at him in wonder. There was something strange in his eyes. Sadness? She would never have expected to find anything so remotely feeling in any of these men.

He pulled a knife out of his clothes, and she thought of Tahn's shirts with the hidden pockets. This man seemed to have one like that.

"I won't hurt you," the man said. "Gonna cut away your gag. Get some water in you. I told them we can't have you drying up and wasting away." He leaned over her and cut at the cloth. "Don't scream. There's nobody out here but us to hear you anyway, and the ruckus would only gain you a beating."

"Why are you doing this?"

He didn't answer, only pulled the cord at the mouth of his waterskin and held it to her lips. "Drink in what you can. Can't say when you'll get another opportunity."

The water was warm, stale, but its wetness was a welcome relief anyway. She drank it in gratefully, never taking her eyes off this strange man. Might he help her even more? Might he loose her hands?

"Thank you," she said when he pulled the waterskin away. "Please—"

"No. Don't be asking for anything. Don't be begging. What happens now ain't up to me."

"Who . . . who is it up to? Burle?"

"I suppose you'll learn soon enough." He studied her again and began to turn, but then he stopped and sighed. "We could get a hundred porthets just for your dress. Ah, Lady. It's a hard way you got ahead of you. And I can't help it none. But I'll see that you eat if you answer me something I wanna know. Do you really love that sorry lunatic, or has he found some way to—"

Netta started shaking. "He—he's no lunatic."

The man laughed. "He's enough of one that you know exactly who I mean, don't you?"

She could feel her heart pounding in her throat. But

she didn't answer. This man knew Tahn, or at least knew something about him. She could not imagine that anyone could call Tahn a lunatic unless they'd reveled in the cruel stories of wicked men, or had been there, like Burle, to mock Tahn's midnight screams in the dark rooms of Samis's Valhal.

"I want to know if you actually love him," the man pressed her. "Or does he have something you or your father want so badly—"

"Stop! He would never coerce me! I don't care if you bring me food. Leave him alone! He's done nothing to you!"

The man shook his head. "What is it about him, Lady? Look at you—all you had—all you *are*. And you sound as though you care."

"Of course I care! He will be my husband. He's a good man. And I love him."

"You dream, if you think you will ever marry now. And you wouldn't call him good if you'd seen him as I have, with his eyes ablaze and his sword dripping blood. You're an innocent fool, Lady, to love something like him. But there's no hope for either of you now."

He turned away and left Netta sitting alone in the darkness, shaking. Her world had seemed so perfect, with Tahn and the adopted orphans around her, and their new house being built. But this nightmare had come and taken away everything. How dare the man call Tahn a lunatic? Tahn was the one who'd left the wickedness behind him to embrace the life and light of the Savior. Tahn was a miracle. A tortured child and a deadly warrior, but now a gentle heart, a life offered to God.

Still, the man's words beat against her spirit. No hope. She certainly saw none in this place. But faith was not born of seeing. There must be some way. She looked about her in the darkness. This little room was halfway beneath the ground and with only one door, locked on the outside. She'd heard the man slide the heavy bolt to secure it again. How could she escape here? The walls were rough stone, impossible to dig through, even if she had full use of her hands. The packed dirt floor would be no better. And if she managed to get outside somehow, there would still be the men to face.

But with God all things are possible. She'd heard her priest say it more than once. She'd even read it in her father's library: "If ye have faith . . . nothing shall be impossible unto you." She'd marveled when she read it. Such a statement seemed unrealistically bold, beyond the reach of this world. But Christ himself, who came into this world that the truth of God might be known, had said it.

"I need your help, Lord," she whispered. Once again she tried to pull her hands free from the ropes that bound her, but they were far too tight, and they did not fall away as St. Peter's chains had done in a prison house. There was nothing at all she could do. Weary and helpless, she leaned her head against the wall and closed her eyes. She should have listened to Tahn. She should have forgotten that silly party and stayed in his arms.

She struggled against tears, thinking of Temas and Duncan and the other children who had known the terror of being captives. She must be strong now as they had been strong. She must be strong for them, for her father, and especially for Tahn. She tried to imagine what it would have been like to be a frightened orphan child, snatched from the streets and enslaved. She thought of the things they had told her, and the things she herself had seen. She thought of the scars on Tahn's back. And yet he'd survived. The children had survived. She must too somehow. Bravely, as they did.

She heard a tiny scraping noise and turned her head to the dark corner nearest her, but there wasn't light enough to see the source of the sound. A mouse, almost surely. Before the thought of it could upset her, she told herself it was a small thing. Nothing worse than a fly flitting past on a warm summer's day. Vari had said once that he used to welcome such things because they were far better company than evil-hearted men.

Still, she drew her legs in close as she continued to hear the mouse scuttle about. She heard voices outside again, but the words were too muffled to understand. She wished she could hear whatever was being said. There must be something she could do to free herself. She felt stiff, and she wasn't sure there was any way to find relief. She struggled to turn a little, but her arm scraped painfully against a jagged piece of rock in the wall. She knew she'd drawn blood, and for a moment she nearly cried. There seemed nothing but pain in any of this.

But then suddenly she lifted herself to her knees as best she could and felt frantically for that jagged edge. If it could cut skin, then maybe, just maybe, it could cut rope. When she found what she was looking for, she had to lift her arms awkwardly and lean back to rub the ropes at her wrists again and again against the hard stone.

It was trying work, and it seemed to be getting her nowhere. She was exhausted. But she could not give up. On and on she rubbed rope against stone. On and on, hoping that no one would come until her hands were free.

And then what? She couldn't answer until the moment came. There must be a way to be free again. There had to be a way, by the grace of God who had spared Tahn's life, and her own, before.

"I believe you, Lord," she whispered. "That nothing is impossible. We want to serve you, but these men would kill us. Free us, oh Lord, that you may use us. Show your grace, your mercy, and your power."

7

Tahn rode alone out of the Trilett gate, glad to do so, glad to be on his way, when he heard Jarel's call behind him.

"Tahn!"

He glanced back to see the young nobleman on his own horse, hurrying toward him. With a sigh he stopped his mount beneath a tree and waited.

"Tahn! Let me go back with you to the searchers."

"They've been hours at it, Jarel. They will have to rest. Before we know it, night will be coming on."

"Would you call off the search? Was that my uncle's word?"

"I am only saying that they must rest. We've seen already that there is no fruit to be had searching in the darkness. Call them in for me as the sun goes down, Jarel. Tell them all to eat and sleep. They may resume when the sun returns."

"You want *me* to call them in? Where are you going?"

Tahn sighed, and chose an answer that Netta's cousin would not be surprised to hear. "To the priest. I must have his prayers, Jarel. I feel as though I could burst apart."

"I'm sorry, truly," Jarel told him. "It should have been a joyous day for you both. Would you like me to come with you? I can send Buris—"

"No. I need to think. To be alone awhile."

"Tahn . . ."

"Don't say more. I know this is heartache for you and for Benn as much as for me. But I promise you that she's not lost."

Jarel looked pale. "I would promise you the same, if I knew how."

"Pray for her, that she will be restored to you. Believe it, Jarel. I need that from you tonight. Even now, please."

"All right," the young nobleman said weakly. "We need her. She is one-third of all the Trilett blood left to this world. The devil did not want you wed. He does not want your godly family."

"The devil be hanged," Tahn replied. "God's will be done."

He started Smoke at a walk toward the town, and Jarel did what Tahn told him and rode in the opposite direction. Tahn waited until a curve of the road would hide him from Jarel's view, and then he turned into the trees and quickened his pace.

Brader's Point would be a long ride. He should have no trouble reaching there by sunup. But he hated that Netta would be so much longer in her captor's hands.

You're being a fool.

The words jumped at him unexpected and unwelcome. He tried to brush them aside, but the voice in his head only continued.

What do you hope to accomplish? You can't trust them! They'll kill you both. Turn around. Why should you die too?

"No. Netta will not die." He said it aloud, as though the sudden arguments came from a living being in front of him.

You're being a fool! How can you rescue her by giving yourself to them? It's senseless!

Tahn rode furiously, trying to still the bitter doubt by his sheer determination. What choice was there? Could there be greater hope by refusing the villains' words? They'd promised to kill her if he did that, or if he tried to alter their demands in any way. Wasn't this small hope better than none? If he stayed, if he waited, if he gathered men to bring with him, or told Lord Trilett and then *he* gathered men, Netta might be lost before ever they could reach her.

Perhaps it was foolish to do as they asked. Blindly playing into their treacherous hands. But he knew he could not do otherwise. Father Anolle had told him a Scripture once about God using foolish things. He wished he could remember the words better.

"Use me, Lord God," he prayed. "Use my foolishness, if that is what this is. Because I have faith that you'll be with me, and with Netta. Cover my lady. Shield her."

Smoke ran almost effortlessly, as though he were glad Tahn allowed him all the speed he wanted. The horse seemed driven by Tahn's determination, as anxious as his rider to put the miles under him and reach their destination quickly. They stopped once only for water until the terrain around them grew rockier and the sun's glowing arc dipped beyond the horizon.

The moon was a bright sliver over Tahn's shoulder. He was grateful for the clear sky. The hills pushed up higher here, the gullies and ditches were more pronounced. The closer they got to Brader's Point the rockier and more uneven any trail would be.

Eventually as he progressed in the moonlight he was able to discern the shape of the Point jutting toward the night sky ahead of him. One tiny light glowed near the top. Someone was waiting. He thought of his cousin, Baron Lionell Trent, but imagined it to be unlike him to sit by a fire's light in the wilderness.

He rode on, but Smoke began to get edgy before they got much farther. Someone was close, Tahn knew it too, though he could see no one in the shadows and he heard only the slightest rustling ahead. Should he call out? Surely whoever this was knew his presence already in the open. But they were a mile from the Point, maybe more. Could this be some other traveler?

He leaned forward slowly, brushed Smoke's neck with his hand, and whispered two words in the horse's ear. "Ready, boy."

He knew Smoke understood. Smoke always understood better than any horse he'd ever known. He walked him ahead just a bit. Tahn thought he heard another horse somewhere in the distance.

"I'm Tahn Dorn," he spoke into the darkness. "I've come for my lady's sake. If you are not the men I seek, clear my way to them, for I'll not be stopped."

With his hand on the hilt of his sword, he continued toward the Point, though he knew there were men ahead of him now. Smoke was tense, his ears pressed back. "Steady," Tahn whispered to him. "Steady."

Suddenly, there was a burst of motion around him. Smoke reared and screamed, lurching wildly. Tahn drew his sword, swung from the saddle, and rolled once on the ground to regain his feet. There had to have been a thrown knife, or an arrow. Nothing but a shock of pain could make his strong horse react like that.

Three men, maybe more, were around him almost instantly, swords drawn. Tahn fought at them, raging inside, until a familiar voice pierced the din.

"Dorn!"

He stopped, his heart thundering. Burle.

"Lay down your sword if you want the lady to live!"

He could hear the bandit leader coming closer. The men who had fought him surrounded him now, standing eagerly, their swords still at the ready.

"You're surrounded with more numbers than you can see. We'll cut you down if you fight us! And she'll die."

Tahn took a deep breath. "I've not come all this way to defy you now." He held out his sword and let it drop. "Let me see my lady."

Burle laughed, and the sound was familiar as old scars. The huge man stepped nearer, followed by others, and the closest men made way for him. Another large man waited in the distance; Tahn could make out his outline. Without a word, that man mounted his dark horse and watched. Tahn stood very still.

"I've seen many a fool in my days," Burle taunted him. "But you're first among them, same as always. Do you really care nothing whether you live or die?"

"I've come for Lady Trilett's sake," Tahn answered him steadily. "Let her go."

Burle laughed again. But then without warning he flung out his fist and struck Tahn squarely in the jaw, sending him reeling backwards. Tahn knew Burle's strength and size. He knew Burle's fighting style, and that he himself was quicker. He could have fought back. He'd bested Burle before. But he would make no such attempt now. He steadied himself to stand straight again.

"That's just the beginning," Burle growled to him. "I carry a scar from your sword. I vowed you would pay for that."

"Where is my lady?"

Just as quickly, Burle hit him again. "You've no status here. You'll ask no questions. Do you understand?"

Recovering himself again, Tahn nodded. "Yes."

"You think yourself someone, I know it. You thought you were Samis's favorite. And now you may be the Trilett lord's favorite. But you're the same pathetic beast you were when I met you. Do you understand?"

"With but one difference," Tahn answered boldly.

"What difference?" Burle raged at him. "You think the lady loves you? Or you have her father's money? What is it? You think you're somebody because the baron's gone half mad to get his hands on you? I don't care what he thinks! Your blood's worth nothing but a few hours' entertainment."

Tahn drew in a deep breath. "I claim nothing but God. He saved me from the beast I was, and from the hell we both knew."

"You're insane." Burle laughed. "That's your problem. But I'm not stupid enough to think you aren't clever still. Give me your knives, Tahn. All of them."

It would have been easier to have only strangers to deal with, who knew nothing of his past or what might be expected of him. But Burle knew much.

Tahn reached one hand slowly inside his shirt and withdrew the first knife. One of Burle's men raised his sword to the ready, but Tahn gave the knife into a waiting hand and peacefully relinquished the others as well.

"Now take off your boots," Burle commanded.

Without a word, Tahn obeyed him, and Burle laughed at him again.

"I'd wear them myself if they fit me," he said. "But you've always been a scrawny pup. I doubt any of us grown men'd fit your measly boots! Maybe some rich man would buy them for his little boy, huh, Tahn? You won't be needing them much longer, anyway." He jerked the boots from Tahn's hands and threw them to one of the other men. "Now stand real still. Cole's gonna tie your hands, and if you move so much as a muscle, I'll slit your throat."

Tahn raised his eyes to the starry sky as his arms were pulled behind him and ropes were wrapped against his wrists. Without a word to any of them, the man on the dark horse rode away northward. And a desperate prayer filled Tahn's heart. *Have you led me, Lord? I thought I could give her a chance. Show me a way.*

Strangely, as the ropes were secured far too tightly, he felt a peace inside him, as though the Lord was answering his plea with one simple assurance. *You came trusting me. Trust me still.*

"Fool," Burle taunted again. "It's going to be a pleasure to watch you die."

8

Lionell Trent paced across the tile floor of his private parlor, his satin cloak making a swishing noise as it brushed against a table. This was one of the most important nights of his life, and he knew already that he wouldn't be able to sleep. He'd longed, he'd waited, and now the time had almost come.

His mind raced over the things that were soon to happen, visiting each step over and over in his thoughts, rehearsing the grand manner in which he, personally, would end the threat to his house and gain the reverence of all Trent generations to come.

The only presence he would welcome in his chamber tonight was a servant coming to tell him of the arrival of another messenger. It would be a bit soon for that, of course, but he could hardly wait. And until then, he longed to stay alone with his elaborate musings, but a soft rapping on the east door nudged his thoughts away from the grand idea of a new tapestry woven in his own honor. He tried to ignore the unwelcome interruption. He'd already instructed Corlis, his servant, not to disturb him until Saud arrived, not to come to his chamber for any other reason. But the gentle noise persisted.

With a sigh, he blurted his response. "I've a headache! Who is it bothering me? Mother?"

For a moment, he heard only silence. But then a soft voice answered. "Most excellent Baron, I crave your company, only for a moment. Forgive the intrusion."

Lady Elane. His wife. He preferred to dictate the moments when he should have her company. And yet he liked her obeisant manner, and her forever pleasing choice of words. She was certainly easier company than Lady Anaya, his mother. So he chose to be especially gracious and allow her audience.

"Enter, my lady," he said, reclining himself upon the divan and throwing his kerchief onto his brow. "Perhaps your soothing voice shall be a balm in my discomfort."

The intricately carved door opened slowly, and he heard the lady's footsteps, but he did not look her way. He pictured her in his mind the way she'd looked when they first married. Slender as a sword, and just as beautiful. But now, he knew, she was large as a tent, carrying his child, and at least temporarily not such a gift to look upon.

"I'm so sorry, my dear Lionell, that you suffer," she said gently. "But I think it no wonder on this night. I'm sure the news from the Trilett manor has been most stressful."

"Yes. Indeed." He almost said something about Netta Trilett's capture, what a shame it was, what a grief to the honorable Lord Trilett. But then he remembered that Elane knew nothing of that. He hadn't mentioned the messenger who'd brought him the fulfilling news earlier that day, nor a word of the worthy plan now in the making. Which meant, of course, that she must be speaking of that now-broken fantasy, the Dorn's wedding.

"I find the whole thing unsettling," Elane continued. "I've known Lady Netta since we were children, of course. My own brother has a fondness for her. That she should choose to join herself with a man raised so barbarously perplexes me immensely."

"Not to mention the danger he poses to your unborn offspring," Lionell added sourly.

"I hope it isn't anxiety over that very thing that causes my own distress this evening. Surely their ceremony of marriage is complete by this time, though I can't picture any priest being willing to perform it. Do you think Dorn himself is responsible for the Triletts' unbelievable neglect of inviting us?"

Lionell smiled. "It was not neglect but design, I can assure you, my good lady."

"You've been very gracious," Lady Elane said, taking his hand. "A lesser man would have been greatly insulted. And far more unnerved, under the circumstances."

"Yes," Lionell answered her slowly, pulling the kerchief away from his face. "But I would not choose to behave as a lesser man."

"Can I do anything to ease your pain tonight?" Elane asked gently. "Before we must call for the midwives?"

Lionell had been about to say something, but he stopped. He dropped his kerchief and sat forward, staring her in the face. "Call for the midwives? You said something about distress. Surely you don't mean . . ."

She nodded. "I feel it has begun. I'm certain. But there is time yet. Perhaps the babe shall not come until morning."

"But . . . but this is not the time you told me! Not yet."

"I know. And that concerns me, but perhaps I was only mistaken before."

"Have you told my mother? Have you told anyone?"

"My maiden Azel. Besides that, I thought you should be the first to know."

Lionell stood to his feet. He stared at Elane for a few seconds, and then he whirled around, laughing. "Ah, yes! It is providence! A lucky omen! Of course the babe would want to come now! He wants to celebrate with me!"

"Celebrate?"

"Absolutely!" Lionell chuckled. "My own son, wishing to greet me when I'm so near to securing his opulent future! This could not be more perfect, Elane. Our worries are done!"

9

Fifteen-year-old Vari led his horse into the Trilett stable along with the last of the searchers, all of them reluctant to suspend their searching until morning. The stable hands had lit lanterns for them, and Vari looked about anxiously in the dim light, hoping to see a familiar mount. "Smoke isn't here yet. I thought you said Tahn was going to meet us after seeing the priest."

"I *thought* he meant to meet us when he said everyone had to rest," Jarel explained. "But he may be long at his prayers. What else can we do?"

"He wouldn't go out again searching alone at night, would he?"

Marc Toddin hung a bridle on a post and glanced their way. "I should think you'd find that far less a surprise than the notion of the Dorn suggesting rest."

Vari paled. "Why would he send us in if he intended to continue?"

Toddin sighed. "Perhaps he didn't think he could push us the way he drives himself."

But Jarel disagreed. "If he's gone out again, then he's too upset to be thinking straight. We can't see any better than last night, and as much as we'd like to, we can't go a second night without rest. Surely he'll be in soon."

"Is Lucas here then?" Vari asked.

Jarel shook his head. "He's gone to Jura on a mission of benevolence with a beggar boy."

"Tonight?" Marc questioned immediately.

"Tahn sent him. This afternoon."

"And you don't think that strange?" Marc pressed.

"Not for Tahn. No."

"At a time like this?"

"I don't think he's able to turn away a need. At any time. I've never seen him do it. The boy came crying to the gate this afternoon while Tahn was here."

"The Lord prosper Dorn and all your means," Marc answered with a shake of his head. "But I wonder—why would anyone attack and steal, if it's known that all they could want may be acquired so simply at the Trilett gate?"

"There is great difference between men's needs and their wants, friend," Jarel answered him sourly. "Stealing Netta was certainly no answer to need. Lust or greed took her from us, and the men responsible are far different from the souls who come here for help. And they'll be dealt with far differently when they are found."

"Without doubt. I didn't mean my words to upset you, sir."

Jarel turned away with barely a nod. "Come and claim a bite and a bed. We are all tired."

Vari walked to the estate house with them and the other men, wondering all the time what Netta was enduring. He'd met only a few of the other noble daughters, and he didn't know any of them well, but he could imagine that there were none like Netta. Beautiful, unerringly proper, yet never too condescending to welcome the peasant-born such as himself into her home or her heart. Netta loved all the adopted children, even though she'd met them when they were ragged, dirty, and without the slightest notion how to conduct themselves in a noble house.

As if called forward by his thoughts, Stuva, Doogan, Duncan, Temas, and Rane came running out with Lorne and Tiarra from the house, surely hoping for some word. With pain of heart, Vari shook his head to them before they even came close, and little Temas burst into tears. Vari would have taken her into his arms, but Lorne reached her first.

"You didn't find the lady?" ten-year-old Doogan asked.

"No," Vari told them with a sigh. "Not yet."

"I'll bet she's found a cave," Temas ventured through her tears. "I'll bet she had to hide. But she's very brave. And smart. She'll be all right."

"If she went in a cave, she wouldn't just stay there," the boy named Rane argued. "She'd come out to the searchers and then come home."

"We don't know what happened yet," Vari told them. "But the Dorn said pray. And he's right that that's what we all should be doing."

"Where is he?" Tiarra questioned, and for a moment everyone was silent.

"Still with the priest, as far as I know," Jarel answered her.

She stared at him, the flame of a lantern in Lem Toddin's hand dancing in her eyes like fire. "But you're not sure?"

Jarel looked at the faces around him, and his answer was somber and short. "No."

"Perhaps we'd better make sure," Marc Toddin suggested. And the little boy Duncan put his hand in Vari's and clung tightly.

Miles away from them, Netta paced in the darkness within the cellar room. Night had returned, and no one had come. No one had opened the door or spoken a word to her for hours. She'd managed to loose the ropes from her wrists but only after scraping one wrist almost raw in the process. And she was still trapped.

How long would they leave her alone? Even the man who had said he would feed her had not come back. And she was powerfully hungry but unsure if she could eat in this place if food was offered. What would she do when someone finally came? She might gain nothing but an angry beating for managing to free her hands this way. They might simply tie her all over again. But she was glad she'd done it anyway. She could not just meekly accept whatever they'd planned for her. She would fight them somehow if she could.

83

She'd tried to find anything she could use for a weapon in this terrible little hole, but there was nothing. And peering through the cracks when she'd had daylight had gained her no real understanding of where she was. She felt useless, helpless, and she hated it. Should she scream again? Trying that before had done no good whatsoever. It seemed no one but her rough captors was close enough to hear. That they'd left the gag off her in this place surely meant that they weren't the slightest bit concerned about that.

With a sigh, Netta stopped her pacing, leaned against the wall, and sank down wearily. There might be nothing she could do until someone opened that door. And then what? Her wrists and shoulders hurt so. And her head too. She was scared. She longed for the comfort of Tahn's strong arms, yet she could not pray for him to find her because that was the very thing these evil men wanted. *Oh Lord, preserve him*, she prayed. *Wherever he is, keep him in the palm of your hand.*

10

Through the blackness of the night, Tahn walked, a rope around his neck and his hands tightly bound behind him. Burle's horse stayed ahead of him with the length of rope tied securely to the horn of the saddle. Burle would stop and then start, slow and then go faster, mercilessly not allowing Tahn to find any rhythm to prevent the rope's cruel pull at his neck.

Tahn knew Burle was toying with him, enjoying this sport. Yet he distrusted Tahn enough even now to keep his men riding closely behind and to each side. They kept on over rocks and underbrush, with Tahn's boots flopping uselessly atop the saddlebag of the man to his right. Brader's Point had been just a decoy destination where they could lie in wait. They were traveling northwest now; he knew it from the stars. The timber grew increasingly dense in this direction, and they were nowhere near the road. Burle had been smart enough to know they weren't likely to encounter anyone here by chance.

One of Burle's men rode suddenly to them from the south, and Burle stopped.

"No sign of anyone following toward Brader's Point," the man reported. "We checked the trail a long way back and to the west and east. There's nothing."

"Maybe he came alone," Burle answered. "But keep a watch till dawn to be sure. If he's got men hidden, they'll wait no longer than that to try and find us."

The man rode away, and Burle turned to Tahn with a smirk in his voice. "Your friends will come riding to Brader's

Point and find nothing, Tahn. I'm clever enough to move you in case your Lord Trilett should search where you told him."

"I told no one," Tahn answered him.

"You're really alone, then? No one but you could be such a bold idiot! Is it a death wish, Tahn? Longing to die for a woman?"

"You will let her go. You pledged sacred honor."

"Sacred? Would I say that?" He gave a jerk of the rope that almost felled Tahn to the ground. "What I told you, back in Alastair, was that you'd gotten yourself a blood grudge. You didn't expect me to forget it while you were cozying up to your sweet lady, did you?"

Tahn took a deep breath and answered him with steadiness. "Should I have let you assault my sister? I did what any man would do."

"No," Burle argued. "You were bent on confounding me and standing in my way, the same as always! You're the reason Samis didn't put me over the other men! You made him favor you. And then you turned and killed him."

"He did himself in. And whatever he bore for me, I'd not call it favor."

Burle gave his horse a sudden kick, and the rope tugged forward as they started walking again.

"Where is my lady?" Tahn called even as he was forced to keep up.

"You think you're in any position to make demands, fool?"

"I have . . . a solemn pledge." He struggled with the words. "She will be set free."

Burle stopped as quickly as he started. Turning in his saddle, he faced Tahn with a curse. "Maybe in that rich man's palace they let you act like some kind of prince! But right now, you're at my rope, and I can drag you till the north wind blows if I want to. You can't command me! You have nothing, Tahn. Less than nothing."

Tahn stood straight and faced him boldly. "Then where are we going? Why not kill me now and be done with it?"

Burle laughed. "That would be far too easy. Too quick. You humiliated us in Alastair, call it what you will. The boys and I have been looking forward to this. And you wouldn't deny us a simple pleasure, would you? We're going to have our fun with you while we can. Isn't that right, Toma?"

A young man to Tahn's left suddenly broke from the others and rode closer. Tahn knew the impetuous youth, barely older than Vari or Marcus yet dangerously tempered and wantonly cruel. He spoke with venom enough to match Burle's.

"I would have liked to catch your horse, Tahn. I would have liked to carve him up for tomorrow's supper. He got away from us, bleeding though he was. But imagine the fun I'll have with your lady when the time comes. I can't wait to get my hands on her. Better than the gold, if you ask me."

"What gold?" Tahn questioned immediately.

Toma gave a laugh. "You think I'd have waited to touch her if there wasn't gold in it? You think any of us would?"

"Shut up, Toma," Burle growled.

But the words had already been enough to give Tahn a measure of peace. Netta might be unharmed, for now, though he wished he could understand what was meant. "Where is my lady?" he dared ask again, though he knew he could expect nothing but an angry response.

Burle kicked at his horse, making the animal jump with such force that Tahn pitched forward and fell to the ground. For a moment a blackness deeper than the night rolled over his eyes, and the pain seemed everywhere at once.

"You see how your life's in my hands, Tahn? You're nothing without the lady and her kin to help you. You've never been nothing."

Tahn lay very still, thinking through their words as he tried to recover himself. These men were cruel. Heartless as their teacher, Samis, had been, and he knew he could expect no mercy. But was there more than what he could see? They were getting gold to hold themselves back from Netta? Was there reason to think he himself would be taken from their hand? *"We're going to have fun with you while we can,"* Burle had said. What would happen after that?

"Get up, Tahn. We have miles to go. You don't want me to drag you that far."

"You won't."

Burle cursed again. "I'll do whatever I please with your sorry hide, you—"

Tahn managed to turn his head enough to look at him. "Are you paid gold for me too?"

Burle was silent for a moment. And then he dismounted with another laugh. "Why shouldn't I sell you? It'd be pleasure enough to kill you myself. But the pay is better if I let it be done by someone who wants you dead even more than I do."

"Lionell."

Burle laughed. "Isn't family a wonderful thing? He doesn't care what shape you're in, so long as he can finish the job himself."

"He . . . he asks that you not harm Netta . . ." Tahn spoke the words of hope. Had Lionell heart enough to make good the pledge of her safety?

"He wants first chance at her," Toma taunted. "Just like a rich man—always demanding the best. But she's no virgin, is she, Tahn? Tell us about it!"

Tahn struggled to his knees, but Burle's heavy boot kicked him down.

"You'll never best me again!" Burle shouted. "The baron will meet us soon enough, and you'll die. Then when he's had his fill, the lady is ours! So much for your rescue! You're a fool, falling for such a trap again. But this time the lady can't muster her friends to save you."

Tahn tried to raise his head, but another swift kick to the ribs took his wind and landed him hard in the dirt. He closed his eyes, trying to form a prayer in his mind, but he could manage only one Name.

Jesus . . .

II

Lucas lay on a mat inside the doorway of a poor home in Jura. The sick woman was breathing better than when he'd first come, though she was still very weak. He had given her medicine, prayed with her, and made a supper of gruel for her and for the boy who had so incredibly come all the way to the Trilett gate for help.

Now both were asleep, and Lucas lay looking at the woven thatch ceiling, thinking of what this night should have been like for Tahn.

Lucas sighed, frustrated by the injustice of this turn of events. He would have preferred to stay at the Trilett estate and attempt to be some comfort at Tahn's side. But he'd been charged with this obligation, and he must do his best with it until the morning.

It could not really surprise Lucas that Tahn would turn his heart and even his friends toward a good deed at a time like this. Perhaps it was his way of making the best out of every hardship. Lucas's mind drifted to the events in Alastair less than a year ago and the good that had come for the street children. But Tahn had come too close to dying, and Lucas would never forget the depth of intercession he'd experienced on Tahn's behalf then.

But now, more trial. With a heavy heart, Lucas uttered a prayer again for Tahn and for the lady. Outside, an owl called in the darkness.

A young man named Britt had told him once that owls always foretell the death of someone you know.

Lucas dismissed the notion from his mind as utter nonsense.

89

Owls hoot every night simply because they're owls. He sighed again, blowing out the single tallow candle. What might Tahn be doing now? Still searching? He hoped not. Like last night, they could do little good in the darkness. Better fruit lay in regaining strength for tomorrow's search with a few hours of sleep before the light.

Give the Dorn rest, Lord, Lucas prayed in his heart. *He shall need his strength tomorrow. Somehow I know that he will.*

Outside of the little dwelling, the owl continued its call. And as Lucas's breathing grew deeper, Alastair's streets filled his mind. Poor children, markets, the bustle of life. But strangely, a new darkness seemed to have fallen over everything. Even beyond Alastair, the hills, the forests, everything was covered with an almost tangible sense of sorrow, of pain, as though the world cried out for a justice long delayed.

Far away through a deepening mist, Lucas heard the creak of wooden wheels, the call of voices. He saw himself crouched down in the shadows of the past, peering out from his careful hiding place at a horrid spectacle. Tahn was chained. Caged and condemned. But who were the men who led him away? They didn't look the same. And there were no city streets this time. It was wilderness he saw surrounding Tahn as faceless men dragged him from the cage. Lucas tried to raise himself from his hiding place, but he couldn't seem to move. The men were beating Tahn, kicking him mercilessly.

"Father! God! What can I do?" With his heart pounding viciously, Lucas fought away the mist, the shadows from his mind to lift himself to his feet again. This wasn't right. Whoever those men were, they had no cause against Tahn. He was made new. Covered by the sovereign hand of God.

"Go to him, son," he heard a voice telling him. "Rise and go."

Netta's tears filled his hearing. The room in Alastair surrounded him with its hanging herbs and potent mixture of smells. And Tahn lay before him so pale, so weakened. He reached his hand to his friend but found nothing but air.

Outside, the owl called, and Lucas jerked awake with his heart thundering in his throat. The dream had such hold on his mind that at first he thought he was in the healer's house in Alastair, and it took a moment to gain his bearings. The ailing woman of Jura still slept across the room from him. The little boy, her son, lay huddled in the nearest corner. Soft whimpering noises escaped him, as though something frightened the child in his sleep.

Lucas sat up, sweating though the night had grown cool. *Go*, the voice had said. *Rise and go to him.*

How he longed to do just that! But he'd given Tahn his word to stay here. He'd promised to wait till the morning light when a kindly neighbor or a clergyman could be found to check on the boy and his mother so they would not be left alone.

He took a deep breath, trying to shake away the dream he'd had. Everything seemed backward, turned about, and he found it hard to remember that it was Netta and not Tahn needing the intercession tonight. Netta was the one in danger, and what could he do now but pray, here or at the Trilett estate? What would Tahn think if he came riding back in the night? Wouldn't he want him keeping his word?

Across the room, the boy made a noise again, a sob, and it struck at Lucas's heart. Truly this was a night for nightmares. "What's wrong, child?" he called across the darkness, but the boy did not answer.

Go. That word from the dream still pressed at him, and the things he'd seen were still tugging at his mind. He rose to his feet. The woman's breaths were slow, still weak. Surely he shouldn't leave them. Not yet. Not against Tahn's word! But the compulsion tore at him. *Lord, is this you?*

The boy's sobs worsened, and Lucas couldn't bear it. The sound reminded him far too much of Tahn so long ago—the scarred child, tormented by nightmares, screaming out in his sleep.

"Boy, wake up," he called out. "Nothing will hurt you."

Cautiously he leaned and placed his hand on the child's shoulder, alert in case he lashed out at the sudden touch as Tahn might have done. But the little boy only woke in quietness and warily pulled away.

"It's all right, lad. You were dreaming badly. No one hurts you."

For a moment the child only stared. But his tears did not stop. "Th-they w-weren't hurting me."

The words, like a freezing dart, pierced Lucas with a dark and icy panic. "Who, child? Who were they hurting?" There was no reason to this, none at all, but he knew how the boy would answer him.

"Y-your friend, th-the Dorn. I saw men hitting him . . ."

For a moment, Lucas could scarcely breathe. Was this some strange madness? A trick of the evil one?

"I don't want him to die!" the boy cried out suddenly. "He's good. I shouldn't have come there! I shouldn't have!"

Lucas felt a tightness welling inside him. "Tell me what you mean, child."

"I can't! I can't tell you—he told me not to!"

"Tahn told you? What? Why?"

The boy tried to scoot away, shaking his head.

But Lucas grabbed him by the arm. What would Tahn have told this child? It made no sense to speak to a strange boy of their circumstances unless there were far more to this than met the eye. "Tell me what you know!" Lucas insisted. "Is he in danger tonight?"

"I-I'm not supposed to say."

Lucas gave him a shake, harder than he intended. "You must! Do you understand me?"

The child burst into tears again. "I'm sorry! It's too late. He's going to die! He went to the men—to save the lady—"

"Went to the men?" Lucas's heart suddenly thundered within him. "Where? How could he know? Why didn't he tell me?"

"He couldn't tell anybody! He had to save the lady!"

Lucas was quiet for just a moment, letting the words flow over him. "You brought him a message, didn't you, boy? Tell me! Everything!"

The boy tried to pull away from Lucas's grasp, and with the noise, his mother stirred awake on her mat and coughed.

In confusion, the woman reached her hand out weakly. "Please," she begged. "Don't hurt my son."

Feeling sick, Lucas released his hold on the boy and knelt beside them with his heart still pounding viciously. "I'll not hurt anyone. But you say my friend is in danger, child. Tell me what you know, for the love of God."

"I-I can't say any more. I don't even know any more."

"Did you bring a message, boy? Tell me the truth!"

"Y-yes. I'm sorry. I didn't know what else to do! I was afraid the man would kill me. Or the lady. He told me they'd kill her."

"Who? Who was it?"

"I don't know."

"Char," the boy's mother called weakly, fear plain in her voice. "Char, what is this about?"

The whole story came out then, and Lucas listened grimly. He knew he would have to go. There was no denying it now. If Tahn would hide this from him, he would hide it from everyone. With his heart pounding, he loosed the bag of coins from his belt and told the woman and her son to get what help they needed by morning's light.

"Wait," the boy suddenly called. He pulled something from beneath his shirt and placed it in Lucas's hand. A necklace. "H-he gave me this. But the lady should have it. Or else the boys and girls if . . ."

Lucas could not hear the rest. He dropped the delicate chain in his pocket and with a silent prayer rushed out to his horse. He felt as though he could explode. Why hadn't he known something was amiss? Why hadn't he questioned Tahn more?

It was a death trap. The boy was surely right. But Tahn would know that. He was no fool, but what could he be thinking? For hope of villains' mercy upon the lady, he would give himself away?

⚊⚊⚊

Outside of the Trilett gate on his dappled mare, Vari blew a signal horn, hoping for answer. He was worried, and he wasn't the only one. Jarel swore Tahn had told him he was going to the priest, yet it hadn't taken long to discover that the priest had not seen him. No one had seen him. Marc and Lorne had ridden into the forest, and they too tried to call Tahn in. But he didn't hear their horns, or he didn't choose to answer them.

But he shouldn't be alone, Vari kept thinking. *This is too much to bear. He can't keep on another night without rest, even though all of us could surely wish to. Where could he be?*

Vari rode out a little farther, hoping to hear Tahn's answering horn. But it was hoofbeats that got his attention. Someone was racing through the trees ahead like a demon-chased madman.

He held back, not sure what to expect until a familiar voice reached out through the trees. "Ho! Ahead with the horn!"

"Lucas?" Vari hurried forward, questions pouring through his mind. "Lucas, what's wrong? Have you found Tahn?"

Panting from the wildness of his ride, Lucas pulled the reins in the moonlight, his face a jumble of emotion. "None of you know where he went?"

"No. But how did you know? We haven't seen him since shortly after you left."

"Hours!" Lucas cried out angrily. "He's far the lead of us, and God only knows which way! If there are men out, call them. Gather whoever you can."

"What's wrong?" Vari begged him, the tension pounding like hammers in his stomach.

But Lucas did not linger for explanations. "Tell the men to meet me within the gate. I must speak to Lord Trilett and Master Jarel. Lord help us, that we are not too late."

12

With the cut of a rope, the bandits let Tahn fall from the back of the horse where they'd bound him. Fiery pain shot from his side to his chest, and he struggled to catch his breath. They'd come at least three miles since the beating, and they'd made him walk until he'd fallen, unable to continue the pace. Now he was dizzy, nauseous, hurting worse than before, but he did his best to look around at the place they'd come to. A house with one candle-lit window sat a short distance away, almost hidden by trees. Another building, surely a barn, was behind it.

Toma stood nearest him, staring down with a smirk at Tahn lying in the dirt with his hands still tied.

Without hesitation, Tahn met his eyes. "I want . . . to see my lady."

The callous young man laughed. "I feel the same way. And you've had your chance with her. It'll be our turn soon enough." As Burle approached them, Toma grabbed Tahn by the arm and jerked him to a sitting position.

For a fleeting moment then, Tahn saw a face at the candle-lit window of the house. It looked like a woman, and she was wider than Netta, more bent over. But then the image was gone.

Burle leaned and grasped the rope that still dangled from Tahn's neck. "Just a matter of time before the baron gets here," he said. "He'll have your head. And he promised me I could watch." He tugged at the rope. "Get up."

Tahn made no effort to move. "Show me my lady."

Burle answered the request with a savage kick. "I said get up."

95

Tahn shook his head. "I came in peaceful trade. My part is done. I'll not do what you say until yours is."

Burle kicked him again. "Do you have any idea how weak you look? How meaningless that is?" He grabbed him by the arm, pulling at the rope at the same time. "Come on, Toma. Let's get this fool ready to meet the baron."

They dragged him deeper into the trees, into a low clearing ringed by the scent of cedar. A circle of men were already there, one feeding a campfire, another lighting a torch, and another hammering stakes into the ground. Burle lifted Tahn and slammed his back against a tree.

"The mighty fall," he said with a laugh. "In your case, Tahn, again and again. How many times is it now that you've been broken? It's a curse. You claim God cares for you, but why doesn't he help you, then?"

With Toma and another man holding Tahn to the tree, Burle punched at him. "You know what your cousin told me?" he taunted. "To subdue you for him. That's what he said. And it's my pleasure. Happy to be of service."

He hit him again. And then he stepped back. Tahn expected others of the men to take their turns hitting him as well. He looked around at their faces. Some were hard as Burle and Toma, but others seemed different. *It's the money they want,* he thought. *More than Burle's revenge. God, touch them. Perhaps they are not too hardened to hear you.*

Burle was walking back to him with a stick taken from the fire. "We were talking about this the other night, Tahn. About what we could do with you. We all remember your fear of flames."

He closed his eyes. "God has freed me."

"Really?" Toma scoffed. "You don't look too free right now."

"No," Burle agreed. "I'd say not." He pushed the stick toward Tahn's chest, but Tahn would not cry out. He would not give Burle that satisfaction.

"Almighty God of majesty high," he began to recite the

words to a hymn that he'd heard both Netta and Jarel sing. "Walked on this earth, and came to die—"

"Shut up!" Burle raged at him. He grabbed him by the shirt. The other men released their hold, and Burle threw Tahn to the ground.

"I want his hair," the man named Eger suddenly said from among the crowd. "The Dorn's long hair for my collection! Would look right nice beside the auburn lock with the green satin ribbon."

Tahn rolled to face him. He remembered Eger. Tall and strange. He was one of the few who had actually liked Samis's Valhal. It made him sick inside to think of this man's hands on Netta, cutting a lock from her beautiful hair or her splendid dress. It must have been terror to her. This whole thing must be a nightmare. *Forgive me,* he prayed. *For putting her through this. I should have left her, once her family was safe. I should never have listened to them. I should never have stayed with them.*

Trust.

The word came plain into his spirit again. *She loves you. She would have followed if you had gone away from them.*

Eger stepped forward with his knife in his hand. With a laugh, Burle shoved Tahn onto his stomach and then planted his boot in the middle of his back to hold him steady.

"Holy Redeemer loveth my soul . . ." Tahn tried again with the hymn as Eger took hold of him.

He'd worn his hair long since he was very little. He didn't remember ever cutting it since it had grown back after the burns, after his mother died and Samis stole him away. But it was nothing to him now, to feel the knife cutting it away. It belonged in the past, in the memory of times he'd tried in vain to hide the scars from himself.

Eger claimed a prize that was worthless now. Tahn took a deep breath and continued the hymn. "By his stripes healed . . . in his blood made whole . . ."

Strangely, everyone had grown quiet. Even Burle, the huge

man, stood over him in silence, the heel of his boot pressing hard into his back.

"I . . . found peace . . . in God," Tahn struggled to tell the men around him. "I found forgiveness . . . and love . . ."

"You sound like another Lucas!" Burle exclaimed. "Did you sell your soul to a priest, like him? Or is that the kind of talk that buys Trilett favor?"

Tahn did not move, did not resist at all as he was jerked upward and dragged across the clearing. Then he was dropped to the dirt again, and one of the men cut the ropes at his wrists. They forced him to his back, stretched his arms outward, and bound them to the stakes they'd prepared. His legs were secured the same way, and then the closest men stood over him, passing a wineskin between them.

"Ever think you'd see the day?" Toma asked with a snort.

"Indeed," Burle answered immediately. "I've always known that I've bested him. Right from the start. And you've known too, haven't you, Tahn?"

Tahn had never acknowledged such a thing, never thought it, and yet a dark memory between them resurfaced in Tahn's mind. But he wouldn't see it, he wouldn't give it a place in his thoughts, even now. Instead, he turned his eyes to the moon peering through the treetops, and his mind to Netta. Dear Netta. *Lord God, preserve her.*

Burle shook his head at him. "Bet you wish you'd died in Alastair." He turned to walk away, and Toma immediately followed.

"Are you going to give him a drink?" one of the men asked.

"No," Burle answered coldly. "Why waste it on him? Keep watch."

With those words, Burle and Toma left. The other men stood silent for a moment. Tahn did not look at them, did not say a word.

"Keep watch?" one of the closest men spoke to Tahn, almost under his breath. "You can't even move. And by now

98

we're sure you weren't followed. Maybe Burle believes the stories. That you're devil or beast, and there's magic that keeps you from dying."

Tahn knew the slightest hint of fear in that voice. Calmly, he answered. "It isn't magic, Bert . . . the hand of God has spared me. And I'm in his hands even now."

The man gave a little laugh, but there was no strength to it. "What do you expect? Fire from the sky?"

"I know not the plan of God," Tahn told him with growing effort.

"But you think something's possible here?" another man asked. "You're all the fool Burle says you are!"

"Where is my lady?" Tahn asked them again.

"It doesn't matter to you now. You'll be dying right where you lay."

"I've prayed for her life," Tahn answered. "Almighty God will set her free."

"Believe what you want," Bert told him. "We've got other plans."

Tahn took a deep breath, and the fiery pain in his left side intensified. "Think, brothers," he said on. "Do you want . . . to meet God with what you do to her?"

"I ain't touched the lady," one of them said. "We're still waiting on the gold."

"Gold can't save you . . . when the judgment comes. Even if you never touch her, you're not blameless if you let her be ravaged."

"You think you'll scare someone into doing something stupid?" Bert protested. "Shut up, Tahn. It's useless."

"Burle's course is useless . . . it will bring you nothing but death."

"I said shut up!"

Bert retreated several yards into the trees. Of the other men, some remained near while others moved away, closer to the campfire. With a painful sigh, Tahn gazed up at the moon again, remembering Netta following him to Alastair, singing to him when he was so sick. Her soft touch had soothed him, her loving voice had called him from the brink

99

of death. *You've given me so much, my Lord. Whether I live or die, I thank you.*

He swallowed hard, thinking of the day he'd given his heart to the Savior beside a flowing stream. The blood of his past, the nightmares and torment, all of it had fled away by the grace of God. Netta and Jarel's familiar hymn filled his heart again, as though all the voices of the church at Onath were inside him. Drawing in the deepest breath that he could, Tahn tried to sing the words. His voice, never good, was worse now than usual in his pain, but this was an offering lifted to the throne of heaven.

"Almighty God, of majesty high . . . Walked on this earth, and came to die . . . Bore on his back the weight of our sin. Beaten and bruised, the Savior of men. Such love as this, I cannot tell . . . He gave me hope, released me from hell . . ."

Strength spent, Tahn closed his eyes. *Thank you, Lord, for the life you've given. I've tasted your goodness more than I thought possible. I'm ready to die, if it is your will. I came willing. For Netta. Set her free.*

Somewhere in the treetops, a songbird twittered. Tahn knew the dawnlight must be near.

It isn't right that she should suffer for her love for me. There is nothing impossible unto you. Give her peace. Loose her and take her home.

The songbird's lilting call mixed with that of an owl somewhere in the woods at his head. Burning pain in his insides made every breath now painful. He thought of his sister for a moment, and Lucas so far away. And Vari and the children. But weariness won over him, and before the light of dawn could touch him he'd faded into the dark mist of dreams.

13

Netta sat back against the stony cellar wall with Jarel's hymn circling in her heart. Because it was Tahn's favorite now. Because she wished she could sing it for him again.

"Oh, Lord," she whispered. "I know he loves me. But he should not give himself up to die! We were to be married. This cannot be your will. Better that he stay away, with the children, and that you give him peace to go on in life without me."

Even as the words left her lips, she knew Tahn would never let them be. In frustration she pulled herself to her feet. What if she rammed at the door or screamed again? Would anybody hear it? Would anybody care? For hours they'd left her alone. Her throat was parched again, and she was terribly hungry. But far worse were her thoughts for Tahn, knowing what these men would do once they had him in their hands.

Pacing about, she tried to continue her prayers, but she was too tense and agitated to form the words.

She'd heard more horses and a stirring of activity outside. She knew someone had come. Was it the rest of the group that had gone another way after the gruesome attack on her guardsmen? If so, there were many men here tonight, she wasn't sure how many. It would take a miracle of God to set her free.

She went to the door, peering out the tiny cracks again into the predawn darkness. What could she do?

Suddenly she heard a voice outside. To her great surprise,

it was a woman. She would never have expected a woman to be here among these horrible men. Was she wife to one of them? Another captive? Or both?

"More stew in the house there," the female voice was saying. "And a cake or two if they've not got them gone a'ready. Go an' claim yourself some now if you would, before it's too late. Never you mind the lady. Been all day an' night without a bite from you. She's got to eat or die away for the weakness."

Netta stood back from the door, waiting for the woman's entrance. What should she do? No one yet knew that she'd managed to get her hands unbound.

The door opened slowly with a creak of protest. The woman carried a lantern in one hand, a basket over the opposite arm. Netta watched in silence as the woman closed the door behind her.

Was this her chance? The only one she might have? Should she rush past the woman now and force her way through the unlocked door?

"Lady," the quiet voice addressed her. "I begged them to let me give you bread."

Netta stepped forward cautiously, near the wall, still thinking of making her way to the door.

"You're clever to loose your hands. They forbade it me and said I'd have to feed you like a babe if you had the will to eat. I've convinced them that you must, or they risk losing their prize."

"Please. I only want to go from here."

"Of course you do," the woman said much more quietly. "I know what they plan, and I wouldn't wish it on a beast."

Tears sprang to Netta's eyes. "Help me."

The woman pulled a skin of water from her pail and placed it in Netta's hands. "Drink. Then tie the rest at your waist. I'll give you bread. You should go quickly before Barnar returns from getting himself a slab of my cake. He's my brother, and too stupid to think I would deceive him, but we haven't much time. Those two men of the baron that were outside—I called them to eat as well, just moments ago, but they'll not linger there. They'll fetch their food and carry it right back here."

Netta drank a meager sip to quench her dryness but wouldn't take the time for any more.

The woman untied the knot in her own shawl and slipped it over Netta's head and shoulders. "Go to the west. Away from the house. Move quickly. But if anyone sees you, pretend you are me going to relieve yourself among the trees. I cannot promise you with so many men that you can slip away, but it is the only chance you have, dear Lady, and I had to give you that much. Come the full light of morning, it will be too late."

"Thank you," Netta whispered. "I pray that you not suffer for your kindness."

"I'll pretend you overcame me. I don't know what will be. But I don't care anymore. Two of these men are my brothers. One is my husband. But I would rather lose my life or watch them die than not lift my hand for you after what your dear one has done. Such a love is all too rare. It should not end in vain."

Netta suddenly felt faint. "My betrothed is here? He's come?"

"Yes, Lady. They brought him bound, short time ago."

Netta's heart was racing. "Where?"

The woman shook her head. "You cannot go to him. He's already wounded, and you won't be able to reach him without being seen."

"Please! Just tell me where! Wounded how? How badly?"

"I don't know, Lady. I saw them spill him from the horse, and he didn't gain his feet. They wouldn't tell me aught except that he still breathes. I offered to take him food and drink, but they refused. He lies bound in the trees beyond the barn, but most of the men are that way. He must love you fiercely. But there's no hope for him now. Save yourself. Please. It is what he would want."

Netta stood numb on her feet as the woman put bread in

her hands and told her the way to the nearest village. But she barely heard the words.

"He came alone?" she questioned.

"Yes, dear Lady. His life for yours. I didn't think any man had it in him. He should have his wish. Go, Lady. Go now."

Netta nodded to her and rushed from her prison, the bread still in her hand. Was this horrible news the miracle she'd prayed for? None of the men were in sight, which surely meant that all who were not sleeping or eating were gathered nearer to Tahn. Why? What would they do to him?

She turned her eyes to the forest to the west. *"Go now,"* the woman had told her. And if she hurried, she could be gone before any of the horrible men had a chance to run her down.

A hoot owl called nearby, but there was not much left to the night. She turned her head to see the slightest glow already touching the eastern horizon. Whatever she did, it must be done in haste.

But the barn lay only a short distance away. And Tahn was in the trees beyond it. So close, but the woman had warned her. *"There's no hope for him now,"* she'd said. *"Save yourself."*

Netta stood shaking. Tahn had come, just like that ogre Burle had wanted. They would kill him. How badly was he hurt already? Was there anything at all she could do? She thought of running away and coming back with help, but would there be time for that? Or would he be dead by the time she got back?

Tahn would want her to run, she knew it. He would want her to leave him and save herself, just like the woman said. But it was an unbearable thought. He would never leave *her* bound and defenseless. Never.

She looked down at the bread in her hand, the waterskin dangling from her waist, and she knew that no one here would give Tahn such comforts. *This is not the first time he's risked his life for me,* she thought. *And he would do it over again, if he were in my place and I were in his. I have to try to reach him. I can't just leave him. Even if we must perish in this place, at least let me see him first. Let us be together. Let me do what I can.*

With the woman's shawl over her head, she moved with quick steps toward the barn, pausing at the corner of it when she heard the sound of voices. More than one man would be guarding Tahn, no doubt about that. Men who knew him, enemies from his past, would not fail to guard him well, even if he was bound and wounded, because he'd survived them before. They feared him, she'd seen it more than once, and not just for his fierce skill with a sword.

Slowly, carefully, she continued, trying to see as best she could in the dimness. The voices were still distant. Would Tahn be near them? If not, then where?

She moved as quietly as she could, from one tree to another, past the barn and into the trees beyond it. Ahead of her, a flame flickered, or perhaps more than one. Campfires? At least one of the lights seemed too high for that. Torches?

With fear welling in her, she kept on. Why would they give light to the forest? Just to watch him? Or were they hurting him even now? She knew she couldn't stop them. She knew she would be powerless against a gang of brutal men. But her feet kept moving anyway, and her heart with them, longing just to see Tahn, to reach him, to give him the comfort of her love. *Forgive me, Tahn,* she said in her heart. *I can't leave you this time. You shouldn't have to be alone. Ever again. I can't just turn away and leave you to die.*

Crouching behind trees, she finally got close enough that she could see the clearing. It was almost like a little valley, down the cedar-covered slope, with another slope rising on the other side. Tahn lay near one of the torches. It took her a moment to realize that he was staked to the ground. Three men stood to one side of him, talking and laughing together. Two more walked near the edge of the trees, weapons in their hands. And it looked like four men lay soundlessly on their blankets at the opposite side of the clearing. Sleeping, yet still not far from their prisoner.

In the direction of the house she heard more voices, many

105

voices raised in a cacophony that nauseated her. They were celebrating. Tahn's capture? Why? This was a game to them, to snare Tahn, to torment and finally defeat him. And they were sure of their victory now. They were beasts, heartless brutes who cared not that Tahn was a man better than they, who loved, and felt, and cared more for the people around him than the lot of them put together could even imagine. They treated him like he was nothing, a dog or worse than a dog. A clod of dirt they could grind beneath their heels.

Fury churned in her as she watched two of the men step nearer to her beloved. One of them had a staff in his hand, and he used it to rouse Tahn with a sharp blow to his side.

"Hey! Dorn!" the man called cruelly. "Who told you to shut your eyes and relax? Maybe we want to have a little more fun. That's what you're here for."

Tahn didn't answer them a word, but she knew he'd wakened. She knew by the slightest turn of his head that he was taking in his surroundings and the placement of the men around him. He'd learned it of necessity long ago, she knew that, and it was a habit he might have always with him: the quick glance at every waking, to see just where he stood and what he might have to face.

But there was nothing he could do about these men now. They had him helpless. Such was their idea of fun, of sport, to torment him bound down that way.

The first man struck at him again. The second stepped closer and brought his boot down hard on one of Tahn's hands. And Netta could take no more. Without thought, she rose to her feet and began making her way through the trees around the clearing toward the torchlight. She couldn't just watch them. She couldn't just sit and let this go on.

"Who's there?" one of the guards called. "You on the slope? Magya?"

Netta pulled the woman's shawl close at her neck, letting its shadows hide her face. "I-I'm sent," she answered, trying to make her voice sound as throaty as the woman who had come to her. "With succor for the prisoner."

"What?"

Netta knew that it was too late for anything but hope that her charade would buy her a moment's time. She only nodded and continued on her course. Once they'd seen her, what else could she do? There would be no running, no escaping them now.

"Succor?" the guard asked. "Who's cockabrash idea was that?"

All heads turned in her direction. The men were suspicious already and soon would be sure that she was not the woman called Magya. It was too late to turn away, because that would arouse their questions, and they would surely follow her. She knew that she was dead now and so was Tahn, without a true miracle from heaven. There was nothing she could do but keep on trying to reach him, to give him what she could of sustenance and her loving touch before her identity was clearly known. *Give him strength, Lord. Give me strength.*

With one hand, she pulled at the cord of the waterskin. She knew what these men were like. When they'd snared Tahn before, they gave him no water, nothing, in all the time they held him. *Just a sip,* she prayed. *Please, let me reach him.*

Incredibly, the men stood still and watched her. Tahn, too, turned his head her way. She could not see his face well enough to know the look that was there, but she could imagine it if he recognized her. She almost expected him to speak, but he didn't. Of course he didn't. What could he possibly say without putting her in more danger than she'd already put herself in?

She was so close. She could see the rope trailing across Tahn's chest, almost surely tied at his neck. *Oh, God! Why did he have to come?*

And then, as she came still nearer, she could see his face, his eyes in the glowing torchlight with fear for her, not for himself. She held out the waterskin, that he might see it.

But one of the guards, a skinny young man, suddenly hollered. "Look at her skirt!"

107

And Tahn closed his eyes, his face contorted with pain, as though the words had been another awful blow.

"It's the lady! What kind of magic is this?" one of the bandits yelled, while with a stream of curses another came running at her. She tried to run to Tahn, but they stopped her. They grabbed her when she was only a few feet from him and pulled her away. She kicked and screamed, flailed her arms and fought with everything she could muster, but one man slapped her, and two others had hold of her so tightly she couldn't break away.

"Stop!" Tahn called to them. "Don't . . . hurt . . . her!"

Only then did Netta realize that Burle was one of the men across the clearing on the blankets. He rose to his feet with booming laughter and strode to Tahn's side.

"You've got yourself quite a wench there," he said as he lifted the length of rope from Tahn's chest. "If we had the baron's gold, we'd take her right now, all of us, right in front of you. It'd be worth all the more, to see your face—"

"Let her go," Tahn said, his voice sounding coarse and broken.

Burle pulled back hard on the rope. "I told you before. You're in no position to make demands."

Netta saw Tahn struggle, saw his arms tense and pull against the ropes that bound him, but to no avail. Still Burle kept the rope at his neck wickedly taut. And then he jerked it even harder, stealing the breath from him.

"No!" Netta screamed, finally successful at knocking one of her assailants away. She strained to get to Burle, to hit at him, to make him let go his hold, but the other men still held her fast. "No!"

"Get her out of here before the temptation's too much," Burle commanded. "I promised we'd ride home with a king's ransom in our bags."

The men who held her began pulling her away, despite her struggle.

"Throw her back in the cellar and find out what in the blazes happened over there!" Burle commanded. "Send Barnar to me. And three of you stay your guard. But don't touch her, you rousters, you hear me? Not till the baron empties his treasury and I give the word!"

They were dragging her, but Netta struggled, frantic, still hearing Burle behind her.

"Ah, Tahn, you never deserved something so fine looking your way. You should have been destroyed long before this."

She screamed again, she fought, knowing Tahn's silence, fearing Burle was killing him even now. But there was nothing she could do.

She kept the fight, the struggle, all the way to the cellar entrance. One of the men shoved her roughly down the steps into the cellar room. The woman, Magya, was still there, on the floor, rubbing her head as though she'd been struck by something.

The tallest man cursed her, told her to go before they beat her for her stupidity.

"Where's Barnar?" another man demanded. "He's got Burle to face for leaving his post."

"I sent him for his barley cake," the woman said, still rubbing at her temple. "How was I to know this one wouldn't be all faded away for want of food and water? I thought she was a proper lady, not a devil wildcat! Stole my shawl too! Will you look at that?"

Magya tore her shawl from Netta's shoulders and hurried away before Netta could see whatever might be in her eyes. Netta could hear the woman's voice continue outside, cursing, as she fled away from them.

One of the men grabbed Netta by the hair. "Burle's counting on enough gold to buy a hundred women like you, and their horses besides. If I wasn't risking the sword to cross him, I'd cut that skirt off you right now. You're enough to—"

Abruptly, forcefully as she could, Netta spit at him, hitting him square in the eye. He jerked back, cursing, and drew his knife.

"Watch it, Jorn," another man stopped him. "Magya won't wanna come back here tendin' a wound if you cut her. And if she's bled weak, or worse, the baron won't give full price, and you'll still be facing Burle's sword."

"Nobody spits on me!"

"Shut up. Take it out of her some other time. Let's go. We'll get Ogden and the Traises to stand at the door. I want to go back and see what else Burle's done with the Dorn."

They shoved her roughly to the dirt floor and bolted the door behind them when they went out. She could hear them laughing on the stone stairs, about Tahn in Alastair taking the whipping meant for his sister, before that taking arrows for some little girl, and now being strangled over his lady.

Netta screamed in fury and beat at the door with her fists. But it gained her nothing but more laughter from the men outside.

"She's crazy as he is! Just think what it'd be like, the two of 'em married! They'd prob'ly end up killing each other! Wouldn't that be something to see?"

She screamed at them again, but their voices only faded away in the distance. She was left alone again in the darkness behind the locked door. Helpless, she sank to the hard dirt floor and sobbed.

14

With heavy heart, Lucas watched Marc Toddin, the tracker, examining the earth in the growing daylight. They were traveling much too slowly for Lucas's tastes, but it couldn't be helped. Everything depended now on Toddin's skill and their gamble that the trail he'd picked up beneath a tree by the Trilett gate was really Tahn's.

It had been Vari's idea to start from the point where Jarel had last seen Tahn and pray that the Lord would give them guidance to follow his trail from there.

"If I can't track the bandits, at least I can track the Dorn," Toddin had said. "May the good Lord hold back the rain this time."

Lucas had worried at first that Tahn might have thought of this, might have purposely made the trail difficult so he couldn't be followed too closely. But Toddin said he'd left normal tracks for someone in a hurry.

Vari rode beside Lucas, his face pale and troubled. Lucas knew this was hard for him. Tahn had saved the young man from certain death at Samis's hands, and had been his best friend since then. Lucas would have preferred to leave Vari at the estate house, because of his youth and because of the way he let his emotions get the best of him sometimes. But Master Jarel had welcomed him along.

Instead, it was Lorne they'd left behind them again, because he was the best choice to try to calm Tiarra Dorn's fiery panic. She'd wanted to ride with them. She'd tried to insist upon it. And Lucas knew how wrenching it had been for tenderhearted Lorne to force Tahn's sister, the woman

111

he loved, to stay behind at the estate house against her will. But it had to be done, and Jarel commanded it. There was no way they could endanger her. Just as there was no way they could have accepted Lord Trilett's presence with them, though he had also wished it.

"We don't know what we're facing," Jarel had told his uncle gravely. "You must stay here in safety. We cannot lose you." For a moment it had seemed that Bennamin Trilett might protest the same as Tiarra, but after the priest's urging and that of other nobles among the still-waiting wedding guests, he'd retreated to his own chambers in silence. Then it had seemed all the more right to leave Lorne posted with them.

The group that now sought Tahn's trail was large. All but Lorne and Amos of the men who had attended Tahn's party, plus additional guardsmen. And volunteers from among the wedding guests, including men from three other noble houses and the father and eldest son of a farm family who had befriended Tahn and the children when they were in hiding.

Lucas drew in a breath, praying for the men around him and their desperate venture. The very air felt sour this morning, as though villainy had turned the world awrong. He thought of the children who'd wakened with the commotion in the night, and he prayed for them too. They'd learned what happened, because Vari had answered every question as though they were adults. And they'd wanted to come too, insisting they'd been trained to fight and could be of help. But Vari and young Marcus with his bow were youth enough to have along. And this was no place for children. Everyone was anxious. Tense. No one knew what to expect.

They rode beneath the rising sun, far too slowly, knowing their cause could become a painfully fruitless one. Tahn had too much the lead of them. He may have reached the villains already. There was no way to know. They may have already done whatever it was they were going to do.

Lucas's mind drifted again to the troubled days in Alastair. Marc Toddin had done all he could to help in that desperate situation. But his words had troubled Lucas's heart back then, and they haunted him still. *"Twice with my own eyes I've seen the Dorn walk willingly into savagery for someone else's sake. It's going to kill him one day."*

Tiarra sat in the corner of the Trilett drawing room, on the floor, her knees drawn up and her head down. She didn't feel like she belonged here now. It would have seemed more fitting to be huddled in the darkness under the barrel maker's shop again with her brother in hiding. The same blackness tried to settle over her, the same fear, the knowing that out there somewhere unseen lurked an evil bent on destroying everything she hoped for.

Why? Now Tahn was missing too! When everything was supposed to have been happiness and light! But such thoughts were a mockery now that her brother was gone. She knew his enemies. She knew what they were capable of. And she wished she could have taken up sword and followed the men who had left before dawnlight seeking his trail. How could she sit and do nothing?

Lorne was pacing in the entryway. She could hear his nervous steps first on one side of the room and then the other. He'd wanted to leave too, and be part of the search. She knew how he loved her brother, how he'd wanted to go with the men every bit as much as she did, and yet he'd accepted the charge of staying here because Jarel said to and because Tahn would want it so. He'd held her back when she'd tried to insist upon going. And she'd barely spoken two words to him since. She'd retreated in anger, in despair, furious at him for keeping her here. And yet she knew he'd acted in love for her, and for her brother.

She prayed that the children all slept long, though the morning was breaking over them. In the night Hildy had taken those who'd waked back to their beds. But this could not be easy for them. Tahn and Netta were the center of their worlds, their teachers, their friends, almost the same

113

as parents. There would not be any children at the Trilett estate if it weren't for them. It was strange to think how so many lives would have been different if Tahn and Netta had never met. Her own life, too, would be vastly different, and she didn't like even thinking about it.

She thought she heard a noise upstairs, and almost at the same time Lorne's furious pacing stopped. *Oh, God, this is like a bad dream.*

She rose to her feet, sure that at least one of the children must be stirring. Hildy would be occupied preparing break-fast already, whether or not anyone cared. And Tiarra knew that early morning with Netta gone might be a sad and frightening time for the children because they always looked for her when they woke. Especially the younger ones. Every morning, because she prayed with them and read to them.

I'm a poor substitute, Tiarra told herself. *But at least I can be with them in her absence. At least that's something to put my hands to.*

With a heavy heart, she moved toward the front stair-case where the children always came down. She heard a voice, tender and quiet. And then another, broken. A child in tears.

Lorne had gotten there before her. He knelt at the base of the stairs with two of the boys in front of him. Little Duncan was the one crying, and Tam sat on the bottom step beside him with one arm around his shoulders. Four steps up were the girls, Temas, Jeramathe, and Rae, clutching hands. And above them stood Ansley and Stuva, near the top of the stairs, both of them looking angry.

Lorne looked up when Tiarra drew close, but he said nothing. Instead it was Tam talking now. "We gotta go on doing the things we should with the day. That's the way to honor them best."

"Like what?" Duncan asked him. "I'm scared."

"Well," Tam answered softly, "what do we usually do? Pray? We can do that, just like when Netta's here. Only we can pray for her this time. And we can do the next lessons she woulda told us . . ."

His voice suddenly trailed off, and he looked away, but his arm still carefully encircled the younger boy.

"I don't think I can do anything today," Duncan admitted. "I thought everything would be okay now. It was supposed to be okay after Samis died."

"But there's more cruel men," Tam told him, sounding nearly grown though he was only ten. "We know that. The Dorn knew that. That's why he always made sure to keep the guard trained and watchful."

"M–maybe they wasn't watchful enough."

"There wasn't no way to be watchful for something like this," Tam went on. "Some things just hit you broadside, and there ain't nothing you can do."

Duncan leaned into Lorne, and Lorne hugged at both boys. The other children came down closer.

"I don't like it," Temas said. "You're talking like Tahn's gone away, like he won't come back. You shouldn't say he *knew* that. You should say he knows! He knows all about it. And he's gotta come back."

"I dreamed he didn't," Rae confessed sadly. "I dreamed we never did see them again."

"Don't talk like that," Temas scolded.

Little Jeramathe hung her head for a moment, and then she looked at Lorne and then straight at Tiarra. "You won't go away too. Will you?"

Doogan and Briant were suddenly at the top of the stairs behind Stuva, followed almost immediately by Jori, Micah, and Rane. All of the children. Tiarra felt overwhelmed just looking at them and too overcome to answer their questioning words, their questioning eyes. Tahn had created something huge here, bringing all these children together, making sure they had a home. It couldn't end. It wouldn't end.

"We won't go," Lorne was assuring them, though his eyes looked stormy and wounded. "We will stay with you."

"Will they be all right, Miss Ti?" Jori suddenly asked her. "Is everything going to be okay again?"

All of them drew closer. All of them were looking at her. Tiarra might have hoped that Lorne could find some way

115

to answer the question for her, but Duncan had burst into tears again, and Temas with him, and Lorne held them both and turned his face to the tiled ceiling. She thought of the rage he'd borne the brunt of, how she'd beaten at him in protest when he'd made her stay here. And now she hoped he realized how sorry she was.

"I know exactly what we must do today," she told them, not sure where the words were coming from. "We must take a hearty breakfast and then go across the grounds to the east and watch the progress on my brother's new house. We have to make sure it goes on, you know. We're going to need it. This one is almost full, and they're about to be married. Maybe . . . maybe we could walk about inside and picture the rooms. Maybe we can help them decide what should go where."

She felt her lips quivering. She couldn't say anything more. Lorne was looking at her. All of them were. "I love you," he suddenly said.

She had to close her eyes for a moment to fight back the tears. "And I love you. All of you."

"Let's do what you said," Rae suggested. "They'll be happy if the house is done when they get back. It's almost done. Let's help the workmen. We can hurry. Then when they're ready for the marrying, they won't have to wait—they can go straight home to their own house."

"And we can go there too," Duncan added. "Any time. All the time, if we want. That's what the Dorn said. Do you think they'll really be okay?"

"We'd better expect it," Lorne answered with the hint of a brave smile. "Can you imagine what they'd think if they got back here and found us brooding, not doing anything?"

"Tahn wouldn't like that," Ansley affirmed. "He says we're supposed to use our days well."

"Netta wouldn't like it either," Doogan agreed. "She told me all our time is lent by God. And we's supposed to steward proper. Do you know what that means?"

Tiarra smiled to see the hope growing in their eyes. "I think it means we should get busy."

116

15

Lionell Trent paced about in the early morning light of the courtyard, hoping to hear some sound from the gate. Lady Elane was still in labor the last he knew, but his mind was occupied elsewhere now, craving to know what was happening with the bandit band and the men he'd sent with them. Finally, he heard horses and hurried closer. After a few moments, the captain of his men, Saud, came sauntering through the gate casually removing his riding gloves as someone else led his horse.

"Well?" Lionell practically squeaked.

Saud's smile was dark, arrogant, contagious. "We have him, my lord."

Lionell clapped his hands together like a child. "Splendid! Ready my horse and a full guard. It will only take me a few moments to—"

"Sir, if you don't mind me saying, you've no need to sully your own hand—"

"Sully? Don't be ridiculous! This is a privilege. I wouldn't have it any other way."

"Then you would have saved much time by going with me in the first place. You could have watched the spectacle of his capture and finished him within a few moments."

"And put myself at risk?" Lionell questioned in surprise. "You know better than that! He would ruin me if he could. He might have tried to kill me, or expose our plot to the other nobles. It would have been foolishness to go before I knew he was properly secured. But now he's not going anywhere, is he?"

"No, sir. I saw him securely in their hands."

Lionell nodded happily. "Then it's been a good thing for the time to pass. The longer those bandits hold him, the more they'll break him for me. He'll be weak and helpless, just the way I want him." He turned toward his estate house. "I will go and get my grandfather's grand ax, and we'll be on our way."

"The bandits would still be happy to kill him for you, my lord."

"True enough." Lionell looked back with a grin. "But that would just not be the same, would it?"

Saud returned the smile. "I understand."

"Of course you do. You'd gladly kill him yourself for foiling you in Alastair. Twice, yes? He does have a way of making enemies."

"So did his father."

"We need no mention of that wretch! Imagine a common criminal daring to couple himself with the daughter of a baron."

"Of course you know she was not unwilling."

"And my father dealt with that properly, dispatching you to rid the world of the miserable wench! If only you'd found her son that night. But if you had, I'd not have this rare treat now, would I?"

"Do you wish me to carry the grand ax for you, sir?" Saud answered almost impatiently.

"No. Fetch me a coverlet to wrap it, and we'll tie it on my own horse. I think I shall like the feel of it near me."

With a jaunty tune in his mind, Lionell sprang up the stone steps of the rich estate and ran inside for the treasured family heirloom. For the lifetimes of at least four barons, the ornamented battle ax had adorned a wall in the Trent formal parlor. When he entered the room, Lionell stopped for a moment and gazed upon it almost in awe. That ax had been in his family for generations, but he'd never actually held it in his hands.

He drew near and carefully lifted the heirloom from its place. It was heavy, solid. He liked the feel of it very much. In a few moments he would be riding across wooded hills in the morning light with this weapon at his side. And then after so many years, the Trent grand ax would have its place in the family history again. *With my name lent to it this time,* Lionell thought, *my act long remembered. Fitting indeed. Perhaps my son will grow to sing a new ballad in my honor! Perhaps he'll commission minstrels! I shall be a legend, because I dare to rid the House of Trent from threat at the hands of the Dorn.*

He hurried toward the front entry, anxious to be on his way. Before the sun was even up, he had placed his riding cloak near the doorway in readiness for this time. As he neared it, Joren, a stable hand, came rushing in with a new saddle blanket. When he saw the ax, his eyes widened.

"Sir . . . Captain Saud told me you had need of this."

"Yes, yes! Help me to wrap this treasure securely for my trip. I do not need it seen, or damaged in any way."

Carefully, they wrapped the ax, and Lionell reached for his riding cloak just as a voice rang from the hallway behind them.

"Lionell!"

With a groan, Lionell placed the battle-ax in his servant's hands and commanded him to wait outside. The door was just closing on Joren and Lionell had begun fastening his riding cloak when his mother came into view.

"Lionell! I thought I heard voices. Where are you going? Lady Elane is asking for you."

"Yes," he said as he adjusted the brooch on his left shoulder and gazed with approval at his reflection in the glass beside the door. The scarlet trefoil pattern at the collar of his cloak always made him look so princely. "Has the time come, then?"

"Indeed, it has. The midwives tell me it shan't be long now."

"Wonderful! I trust she'll give me a son. Today of all days! When I shall finally have what I've longed for." He placed his hand on the door handle. "I am twice blessed, Mother. We'll not have to worry—"

"Lionell," she interrupted him sternly, "you've no business going anywhere. Lady Elane is asking for you. You're about to be a father."

"To my great joy, Mother! But I was with her through much of the night, and that should be good enough. We've the best of midwives at her service. It's not something I can *watch* anyway, and it could be hours yet. I can't linger. Today is far too important! This is the triumph I've been waiting for."

"Lionell Ennaysius, what are you telling me?"

He smiled. "You shall have your grandson, Mother. The heir to all things Trent. And I shall secure his wealth and power for him. We will never be threatened again."

He was almost out the door, but his mother caught him by the arm.

"Lionell, what have you done?"

He pulled away from her and brushed at his sleeve. "Secured us, as I told you. And I shall finish the matter myself. A most fitting birthday gift for my firstborn child."

"What have you done?" his mother blurted out again, her voice rising to near panic. "Where is Tahn Dorn?"

Lionell laughed. "Why in the world would you want to know about *him*, Mother? It isn't proper for gentle ladies to concern themselves with such vermin."

"Son! If you harm him, you bring the wrath of Lord Trilett down on our heads! Better to let it go than to risk our destruction. We've talked of this before."

"Yes, Mother. We have. But snakes and scoundrels cannot be ignored. I'll not be bitten by him when he decides to pick his moment. I've waited long enough."

"Lionell—"

"Your grandchild shall thank me."

"Or rue the day of your folly!"

"Mother—"

"There's something more worrisome about that man than his rights, should he pursue them! He never should have lived long enough to grow up. It's a curse, perhaps. It isn't safe to touch him."

"I've heard the nonsense," Lionell scoffed. "Thrice

charmed. Samis couldn't kill him. Father didn't manage to hang him. And we failed in Alastair, but I don't believe the foolishness. This is mine to do. My privilege. For the Trent honor."

"Where is he, Lionell?"

"It is no more of your affair, Mother."

"Where is he? By all that's holy—"

He smiled again and broke from his mother's grasp. "Right where I want him. And that is all I shall tell you. He's the same as in my hands. And no charm under God's heaven will stop me now."

16

Tahn lay on his back with the rope still at his throat. He knew where he was, staked to the ground like a hide waiting to be tanned. With a circle of trees around him, and above that, the brightening sky with a swirl of clouds. He knew the reality of this newest pain, and yet another reality encroached upon him—a dark room, a memory he'd never chosen to face.

Helpless, he had tried to pull against the ropes back then, but it did no good. He was just a little boy, but the pain of those days was dreamlike in its endlessness, and so intense that he trembled uncontrollably. He screamed, but that, too, did no good. He'd heard them say it must be like this, for his own good. He must lie still. But he did not understand. He tried to think of his mother, but the memory of her was becoming lost in Samis's cruel words. *"You've nothing in this world but what I give you, boy. You belong to me."*

The burns were extensive across his back and neck. Excruciating. And every night they bound him down when he was unattended so that the nightmares could not toss him and tear open what healing progress his skin had managed to claim. On his stomach, his face to the bench that had become his bed, Tahn sobbed, night after night, with the balm spread on his back and Samis's bitter tales in his heart.

"They didn't want you in that town. They know what you are—born to the sword and to blood. You'll never be welcomed, never live a normal life. But I can use a beast like you."

No. He only wanted to get away—to run through Alastair's streets again, searching for the mother Samis claimed he must forget. But he had no part with her; she wasn't even real. So he was told. And yet he longed for her still, for nothing more than her kind touch upon his brow, just to have her near him. He dreamed of her coming into the room, standing in the darkness. He cried out to her, begging her to take him away from this place.

But the hand that touched him was not his mother's. He screamed at the sudden shock of weight upon him. He shook at the pain of it, at the childlike voice warning him not to tell anyone.

No. He tried willing the scene away, taking his mind forward again to the desperation of the clearing under the trees. And Netta. He must think of Netta.

But Burle's face drew him back to the nightmare. He'd been much bigger than Tahn even then. A teenager, but already the darkness had owned his heart. His eyes were savage as he spoke the words Tahn had been careful to forget. *"Samis is not the only one who owns you now."*

No.

Tahn shook his head, shoving away the bitter vision. *Help me, God.*

He was shaking, aware of being on his back again. He could feel the ropes at his wrists and ankles, and the pain in his head and his ribs. But it seemed like he was caught between two illusions, two bitter horrors too awful to be true.

Help me . . .

The light of the sun was edging toward the treetops to his left, and the sky seemed to be streaming with light despite the swirling clouds directly above him. *I belong to you, my Lord. And with Netta it is the same. They cannot claim her. They cannot have her. Set her free!*

The sky seemed to shimmer like light on water, and it was endless, as though one could look upward and see into eternity. He'd never seen such a sky before, with a brilliant dancing blue and streaks of golden light. He knew this was

123

not the way of things on earth. He tried to reach upward, to touch the shimmering light, but his hands were still bound, tingling with pain.

Lord God . . . I don't understand . . .

Out of the light came one fluttering being, suspended above him and yet somehow at his side. And then he saw more like that first one, in the light and part of the light—a whole company of glistening angels, not unlike a painting in Benn Trilett's formal hall.

"Receive me, God," Tahn prayed. "I'm ready to fly away with you now if it is the time. And yet I ask you for Netta's sake—spare her the pain, Lord. Please."

He didn't know if he'd spoken the words aloud. It didn't matter, except that someone was coming toward him. Someone of earth, of the darkness.

He turned his head and saw Burle's sickening grin. "You passed out on me, Tahn. I would've kept on, but it's too soon for you to die."

As Tahn looked at Burle's face, the dark room tried to close over his mind, so he turned his eyes to the sky again. The radiant, endless light was still there, and it was filled with wings, far and near.

"You think you're going to ignore me?" Burle's voice continued.

One bright angel swooped down over Tahn. He was a huge and mighty being but with a glowing tenderness and somehow sadness shining from his eyes. One of his glistening wing tips brushed Tahn's face, and from that spot Tahn could feel a healing warmth spreading through him. "Are you . . . are you the angel I saw on the Trilett rooftop?" Tahn managed to ask him.

But Burle's booming voice rang out in answer. "You've gone mad this time! You've truly gone mad!" Toma appeared at Burle's side, and Burle nudged at him roughly. "He thinks I'm an angel. Can you believe that? Oh, Tahn! I come to you when you're bound down. When you're useless and weak. Tell me your prayers, and I'll dump them down a hole somewhere!"

Burle's laughter rolled over Tahn like a choking wave, but the angel's eyes held him. *"Peace. Your prayers are in heaven already. And heaven is here with you now."*

"We may have to do something to get his attention," Toma suggested. "Looks like he's trying to pretend we aren't here."

Burle grunted his agreement. "We're your angels of death, Tahn. Sent to make you pay for your arrogant ways." He walked to the remains of the fire, to the pile of wood beside it, and picked up a length of brush not yet broken into kindling pieces, with dead leaves still attached. "Stir the fire up for me, Cole," Burle commanded. "We all know how to make this boy scream."

The man called Cole added tinder to the embers, then more wood, until he had a roaring blaze. Burle shoved the end of his branch into the fire, and the leaves sparked and burned. Brandishing the flaming branch like a torch, he returned to Tahn's side and threw it at his bare feet. But the angel, with unearthly calm, turned his head and waved one hand toward the flame. Tahn could feel the gentle breeze blow across him and extinguish the fire before it could do its damage.

Toma stared. Two other men nearby stood to their feet. One of them walked anxiously away.

"Thank you," Tahn whispered to the angel and then turned his eyes to the sky again. "God, I thank you . . ."

His body shook; he didn't know why. The angel brushed one wing across Tahn's face again, and the shaking subsided.

Burle cursed and took his branch to the fire again. "Nobody ever said you weren't lucky, Dorn. But I'm not having any of this 'charmed' business. You hear me? You're just a man. Smaller than most. Stupider than most. And I can do to you whatever in blazes I choose!"

He lit the branch again. He brought one of the torches too, glowing red from the fire. But the torch went out in his hand, and when he threw the burning branch across Tahn's legs, another tender breeze put it out.

"The wind's contrary!" Burle shouted to one of the other men. "It means nothing!"

125

"He's a demon," that man answered. "Covered by strong curses."

"Then why did he thank God?" another man demanded with a hint of fear in his voice.

"Because he's a fool!" Burle shouted. "And a trickster! He only wants to scare us!"

"I thought you said he was helpless," another man said. "I thought you didn't believe such talk."

Burle cursed and ran at Tahn in a rage. "I don't! And I'll prove it to you. He's nothing! There's no power in him at all."

The angel spread both his wings quickly over Tahn's full length as Burle rushed forward and struck out hard with the torch club in his hand.

"I'd kill you now if it wouldn't cost me a king's ransom!" Burle raged. "You've vexed us long enough, miserable dog. It'll do you no good to pretend God cares for you. If he cared a wit, you wouldn't be here. You're cursed. More than any man I know—covered with scars and left for God's dung heap. You're nothing! Don't you know that by now?"

Burle hit at him again as he continued his tirade. And out of the sky's amazing brilliance another of the shimmering angels winged swiftly down. And another. And then still more. Soundlessly each of the majestic creatures huddled with the first one, spreading their radiant wings over Tahn's bound body. Burle kept hitting, and then he was kicking, cursing, but it was as if Tahn watched it all from the sky. He didn't feel the blows. The light of the angels blurred together, and Burle looked like nothing more than a tiny child out of control, kicking and screaming at a ball of light bright as the moon.

Tahn thought it must be a dream. He wasn't dead. Though he seemed to be above everything, he could still feel the ropes tight at his wrists and ankles. His hands and feet felt stiff, almost numb. But except for that, he didn't hurt anywhere, despite what he'd already suffered.

Cover Netta this way, Lord. Even in her waking moments. Pour upon her your love.

"Do not fear," the first mighty angel suddenly told him. "We'll not leave you."

With surprise he realized that the angel had whispered the words into his ear. And he was on the ground again, looking up through a shimmering haze.

"Heat a pot of water, Jeth," Burle commanded, his eyes looking strangely wild. "I want a scream out of him. You all know a bit of boiling water'll get us a good one."

But the man called Jeth rose to his feet in protest. "Don't you think it's enough, Burle? Look at him. You've broken ribs, who knows what! He's going to die! What more do you need?"

Burle stared at the man in furious shock. "Are you too soft for this? You knew what we were going to do."

The man nodded. "I knew we'd snare him and rough him up. Sell him to the baron and let him die. But all of this? It's past vengeance! It's senseless, Burle. He's helpless."

"He's breathing. And as long as he stays that way I can do what I want without endangering your sack of gold. So why do you care?"

The man stood for a moment in silence, looking at Tahn with sweat on his brow and pain in his eyes. One of the angels fluttered down and stood beside him, reaching his shimmering hand to touch the man's chest. "He was right all along," Jeth answered Burle boldly. "We've been doing the devil's work, terrorizing people and stealing whatever we could. He stood in our way because we were wrong! We're cutthroats! And you torture him for opposing us? We're fit to be hanged. All of us."

Without a word, Burle drew a dagger from his belt.

No, Lord, Tahn prayed. *No blood.*

"You can't deny that he prays!" Jeth continued. "You can't deny that God has kept him alive this long. Remember the church bells at Onath? And the turn of the crowd? We should have seen it then. He reached to God, and God answered him."

"I told you to heat a pot of water," Burle snarled. "Are you going to do what I say?"

127

But another man stepped closer. "Burle, it's no good us fighting each other. Jeth's right that Tahn's good as dead. What's the use wearing yourself out on him? He can't take much more anyway. You don't want to kill him accidental, do you? Just let him lay! The baron'll be here soon enough, and we can leave this behind us."

But Burle shook his head. "I ain't heard him scream."

Tahn closed his eyes, remembering Burle from those early days in the darkness of Valhal. It seemed he'd always relished screams.

"You're the demon more than Dorn," Jeth said soberly.

"I thought this was about gold," the man named Jud addressed Burle quickly. "The pay's the same if we just wait it out now. Get some rest. And feed on more of Magya's cooking—"

"Nobody defies me," Burle insisted. "I want a pot of hot water, Jeth. Now."

Some of the men gathered closer, anxious to see how this conflict might be resolved. Others backed away, wanting no part of Burle's rage.

With the unseen angel still beside him, Jeth shook his head. "Let it go. There've been enough screams."

Burle turned his eyes toward Tahn for a moment, and they were like looking into a wild blaze. Something deeper than Burle was there; Tahn knew it. He could feel the coldness of it, and see the dark horror staring out of the bandit's eyes at the angels no one else could see.

"No," Burle growled his response. "They'll not win." With his dagger at the ready, Burle ran at Jeth, who had barely time to pull out his own weapon.

Tahn shook. This was no dream. And yet it couldn't be real. The first of the angels laid a warm hand across his forehead, and he closed his eyes and prayed. The words came out almost on their own. "Dear God! Jeth has been wicked as the rest, but don't let Burle kill him. You've wakened his conscience! He'll hear your voice! Let him know you before he dies."

Suddenly, a scream flew out over the sky. And Burle lay on the ground with Jeth crouching over him.

No one spoke as Jeth stood to his feet, bloody dagger still in hand. Fear shone in his eyes as he turned to Tahn. Beside him, Burle moaned; he rolled just a little. But Jeth paid him no attention and hurried to kneel at Tahn's side.

"I'm sorry for all this," he spoke hurriedly as he sliced the ropes that held one of Tahn's wrists. "God, forgive me."

"He does," Tahn told him. "If you ask it truly."

"I do," Jeth answered, reaching toward Tahn's other hand. "Christ, save me, I do."

Suddenly, a shadow. Darkness falling over them. Before Jeth could cut any more of the bonds, Toma came from behind and struck him down with his sword.

"What do you think you're doing?" Toma yelled at the fallen man. "You loose him and then what's next? Loose the lady too? Before we have our turn at her? Not while I'm alive!"

Tahn tried to reach his free hand to Jeth's fallen knife, but Toma kicked at his arm and then stomped down hard on his already bruised hand. Standing over him, he shoved the tip of his sword at Tahn's throat. "Come and retie him, Cole," Toma commanded. "And then take Burle over to Magya for her bandaging. This little game is over."

Tahn closed his eyes again, suddenly struggling for a breath. Jeth was so still beside him. Dead. The shock of it was like a wound.

"You thought you'd won one of us over, didn't you?" Toma demanded. "Well, it gained you nothing. And I can assure you, the rest'll think twice about showing you any sympathy. Burle'll be all right. And we'll be even quicker to kill the next man who takes your part."

Why? Shaking, Tahn formed the question in his mind. *Why, Lord God, should a man die because of me? I thought you helped . . .*

"*Peace,*" came the angel's quiet voice. "*Though breath is gone, he lives. God's help is with you. And your prayers have opened a path of grace . . .*"

17

Lucas rode in the midst of the column of solemn men. *Tahn has more to give.* The words circled desperately inside him. *He has more to share with this world. I don't know where he is. But you do, Lord! Show us. Save his life again! We are not ready to be without him.*

"I don't understand it," Lem Toddin was suddenly saying. "How could Tahn hope to accomplish anything good by running to them alone like this? They're surely minded to kill them both."

"Did any of us know which way to travel before?" Lucas asked him sharply. "He's leading us, whether he knows it or not! By that alone, he may save Netta's life."

"If they're not already dead by the time we get there."

"Shut up!" Vari suddenly yelled from behind Lucas. "Why feed demons of doubt? Go away if you can't hope for good!"

Lem stared at the young man. "I'm sorry. I didn't mean—"

"You didn't mean God could use the Dorn's heart for good in this! Or reach his hand down from heaven to save—"

"Forgive me. I am just beginning to understand the importance of faith to all of you."

"And to you. One day," Vari continued bitterly. "When you begin to learn sense." He turned his face away and kicked his horse to move faster toward the head of the column.

"His love is deep for the Dorn," Lucas remarked solemnly.

"I can see that," Lem answered. "May I ask forgiveness of you too, Father? I know your love is great as well."

Marc Toddin brought the line to a sudden halt. Stepping from his horse, he scanned the ground. "We go in the direction of Brader's Point," he told the others. "If that's where Tahn's path takes us, be prepared. We'll not come on them unseen."

Lucas's heart pounded within him. It took only seconds to slit a captive throat, if a group of this size were seen to be approaching. *Keep us hidden from them, God. Let us come upon them by surprise, at Brader's Point, or wherever they may be.*

It didn't take Marc long to be sure of his trail, and they were moving again, always slowly. The Point was still far in the distance, and the sun was already high in the sky, warming the air around them. Men were already drinking deeply of their waterskins, with no idea yet how far they had to go.

Lucas looked ahead of him at Vari, who was pale and restless. His anxious horse seemed to be responding to the tension of his rider. The animal wanted to gain speed, and Vari had to hold him back. With a sigh, Lucas rode forward to the boy's side.

"Peace," Lucas told him. "Tahn has placed himself in God's hands."

Vari glanced at him and took a moment to reply. "But it's never going to end. Not till the baron is dead."

"We can't be certain that Baron Trent is involved in this," interrupted a nearby man, one of the wedding guests, a cousin of the hostesses of Netta's party.

"If he's not responsible then he cheers the man who is," Vari answered him angrily. "We all know the truth of that."

"Perhaps such words should not be spoken without proof," the nobleman continued. "The violence of Lionell's late father against Triletts is well known. But what could the baron now gain by kidnapping a Trilett bride? And then calling the groom to him? What could he want with the Dorn?"

131

Lucas turned his eyes to Jarel Trilett, mindful for the first time that none of the other nobles knew what the Triletts and the baron knew about the Dorn. No one had made Tahn's parentage widely known; no one else understood the noble birthright that had been so viciously denied him. Lucas took a heavy breath. Should he answer the nobleman's question? Was it his place to speak of such things when Lord Trilett had remained silent, at Tahn's own request?

But Jarel answered the question in a grave voice. "It's time you understood, Caden, that Lionell would like nothing better than to have Tahn Dorn dead."

"Why? To deny Benn Trilett grandchildren?"

"To preserve his own barony from a threat he only imagines. He is afraid of our groom, because Tahn Dorn is a Trent."

"What?"

"His mother was daughter to Baron Klonten Trent, and sister of Naysius, Lionell's father."

"Karra Loble? The mistress's daughter who disappeared? It can't be true."

Jarel frowned. "Then I've chosen a merry time for spinning lies."

The nobleman stared at Jarel in silence for a moment as they rode on. His brother Irzam and two other young noblemen rode nearer.

"Why weren't we told of this?" Caden finally asked.

"Our friend the Dorn had hoped to avoid outright war with the baron. He has seen enough of bloodshed."

"This begins to make better sense now," one of the other men spoke up. "I could not quite imagine how Benn Trilett could give his daughter to a commoner."

"You misunderstand him then," Jarel told them. "My uncle doesn't care so much anymore about lineage. He had accepted Tahn before we learned of his parents."

Caden gestured toward Lucas and Vari. "How is it that others know of these things when noblemen are kept in the dark?"

Jarel sighed. "Some were there when the truth was first found. Others are simply in our house and in our confidence."

Irzam looked troubled. "Why would Lionell fear the son of his illegitimate aunt? Is not his own claim far greater?"

But it was Caden who shook his head. "You know the saying about Trents: Pity Trent mothers when there are two boys in a generation. One will be a murderer, and one will die young. Perhaps Lionell believes that far too well."

"But the Dorn has made no threat, has he? And Lionell's claim *is* greater," Irzam argued. "Why would the baron risk himself with villainy? Even if he feared a plot against him, he could disclose it openly and call on the other nobles to stand with him! We'd have to, if it came to that. Not only is he older, but no one can deny his privilege. His father, Naysius, was adopted, but he was still a Trent son. And the bloodline touches Lionell at least in a measure through his mother, a distant cousin. So he has almost a double right. Karra Loble's waif could gain nothing against him."

"Until you understand that she was given the birthright," Jarel answered him soberly. "Naysius was disinherited for his evil ways, but he killed his father and claimed the barony before the matter could be known. Lionell knows it is true, and he would kill to keep the secret. By blood and by justice, Tahn is the rightful heir."

"This is like a strange dream, such a tale."

Jarel sighed. "It has been much trouble to a good man. I am sure the Dorn has wished that he never heard the name Trent."

"But would your uncle attest to his right, should this come to conflict?"

"It has already come to conflict. And my uncle would gladly have made this known, but Tahn prevented him for our sakes."

"Then he must hope for peace with his cousin."

"He did. I fear it may be too late for that now."

The weary group continued in silence over the worsening terrain as the sun's warmth bore down upon them. Then suddenly Caden shook his head again.

"Despite all this, it may be only bandits or Dorn's old enemies at the heart of today's trouble."

133

"And then we would be back to the boy's words," Jarel answered. "If Lionell is not responsible, then he cheers whoever is."

"What will your uncle say, or the Dorn," Irzam questioned, "when they learn you have told us?"

"I don't know. I am weary of keeping the matter hidden." Jarel stared ahead of them to Marc Toddin, who kept his eyes searching for any sign of Tahn's trail.

"Lionell may say that you made all this up," Irzam pressed him. "That it is Trilett revenge against the House of Trent."

"What revenge?" Jarel's voice was angry. "No one takes from him! No one asks anything of him. Except that he leave us alone."

Lucas watched the young noblemen ride on ahead of him in silence. Vari too was quiet, still at his side. How might it change things for all this to be known? Lucas's heart was heavy. There would be no avoiding another confrontation with the baron now, even if he'd kept himself away from this latest assault. Vari was right. He would never let the matter rest.

Lucas turned his eyes to the sky, which seemed strangely, unusually bright. *Help my friend,* he prayed in silence. *All he wants is a chance at tomorrow with the woman he loves. I know it is not too much to ask, Lord. Nothing is impossible with you.*

18

Tiarra and Lorne were at the site of the new house. The children scurried about almost in the workmen's way, sweeping dust from wood or stone and fetching whatever they could think to carry. But no one halted them. No one tried to send them away. Their voices carried with excitement, naming the various rooms and predicting all the glorious moments to take place in them. Tiarra knew she could not quiet them, though their words were difficult to bear. She knew the children's hearts were as fragile as her own this day, and if anyone silenced this game of hope it would be replaced by tears.

She stood in an unfinished doorway just watching them, but her thoughts drifted far away. Her brother had ridden away alone. Bidden to a trade. His life for Netta's. It made her heart ache, remembering his stripes in Alastair on top of all the old scars. He was far too quick to put himself in danger.

And why? Did he love everyone else more than he loved himself? Didn't he see what he'd become to so many people? A deliverer, a hope, an inspiration. Or did he still think he was a trouble to them? A terror? He used to believe that. She knew it. He used to think he could never deserve anyone's love.

She could feel the familiar fury swirling inside her as she thought about the baron and Alastair, Burle, and Samis, and what they'd put her brother through. The anger had never died in her completely, and she felt it rising again now, so much that she withdrew from the children to an inner room away from their gaze. She might have lingered there alone. She might have sunk into tears again, but Lorne stepped behind her so quietly that she didn't realize his presence until he laid his hand softly upon her shoulder.

His tender touch was warm as always. Most of the time, she had welcomed him and longed to be held by him. But right now she didn't think she could bear him so close beside her. She began to pull away, but then he whispered her name.

"Tiarra . . ."

She turned to face him. "I can't talk right now. Please, Lorne. You know me. I feel such a fire to help somehow. And there's nothing I can do."

"You've already given the children a hope to hold to."

She shook her head. "My brother did that long ago."

His voice was gentle. "Yes. By God's grace. But your encouragement has helped them. And me. Thank you."

For some reason his words only served to fan the wrath she was trying to squelch within her. "But we shouldn't even be here, you and I! Hildy and the other hired servants could see to the children! We should be searching. My brother wouldn't linger here—"

"He would not want you anywhere else. You can't place yourself in danger."

"But doesn't *he*?" she demanded. "And what about Netta? Is it right for us to wait in comfort while they suffer? Do you think my brother would wait if I had been the one to disappear into the night?"

"Tiarra, that's different."

"Because he's a man? You know that I'm as good a fighter as half the men who rode off with Lucas last night!"

"I'll not argue that."

"Then why couldn't I go?"

Lorne grew quieter, trying to reason, or to calm her. "I kept you here for Tahn's sake. And for the children, because they need you. And because I love you, Ti. I don't want you hurt."

She stared at him. He'd never called her Ti before, though they heard it often enough from some of the children. He took her hand, and she saw the sadness, even fear, in his bright blue eyes. It made her feel weak.

He hung his head. "I've been afraid for Tahn, and for you, since we discovered your kinship. Lionell is the son of his father, a ruthless man."

"If he's responsible for all this," Tiarra answered bitterly, "may God judge him this very day."

Lorne folded his arms around her and held her close. She laid her head against his shoulder and closed her eyes. But she could not stop her mind from racing. Netta should know such comfort as this in Tahn's arms. Were they together somehow? Where? And what could be done?

"I'm sorry," Lorne told her softly. "Please believe me, I would have given anything to go with them last night. I know how you feel. I hate being here helpless. I feel like I'm betraying Tahn because I'm not out there looking for him. But he would want you safely guarded."

She reached her hand to touch his short blond hair. "I can't fault you. I know you were commanded to stay. And your presence is good for the children." She took a deep breath. "They will need you . . . if . . . if Tahn does not return."

"No, Tiarra. Don't—"

She placed her fingers gently against his lips before he could say more. "I have to say this. Please. If he cannot return, he would want you to take his place, as nearly as you can, in their hearts."

"No one could do that."

"You know what I mean. Don't you?"

Lorne only held her in silence, unable to answer.

"And I know it's the same for me. I could never take Netta's place for them. But she . . . she would want—"

"Please," he begged her. "Stop."

Tiarra sighed. She knew the words were painful ones, but somehow speaking them was better than letting them silently eat away at her heart. She took Lorne's hands in hers. "Death has always been but a step away from him."

"But that is past."

She bowed her head. "God has not kept us from pain.

137

He has brought us through it. And now—I don't know how much there will be this time—"

"Tiarra, please. Don't lose hope."

She took a deep breath. "Only nine months I've been with my brother. Some of it has been a frightening time, but these have been the best days of my life. God has given me family, and future. And you. I won't lose hope, Lorne. Even if I think it is his time to die."

Lorne pulled away enough to look into her eyes, and she could see the pain, the protest, in him over her words. But she continued. "I mean that, by some evil plan, we should have to go on without him. Without both of them. But God is greater than times or seasons or plans of men. And I think the death that would hold him cannot win."

"Death has no sting," Lorne agreed, leaning closer into her again. "It has no victory. Nor do evil men."

"For God Most High has graven our names on the tablets of life." Tiarra repeated the words she had once heard the priest say. "Whatever happens, I think this time it is finally over."

He nodded his head and placed his hand against her hair.

"Will you wish to marry me one day?" she asked him boldly, strangely. How could she dare think such thoughts right now?

But he did not seem the least bit surprised. "With all my heart."

"My brother will be pleased."

"I know that."

"If you're very sure, perhaps we could mention it to him."

He smiled, just a tiny smile. "In good time, Ti."

"When he comes home?"

Lorne's smile grew larger. "Yes. After he marries Netta."

Now Tiarra smiled too. "When they're moved in here, that would be a good time. With the children all crowding around them, telling them the names they've given to all these rooms."

Lorne leaned and kissed her cheek. "I would rather speak of it to him for the first time alone. Once he's home. In good time."

Her face darkened for a moment. "He might be hurt."

He nodded. "I know."

"But God brings him through."

"Yes. He does. He will."

Tiarra lifted her face toward Lorne's and kissed him softly, lingering for a moment at his lips. "Will I ever learn to love as much as my brother loves?"

"I think you do."

Doogan's voice suddenly called out to them, joined almost immediately by others of the children.

For a moment, Tiarra's heart pounded, but there was no fear in the voices. She drew in a calming breath. "Do you think it would be right for us to pray with them again?"

"I think it would be a comfort."

Tiarra sighed. "Do you think my brother will ever be a father?"

"Many times." Lorne put his hand in hers. "And not just to these. He'll have his own. It will be over, just like you said. He'll have peace." He kissed her forehead softly, and they went together to the children again.

Tiarra looked around her at the grand house this was becoming. With many spacious rooms, two sets of winding stairs, and many windows looking out over the lovely estate. In her mind she could picture the place all finished. The walls in merry colors, and the rooms filled with the marvelous Trilett taste in furniture. Even tapestries on the walls, and music somehow floating over everything. And Tahn holding Netta lovingly in his arms.

She closed her eyes, drew in another long breath. *It will be over.* Lorne's words echoed within her. *He'll have peace.*

Oh, let it be so.

Netta heard them coming before they even reached the steps outside her cellar prison. Two men, talking. About Burle, somehow lying bandaged in the house.

What could have happened? Could she entertain the hope

that Tahn had broken free? She didn't know if it was possible, even for him. She didn't know if he yet breathed.

She moved to one side of the door in the dimness, wishing there was some hope of wrestling her way past them and running out of here. She would go straight to Tahn again, praying to reach him, to touch him, one last time. She ached terribly, but still she longed to fight the men when they opened the door. What else could be for her, futile as her small struggle might be? They would not do her good.

She heard the heavy bolt moved from the wooden door. Again there was a creak as the outside light broke in. With a cry, she hit at the first man, who simply shoved her back with a curse.

"What did I tell you? She's turned wild as a demon. Too much time spent with the Dorn."

Netta struggled to her feet, staring at them. They were big men, both of them. And one of them held ropes in his hand.

"Maybe so," the second man said blandly. "But being locked in this hole could make the sweetest noble lady crazy after awhile. Ain't much of a palace."

The closest man took a step nearer, and Netta tensed, still hoping to fight them though she knew it would only cost her pain. "We've got to get you ready for the baron," the man told her. "Can't have you scratchin' his eyes out, now can we? He wouldn't like it. He was pretty careful to say about prisoners being subdued, but we didn't think we'd have so much of a worry with you."

Netta swallowed down the anger rising in her throat. "He will come here?"

One of the men smiled. "Personally. I hear it's an honor. You should be proud he thinks so highly of you." He grabbed for her arm, but she backed away and then struggled when he grabbed at her again.

"You see?" the man said. "I told them you'd be fightin'. I told them we'd have to tie you good, or you'd be lightin' into the baron. He could charge us each a gold piece for that."

140

The man wrestled to hold her arms as the other struggled to tie her hands behind her back again. "The Dorn teach you this kinda fight?" the man with the ropes asked her as she continued to strain against him. "I thought noble ladies was weak and delicate, kinda like them flowers they like in them gardens of theirs."

Father God, help, Netta prayed as he tightened the ropes at her wrists. *Oh, please.*

When her hands were secured, the men forced her to the dirt floor. One of them placed his grimy hand against her neck. "Ah, if we could take her now," he mused.

"Later. When the baron's had his fill. Right now we're only to see that she don't kick him in his manlies 'fore he gets a chance to do what he will."

They tied her feet securely. They wound an extra length of rope around her arms. Staring up at them, she felt suddenly choked by tears. "Tell me—is my beloved alive?"

"Don't matter," one of them told her. "If he is, it ain't for long. Good thing Burle's over there with Magya nursing a hole in his side. He's mad enough to cost us half our pay."

"Did Tahn fight him?" she pleaded hopefully.

One of the men laughed. The other didn't answer at all. They rose to their feet, and one of them pressed his waterskin against her lips. She took a sip with pain of heart. She had not been able to give Tahn even this small benefit. "Please . . . is he—"

"Forget your lover, lady. He'd been better off if he was never born. And you shoulda stuck with one of them puffed-up rich men with rings on their fingers. Ain't no helpin' you now."

Netta stared up at them, feeling utterly broken.

"Are we supposed to gag her too?" the shorter of the two men asked.

"Nah. Let her scream. Who's gonna hear? Diggen just got back from the south trail as far as Brader's Point, and there ain't a sign of nothing. Even if the Dorn told 'em that much, they ain't gonna find us now."

He wouldn't have told. Netta let the words sink over her

as the men turned away and left her alone in the darkness again. *No one knows where we are. Except the baron. And he will be here at any moment.*

She leaned her head back against the wall behind her. The ropes cut into her, and it was hard to put one thought after another. Perhaps they would truly die. Both of them. Separate like this. Helpless.

She remembered her dream, of Tahn in the cage, wounded and broken. But still brave. Still faithful. She closed her eyes, drew another deep breath.

"Our Father, which art in heaven . . ." She forced herself to remember the holy words, to say them steadily, despite the temptation to despair. "Hallowed be thy name. Thy kingdom come, thy will be done, on earth as it is in heaven . . ."

19

Tahn lay with his eyes closed, conscious of each breath and the burning pain that accompanied it. The sky above him had grown too bright to look upon, but he could still feel the glow of it, the warmth that seemed to soak inside him. Perhaps the pain was touching his mind. The heat of the sun and the lack of water. But he still felt the oddest sensation of touch, a cool hand, not on his forehead but somehow within it.

"Dorn, look at me."

Something hard nudged against his side and then kicked at his arm.

"Dorn, wake up."

He opened his eyes just a crack, just a squint against a light greater than he'd ever seen from the sun. A dark shape loomed over him. A demon, it could have been, but its voice was Toma's.

"Don't keep going out like that. You make me think we're gonna lose you before the baron ever gets here."

Memory rushed over him, of Jeth falling at his side. He turned his head, he tried to look, but the body was not there.

"The men've been telling me you ain't got much left. Maybe they're right. Hard to say with you, I know that." Toma squatted down. "But I've seen you looking better. I tried talking to Burle, you know. 'Bout being sure we ain't killed you before the time comes. You wouldn't die on me, would you now?"

Tahn drew in another aching breath, and it seemed to take

143

extra effort. He'd known since the beating on the trail that something was broken. Ribs. But the pain was so much worse right now, making it harder to breathe. He closed his eyes.

Toma's hand was suddenly on his chin. "Come on, Tahn. I thought you were a fighter." He pushed a waterskin forward, pressed it against Tahn's lips. "Drink. Come on. Just enough to keep you here for the baron."

"My lady—"

"She's not here. Forget her. You'll not be seeing her again."

Toma splashed the water across his lips, and Tahn took in what little he could.

"Free her . . ."

"Are you mad? You're talking to the wrong man now."

"She has no part in this."

"Well. Maybe she wouldn't have. If she hadn't tied herself to you. Should have known better, that's what I say."

"God loves her."

Toma laughed a little. "Oh, sure. The rich are always his favorites, aren't they? While poor men have to steal to survive. And then they go to hell for it."

Tahn shook his head. "He loves you too."

"Now I know you're mad! You know what I am, Tahn. I don't care, and I'm not sorry. I'm gonna take the lady when I get the chance, and I'll laugh at her prayers. I'll watch you die with no regrets."

"He loves you," Tahn said again.

"Then he's crazier than you are."

Toma pushed the water at Tahn's lips again. Tahn tried to look up into his eyes, but he saw only darkness surrounded by the halo of the sky's light behind him.

Toma set the waterskin aside and reached his hands toward the rope at Tahn's neck. Even the slightest movement of it hurt, and Tahn closed his eyes again, expecting the coldhearted young bandit to pull it tight, tormenting him as Burle had done. But he could feel the cool hand at his forehead moving down across his cheek and then touching the raw soreness at his neck. The angel. Still with him.

144

Toma's hands pulled the rope, but it did not tighten. Tahn opened his eyes again just as Toma loosed the rope enough to lift it over his face, jerk it loose, and then toss it to one side.

"Thought I'd better remove the temptation, Tahn. If Burle gets himself back here, he'll get a hold of you again. And I don't think you'd take one more strangling. Do you?" He poked at Tahn's side. "Not that I'm going soft, you understand. I'm just protecting my purse. You know what I mean. Same goes for the boiling water. Nice idea. But you're too weak right now. I might suggest it to the baron."

Tahn stared upward into the darkness where he knew Toma's eyes must be. "I remember . . . when you were captured. Samis took you from the streets of Alastair. Like me."

"Not like you, Tahn. Not like that."

He managed to nod, a little. "No burns. I know. But you . . . you were scared."

"Oh, shut up. I was a boy then. And he was—"

"Tyrant . . . devil . . ."

Toma stood tall again. "No use speaking of the past."

"You can . . . be free."

"What are you talking about? I am free. Since before Samis died. You know that! He doesn't rule me now. Your mind's gone, Tahn. You're fallen into the past."

"He rules you . . . if you're like him. But you can be free. You were innocent once."

Toma laughed loudly this time. "Once? Weren't we all? It doesn't last. You know! You've got as much blood on your hands as any of us."

"God forgives . . ."

"The noble ladies, maybe. Babes in the churches, saying their prayers. But not grown men. Not killers like us."

"Samis made you . . ."

"Oh, I know. He made me a killer. Just like he made you. But now that we *are* that, there's no going back. Even for you, with all your trying. If I loosed you and gave you a sword, you'd kill me gladly for a chance to get away."

"No."

"No? You're telling me you wouldn't want to leave?"

"I would . . . find Netta."

"Oh yes. Your true love. That's pathetic, Tahn. You were very good once. Some of us even feared you. But you're pitiful now. Weak on the inside. You can't care what happens to her if you're going to be strong! You live for yourself. Take what you can."

"Toma, you had a mother—"

"Shut up."

"She was good. You told me—"

Toma's boot smacked against Tahn's side without warning. The jarring pain of the blow ripped through him, tearing through the other pain and taking his breath away. Above him the sky seemed to tilt crazily.

"See what you've done? You bring it on yourself. I told you to shut up."

"Please—"

"You're not going to talk me into going soft!"

Tahn lay struggling for air as Toma walked away from him. Gray spots floated across his vision. Through them, the sky continued to waver even as he closed his eyes again. The world around him faded into a hazy darkness, and the ropes disappeared. He was walking in the past, in a forest near the road to Alastair. *It must be a dream. The pain has sent me beyond myself.*

He was surrounded by other young men waiting for Samis. The master had gone into the city for provisions, but when he came back it was with more than the necessary bags. A dusty-haired boy cowered in front of him on the horse, his dirty cheeks smeared with tears. Toma. Barely seven years old, and snatched from Market Street to begin the horrors of training.

Years rushed over Tahn's mind. Samis's Valhal, the blood, the pain. Children were turned into beasts by the ruthless hand of evil. The crushing weight of it pressed against his chest. *Oh, Father—God, you know. He was a little boy. A scared little boy . . .*

"Do you plead for your attacker?"

146

A sudden voice asked it, softly, gently. The angel still at his side.

"Yes." Tahn struggled to get the word out. He wasn't sure if he'd said it aloud, even in the strangeness of this dream.

"Why?"

"I was . . . a scared little boy too . . ."

"But now you're a man of faith."

Tahn remembered the hope he had reached for, the light of God that had taken him from the darkness and given him a measure of peace. Only in that light, only in God, would Toma have a chance for anything but destruction. "Touch him, God . . . please."

"We cannot make a man give his heart to the almighty. He would ravage the woman you love. Gladly. He longs to."

Tahn started shaking. "I know."

He felt the angel's cool hand suddenly upon his side. "You are a saint among men, Tahn Dorn. For all the darkness you've known, yet you are able to love greatly."

"Toma is blind. They are all blind."

"They will not all hear the voice of God."

Tahn could see Cole bowed in the face of Samis's raging, Judson beaten on his first day at Valhal, Eger cowering in a corner. "Touch them, Lord. Give them . . . every chance . . . even the baron, oh God, may he hear you . . ."

The haze lifted away, and Tahn was aware again of the brightness of the sky. Everything above him seemed to quiver, as though the light was in motion. Angels filled the heavens, their wings seeming to feed the winds and make the entire sky alive. This dream, if that is what it was, seemed suddenly full of them.

"Are there more of you with Netta?" he asked, his heart heavy for her sake. He'd failed her. He'd come as commanded, but it had served for nothing but to add to her pain.

"There are more with her," the angel at his side confirmed. "She will not be alone."

"They would keep her when I'm gone," he said with pain of heart. "A hopeless slave to them, ravaged every day. It mustn't be so. Better that she die—"

"She will never be hopeless, Tahn Dorn."

"Take her away."

The angel sat beside him, laid his large hand across Tahn's brow. "There are some things I cannot do."

"Why?"

"If I take her up, her life is done. And it is not time."

Tahn breathed in, and the air felt strangely like water moving inside him, filling him with coolness. "Then she will live."

The coolness spread within him, numbing him. At the same time the brightness seemed to be settling upon him, covering him with a layer of soothing warmth. He'd never had such dreams as this. Not even the other times when he was in pain. He could look through the sky now like it was a pool of water and see not only stars beyond it, but cities, worlds. And a beautiful place brighter than the sun where a woman stood beside a crystal palace and reached her hand toward him.

"Mother?"

As soon as he said it, she was gone. He'd not seen that face since he was so very small. And he'd not been able to pull it into his memory through all of the torment that had followed. But he knew it was her. He shook again, suddenly feeling her tender touch against his cheek.

"Mother."

But it was the angel beside him. The light of the sky seemed to pulse around him.

"I've seen . . . a glimpse . . . of heaven."

"Do you know there are those who love you there?"

"It is hard . . . hard to fathom."

The angel smiled. "Perhaps so. But you know your Savior loves you. He is all places with you. And he is there, where there is no more pain."

No more pain. Tahn could see through the crystal-clear sky above him to the place of peace, comfort, and boundless love. He knew he was broken of body again. He knew he would be many days in pain, perhaps weeks at recovering, if he survived. But perhaps he wasn't meant to. Maybe this dream, this glimpse of heaven meant that it was time to go home. He was so weary inside. So tired of body. So scarred.

The sky was suddenly blurred, but still he could picture his mother's outstretched hand. And he felt a hunger he'd never known before, to step away from this world into the brightness and the waiting peace. It all seemed so close, like he could touch it, like he could simply choose to shed this pain and walk into his Savior's arms. He wanted it, and yet he could not wholly embrace the thought with Netta here somewhere, needing help.

Tahn trembled. He could still see the brightness extending above him, the shimmering angel's wings. But they seemed farther away somehow, as if driven off by his thoughts, his doubts. *How could I leave her?* he questioned in his mind. *And yet I long to be with you, Lord, and for all of this to be over.*

He could not hold back the tears as the painful awareness of his bitter surroundings returned in its fullness. He could feel the ropes again and hear the bandits somewhere nearby. Perhaps he'd wakened. He could not be sure now. Nothing seemed real. Under the sunlit sky he wept. And his angel stayed beside him, holding gently to his bound and wounded hand.

20

Marc Toddin leaned down to the dirt, a frown on his face. Brader's Point rose beyond them, less than a mile away, but he had stopped the troop of men, studying the signs here, trying to read what had happened in this open place.

Lucas rode nearer and dismounted from his horse. "What do you find?"

"More tracks. He's not alone here."

"Did they go on together?"

"I know Smoke's hooves. We've been following him for hours. Something's happened here. A group with horses, many, it seems. But there are boot tracks. They dismounted, some of them."

"Tahn? Can you tell?"

Marc shook his head. "Smoke's tracks are different suddenly. Like he's prancing, jittery. And I don't know Tahn's boot track. I can't be sure."

"Which way do they go?"

Marc pointed to the northwest. "Most of them that way. Some back the way we came, but not on the same trail. Smoke—I'm not sure—he's circled around . . ."

Marc looked at the imprints on the soft ground in front of him, glad that the rain had not returned. He studied the horse tracks for a moment until he saw something that made his heart heavy. "Look," he told Lucas. "Here. This indentation. Somebody or something hit the ground here."

Lucas shook his head. "I see no sign of blood."

"No. There's none here. And that's a good thing." He

followed the track just a few steps farther. The way the boot tracks scattered over each other, around each other, there must have been a scuffle. This was the place Tahn had encountered their villains. He felt sure.

Lucas glanced up at the sun. "Are you sure of the way enough that we can continue? Which direction has Smoke gone?"

Marc did not answer quickly but still studied the ground before him. There was a bootless footprint, plain as the dirt itself, in a low place where the mud had not completely dried since the rain. "I'm not sure he's still with Smoke."

"What do you mean?"

"He may be the one who hit the ground. I'm not sure he remounted."

Lucas seemed confused. "Then what? He's walking?"

With heaviness of heart, Marc followed the trail for several yards before he answered. "Someone is. In the direction of the horses. Bare of foot."

Lucas shook his head. "That can't be Tahn."

Marc sighed. "The gait is uneven. Long steps and short. I saw this once before. A stumbling slave, pulled along."

Lucas turned his eyes heavenward. "He's captured."

"I can't be sure. But his other track stops here where this one begins."

"What about Smoke's prints?"

"They're lighter. Erratic. I can try to pick his out, but they mix with the other horses."

Lucas looked like he was in pain. "Try."

Marc took some time studying, following the prints he saw, praying. He went away from the trail of the other horses for a time, stopping at an especially imprinted spot and then going on again to see Smoke's prints circle back until they were planted atop the prints of other horses. "I think he's following them."

Lucas nodded, slowly. "Tahn must have found them and seen them with a captive. He would follow, until he could find a way—"

Marc shook his head. "Smoke lay to the ground a few

151

feet yonder. He rolled. But there are no boot tracks there. He's riderless. And bleeding."

"Bleeding?"

"Look." Marc pointed out the dark droplets near the track of the single horse before it joined behind the others. "There was more where he rolled. Not bad. But bad enough. And look. He only follows a short way and then crosses to the trees again."

"Might he still be there?"

"I don't know. But he's riderless. And our trail's pretty plain here. Let's get moving." He turned to his horse and mounted without a word but then glanced at Lucas again. "You know how bad this looks."

Lucas shook his head. "We've seen only horse's blood. No bodies."

Marc nodded gravely, pointing out another trail. "One more rider. See? Straight north."

"I don't want to separate," Lucas answered him. "We'll stay where you think Tahn's trail is."

"The group," Marc told him soberly. "The shoeless tracks."

Quickly as they could, the men progressed with Marc ever at the front, studying the ground. Most of what he saw he said nothing about. The human footprints, partially obscured by horse tracks, were still uneven—a stumbling, faltering gait—close together and then wide apart. Walking, running. It was more than Toddin wanted to see. If this was the Dorn, he had been treated like an animal, pulled behind a horse until finally the unmistakable point at which he fell. Here Marc stopped again. Here he saw blood.

He said little of the things he could read. The fall, the boot tracks again, the dark stain on the sandy soil. But the trail went on. And they must hurry to follow it.

"Look!" Vari suddenly called from behind him.

Marc turned his head to see Vari pointing away to their left. A shape, a horse, stood in the shade of the trees. It took one step, and then another, limping, head bowed, clearly in pain. The animal wasn't bleeding now, but it wasn't hard to see the encrusted blood over a wound in his chest. Vari quickly rode closer. Smoke knew him. He made a sound. And then as if he couldn't stand strong any longer, he rolled to one side and flopped wearily to the ground.

With a cry, Vari jumped from his horse and ran to the animal. Lucas hurried to join him. And feeling heavy, Marc followed. The horse was hot to the touch, glassy eyed.

"Knife wound. Very deep," Lucas said, his voice sounding somehow wounded. "There's another, on his left flank, but not so bad as this on his chest."

"He'll make it, won't he?" Vari asked.

"Can't say. It looks enflamed. And he's a long way from home."

Vari shook his head. "We can't kill him! Not Tahn's horse! Surely he'll be all right."

Lucas bowed his head. "I can pray. But it doesn't look good with him down."

Marc took a deep breath and turned away from the animal. "We can't bring him with us in that shape. End his suffering or leave him. We have to go on."

"We can't kill him," Vari protested again. "Lucas, we can't. He was arrow-shot once. And he healed up all right."

"Would you stay with him?" Lucas abruptly asked the boy.

Vari seemed stricken by the question. "No. No, I can't. None of us can. We might—all of us—be needed."

"Then if you can leave him alone this way, very well. Otherwise . . ."

"No! We'll have to leave him, Lucas. But he'll be all right. You said you'd pray."

And pray they did, as they continued on the trail, but the group was very quiet after that. Marc knew they were troubled to find Tahn's horse in such shape. It seemed a shame to leave him suffering, but whether they should have mercy killed, Marc did not know. None of this boded well for Tahn.

Still, Marc said little of the things he knew and only led the group forward. Who could tell now what they would

153

find? Marc thought of the first time he ever saw the Dorn, the day arrows had felled him to the dust. And then a year later in Alastair's bitter streets he saw the Dorn hold himself against the post for a brutal whipping he did not deserve. *It's going to kill him.* The words of his solemn warning to Lucas echoed through his mind. *It's going to kill him one day.* But on any of the occasions, including this one, there'd been nothing any of them could do. With a deep and anguished breath, Marc kicked at his horse and hurried forward.

⚊⚊⚊

Victory by blood. The words repeated themselves again and again in his mind like a drum cadence joining its rhythm with the pound of his horse's hooves. *Victory by blood.* Lionell remembered his father's brief interpretation of the family motto. "You risk your own for what's important. You take another's to gain what you must."

He thought of the day he'd hired his father's death by Samis's hand. And his father before that slaying his grandfather to prevent the Trent wealth from going into the hands of a commoner's daughter. Blood had always been necessary. Sanctioned by generations. Ordained by God, perhaps, who had given him a noble station to protect.

Strange how his mind turned about as he rode. For a moment, he'd seemed almost light enough to be floating, as though a dream of brightness had touched upon his mind. And with that strange sensation had come an even stranger thought. Tahn Dorn was his cousin. Perhaps he could free him. Let him live as he wished to, even claim him as a relative. He shook his head, laughing at the folly of such a preposterous thought. The Dorn? Openly recognized? Turned loose and left to his own devices?

It could not be. Killer, street urchin, mercenary dog. Dorn could never be trusted. More than that, he could never be worthy.

"We're drawing near, my lord," Saud called to him.

"Good. Good." He laid one hand against the bundle at

the back of his saddle. The grand ax. Emblem of power. How comfortable he would feel when he could lift it in his hands again. What would the Dorn look like when he saw it? Would he be defiant, or spineless? He'd seen him only once before. In Alastair, at a distance, sitting on the stone rail of the church steps. But he knew he would know him. Just as the Dorn would need no one to tell him that Baron Trent had come.

Lionell sucked in a mighty breath. Country smells he could not identify rushed through his nostrils. He would be glad to be home again. But he was even more glad to be here now. This was his moment. The beginning of his future.

Saud slowed, taking his horse deeper into the trees, and all of the other men followed suit. *We're drawing near.* Lionell echoed Saud's words in his mind. *Almost there. Almost there.*

The trees grew denser, but still the unerring sunlight beat down through them. Maddening, all this summer sun. It was enough to make a nobleman perspire, for goodness' sake. He should have thought to bring his fanners, but perhaps they would be too squeamish for this sort of quest.

Eventually, he saw a house peeking at them through the trees. A man ran eagerly to meet them from the large barn behind it. This must be the place. There were many men. A few he recognized as his own, which he'd sent for this duty. The rest were the bandits he'd bought. Twelve or fifteen of them. Maybe more.

"Where are my prisoners?" he asked no one in particular, wondering again what he might do with Lady Trilett, who had served so worthily as bait. He had not seen her for a very long time. But she was lovely, he remembered that. Deeply lovely. It would be a pleasure to touch her.

And then the bandits would want her given up to them, of course. How could such red-blooded men resist that desire? But if he paid them well enough, and perhaps even promised them a wench or two, he could keep her hidden away for himself. Lady Elane would be busy with her infant now. She need never know.

"We've been riding a good while, my lord," Saud told him. "You should take refreshment before the business at hand. I've stocked the house with wine. And there is a passable cook—"

"I'll take no wine before the job is done," Lionell declared. "I would be in my fullest senses, to remember and appreciate every moment."

"Of course, my lord. I do not mean—"

"Afterward. That is the time for the celebration and feasting. I require now only a leg or breast with a chunk of bread. And fresh-drawn water."

"Yes, my lord."

The horses were stabled. Lionell was given his chosen morsels. Burle, the clearly uncivilized bandit leader, approached him with his shirt off and his side generously bandaged.

"Did you have trouble with the vermin I sent you to fetch?" Lionell asked him.

"No, sir. Nothing we couldn't easily handle."

"Then he is well?"

"Well enough for your needs. When do we see the gold?"

"When the deed is done, man. That is the way of good business."

"What about the lady?"

"The same, of course. You have kept her untouched?"

"It weren't easy, sir. But we kept her. And she'll be well worth the wait. But she's a wild one. Taken to the Dorn's ways, I don't know. We had to tie her well."

"Fine. I can handle her. Make no mistake."

"Which would you see first?"

Lionell smiled. "Pleasure tempts me to go to the lady. Of course. You understand that yourselves. And yet when Dorn is dead, she's fully ours, with no groom to long for, nor hope of rescue. I think my duty calls me first, as befits a man of my station."

Burle was staring at him oddly. "There's a bit of the pleasure in that too, being rid of the plague of the Dorn."

"Yes. Indeed. I see you understand me very well."

Lionell finished his leg of lamb and tossed the bones to the ground behind him. "I believe it is time I met my cousin." He turned to one of the men who had ridden with him. "Cherlan, bring the grand ax for me."

Desperately, Netta worked at the ropes that bound her, backed against the sharp-edged rock in the wall she'd used before. It was much harder this time, bound as she was. But her heart raced with new urgency. She'd heard the horses, the new voices. And she knew whose arrival had been expected. The baron had come. He was here. And if Tahn yet breathed, the baron would not let it remain so, not for more than a few moments at best.

She screamed, still working at the ropes. But what could she do, even if she got them loosed? By the time anyone came to open her door, she would be too late, she knew it. Lionell would destroy Tahn first, and then he would come to her and gloat about it. And do whatever he fancied.

Such thoughts made her scream again in anger and despair. But behind the screams a prayer rose. *God! God! Where are you? Help us!*

For a moment the room seemed brighter. A draft filtered through the cracks of the door and blew a soothing coolness across her face. *God of the wind, help us,* she prayed again. *We are your servants. We are in your hands.*

The tears at her eyes were suddenly gone, as though stopped in an instant by some unseen hand. *Scream on,* a voice in her heart told her. *Until the door is opened.*

21

Tahn felt the angel's wings over him like a satin coverlet. The hard ground beneath him seemed now as soft
as cushions, and he felt no pain. *I am sleeping again,* he
thought. *Another heavenly dream.* The smell of roses floated
around him. He must be in a garden. Netta liked roses. She
planned to plant many of them in the courtyard of their new
home when the workmen were finished.

Tahn drew in one more heavenly scented breath and then
opened his eyes to the world in the clearing. The angel sat
beside him, with one hand on his shoulder. His words were
low. "The baron is here."

The hard ground was beneath Tahn again. The pain came
rushing back. It was harder to breathe here. Much harder.
"Then . . . if I am to die," he struggled to answer, "the time
has come."

"The Lord is with you. Always," said the angel in a quiet
voice. "You are in his hands and no one else's. He has made
you free."

Staring into the angel's eyes, he pulled painfully against
the ropes and trembled. "Look at me. Do I look . . . like I
am free?"

"In God, things are not always as they appear."

He could not feel his bound feet. His hands were strangely
cold in the sunlight. The left one, the one Toma had stomped,
throbbed now. But the right one seemed dead. His arms, his
shoulders, his sides all ached. Especially his sides, where the
pain seemed to burn deep into his being. He drew another
difficult breath. "Can you not loose me?"

"No, my friend."

Tahn closed his eyes for a moment. "You do me honor . . . to call me friend."

"Are you not a friend of God?"

He felt a sudden welling of tears. "I hope so . . ."

The angel placed one hand upon Tahn's forehead, the other on his chest. "Then you are also my friend."

"I choose Netta's life . . . it's all right if I die . . . so long as she is spared."

"I know your heart."

"God's will for me . . . I'll be free . . . in his heaven . . ."

The angel nodded solemnly.

And a sudden scream in the distance jarred Tahn. Every muscle tensed. "Netta!"

"Peace," the angel said quickly. "She's all right."

"Then why . . ."

Another scream rang out. Another.

"God!"

He felt the angel's hands still upon him, but now other hands too, unseen, one on each side of his head. He breathed, and the breaths came easier. The pain lessened. Someone was moving to his left. He turned his eyes to see first a group of the bandit guards, and then behind them the dark clothes of Trent soldiers. He swallowed hard, knowing Lionell would be with them. In the distance, Netta screamed again.

The baron strode forward in blue riding garments, complete with a cloak even on this warm day. Tahn had never seen him this close before and had never longed to. The baron was tall, strong. Older than Tahn, but far from old. Easily capable of doing, and having, whatever he wanted.

From the corner of his eye Tahn saw more angels moving to his side. One of them knelt and held his right hand.

"Well." Lionell stretched his first word out long. "I finally have the opportunity to meet the Dorn." He stepped closer and nudged Tahn with the tip of his boot. "You don't look as formidable as I've been told. A pitiful mongrel, actually. And a fool, as your friend Burle tells me. Do you think I would have given myself to *you* for the sake of a woman—even one so fair as Lady Netta?"

Tahn's breaths were suddenly harder. Steadily, he forced himself to meet the hard gaze of this man. This cousin.

"You can't be faulted, I suppose, if you know nothing of how to conduct yourself," Lionell continued. "You were born to be dirt, and to die in the dirt."

"I never wanted . . . what is yours."

Lionell smiled. "And you shall never have it. But do you think I'm fool enough to believe your lies? You can't threaten me now, but if it were you standing over me, you would tell me that all I have is not mine, but rightfully yours. And you would kill me to make it so."

"No . . . I don't want—"

"So your Lord Trilett has told me! You don't want my wealth, my position. You don't lay claim to anything of the House of Trent for yourself. So you say. When you're helpless. When you're beaten and desperate. But I know the greed in men! And I know the grudge Lord Trilett has against me because of my father's deeds. He would be pleased, once you've married his daughter, to see you rise up and claim the barony he thinks you're entitled to. Why else would he let vermin like you have his daughter, except for the anticipation of my ruin? You think he honors you for yourself?"

Tahn closed his eyes. *Samis always raged like this. Always tried with his words to break me apart.*

"He thinks he shall own the Trent power because of you," Lionell continued. "You're nothing but a street thug without that. He would have cast you aside long ago."

Tahn shook his head, opened his eyes again. "He is a good man . . . a man of God."

Lionell only laughed. "Good to *you*! Because he knows what you really want, the same as I do. And he was eager to help you get it, wasn't he? How long would I have lasted before your attack came to me, cousin? A week after your marriage? Or a month before you declare your right to Trent lineage and bring war to my gates? You know how necessary my action is. For the sake of my future, I do away with you."

160

Tahn looked away from him, into the brightness of the shimmering sky filled again with angel's wings. Perhaps he would be part of that sky soon, flying through it toward his mother's arms. But now, at least for a few more moments, there was earth to face. And a cousin who had never been a cousin. It was folly to claim they were family, because family was made of more than blood. He struggled with the words. "Would God . . . there were no kinship between us."

"It is too late for that now."

"I threaten no one."

In the distance, Netta screamed again, and Tahn tensed. *Jesus! Lord, help her!*

Lionell turned to one of his men in disgust. "There she is again. Screaming, distracting me. I told those bandits! Go, Rolin. Go and make sure that none of them touch her until I am there. Command her to shut up in the name of Baron Trent." Lionell turned his eyes to Tahn again as the man hurried away. "I believe I was having a conversation with my cousin, wasn't I?"

Tahn didn't answer.

"I know you don't threaten me. Because you can't. And neither can the Triletts without you. Unless you've already gotten the fair lady pregnant to spite me."

Tahn turned his head away, but Lionell kicked him sharply. "Well, have you?"

Struggling against the sudden rush of pain, Tahn forced the words out. "No . . . please . . . let her go . . ."

"Ah, you're not too proud to beg." Lionell turned his face toward one of his men. "Cherlan, bring me my battle-ax."

Tahn had not noticed the bundle before, across the shoulders of one of Lionell's men. Quickly the soldier unwrapped it, a jewel-speckled, shining, horrible instrument. Lionell set aside his riding cloak and then received the ax gladly into his hands.

Tahn gave a glance toward the angels still beside him and then turned his gaze squarely upward again into the baron's eyes.

Lionell smiled and coolly moved the toe of his boot over Tahn's neck. "Do you beg me for your own life?"

"It would . . . gain me nothing from you."

Lionell laughed. "Then why do you think I would hear you for Netta Trilett's sake?"

"She's a lady," Tahn stammered. "An innocent . . . good lady. I'm the one . . . who troubles you. Not her. Let her go."

"Oh no. Not such a rare specimen. I intend to make good use of her. And no one will ever know I've had anything to do with her unfortunate disappearance." Lionell's smile widened. "A scourge of bandits in our land is not *my* fault! Obviously, they carried her off. That is what everyone will say. And if we leave a bloody piece of her dress here, all will assume they've killed her. We can hide her away and do what we wish. A good plan, don't you think?"

Again, Netta screamed far away, and Tahn could scarcely bear it. "Why would you hurt her?"

"Surely you know, Dorn. How can a man resist such a fine toy? I expect she'll provide much enjoyment for me."

Tahn struggled against the ropes, his heart thundering wildly, painfully.

"Peace," his angel whispered to him.

"You'll not be loosed," Lionell said. "You can be quite sure of that."

"Let Netta go," Tahn pleaded again, though he knew his words struck ears that were deaf to reason. Netta would be loosed. He believed that somehow. But her deliverance would not come from any mercy of Lionell's, or any of these men. God had heard him. God would set her free. Tahn heard her scream once more, but this time, he did not fear for her. She wanted to be heard. That's why she screamed. She bore hope of rescue, and rescue would come to her.

Lionell's eyes were cold, deathly evil. "You've been a skillful adversary, Dorn. But it is over now. I will lift our great-grandfather's battle-ax and sever your sorry head! Did you know it is a family tradition? Great-grandfather killed his brother Alfan. Grandfather killed his cousin Markel.

162

And now there is a cousin for me to dispose of, though you are not worthy to be called that. Your father was a rogue bandit, your mother an illegitimate wench, a traitor to her family. You are not true Trent."

Tahn licked at parched lips and turned his eyes to the sky again. "Blessed thought."

Lionell kicked at him again, hard. "Fool! Do you scorn me? Do you scorn my name? I hold your death in my hands!"

Tahn could see all the way to the crystal palace beyond the sky. There were meadows. Sweet grass and another sky even more brilliant than this. The smell of flowers. Comfort. And painless peace. All waiting for him beyond the shimmering river that earth's sky had become.

Netta screamed again.

Lionell lifted his ax. "It is my pleasure that you die not knowing your lady's fate. Perhaps I'll give her to the bandits. Perhaps I'll keep her. Perhaps I'll kill her when I tire of the game."

Again, the scream in the distance.

Lionell raised the ax above his head.

Heaven was close. Tahn could see it, even taste it. It seemed that he could just reach out now. He could be there.

"You can do nothing," Lionell taunted. "Nothing to stop me."

A welcome thought. Heaven so near—so beautiful. No more pain. The longing washed over him. But then Netta's name drew his heart.

Netta. A house being built. And children . . . so many . . .

He turned his eyes from the glory of sky to his angel's face. Strangely, he saw tears there. And joy, mingled together with a strength he'd never seen before. But he knew he could touch such strength, even in this world. In faith he could claim some part of it for his own.

Carefully, deliberately, Tahn breathed in as deeply as he was able and moved his eyes to face the baron again. He would not flinch, or close his eyes now, or turn away.

Jesus, I am in your hands . . .

"Die, unworthy vermin! By Trent power and will!"

163

Tahn saw the ax as though it were timelessly suspended. It began its descent. He couldn't move. He couldn't pull away. His hands grasped at the ropes that held him, but he knew he would never be able to pull himself free. Such a blow should be swift, but it seemed as though time had stopped. And the baron's cruel face stared down in anticipation of the blood.

I am free, Lord . . . you have set me free . . .

As the words sang in his mind, Tahn drew in another deep breath and felt heaven's peace within him. Here.

The face above him changed. A look of surprise, even terror, spread over Lionell. The ax stopped its deadly arc and plummeted downward, tilted off its course. Tahn did not understand what could have arrested the baron's motion. But then he saw that the baron, too, was falling toward him, with a length of feathered shaft protruding from his throat.

The ax crashed down at an angle against Tahn's shoulder. The baron sank to his knees, then pitched sideways and toppled to the ground beside Tahn, his breath wheezing raggedly past the blood and the wood. Tahn turned his head as the baron fell, and for a moment their eyes met. With a choking gasp, Lionell's life fled from him, and Tahn closed his eyes with a shudder. Once more, he had stared death in the face.

Vari rushed forward, unable to hold himself back for even a moment after Marcus's arrow hit its mark. It had been a miracle shot. They all knew that. The only desperate chance they had to stop what they'd come upon almost too late.

"Tahn?"

Chaos broke over the camp as he ran, far from alone. Trilett guardsmen and friends rushed at the bandits, some of whom fought, many of whom fled. Some of the baron's soldiers were here too, and most of them fought because someone was yelling to them, urging them to. Vari cared nothing for that. He only wanted to get to Tahn.

164

He looked so still. How badly was he hurt? With dagger in hand, Vari ran, his heart nearly beating out of his chest.

But someone reached the bound figure first. The tall man with the booming voice who still commanded the dead baron's men. Saud. He had hurried forward to stand over Tahn. He had drawn his sword. Vari could not wait to see if any of the others could stop him. Tahn had taught him things he'd hoped to never use. But use them he must. Now.

He jumped upon Saud and thrust the dagger into his back. But it wasn't enough. The man didn't fall. He slumped a little and tried to turn, his sword still in hand. So with teeth clenched and a prayer in his heart, Vari plunged the dagger again and again until the man staggered, dropped his sword. Vari quickly grabbed it and finished him with one quick blow. *Oh, God! God, forgive me!*

I had to do it, he told himself quickly. *I had to. He would have killed Tahn.*

Vari dropped the sword and fell to his knees at Tahn's side while the struggle still raged around them.

"Oh, God, Tahn. I was so scared we were too late."

Tahn looked horrible. Bruised. Beaten. Vari reached to pull his dagger from the bloody body and then shoved it away. He had to push at Lionell's body too, to get it off one of Tahn's arms. *Oh, God, what they've done!*

"Go to Netta . . ." Tahn pleaded with him, but Vari shook his head.

"Jarel's gone to her. We heard her screaming."

He laid the dagger down and pulled a smaller blade from his pocket. The knife Tahn had given him so long ago. It was more familiar to his hand than the larger weapons, but still he struggled with it, trying to cut Tahn's arms loose. The ropes were so tight. He was afraid he would cut him. And Tahn was breathing in strange, difficult gasps. He was hurt badly.

"It's all right," Vari spoke hopefully. "You're going to be all right."

Finally, the right arm was loose. It was even harder trying

165

to cut loose the left. Tahn's arm and hand were both swollen, and Vari worried that they might be broken. Tahn looked up at him almost as if he didn't know him, but then his eyes turned beyond Vari, behind him. Vari's gut wrenched. He saw something in Tahn's eyes change. There was a hardness suddenly, like the old fury but mixed with a sudden desperation. Fumbling, with quick and awkward effort, Tahn pulled his right hand forward and grasped hold of Vari's dagger. His dark eyes were frightening in a depth raw with pain.

"Tahn?" Vari tensed. Did he know him? Did he know what was really happening? Or had the pain stolen his mind for an instant, as Vari had been present to witness before? "Tahn—"

With arm shaking, Tahn raised his head and shoulder enough to lift the dagger and let it fly past Vari's shoulder and behind him. Vari whirled to see Burle suddenly drop to the ground, sword still in hand and the dagger in his chest.

"Oh, God." Vari breathed the words out. "Oh, Tahn. You saved my life, even now."

He turned quickly back to his friend, but Tahn had sunk to the ground again. His eyes were closed, and he was far past answering. Feverishly, Vari struggled to cut the remaining ropes. By then, there were no more bandits or soldiers fighting near them in the clearing. They were defeated or run off, and some of the Trilett men gave chase. Lucas hurried to join Vari at Tahn's side. He tried to rouse him enough to give him water, but with little success.

Lucas was quiet, grave-faced. They moved Tahn quickly to the shade, and Vari wanted to ask if there was any way to know the extent of his injuries. But he couldn't force the words out. Lucas opened Tahn's shirt, and they saw the purple bruises, deep and horrible, covering Tahn's abdomen and sides.

Vari glanced over at the man he'd killed. He'd never killed before. Never, even in all they'd come through. But this was Saud. Vari knew it was the man who'd killed Tahn's mother. For the sake of Lionell's father he'd hunted Tahn's family, and ordered the burns that had almost killed him. Now he'd come here. To be part of torturing Tahn again.

Suddenly overcome, Vari pitched forward and retched onto the bloody ground. Lucas reached one hand over and gave him just a short pat. And Tahn suddenly jerked and tried to roll.

"Peace, my brother," Lucas spoke gently. "We're here with you."

Tahn opened his eyes and only looked at them, still breathing in gasps. Lucas held a waterskin and helped him drink.

"Netta . . ."

"She's not far from here," Lucas told him with a soothing voice. "Her screams called to us, but Toma told us she was unhurt. Jarel and Tobas will be bringing her. It's all right."

Tahn looked confused. "Toma?"

Lucas smiled, just a little. "There are things possible in God that we might never have dreamed of. He'd taken the lookout's place. He saw us coming, but he let us through without alerting anyone. He even pointed the way to you, Tahn. He said he felt like he'd been torn in half, and not even gold would fix the rift. I'm not sure what he meant, but seeing us coming, he knew the gold was lost. He just rode away." Lucas carefully took Tahn's hand. "I pray he doesn't get himself back together, whatever it is he means. I pray that the Lord continues to melt in him what used to be a heart of stone."

Tahn closed his eyes again. His voice came out nothing more than a whisper. "Thank you, God . . ."

22

Netta burst into tears when she saw Jarel and Tobas open her cellar-prison door. It was her miracle, an answered prayer! But she was so overwrought with worry for Tahn that the tears continued as they untied her. She wanted to run to find him as soon as she was free, but Tobas rejoined the fight outside, and Jarel would not let her leave until all sound of battle had stopped.

When finally Jarel opened the door, Netta would not be held back. She ran as fast as her legs could carry her, praying that Tahn would be all right. As she ran past the old barn and then behind it and into the trees, Jarel and Tobas had to struggle to keep up with her.

"Netta!" Jarel called and then finally took her arm. "Netta, please. We don't know what we'll find over there. Stay at my side."

She stared at him for a moment. What could he mean? That Tahn might be dead? She could not believe that, but even if it were so she would still go to him. Fighting back tears, she ran again. *Lord God, hold him. To be hurt again, abused again . . . why can it not end?*

Holding her now torn and filthy skirt, she hurried on through the trees to the little clearing a few yards away and down the slope. She glanced at the sky for just a moment, thinking that it seemed unnaturally bright, even for a sunny day. But she had no time to put her mind on such things as that. Tahn lay just ahead.

Thankfully, Lucas and Vari were with him. Marc Toddin and his brother were approaching from one side, and other men she recognized were not far away. Except for scattered bodies, she saw none of the bandits and none of the baron's men. Ignoring the grisly signs of the battle, she ran down the slope, almost tripping twice and refusing Jarel's arm when he tried to take hold of her again.

She could not say anything when she sank to her knees at Tahn's side. She would have leaned across him in an embrace, but she was afraid of the way he looked, afraid she would hurt him. He breathed, but his eyes were closed. They'd untied him and moved him from the sun, but he lay on his back still, with his knees up and one wounded arm now drawn in close to his chest. Gingerly, she reached out her hand to touch him. It had not been bright like this when she saw him before. Now she could see that his face was discolored with bruises and his neck was even worse. Swollen and purple, rubbed raw with rope burn.

She started shaking. Jarel knelt beside her and held her as tears filled her eyes again.

Vari put his hand on her shoulder. "Netta, are you really all right?"

She looked up at him but couldn't manage to answer his question. "Oh, Vari! Look what they've done."

"He's strong," Tobas said behind her. "You know he recovers well."

But the words were little solace. Why should he have to suffer again?

"Netta . . ."

Her heart thundered as Tahn's eyes opened. "Oh, Tahn."

He lifted his right hand toward her, and she moved her hand quickly to meet his. His voice was low, strained. "Are you hurt?"

That simple question, so like him, only augmented her tears. "Oh, Tahn—you're the one that they—"

"Please . . . did they hurt you?" His eyes were so deeply pained. Like that dream she'd had of the awful cage.

"I'm all right," she assured him quickly, knowing he would not be at ease until he heard those words from her. "I'm not hurt . . ." Truth be told, she was aching badly. But

169

she could not tell him that. She leaned and kissed his cheek. "Thank you, my love—" She had to stop. The tears got in the way of her words.

"Peace, my lady." He drew her hand to his lips for a gentle kiss. And then he smiled, a tiny smile, but to Netta it seemed big as the world.

But then he tried to roll just a little, and she saw the pain in his face. "Thank God . . . that he is with us here . . ." He turned his face for a moment to Lucas. "Help me up . . ."

"Are you sure?" Netta asked immediately.

Tahn nodded and turned to her again. His eyes seemed to shine. "Been here . . . long enough."

She had to smile. "I love you."

Carefully, Lucas helped Netta pull Tahn forward enough to sit. He seemed to be trying unsuccessfully not to show the pain in his movement, and Netta put her arms around him to lend her support.

"Take a man to the nearest village," Jarel told Tobas. "Secure us a wagon. We'll need it getting them home."

"I can ride," Tahn told him.

Jarel shook his head and motioned Tobas on. "I'm not even going to put that to the test."

At his home estate, Lord Bennamin Trilett stirred himself to his feet after a fitful rest. Two almost sleepless nights had passed, and he was exhausted. But even so, he bitterly upbraided himself for the decision not to accompany the searchers tracking Tahn. He shouldn't have listened to Jarel, or the priest, or the other noblemen. He should have followed his heart and tried with everything in him to get closer to his daughter. They would find her, he was confident of that somehow, but it still plagued him to think of what she'd been through, frightened and alone.

The lawlessness in Turis had gone on long enough. A woman was not even safe under heavy guard a few short miles from her home.

"We should have a king again," the noble Lord Eadon had told him only a few days ago. "After the wedding, at the next council of nobles, I shall broach the subject once more."

Benn was not sure how he felt about such words. Ambition for the throne had been the driving force behind Lionell's father's attack on Triletts not so long ago. Since then, the nobles had become more unified, in part to deter any further Trent aggression. But kingly hopes might still stir passion, and violence, among the nobles.

What if the attack on Netta had stemmed from jealousy? He knew the talk circling about in the streets of not only the nearest city.

"Lord Trilett has shown God's honor. Lord Trilett cares for the needs of the people . . ."

He knew he was favored, and had been favored all along, by many of the common people and a fair representation of his fellow nobles. Far from exciting him, such was cause for considerable trepidation. It had been nearly ten years since the unexpected death of the former king. There were no direct heirs. Only distant cousins—women who had married into other noble houses—and their sons and grandsons after them. Such as himself. But almost every house in the land could claim at least a strain of the royal blood somewhere, including the Trents. That only added to the difficulty. They could not have the stability of organized civil law in Turis without a head. But there could be no head without greater stability. Every time the council of nobles had addressed the matter, unrest had broken out somewhere. Many of the nobles seemed afraid to try again.

Perhaps I am afraid too, he thought. *It has already cost us far too much.*

Pacing in his marbled meeting room, Benn was suddenly drawn to his grandfather's tapestry hanging behind the great oak desk.

Faith exalts. Fear demeans.

The words were woven into the flowery border, repeated again and again as though the weaver were insistent that they should not escape notice. And the scene—his royal-blooded ancestor at the battle of Dabair—seemed designed to stir courage. It was said that Bennamin Bannerwood had risked himself against considerable odds for the sake of his fellows.

Like Tahn, Benn thought suddenly, who himself carried Bannerwood blood from his great-great-grandmother, though he almost surely didn't know it.

Ah, Lord God! There has been too much injustice for too long. Bring them home in safety! Show me the way to go from here. Nothing like this must ever happen again!

He knelt, praying, until he heard a sudden rapping at the chamber door that jolted him to his feet again. Could they be back?

But it was Tiarra who opened the door at his invitation. Looking tense and pale, she took two steps into the room and stood looking at him.

It was not like her to approach him this way. They had talked only little since her arrival here, and he'd always assumed that he made her uncomfortable. She was not raised accustomed to noblemen, that was certain, and even though he'd welcomed her as a part of his family, she'd still seemed distant. At least from him.

"How can I help you?" he asked her, hoping she had not heard more troubling news.

"I—I had a dream. Lorne insisted that I lie down after . . . after not sleeping." She turned her eyes from him and let them rest, strangely enough, on his grandfather's tapestry.

"Worry assaults us sometimes in our dreams," he said softly. "It is rare that they portend reality."

"I've been trying to hide my worry all day. And I don't think this dream came from that. I don't understand the things I saw. But I thought . . . I thought I should tell you."

Her eyes, dark as Tahn's, were damp with tears and strained with the pain of uncertainty. She looked exhausted, despite the sleep she spoke of. And he knew he probably looked far worse. "Come. Sit. Tell me this dream."

He motioned her to a chair, and she hesitated but then slowly moved to join him.

172

"In a way, the dream speaks good, because Tahn and Netta were in it. But I was afraid because it also seems to speak bad."

She turned her eyes away from his gaze and bowed her head. "I am sorry. It is surely not the time for this."

"You do not trouble me. Please feel free to tell me what you wish."

"But you . . . you were . . ." Again, she hesitated.

"What, daughter? Don't be afraid. I told you that I take only little stock in dreams."

"But you were gone—I mean passed on from this world. And your body lay in the largest banquet hall." She looked up at him, her eyes bearing more than a hint of fear. "There were so many people in mourning. Inside and outside. I've never seen so many people."

He sighed. "I am not young. And we all have a day to face."

"I don't want to face such a day as that! I think none of us would. What would happen, if something happened to you?"

"My daughter, my nephew, and all of you, would carry on."

"It wouldn't be the same here."

"Nor was it when my father died, or his father before him. But I expect I have some years yet, Lord willing. Did the dream bear you some cause for present concern?"

She shook her head. "I didn't understand the rest of it. I saw many three-leaf clusters spreading like a cape over the shoulders of a lion. And a baby—a little boy—lay kicking his feet and crying. And then a golden flower floated down from a clear sky and came to rest upon him."

He was quiet for a moment, only looking at her. This was no ordinary dream. Finally, he found his voice. "You said your brother and my daughter were in this dream."

"They were standing one at each side of the child."

He smiled. "Yes. That would make sense."

She brightened a little. "I—I hoped that meant it was their

173

son, that they would be well and give you grandchildren before . . ."

She couldn't seem to finish.

"Before I leave this world. I understand. And it is my great hope for that part of your dream to come true, at least. But there is more to what you've seen. Perhaps the Lord has chosen to show me the matter as he has had it in mind all along. What kind of flower was it that you saw?"

She seemed clearly puzzled by his response, but she turned her eyes to the tapestry again. "I don't know the name. I'm not even sure whether I've seen it before. But it looked like those." She pointed. "Around the edge of your beautiful picture."

For a moment, he couldn't say a word to her. The tawny laurel. For generations a part of the Bannerwood crest. What could he possibly say? This girl knew nothing of what that meant. Perhaps it would not even be right to explain it to her. Not yet, at least. "Thank you," he said simply. "On a day when my heart aches for my daughter, you've given added hope."

She stared at him. "There's a lion on the Trilett banner."

"Yes."

"From where comes the cape of leaves?"

He took a deep breath. "You're not one to let a matter rest. There's much strength in you."

"You've understood something of what I've said."

He nodded. "The triple leaves—blood red?"

"Yes. But I didn't tell you they were red."

"It was not hard to surmise. The scarlet trefoil. It is the Trent insignia."

Tiarra's face changed, growing almost ashen at the same time that her eyes flashed with new fire. "Upon the lion? Do you mean that dog, Lionell? Will he attack you? Or Netta?"

"No. You said the leaves in your dream spread like a cape. It seems a peaceful thing to me. And I think it speaks of Tahn, not Lionell."

"Tahn?"

"The symbol of Trent becoming a covering to Trilett."

174

"But Tahn would never bear the banner of Trent!"

"He bears it whether he chooses it or not."

She was silent for a moment, staring down at the marbled floor. Finally she spoke. "You seem to accept this dream as more than an assault of worry."

"You could not have invented things you haven't understood. I believe that the Lord gives me peace and a great understanding of the future."

"What does the flower mean?"

Benn studied her for a moment, but he could not bring himself to explain anything further. Not now. It was enough to hold such a thing in his own heart. He could not speak of it yet to anyone. "Perhaps it speaks of new life. Of growing things, in the order of God."

"I don't understand."

"That's all right," he told her, standing to his feet. "You have given me a gift."

23

On the creaky wagon, Tahn hugged at the wad of cloth Marc Toddin had given him. A riding cloak, he knew. Lionell's. With a velvety lining and a scarlet trefoil pattern upon the collar. But now it was nothing more than a bit of cushioning to press against his side in the hopes of softening the bump of the wagon over uneven ground.

He knew he had broken ribs. How many, there was no way to tell. They would heal in time. But now the pain was like fire in his insides. It would have been easier to linger a while longer before traveling, but it would not have been right to make Netta wait in that place.

He wasn't sure about his left arm, from the bruise and glancing ax cut on his shoulder to the kicked-at forearm and the swollen and throbbing hand. He didn't know if anything had been broken. But Lucas had wrapped it down securely to his chest, which also helped, at least a little, against the ride's bumpiness.

"Are you doing all right?" Netta asked him. She lay beside him, and he welcomed her soft body next to his as she held him as still as she could. It was joy and relief to have her here, alive and well.

But she'd asked a question. He gave her a nod, choosing not to speak because he knew the pain came through in his voice.

"Please," she whispered. "Don't ever do such a thing again. Oh, Tahn, I love you so much. Don't risk yourself again. Not even for me."

Looking into her bright green eyes he knew the sincerity

of her plea. But it was foolishness. If ever she needed him, if ever she were in danger again, he would do what he had to do. He could not claim to love her otherwise.

"I was afraid he'd killed you." Her eyes still held some fear when she said it, and he wished he could brush all of that away. Gingerly, she moved her hand to touch his neck, and the turmoil in her eyes increased. "Oh, Tahn . . ."

The lightness of her touch hurt him. Every movement of his head, and even swallowing water, hurt his neck. God alone had spared him. Perhaps he had even been dead. He wasn't really sure. All that he'd seen—the angels, the brightness—he didn't know how much of it was real.

She took a cloth in her hand and bathed his forehead. "You should try to sleep."

"You too." He forced the words out steadily. "Rest."

"I'm not sure I can. Not till we get you home."

He shook his head ever so slightly. "Till . . . I get *you* home," he told her.

And she smiled.

But he saw what he thought he'd seen earlier. The slightest discoloration on her cheek. He took a deep breath, praying he could speak on with the strength he wanted. "Tell me . . . what they did . . ."

"Oh, Tahn."

"You're . . . bruised."

Her eyes filled with tears, and he was almost sorry he'd asked. Perhaps he only troubled her with things she hoped to quickly forget. But she laid her hand across the side of his face and did what she could to answer him.

"They were horrid. They tied me, tossed me about like a sack of grain. But God covered me and kept them from anything else." She brushed at a strand of his hair. "The worst thing was knowing they were hurting you."

"I'm sorry . . ."

"Why? It was not your fault."

"I should have—"

"You did all we could ever ask. More than we expected.

Tahn, you even warned us. What happened was not your fault."

"I should . . . have stayed with you."

"No! You might have been killed on the road or captured then."

A sudden sprinkle fell against his forehead. He was surprised to notice that the sky was now nearly filled with clouds and the sun's glow was sinking lower. The world still looked bright to him. Almost as bright as before.

But another raindrop fell. And another. And then more, in a gentle but unexpected shower. Painfully, with only one hand, he pulled Lionell's cloak straighter and caught another glimpse of the triple leaves at the collar as he spread it protectively over Netta's shoulders.

At the same moment, he felt a familiar touch across his forehead. The angel's wing. Soft and light. He closed his eyes, and strangely he could see it.

"Thank you, Father," he spoke toward the sky.

The angel smiled. And Netta snuggled beside him, resting her head on his right shoulder. He didn't feel any more raindrops. It was peace that washed over him, and a gentle, healing sleep.

The pitch of the wagon woke Tahn hours later. Darkness had closed over them, but the clouds were gone, and the stars shone brilliant white above him. He could feel Netta warm beside him, and he knew that she still slept. He was glad for that. In her concern for him, she paid too little heed to what she might require after such an ordeal.

He thought of the men Jarel had sent toward the Trent estate with the bodies of Lionell and his men. It was a gesture Tahn approved, to not leave the bodies where they lay, but he wondered what reaction the Trilett men would receive there. Some of the soldiers had escaped. A few of the bandits too, Lucas had told him, though they were being sought after. But surely they could not be so foolish now as to try any new assault. With Lionell dead, nothing could be gained by it.

A handful had surrendered to them, including a woman and her wounded husband. Jarel had not known what to do with them, so he'd brought them along. For Benn Trilett's judgment, presumably. Tahn thought of one man in particular, Bert, who had carefully helped bury the bodies of Burle and his fellow bandits. That man's heart was changed, Tahn had seen it in him. Somehow what had happened had gone deeper than mere consequences for a wicked plot foiled.

It made Tahn think back to the first time he had met Netta. Trapped in darkness, he'd been sent on a wicked quest, but Netta was protected by an angel. God's own messenger, sent by God's own hand. That anyone could be so loved and watched over had stirred in his depths a painful longing. And now Tahn hoped that all the surviving bandits might come to know that longing too.

Even now on this bumpy wagon, he knew that God's angels were with him. That he was loved, as Netta was loved, and it was an awesome feeling. The change in him had been great, he realized that, and he hoped that the bandits had seen it and taken to heart the grace available to them in God.

And yet he wondered why he should feel the presence of God so distinctly. Even still.

Why do you linger with me? he asked in his mind. *Is there more danger for us?*

He knew the answer in his heart, and it filled him with peace. "I will never leave you or forsake you."

He closed his eyes and felt the soft satin of Netta's dress against his arm. Her breathing was slow and even, a comfort beside him. But he could not help a continued concern for her.

Does she tell me the truth? Or does she hide her pain until I am stronger?

He could envision an angel sitting beside them in the wagon, stretching out a steady hand to touch the top of Netta's head. Tahn could feel her tremble slightly in her

179

sleep and then relax again as though a heavenly peace were washing over her.

"*Your days are just beginning,*" the sudden words floated in his heart. "*You have thought that your call was tied only to survival. Your own and so many others you have touched. But there is more now.*"

Tahn drew in a quick breath as the wagon hit a bump beneath him. *Always,* he said in his mind, *I am in God's hand.*

He looked up at the brilliant stars again. *Have I been dreaming everything? Am I even dreaming now?* He heard voices talking somewhere nearby, voices he didn't recognize. For a moment he tensed, but he could see Lucas beside him in the darkness to his left. Tobas and Vari had been on the wagon seat. He couldn't see them the way he lay, but the wagon continued on its slow journey, and he knew they were there.

"You know what this means as much as I do," Jarel's voice was suddenly saying in answer to someone. They were in front of the wagon, Tahn could tell that now, and their voices were barely loud enough to be heard over the creak of the wheels.

"How can the nobles accept him? He was raised not only as a commoner but as a villain."

"Will that matter?" Jarel pressed his unknown companion. "He has not chosen villainy. And nothing can change what he is."

"But can it be proved?"

"Do you doubt my uncle's word? Do you think anyone will?"

Tahn did not analyze the words they were saying. He let the talk float over him and tried to move his right arm just a little without waking Netta. It had gone to sleep as she lay on his shoulder. His other arm was still wrapped against his chest. It suddenly occurred to him that he was without his sword. His dagger too, and knives had been taken by the bandits. Strangely, it did not bother him.

My days are just beginning, he thought. *Perhaps I can learn new things.*

"Are you all right, Tahn?" It was Lucas suddenly asking. He must have noticed the small movement. He must have been watching.

"Yes. Better. Thank you."

"Water?"

"When Netta stirs. Please. We must let her sleep."

For a moment Lucas said nothing in answer. And when he spoke again, his voice was strained. "It was too close, Tahn."

"We're both all right."

"You will be. I know. But if we hadn't been able to follow your trail, or if we'd waited even a minute longer—"

"God held the timing."

"I know. And I thank him for your lives! But it was too close. Seeing Lionell standing over you that way—it was like the world had tilted off balance, and there was nothing left for any of us—"

Tahn stared up at him. "You make overmuch—"

"No. So long as you were always the target, through no fault of your own, nothing in this world could make sense. Surely things will be different now that Lionell is dead."

"Was it Marcus?" Tahn asked, remembering the arrow.

"Yes."

"A fine shot. Far better than our apple would have been."

Lucas's voice sounded lighter. "He said he was aiming for the chest."

"He did one better. Where is he? I'll go to thank him."

"Riding behind with the Toddins. Watching our backs."

"He is to be commended. All of you are. A bold rescue."

Lucas was quiet again. "What about you?"

Tahn sighed. "I seem to always need rescuing, don't I? I'm sorry. I couldn't tell you."

"I understand. But it might have killed you this time, Tahn."

"Better than leaving Netta alone to their whims."

"I suppose you are incurable."

"I suppose I could say the same of you."

181

Jarel's voice suddenly called a halt, and the wagon stopped. He yelled for Vari, who leaped from the wagon seat and disappeared into the darkness.

"What is happening?" Tahn asked Lucas.

"I think they've found your horse again. This is about where we saw him before."

"He is injured . . ."

"We know."

Tahn could hear Vari's voice in the distance, talking soothingly to the animal, trying to lead him toward the wagon. Apparently, Smoke wasn't cooperating. Tahn raised his head just a little and whistled. In moments, Smoke was at the back of the wagon with Vari at his side.

"Good boy," Tahn told his horse. "How bad is he, Vari?"

"He's limping. He probably lost his share of blood. But he seems stronger now than he did yesterday."

"Then he'll be all right."

"Jarel said to tie him behind the wagon."

"Good. I like him close."

Soon Vari was moving around to the side of the wagon, ready to climb up again to the wagon seat.

"Vari," Tahn called. "Come here."

Without a word the boy climbed in the back and sat beside Lucas as the wagon began to move again.

"Are you all right?" Tahn asked him.

"Of course," he said weakly. "Why wouldn't I be?"

"I know you. You've never wanted to fight."

"Neither have you!" Vari suddenly burst out. "But nobody asked us! And I couldn't just sit back and watch. Saud would have killed you. I was the only one close enough."

Tahn nodded a little. "Thank you."

"You did practically the same for me, twice now."

"But it was not my first kill." He sighed, suddenly very weary. "I'm sorry, Vari. I had hoped . . . that you would never have to—"

"I'm not sorry." Vari looked down for a moment. "He gave us no choice. Maybe you should sleep again. I can tell

182

you're still weak." He glanced toward Netta. "Is she really all right?"

The same question would not quite leave Tahn alone. "You think like me sometimes," he answered quietly. "She will be. When she's home again."

────

Home again. The wagon continued its progress in the darkness, and Netta dreamed of the old Trilett estate that Samis's men had burned. Her mother sat in the sunny garden surrounded by roses. Her cousins Anton and Jarel were across the courtyard leading their horses toward the gate for a ride. This was a peaceful day. Beautiful. And Netta wanted to do nothing more than stroll among the flowers until Ananda Stomer came to give her another harp lesson. She'd thought she would hate the harp. But her father had insisted she learn it, and she'd begun to enjoy it more and more. Especially on a day like today. There should be music floating over the flowers because summer seemed born for song.

"Netta?" her mother suddenly called from across the garden.

"Yes?"

"Please. Come to me."

There was something different in her mother's voice. Netta looked up and saw her gentle smile. But something was different in her eyes too. And Netta hurried to her mother's side. "What is it?"

Lady Trilett sat upon one of the stone chairs that Netta's father had commissioned for the garden. She leaned forward just a little and reached for Netta's hand. She was so thin. She'd always been thin. But lately, she seemed even more so. "Netta, I must speak to you about something."

Netta knelt beside her mother and listened to her tell of the sickness she'd been hiding, a sickness that only grew worse until she knew she could hide it no more. Netta's eyes filled with tears to hear her mother's words of acceptance.

183

"I'm going to be leaving you, child. I don't know when. But I know it is coming, far sooner than we thought. I had to tell you. There are things I wish to share while we still have time together, and I knew that I must be honest with you."

That was the beginning of some of the worst days of Netta's young life and yet also some of the best. She was with her mother almost constantly until the day of her death. Lady Trilett told tales of her grandmother and her great-grandmother, and even grandmothers before that. She told of the day that she first laid eyes on Bennamin Trilett. They were already betrothed, but she had not yet decided whether she could ever love him—until she found him to be far more nervous than she was. She told of parties and feasts and Uncle Winn riding his horse into the estate house once just to gain his beloved's attention.

And then one day, not long before the end, Lady Trilett finally told her where she had gotten the name "Netta." It was a tale not told before, and Netta listened in rapt attention.

"When I was a little girl, my father stole a great deal of money from his father because he thought he could win much more with a foolish gamble. He lost it all and was disgraced. My mother and grandfather turned from him. He stole me away because he thought I was all he had left, and we fled to a place where they wouldn't know us. We had no money. Father tried to work, but he had no skills. He took ill with a fever that had killed many people. I was afraid because I thought he would die and leave me alone. But an old woman took us into her home and nursed him to health. She took care of me like I was her own grand-daughter. She convinced my father that he must go back home and beg forgiveness. She even gave us all we needed for the journey, though she had so little. Her name was Netta Willow. And she must have known we would be received at home again with joy."

"I am named for her," Netta had said. "Who better? Why didn't you tell me this before?"

Her mother's answer was low and solemn. "She was not

only a commoner, but of a different people and manner of worship, with a very poor reputation. I wanted to give you her name, because it will always mean "angel" to me. She saved our lives. And yet I thought that if the story were told it could embarrass your father. He wanted to name you after his grandmothers."

"He did! Those are my middle names."

"Yes. But I insisted upon your first name. Because someday you will need to know that we are all the same, despite the reckoning of men. Netta Willow was despised even in her own land, but she was better to me than a hundred noblemen when we needed her."

The wagon creaked, and Netta stirred just a little. Her mother was long gone now. And Netta was engaged to marry the Dorn, a man she'd once thought to be a commoner. He'd been enslaved by the ruthless Samis. He'd been hunted, tormented, and forced to kill. She was marrying far beneath her, some people had said. Perhaps they would change their minds if it became known that he was Trent as well as Dorn. But some might never understand that none of that mattered. Because he loved her. And she loved him.

Suddenly the events of the last few days rushed over her, and she could scarcely breathe. He'd nearly died. He was so wounded again! His ribs. His arm. His neck. She could feel his warmth beside her now, but she was afraid that he might have worsened as she slept. "Tahn?"

His arm beneath her moved just a little, and he brought his right hand to her shoulder. "My lady."

"Oh, Tahn, I've told you so many times, call me Netta." She eased forward enough to kiss his cheek carefully, and then sat up at his side. "Is the pain any better?"

He made no attempt to answer the question. "I'm glad you could rest."

Lucas's earnest voice interrupted them. "Can I give you water now, Tahn?"

He nodded, and she moved carefully to help support him enough to drink. "I love you," she whispered.

185

Under the clear light of the stars she saw him smile, just a little. "Marry me, Netta."

"You've already asked me!"

"It . . . seemed right . . . to ask again."

"Of course I'll marry you! As soon as we can."

"This coming day."

In part she was glad that he was so anxious. And yet she worried for him. "Are you sure you'll be ready?"

"The devil took one day . . . two . . . or three . . . I don't know. But I don't want to give him more."

"He won't take more. He can't. We are together now."

She could picture them at the beautiful church in Onath. Surrounded by friends and rejoicing. She knew that some would still shake their heads, wondering why Benn Trilett had ever agreed to such a wedding. And now it made her almost wish to hide Tahn's parentage forever, to spite those who refused to see him for the man he was.

But then a new doubt crept in. How would all of the noble houses react if the matter were finally disclosed? Would there be some among them like the old woman in Alastair who had feared that Tahn wished to marry Netta only for the power it could bring him? Would they fear his motives, his ambitions, in tying himself to the venerable name of Trilett?

It made Netta's heart hurt to think such things. Violent treachery could be born of the fear that another's ambition stood in the way of one's own. Lionell was the best example of that. The announcement that Netta Trilett's groom was really a Trent could create a far greater stir than she wanted. And if it bred jealousy, or fear, it could also bring the threat of more trouble.

Trent joined to Trilett! Very possibly the wealthiest house, with the one most revered for generations. Some could fear such a joining indeed, as though Tahn Dorn and Benn Trilett had made a pact to draw power, and perhaps even the throne, to themselves.

Netta clutched Tahn's hand, unable to share with him the sudden fear that pierced her heart. Would he be in danger

186

all over again, from men incapable of understanding that he held no such lofty ambitions? Something close to panic surged within her, but she leaned and kissed his cheek again, refusing to show him her turmoil. *Lord! Perhaps we can continue to hide who he is. It makes me wish that we had both been born peasant farmers. Help us!*

24

Tiarra lay curled on a divan in the drawing room of the estate house. Unwilling to go to her bed but too weary to stay on her feet, she had settled there for a few moments as she waited for some word of Tahn and Netta as the night progressed. Lorne, who seemed not to trust her alone right now, sat in a nearby chair with his head tilted back. From another room, she could hear the voices of Lord Trilett and the priest praying together.

Many guests who had come for the wedding still lingered to hear news of Benn Trilett's daughter. Many had family members who had gone with Jarel and the searchers. Tiarra didn't like the house being so full of strangers, even though they were supposed to be friends.

Somewhere outside a hoot owl called. Tiarra sighed and stared out the open window into the darkness. In a way, she longed for the morning light again. It seemed oppressively dismal to think of Tahn and Netta gone in the blackness of night. And yet if the sun rose already, it would only mean that they had been missing that much longer. The devil had played a cruel trick, to snatch a bride on the eve of her wedding. And then the groom not long after.

They would be back. After her strange dream, Tiarra felt certain of that. But she was still afraid for them with a bitter fury inside that she'd managed to keep in check only because she had no real outlet for it.

Lorne sat up suddenly. She didn't say anything, only watched him, expecting him to have something to say to her. But he was quiet, turning his head toward the window.

Tiarra's heart pounded as she listened to the wind outside and strained for the slightest indication of what he might have heard. And then she knew. A signal horn, like heavenly music floating out of the forest. And then another, much closer, an answering call from the gate.

Tiarra jumped to her feet.

"Stay here," Lorne told her quickly. "Let me go first and discover—"

"No! It's the searchers returning, isn't it?"

"It's their signal. I can't tell if it's one man or many."

"I'll not wait!"

Lorne took Tiarra's hand before she could get past him. "All right. Come with me then."

She heard the heaviness in Lorne's words. He would have gone first to discover the kind of news they brought and then ease the word to her gently, whatever it might be. But he did not argue. Perhaps he knew that it would have done him no good.

Together they hurried into the hallway, where Lorne rapped on the door of Benn Trilett's meeting chamber. "My lord! Searchers, at least some part of them, have returned!"

Tiarra could not wait for any reply. She ran for the front door with Lorne still at her side. He threw open the door without even slowing down, and her knees felt like butter as they hastened down the steps outside.

Oh, God, let them be home! Let them be all right!

Behind her she heard someone else shove at the door and rush down the steps. Netta's father? If so, he was moving almost as quickly as they were across the courtyard because the footfalls did not fade behind them as they ran.

In the clear moonlight, Tiarra could see a wagon and several horsemen already progressing through the gate. But the searchers had not left with a wagon. Tiarra's throat tightened. That meant they were carrying dead or wounded.

She couldn't stand it any longer. She broke from Lorne's hand and ran with every ounce of speed she had.

A big man drove the wagon. She couldn't tell who it was by the shape. But the man beside him was tall and lanky,

189

and suddenly leaped down like a boy. She knew that form. "Vari!"

She screamed his name again, and he turned toward her. "Miss Ti! Miss Ti, we found them!"

The wagon stopped. With her heart pounding almost through her chest, she ran to meet them. It looked like Lucas helping Netta carefully from the back of the wagon. And then Tahn.

She wanted to rush at them both, to grab them up together in a crushingly joyful embrace. They were alive! Standing on their feet, and home!

But something about the way they moved, especially Tahn, held her back. She stopped her run abruptly and stood stock still, tears suddenly filling her eyes.

But Lord Trilett did not stop. Tiarra had never heard him sound like he did when he called his daughter's name. Frightened, overjoyed, and yet somehow small. Netta stumbled forward into his arms.

Tiarra took a step closer to her brother, realizing that Lucas was staying carefully at his side. She didn't venture to hug him. She only moved enough to take his hand.

"Tiarra." Tahn spoke her name like it was a blessing, a gift he'd just now been given.

But she was shaking inside. She knew he was being strong. Standing to greet her before he really should. He was hurt. She could tell. And the tears rolled down her cheeks. "Sit. Please."

"I'm all right."

"No, you're not."

But he took a step forward and pulled her carefully to him. She shook as he held his arm around her. She'd almost lost him only days from their first meeting, and now again. He was all the family she had in this world, at least all the family she could claim. She didn't want to cry, but she couldn't help it. And he only continued to hold her, though one of his arms was wrapped with something stiff, and his breaths were somehow different.

"Thank God," she whispered.

He kissed her forehead. His lips were strangely warm. She almost panicked, remembering his fever in Alastair. "Tell me what's wrong! Oh, Tahn, please, we must get Amos Lowe—"

"Tiarra . . ." He squeezed her hand. "I will be all right."

Netta was crying in her father's arms. Tahn moved one hand to meet Lorne's almost before Tiarra realized he was there beside them. "God has answered our prayers," Lorne spoke in a solemn voice.

"He is with us," Tahn quietly agreed.

"They need rest," Lucas said almost urgently. "Warm water for washing. And food. The wagon can take you closer to the house, Tahn. Both of you. You need not walk so far."

Tiarra knew the gravity of his words. She knew that Benn Trilett would recognize that as well. Wherever they'd been, whatever had happened, none of it was good.

"What of the villains?" the Trilett lord suddenly asked, his voice sounding tight.

Tiarra had not even noticed Jarel coming toward them from among the horsemen until he spoke. "Most are dead, Uncle. Including Lionell of Trent."

A coldness suddenly fell upon the night's warmth, and Tiarra could almost have thought she dreamed again. With the sudden mention of that name, nothing seemed real.

"We will speak further," Benn Trilett answered his nephew abruptly. "First we must see to the present needs. My most solemn thanks, all of you. Lorne, please hurry ahead and tell Amos Lowe we have need of him. Ask Hildy to heat water and prepare bread."

"Yes, my lord." Lorne hurried away.

Netta looked exhausted. She seemed glad to return to the wagon and not have to put one foot in front of the other across the courtyard. Tahn, too, agreed to sit at the back of the wagon. Tiarra noticed the way Netta lent her support as soon as he was beside her. He seemed to lean into her, and Lucas climbed to the wagon too, as though he thought they might need him.

191

"How bad is it?" she whispered to Vari, who still stood near her.

Vari was silent for a moment before he could answer. "You won't like the looks of him in the light. But he's standing. That's a miracle, Miss Ti."

The rest of the night was taken up in care for Tahn and Netta: washed wounds, clean clothes, food for them and for the searchers, and then rest. Much rest. In between everything, Tiarra learned what snatches she could of what had happened, most all of it horrible. Lord Trilett eventually told her and everyone else to try to sleep, so she went to her bed, but it was hard even to lie down with her thoughts whirling continually.

Vari was right. Tahn looked terrible. She could not take her mind from the ghastly raw sores and bruises on his neck. He hadn't talked about what had put them there, but she could imagine, and it made her blood cold with rage. She'd seen the bruises of a hanged man once, and this was something else. Someone had tormented him with a rope at his throat, had made him feel the pain of it again and again until it tore even the skin.

She sat up and threw her cushions viciously across the room. But that wasn't near the release she needed. So she got up from her bed and kicked at them. She felt like screaming, but she knew that would not make her feel any better. So she ran from her room and toward the stairs to go to the room where Tahn lay. She could not bear to be away from him right now, even though he had told her she should try to sleep. Why did he have to be so strong? She would understand it if he wept. If he raged. Anything.

She found she was not the only one who could not rest alone right now. Netta came from the other end of the long hall in her flowing gown, looking as beautiful as ever despite her bruised cheek and disheveled hair.

"I have to look in on him," she said with tears in her eyes.

"Me too." Tiarra could barely get the words out.

She didn't take another step before Netta hugged her. Netta had been crying almost the entire time they'd been back. Tiarra hadn't tried to talk to her. Who could tell the things she'd been through? She was crying again now, clinging to her.

"Your father wanted you to rest," Tiarra prompted.

"He's not resting himself! He's in his chambers talking to Jarel and Tobas."

"I'm so sorry for what happened to you—"

"It's nothing of yours . . . to be . . ." Somehow Netta couldn't finish. "Oh, Tiarra . . ."

Netta suddenly seemed so fragile that Tiarra was afraid she might collapse. "Maybe we should sit."

"I want to sit with Tahn."

"I know. But wait. You know how he'll feel if he sees you worked up like this."

"I know." Netta's legs seemed to give out beneath her. Tiarra did the best she could to stop her fall, easing them both carefully to the floor.

"Oh, Tiarra, I wish I could make him stop worrying about me."

"Tonight everybody worries about you. Maybe tomorrow it will be better."

"You know what I mean! He can be dying inside, trying to hide it from me, and still fretting for me about some small thing!"

"This has not been a small thing."

"You know what I mean. He cares overmuch. I almost killed him! He should not have come for me!"

Tiarra petted at her hair, felt her shaking. "Do you want me to get your father?"

"No."

"Tahn loves you. Maybe it's hard to understand such a love. But you can't ask him to stop. I think you feel the same things for him."

"I want it to be over," Netta cried. "I want him to be safe. Here or anywhere! He should not have to watch his back everywhere he goes!"

193

"Maybe it *is* over. Surely it is. Lionell is dead." Speaking the words was powerful for Tiarra. She could believe that the threat was gone.

But Netta shuddered. "Is he the only noble to succumb to fits of jealousy? Or violent ambition? Even madness?"

Tiarra didn't know how to respond. She'd never seen Netta like this. The lovely and poised daughter of a lord seemed to have fallen apart. But it wasn't any wonder. "I know one thing," Tiarra said as calmly as she could. "You are safe now. So is Tahn. And your father and Lorne and all the other men are going to make sure that you stay that way. Both of you."

Netta couldn't seem to answer. Maybe she just needed to cry it all out.

"Do you want me to get Hildy?" Tiarra asked, knowing how close Netta was to the kindly woman.

"No," Netta stammered. "She was here just a few moments ago. She was a dear, doting on me like she always does. But—but I don't need that, Tiarra." She wiped at her eyes.

"What do you need? How can I help?"

"I want everything to be right again! Roses and sunshine, like it was when I was a child. Before my mother died. But you—you and Tahn never had things right. Even as children . . ."

"Things are right *here*," Tiarra assured her. "With your family and all the little ones. My brother's been happy. I never thought we could be so blessed."

"Until you step away from this estate," Netta answered her bitterly. "Until someone else learns who you are."

"It will be different now. Don't be afraid."

"I'm so tired of all the troubles! And the pain in Tahn's eyes that he doesn't want me to see!"

"I know." Tiarra knew nothing else she could say. She understood. She felt the same way, but in anger more than this brokenness. *Netta is a flower,* she suddenly thought. *But I am more like a stone clinging to a hillside, wishing I could hurl myself furiously at the wicked souls responsible for the pain I see.*

They sat quietly, neither of them saying anything more until Netta began to seem herself again. She dried her tears. She took a deep breath. She gave Tiarra another abundant embrace. "Do you think . . . that we could go to see him now? I just want to check in on him one more time before I try to sleep again."

Tiarra nodded and helped Netta to her feet. "Yes. Me too."

Netta smiled a little and hugged her again. "You're such a blessing."

"I don't know why you say that. I'm just so glad you're home."

Together they went down the stairs and into the room Benn Trilett had given Tahn tonight. He rarely slept in the house, having quarters of his own to the side of the guard-house. But nobody wanted him there now.

Amos Lowe was with him. And Lucas, who had refused a bed and insisted upon spreading his bedroll at the base of the window in the room where Tahn would sleep. Tiarra thought she understood. Lucas knew her brother's battles better than anyone except perhaps Vari, who would be here if Lucas was not.

Tiarra was still afraid of the warmth she had felt in her brother, that he might take fever the way he had after the whipping in Alastair. She almost reached her hand to touch him first thing, but he was so still, his eyes closed. She didn't want to wake him.

"What can you tell us?" Netta whispered to Amos.

"He rests well. Breathes stronger. They are good signs. You needn't fear."

Tiarra shook her head. "He struggled with his breathing when he was awake. I could tell."

"There is pain in it. He has ribs broken from a fierce beating, though I'd rather not tell you such things."

Tahn's neck was covered with a bandage now, but by the oil light, Tiarra could see another line of rope burn on his right wrist. The swollen left arm and hand were completely wrapped in bandages. She already knew that Amos believed a bone to be broken in his hand, perhaps in his lower arm as well.

Netta knelt at the bedside. "He wants to marry in the morning light."

Amos sighed. "He should sleep through the morning. He needs it. So do you."

Lucas was leaning against the wall beneath the window, his eyes closed. But Tiarra knew he did not sleep. "Thank you," she said to him. "If you had not come from Jura when you did, they might have been lost."

He opened his eyes for just a moment. "God kept them. His hand is with them. He has a plan for Dorn and Trilett. I've no doubt."

Such a pronouncement made Tiarra think of her strange dream. The lion and the scarlet trefoil. Trilett and Trent. Or better said, Netta and Tahn Dorn. And a baby. A beautiful little boy. But what was the flower in the dream? She hadn't understood that part. And Netta's father, if he knew, had not truly explained.

"Praise our sovereign God," Lucas spoke on as he closed his eyes again. "Lord of answered prayer."

"Amen," Netta said with her head bowed only for a moment. Then she turned her eyes again to the healer. "I was afraid for Tahn on the way, that these injuries might be deep or bring sickness."

Tiarra tensed to hear her admission. And Amos Lowe's answer was not as reassuring as she would have liked it to be.

"I know he has bled inside, or the bruising would not be so large across him. I can help, but only God knows fully of such things."

"He seemed warm," Tiarra ventured fearfully.

"Yes. But not bad. I do not think there is great danger."

"Should he stay abed?" Netta questioned.

"As much as he will. Until the ribs are strong."

"He'll not like that," Netta said softly. "But I'll try to persuade him."

25

Morning light began its gentle dance upon the windows as Benn Trilett lay back against a pair of cushions in his private chambers. The children would be stirring soon, if they were not already. But they were almost the only ones. He sighed, knowing he should sleep at least for a little while. He'd had so little of it since Netta disappeared. Yet the events of last night churned in his mind and kept him from being able.

Jarel had brought six prisoners. One a woman. They were the only ones among the large group of bandits and Trent soldiers to surrender themselves when his men broke in upon their villainy. It was not easy to know what to do with them without a formal law in the land. The council of nobles was a possibility, but Benn knew that any commoner set before them would receive the judgment of death almost without discussion because none were ever brought before the council except for some notable crime against nobility.

Most questions involving commoners were simply resolved by the individual noblemen themselves, in whatever manner they personally saw fit. It had always been rare for anyone to be brought to the council's notice. This case certainly qualified. But Benn felt considerable heaviness about it. These six persons might actually possess conscience more than any of the others who'd been involved. That may have been why they chose not to fight, or at least not to persist at fighting, the rescuers. Two were Trent soldiers, who might have been under orders they were not at liberty to refuse.

And the woman. She might have had no choice in the

matter at all, under the rule of her husband. Netta had told him briefly how the woman had tried to help her escape.

He had not ventured to see any of them. He was not sure he could maintain his composure even looking at them. Jarel and Tobas had told him how many bodies were sent back to the Trent house and how many were buried in the wilderness. Some had escaped. Only a few. So it was entirely possible that these six may only have surrendered to save their own lives.

He knew he would have to discern the truth case by case. He would also send men to hunt for those who'd escaped. Tahn might be able to supply their names. Or Lucas, who'd seen some of them. Or even the prisoners, should they cooperate.

Lord Trilett lay back on the cushions where he was supposed to be resting and let his mind turn to the difficult time, almost a year ago, when he'd left the baron and his men behind him in Alastair. And the bandits. He'd not pursued justice with them then because there would have been a brutal battle, and he could not risk the women and children who had been with him. But the battle had come to their doors, and he could not neglect the pursuit of justice now.

His thoughts turned suddenly to the women of Trent, and what their grievous reaction must be this morning to the return of Lionell's body in disgrace. Many of the other noblemen already knew he was dead. And why. Benn knew that even more would know before the day was out, whether or not he personally spoke to any of them.

Some also knew about Tahn now. And that news, too, would spread. Because of that, he supposed that a formal announcement should be made. But he would not take such a step without talking to Tahn.

He had no idea whether the house of Trent would choose to acknowledge Tahn and Tiarra as kin, nor whether the other noble houses would be willing to accept the birthright of such a pair. But he didn't care for their opinions. Right was right. He rose up off his bed and took parchment from the drawer of his dressing table. Dipping his goose quill in the ink he kept in the same drawer, he began a stern and careful letter to the matrons of Trent. It didn't take him long. And then setting it aside to dry, he began a letter of announcement that could eventually be presented to the other noble houses, if Tahn would permit it.

With another sigh, he realized that the time had come for even Tahn to accept who he was, which Benn was certain he had so far been unwilling to do, not just for the sake of his loved ones' safety. Tahn had struggled from his first knowledge of the truth that he had villainy, even vicious evil, tied to both sides of his family. The Trents were no more welcome in his mind than was his father's brother, the heartless Samis.

A sudden noise outside his chamber caused Benn to set aside his quill. The children. At least some, already on the stair. He had told the servants to keep them all occupied, outside if necessary, to prevent them from waking Netta or the others. But now he imagined how hard it would be for Stuva, Temas, or the others to be brushed aside without a chance to see Tahn and Netta, whom they loved so well. *We owe them as much explanation and assurance as we can give,* he thought. But everyone else slept. Hopefully.

He rose from his chair and drew his chamber coat about him, tying the belt as he strode to the door. Temas was the first child he saw in the hallway. And she looked frightened.

"Where is everybody?" she asked with her dark eyes wide. "I was already downstairs, and I could see more of those wedding guests around, but nobody else at all."

Benn knelt down and took the girl in his arms. "Our searchers came back last night, so late that it was almost morning. They sleep now. Tiarra and Lorne, and perhaps Hildy and the others too, because they were up with us."

She looked even more frightened, her eyes filling with cautious tears. "Did they bring back the lady? And Teacher?"

Benn smiled a little. Some of these children might always call Tahn "Teacher," the name they'd had for him even before he'd stolen them away from Samis. "Yes, child. But

199

they're sleeping too. And we will need you all to be quiet today because they need the rest very badly."

"Are they hurt?"

He drew a deep breath. "They'll be all right. It isn't so bad as it could have been."

He took the little girl's hand and went quickly to gather any others who were awake and explain all that he could. Ansley and Stuva, the oldest among them, and the little girl Rae, always a leader, offered to keep the other children occupied at their lessons or quietly playing outside.

"When can we see them?"

Benn had known the question would come. It was little Duncan asking, his big blue eyes wrought with cares.

"I don't know," he answered honestly. "We must wait till they wake. And then until they're ready. It has been a difficult ordeal."

"I don't like that Tahn's hurt again," Briant said sadly. "He has too many scars."

"I know, son. I feel the same way."

"I bet Netta was very brave," Temas said. "She's always brave."

"Teacher too," Doogan added.

"They were brave," Benn told them, hugging the nearest few. "You are right."

It was Tam, with his young brow scrunched into thoughtful furrows, who asked the question Lord Trilett had not thought to discuss with them. "Did the baron get away?"

He had not even told the children that the baron was involved. But they knew who had posed a threat. They'd known all along. "No," he told them solemnly. "He was killed. With the other kidnappers. Yesterday."

Benn did not expect the cheer that went up from these children who had each known their share of pain. But quickly, quickly, they shushed themselves. Several even apologized for the sudden outburst.

"I hope we didn't wake anybody," Temas whispered.

"But I'm sure glad he's dead anyway," Duncan added, pumping his head up and down in a sincere gesture of relief.

200

"Now they can get married in peace," Doogan announced.

"Yeah," said Briant. "Finally."

Benn could not tell them anything else. In a way, he felt as they did. But there was more to the grown-up world than these children understood. Lionell's death would change far more than they realized. He wondered if Tahn had had time to consider that. Or even knew how.

The day progressed with a radiant sunshine and warmth. Tahn slept through the entire morning. Netta did too.

Virtually all of the wedding guests lingered on, though there was considerable uncertainty as to when the ceremony would take place. Benn knew that many of them would wait for a glimpse of his daughter after such troubles, even if he tried to send them away to be called at another time for the marriage. It was something of an annoyance to have so many guests about, asking questions, making him repeat the same answers.

Finally he retired to his chambers, giving strict orders that he not be disturbed until Tahn or Netta or Jarel awoke. But he still couldn't sleep. He called for a messenger and sent on its way the letter he'd written to the matrons of Trent. With its absence of condolences, the correspondence might seem uncharacteristically harsh, but so be it. He didn't think he could ever again say something to the other nobles that he did not truly mean. And he was not sorry, not at all, for the Trents' loss.

He watched from the window until the messenger left the gate. And then finally he could manage to lie down again for a few moments' needed rest.

"Father, help me. Guide me," he spoke his earnest prayer. "Why do I feel so tense about the days to come? You have saved the Dorn alive. It must be for your purpose. And I'll not have him denied."

26

Tahn woke expecting to find himself flat on his back and bound to the ground in the bandit's clearing. Instead it was a soft bed where he lay in one of the Trilett estate blue rooms, in finery he didn't think he'd ever get used to. He remembered that Amos Lowe had been here last night, but he was gone now, and in a small measure Tahn was glad. He knew there was little the healer could put his hand to for helping him. This healing would just take time.

It was fully day. The sun was bright outside the high-arched window, though the draperies had been drawn to keep as much as possible of it out of his eyes. He saw the bedroll on the floor beneath the window and knew that Lucas had been there and had probably only stepped out for a moment. He, and others, would be reluctant to leave him alone when hurt. They always were.

He slid his feet toward the edge of the bed, hoping to manage sitting up before anyone came to ask him not to. Something uncomfortable bound his neck. He pulled away a white bandage, but he could not remember when it had been placed there. Everything was quiet in the house. The bandage slid from his luxurious bedcovers to an intricately woven rug on the floor. *Lord God, it feels strange to be back here. Almost like I don't belong.*

His eyes were drawn to the slivers of light around the stunning blue drapery at the window, and he pulled himself forward, longing to part the drapes and let that light flow in unhindered. Perhaps it would not be like the brilliant light of heaven he'd seen in yesterday's angelic sky, but just a taste, just a burst of it upon his face would be welcome indeed.

"Thank you, God," he whispered as he managed to bring himself to a sit at the edge of the bed. He stopped there for a moment to rest and take in as much breath as he could. He felt strangely light-headed. Weak. And sore as he'd known he would be.

Grasping the bedside chair to pull himself forward, Tahn slowly rose to his feet. He was dizzy, just like last night. Maybe worse. But he could feel strength in his legs and warmth down his spine as though he had been touched and blessed by an angel again. Slowly he moved to the window, stopping once and bowing just a bit when the room tried to whirl. Had he been hit in the head? He couldn't remember. Punched, probably. Slapped about by Burle and his men.

It was with happy relief that he reached the wall and then pulled the drapery cord, allowing even more sun than he'd expected to cascade over him. That much motion had hurt. Terribly. But he ignored the pain, leaned against the window ledge, and turned his face to the sky.

He thought of the many magnificent angels, radiant and strong, with shimmering wings and compassion in their eyes. Were they always reaching their hands that way, ministering to the souls of earth? Or were they sent only for that precarious occasion, bidden by the voice of God for a rare moment never to be repeated?

Why could I see them so plainly? he questioned himself. Did *I see them?*

Closing his eyes for a moment, he knew the answer that would settle in his heart about all that. He'd seen them. He'd felt them. There could be no denying that they'd truly been there and all of it was real. Maybe he wouldn't have believed such things before. Maybe he'd been closer to the reality of his death this time. He didn't know. Death had been close to him before. But this time, a gift of angels.

He drew in another deep breath and felt as though the sun's warmth rushed inside him along with the air. *You have been with me all along, God of light. You have had your angels with me, even when I couldn't see them. Even now.*

He opened his eyes, feeling suddenly as though he were in the midst of a great crowd, as though heaven and all its hosts were somehow all around him, or he were already there in their midst.

But it was a Trilett blue room where he stood, in the heavenly sunlight at the window. And he was still alone, though he would never feel truly alone again.

The door opened behind him, and for the first time in his life he did not feel compelled to turn and discover who was at his back. It was peace, and a sense of security, that he wasn't used to.

"Tahn—are you sure you should be up by yourself?"

Jarel. Not who he might have expected to come in first.

The voice continued. "Netta told me you might be fiercely anxious to be up too soon."

"How is she?"

"Very well, considering. Can I help you to the chair?"

"I would rather . . . that you bring the chair to me."

Jarel was quiet for a moment, but he did as he was asked. "I'm sure Lucas will be back in a moment," he finally said. "There are plenty of others who wish to see you as well. When you're ready."

Tahn eased carefully into the chair. Jarel took his arm to try to be some help, and Tahn closed his eyes again when he was settled, letting the heavenly warmth push some of the sudden pain away. "Why did you come?" he asked Jarel. "I might have expected Vari. Or Tiarra. Or Lorne."

"They'll be here. I was just checking in on you, to see if you'd stirred. And you have all right, all the way to the window. You certainly don't wait to be waited on."

"I know you," Tahn spoke the words slowly. "You don't often seek me unless you've something you need to say."

For several moments, Jarel was quiet again, and Tahn waited, a silent prayer suddenly in his heart. For Lionell's widow, strangely. And for Jarel, though that seemed to make no sense at all.

"Tahn, maybe you're prepared for the changes, I don't know. I wasn't sure you'd even be awake now. Lord knows you're in no condition to be hearing words of instruction from me. But I did want to tell you that you will always be who you are, and one family name, no matter what it is, doesn't change that. To everyone who knows you, you're the Dorn. And there's not much else to be said."

"I'm not sure I understand you."

"You will."

Tahn bowed his head. "Thank you. For following me northward."

"It was Vari's idea. And Marc Toddin's skill."

"But you did not have to come with them."

"For my cousin—and my friend—I did. I can't tell you how much I admire your courage—"

"Not blind folly?"

Jarel smiled. "Perhaps. But when it is for Netta's sake, folly is a virtue."

"Will you help me? I need to go and speak to your uncle. With his permission, we should continue with the wedding . . . if Netta is ready."

"You mean today?"

"It is no longer morning. I can tell by the sun's light. I have lost more time than I wanted already."

"We thought you might need a week or two to heal. At least take a day. Our men are not yet back from delivering bodies to the Trent house."

That was a grave and uncomfortable thought. "All right," Tahn agreed. "But we should not let ourselves be slowed more than necessary. I'll let Netta decide the hour. Perhaps we should send some word to the priest."

"He's here. With Evan and Amos Lowe, I think."

Evan. He'd forgotten. And that bothered him considerably. "How is Evan? And Jarith?"

"Evan is much better but still weak. Jarith has had trouble with one of the wounds festering, but his recovery is expected."

Tahn nodded. "I wish there were something I could do for their families. And the families of those who died."

"There will be a memorial vigil."

"When?"

"I don't know yet. There's been no time set, because of our circumstance."

The door opened, and Vari rushed in without knocking. Almost as quickly, he stopped. "I didn't know you were here, Master Jarel. I thought I should sit with Tahn until Lucas gets back."

"Where has he gone?" Tahn asked.

Vari seemed to hesitate. "One of the prisoners asked for you."

"Prisoners?"

"Yes. I'm not sure why, but Lucas went to talk to him."

"Who is it? One of Burle's men?"

"Yes. Bert."

"How many prisoners?"

Vari stepped closer, his green eyes plainly revealing his concern. "Six, Tahn. We brought them with us. You don't remember?"

He shook his head. Was something wrong? It was strange, if Vari thought he should know these things. "All of them bandits?"

"One is wife of a bandit. And two Trent soldiers."

"Don't concern yourself," Jarel added quickly.

Tahn turned to him. "Why did you bring them?"

Jarel sighed. "They gave us their weapons. It didn't seem right to slaughter them, even after what was done. But I couldn't just turn them loose to their own devices."

Tahn nodded. "I've never known Benn Trilett to hold prisoners."

"Nor have I, and I don't expect it will be long."

"What will he do?"

"I told you not to concern yourself. Please, Tahn. You've had more than enough part in this."

Tahn turned his eyes to Vari again with a heaviness now over him. "Where is my sister this morning?"

206

"She slept the morning, like most of us," he answered with some hesitation. "She is with the little girls this afternoon, but if she knew you were awake, she would be here."

Tahn stared out the window, frustrated with himself. He had known only moments ago that the morning was gone. Why had he forgotten? His thinking was cloudy somehow. But surely not badly. "She greeted us within the gate last night, didn't she? Or was that a dream?"

"It was no dream. Tahn, maybe you should lie down again."

With his right hand he gripped the arm of the chair to pull himself forward. He could not use his left effectively. The bandage around it was hot, cumbersome, and he felt like tearing it off, but he didn't. The throbbing pain was enough for him to know that the healer's handiwork there served him well.

"Let me help you," Vari said quickly, jumping to his side. "You should rest all you can. Amos made that direction very plain."

"I'm not going to the bed."

"Then what?" Vari protested. "If you want to see Tiarra, I can go and get her for you."

"I'm going outside."

Neither Vari nor Jarel seemed to know what to say. Jarel only stood watching. Vari took hold of Tahn, lending his support.

"The bench . . . by the pond . . . I think it would be in the sun at this hour."

"Maybe." Jarel found his voice. "But do you think you should walk that far?"

"I think it would not help me . . . to decide I can't try. Enough of everyone thinking I must be coddled today."

He moved toward the door, giving them no time to complete their protest. This was a good room, and he appreciated that it had been given to him, but he wanted to be outside where Tiarra and the children and anyone else could feel free to approach him if they wished. And the light of day could wash over him unhindered by walls. Strangely, he noticed the plush feel of the rug beneath his toes. He was barefoot. Why hadn't he reached for his boots when he first got up? But they weren't by the bed. Might Amos have pulled them off and set them someplace else?

It didn't matter. He didn't ask. The grass beneath his toes would feel even better than this. He went on, trying to remember if this room was upstairs or down. He didn't ask that either. He'd find out soon enough, once he got to the hallway. He should have known already, from his view out the window. He didn't know why he didn't know.

Vari was at his right hand. Someone else was at his left. But it wasn't Jarel. Jarel moved ahead of them and opened the door. "I'm not sure Amos will be pleased with you," he warned. "Nor Netta."

Tahn didn't see anyone else beside him, but he didn't have to see. "Angel, something is wrong." He stopped and took a careful breath, not sure if he'd spoken the words aloud. "Is there a fog in my mind?" He heard no answer, but he still felt the steadying hand at his left shoulder. Vari was looking at Jarel. Neither of them said a word.

They were downstairs. He should have known they would not have given him stairs to manage when they came in last night, though he did not remember coming in. Had he been carried? He could vaguely remember someone carrying him—Marc Toddin, he thought, but that had been long ago.

"Lord God," he whispered. "I yet need your touch."

The hallway seemed acres long. It opened into an exquisite room with cushioned chairs trimmed in gold. Tapestries on the walls. A beautifully carved table with feet like lion's paws, and on it an oil lamp with hundreds of pieces of dangling glass. He'd never seen anything like it. Had he? There was something familiar about the delicate loveseat and the tiled fireplace along the opposite wall. Had he been in this room before?

"Maybe we should stop to rest," Jarel suggested.

He shook his head, hearing the sounds of people not far away. Other rooms, just down the hallway. Or more than one hallway, it seemed like, leading to rooms even larger and grander than this one. "Please. I want to go outside."

"Tahn, are you all right?" Vari finally asked him, sounding more than a little anxious.

The painful moving had brought on beads of sweat. He could feel their dampness on his brow. "Yes. Please, Vari. I want to go on."

"Why?" the teen protested again. "You drive yourself too hard! You've got to rest. What can it hurt just to stop a few minutes? Let me get you a drink."

"Are we halfway?"

"To the door, more so. To the pond, not near."

Tahn took a deep breath. He winced, it hurt him so. "To the steps, then. I'll rest there. And take your drink." He breathed in a few more gasps, trying to collect his strength.

"Did anyone ever tell you that you are uncommonly stubborn?" Jarel asked him.

"I think so. I think it was you. You shoved me against a tree. But you're not angry now."

Jarel moved in front of him, and his face seemed pale. "By the Lord in heaven, Tahn. You mustn't push yourself. You need help. Let me go get Amos."

Tahn shook his head. "Don't go alone. Samis is still watching."

Vari gasped beside him.

"Get him back to the bed if you can," Jarel said urgently. "I'll be right back with the healer."

"Outside," Tahn protested. "On the steps."

"Samis is dead," Jarel told him. "You were there to see the body."

"Yes. You're right." Tahn looked from one face to the other, both of them afraid for him. *Lord God, what's wrong with me?*

"I can lift him," Vari offered. "He's not that big. I can take him out in the sun if that's what he wants. Amos can meet us there."

Jarel nodded. "All right. God have mercy."

"God have mercy," Tahn repeated. "I . . . need his help. My thinking is . . . a little muddled."

"We've noticed, Tahn."

"I can walk. Don't carry me, please. If Netta sees, or my sister, or the children—"

"Then what?" Jarel demanded. "They already know you are hurt. You can't hide from them! They know every bit of the pain whether you tell them or not!"

Tahn closed his eyes. Jarel was yelling at him, out in the trees somewhere with their horses waiting. But that was in the past. It wasn't real now. They were still inside, in the room with the tiled fireplace and the glass-ornamented lamp. "It was a long time ago," he said softly. "When you were angry with me."

"Yes," Jarel acknowledged. "Before I understood that you weren't the evil I expected."

"Lionell is dead."

"Yes. And you have a lot of people very concerned about you right now."

"Stand here with the angel, Jarel," Tahn said. "On my left. Both of you, walk me outside. I'll be all right."

Once again, Jarel and Vari looked at one another. Jarel hesitated. But they did what Tahn said. They made careful progress down another hallway to the entry at the base of a curving staircase. This Tahn remembered—children running down it, bursting into his arms.

Someone was in the room to the side of the entry, someone who stood to his feet as they walked past. But Jarel waved him back. Whoever it was did not approach.

"There are still many guests here," Jarel said quietly.

"Where are they?" Tahn asked him.

"Most of them are occupied with the entertainment my uncle prepared to keep them out of Netta's way. She didn't seem in a mood to talk to any of them. Do you remember the musicians at your party?"

He nodded. "They had some pipes or something."

"Among other things, yes."

"Where is Netta?"

"With her father. Or Hildy. I probably shouldn't tell you this, especially not now. But she's been crying a lot."

"Ask her . . . ask her to meet me by the pond."

"Tahn—"

"I'll rest on the steps first. We're almost there."

"Stubborn," Jarel muttered under his breath.

The Trilett front door opened before they got to it. Lucas stood for a moment in the doorway and then shoved the door wider. He didn't say anything, only watched them move out into the sunlight.

Vari stopped on the top stone step and helped Tahn sit.

"I'm glad you've come," Jarel said quickly to Lucas. "I need to speak to Amos, and to Netta. Vari is going in a moment to get Tahn some water. Stay with your friend, please. He's not quite himself."

Lucas didn't speak in answer. He only nodded and moved to sit on the step beside Tahn. Vari looked down at him gravely but didn't try to explain.

"Good to see you up," Lucas finally said. "How are you feeling?"

Tahn stared out across the courtyard. He didn't really want to answer. He didn't want them to focus on him this way, to persist in worrying. "I'd have to expect to be sore."

"Yes," Lucas answered him simply.

And Tahn sighed. Lucas knew there was more. It seemed he could always tell such things as that. "Do you remember the dreams I used to have?"

Lucas's face was grave when he nodded. "I could never forget."

"Sometimes as I woke, for only a few moments, things got confused together, and I wasn't sure what was real and what was dream."

"I think I've seen that."

"It's not the same—but there are things today—I'm just not sure."

Vari heaved a sigh. "I'll be back in a minute with your water, Tahn." And he disappeared.

"What things?" Lucas asked.

211

Tahn leaned against the stone rail. "I don't know. I don't want to worry you. I already worry them."

"You had nightmares?"

He shook his head. "I don't remember things. Or I'm not sure if I remember or not."

"I can understand that. You weren't awake for all of the ride back. And I wouldn't be surprised if you'd lost consciousness before that. They beat you badly." He watched Tahn's eyes as he continued carefully. "And I think you were strangled. Do you remember?"

He shook his head.

"The marks on your neck tell it."

"I lost my boots."

Lucas nodded. "We noticed that. A long time before we found you. We followed barefoot tracks for a considerable way."

Tahn looked down at his feet. He couldn't seem to say anything.

Lucas put a hand on his shoulder and sighed. "Where the foot tracks stopped, there were other marks Toddin didn't talk about. And then only the horses. I feared you were fallen. Dragged. And then thrown on a horse, dead or alive. It was unspeakable relief to find you breathing."

Tahn closed his eyes. "Where is Netta? I want her here."

"Jarel said he would speak to her. I'm sure she'll be coming."

He tried to pull himself up. "Walk with me to the pond."

Lucas took his arm. "Give yourself a few moments first."

Tahn sat in silence, so many things racing suddenly through his mind. Burle with the rope. Lionell with the broadax. And Burle in a dark and dismal room, so long ago. Was that part even real? He shuddered. "Did Burle ever hurt you?"

"You know there was no love between us. He hit me more than once when we were boys. But nothing like what he's done to you, Tahn. It was an obsession born of the devil."

Tahn licked his lips, suddenly dry and shaky inside. "Born long ago."

212

"But it's over now. Push him from your mind. He's dead. No more concern."

"Did I kill him?"

Lucas nodded. "I'm not sure how you had the strength, but thank God for it."

Tahn bowed his head. Vari's dagger. He remembered now. But at the time Burle had seemed almost vaporous, like a cloud of evil rushing toward them. Tahn could still hear Burle's grim laugh, not only from the wilderness clearing but also from that awful room at Valhal, a more boyish laugh but just as cruel. *God, help me push him from my mind, as Lucas said! I don't want to think about this! I don't want to know if it was real.*

"Everything will be all right, Tahn. It just takes time sometimes."

"I know," he said with a sigh. "For the soreness to fade."

"And the mind to be at rest. You were hurt badly. I feared what we'd find. If you don't remember things, it's nothing more than can be expected. It doesn't matter. Some things are better forgotten."

Tahn opened his eyes and looked at the bright sky above them. There seemed to be a shimmer behind the clouds, a promise almost, of what lay beyond them. "I saw angels, Lucas."

"Then perhaps you were as near to heaven as I feared."

The estate door opened behind them, and Vari hurried to them with a chalice of water. Netta came rushing out behind him. She knelt on the step in front of Tahn, and he leaned to pull her into his embrace.

She was weeping, he could tell. Little, quiet tears. He hoped it only meant that she was joyful to be home. He held her as tight as he could stand, breathing in the scent of her hair. She was dressed so beautifully in a daygown. She seemed to tremble just a little. And he remembered her coming so boldly toward him down the slope and across the clearing even with the bandits all around, as though she could pretend to be somebody else.

"Netta—never, never do that again."

213

She drew back and stared at him. "What? What, my love?"

"You put yourself in danger . . . coming to me there, when they were all around. Never again. Please."

"Tahn." She shook her head. "What about you? What if I told you the same thing?"

He only looked at her, and then drew her close again.

"I don't want you ever to put yourself at risk again either," she persisted. "Even for me, Tahn. No more."

"I can't promise such a thing."

"Then God shield us! I'll die if ever I have to see you like that again!"

"Sshh." He held his arm around her, wishing he could still her quiet tears. "I'm sorry. It never should have happened."

She kissed his cheek, so softly it felt like the brush of an angel's wing. "Jarel told me you were up too soon," she whispered. "He said you weren't well."

"He worries overmuch."

"And you push too hard. Please, let yourself rest."

He drew several difficult breaths. "A blanket. By the pond. Is that all right?"

She nodded. "Vari, can you get us a blanket? Our picnic spot, Tahn?"

He smiled. "Yes. Join me?"

She smiled too and kissed his cheek again. "If you'll lie down, and not let the children climb on you."

The sun burst from behind ethereal clouds. He could picture the angel's wings again filling that sky. *You're with me,* he said in his mind. *Thank you, God, that heaven is with me now. Thank you. For Netta. For sparing her life . . .*

Vari held the cup forward, and Netta took it in her hands. "You need a drink, love."

He let her hold it for him. He wasn't quite sure why, but he wasn't certain if he could have held it for himself. He felt peace again, far larger than himself, yet at the same time an overwhelming weariness. He let both Lucas and Vari help him to the grassy spot beside the pond. He didn't protest when Amos came to see him there. Or the children, most of them far too quiet, and acting as though they were afraid to touch him. Tiarra, too, did not hug him but only sat for awhile and held his hand.

This was a happy place, site of a hundred picnics, or so it seemed, and romping and laughing with the children on the spacious estate grounds.

Laughing. He suddenly stopped and wondered about that. Had he laughed? Jarel had said at his foolish party that he could not recall such a thing. But at least the children had done it, and it didn't seem so awfully far away from the memories that he had in this place.

A gentle breeze tossed his hair, and he wiggled his toes, thinking he would have to get boots before the wedding. But he didn't want to ask Benn Trilett for them. Benn Trilett did so much, taking in all these children and providing for their needs. Paying for every detail of the wedding. And now for a healer again . . .

Rest.

The single word seemed whispered into his spirit.

Rest.

He thought of Evan and Jarith, and the families of the dead. Even Lionell's widow again, though he'd never met her and didn't expect that he ever would. Benn Trilett had so much to think about, he suddenly considered. Even those prisoners . . .

Rest.

But he hadn't asked Lucas about Bert. He'd meant to. Where had Lucas gone? He thought he might lift his head to look for him, but he couldn't quite bring himself to do it. The sun was warm on his feet, but his eyes were now in the shade. He thought of the clearing where he'd been bound, and he curled his body just a little, turning to one side as much as he could bear.

Burle was dead. Lionell was dead. Samis, too, longer ago. Not far from here. And peace rested over the Trilett estate. Perhaps there would be a wedding tomorrow. And then heaven after that, right here on earth. He drew in a

215

deep breath, and the pain seemed to have eased. Light and shadow mingled in his mind with the voices of children, and then it all faded until he was no longer aware of anything but the breeze. Cool and restful, it carried him away into a peaceful sleep.

27

He'll not be happy about it, I can tell you that right now." Jarel paced in his uncle's meeting room, his boots thudding against the marble with every step. "Any communication demands some kind of response!"

"I want a response," his uncle answered soberly. "I want those who remain of the House of Trent to tell me plainly whether they will receive him properly as a relative or not."

"As another nobleman pointed out to me so carefully today," Jarel said with a sigh, "Tahn's mother was illegitimate. It's not like he can demand an acknowledgment. Or, in this case, that you can demand one for him."

"Karra Loble was acknowledged. Plainly. All of the nobles know that. Her father claimed her and gave her inheritance. He has rights."

Jarel shook his head. "He doesn't want them! How dare you act without asking him?"

Benn Trilett's eyes were suddenly fire, and Jarel swallowed hard, realizing what he'd said. How dare he talk to his uncle that way? He'd never done it before.

But Benn Trilett only sighed. "Tahn has not been in a position to see how this decision affects far more than only himself. We will have to help him to understand."

"What is it you want?" Jarel asked his uncle. "All Tahn needs now is Netta and the chance to peacefully share his life with her."

"And the children he has loved and rescued. The children Netta will bear him. Perhaps far more than that, even. He does not see how far his influence can carry."

"Do you?"

"Lady Elane of Trent is expecting a child, as I recall. Tahn, as a kinsman, could be an example of mercy and humility sorely needed for any child of Trent."

"And you think Lady Elane would bring her offspring to sit at Tahn's knee?"

"The lady has not the same heart as her husband."

"But he *was* her husband."

"Because her father sorely needed money, and Lionell needed marriage to better his image. Elane of Fontner gave Lionell new dignity and acceptance as he was trying to save face for his father's sins."

"She *is* dignified," Jarel acknowledged.

"And widowed in a house of women who may be exceedingly unpleasant company. Bitter dregs to raise a child upon."

"What are you saying?"

"Can you picture Tiarra as nobility?"

Jarel smiled. "I'm used to her being here by now. But no. Not any more than I can Tahn. Not if you mean nobility as we generally know it in this land."

"Then they are just what our nobility needs. What would Tahn do with a portion of Trent wealth?"

"Give it away, probably. To the families of our dead, for starters. Street orphans. You know him. He wouldn't even want to keep it for himself."

"Indeed. Untold good. Even if he didn't realize it."

"My lord—"

"Jarel, Lionell was as wrong about *me* as he was about his cousin. I am not ambitious for what was his. I only want to see justice served and good come out of what has been a grievous injustice for a very long time."

"I still say you should have talked to Tahn before sending that message."

"I could not wait, under the circumstances. How much have you thought about this, Jarel? What will the Trents do about Lionell's death?"

"They can do nothing! He was caught in murderous intent. They would have no justification—"

218

"They cannot retaliate, even with what soldiers they have left. I wasn't speaking of that. What will they do now? Without their head?"

"Mourn." Jarel paced about a bit. "For a customary time. Then they must declare a new baron. If Lady Elane's child is a boy, it shall be him, with a proxy appointed until his maturity."

"And if it isn't a boy?"

Jarel was quiet for a moment, his mind racing over the possibilities. "There are cousins of Lionell's mother."

"Products, all of them, of marriage to Trent cousins already far removed from the lineage. But the baron must be a direct descendant of a baron. Or else, without a king to appoint their lands, the House of Trent is dead."

Jarel dropped heavily into a chair. He stared up at his uncle. "They could attempt appointing a relative not of direct lineage. If no one contests them to the council."

Benn crossed his arms. "If someone does, the appointment would be found invalid."

Jarel stared at his uncle. "Would you truly? Oppose them before the council?"

"I might not need to. There are others now who know the truth. But if I did, why would that trouble you?"

"Because it's Tahn's life you speak of! You can't put him in this position!"

"He's in it regardless of what I do. If we say nothing, it will still be spread about who he is. Even if Lionell's child is a boy, the Trents shall have to acknowledge Tahn or explain why they do not."

For a moment, Jarel couldn't speak. He felt as though all the wind had been sucked away from him. "Then he can't escape this?"

"No. He cannot. Too many people know now. The noble fellows you spoke to on the trail have noised it throughout the house."

"May he forgive me."

"It wasn't only you. The Toddins have known. The priest has known. Lionell's wife has known."

219

"Surely Lady Elane would tell no one what her husband thought to be his greatest danger."

"On the contrary, she told her brother. And Master Fontner in turn told one of our guests of the House of Eman. He came to me even before the kidnapping and asked me what I intended to do."

Jarel sucked in a quick breath. "What did you tell him?"

"That I shall marry my daughter to an honorable man. What more besides that shall depend on what the Trents may do."

28

Lucas could not be certain why it was so important for Tahn to be outside, except perhaps that it had always been a little difficult for him to accept having a place in Lord Trilett's grand mansion. When evening came, they tried to get him to go back inside, but he didn't want to, telling them he wanted to stay where he could look at the stars. Despite their concerns, they let him have his way because the sky was clear and no one wanted to argue.

Perhaps it is still a bit too much for him, Lucas considered. *To see himself as part of this world. But he never belonged in Samis's world, and maybe the best he can find in between is a piece of ground beneath the open sky.*

Lucas sighed and stretched out on his bedroll, now moved to the pond's edge not far from Tahn. Netta was born for noble houses. When the darkness had come, she'd wanted her father, her home, and all that was familiar and proper for her. She could not stay with Tahn, yet unmarried. So with a kiss, she'd left him on his blanket and asked Lucas to stay with him once again.

They were not the only ones under the stars tonight. Vari and Lorne were a stone's throw away, closer to the house, should they be needed. Tiarra and the children had not wanted to be even that far; they'd offered to camp with Tahn, all clustered happily about him. But Tahn had asked Tiarra to give him the night's solitude and the children a better rest.

"We can better camp another time," he'd said. "When all of you are done with your worrying. Only for tonight, please, let me rest alone without a roof between me and heaven."

It was a strange request, and one that no one, especially not Netta nor Amos, could completely accept. Alone? Not when every slightest movement hurt him and he still seemed just a little past himself somehow.

"Forgive us, brother," Lucas whispered. "I know you despise the worry. But it is our love for you that makes us watchful."

Layers of blankets had been brought to go under him, and one coverlet, should he need it on top. And cushions, many, many cushions, to ease his aching ribs. Tahn slept now, or at least he appeared to, among the careful arrangement. He made no sound, nor the slightest movement, and Lucas lay quietly staring up at the stars.

Years ago, when he'd been eleven and Tahn perhaps ten, they'd camped beneath the stars with Samis at the base of the northern hills. There were only the three of them that night, and Samis had wanted the company of his bottle more than the boys. So Tahn and Lucas were left alone while Samis drank and then stretched out to sleep a few yards away.

They might have escaped him, if he'd ever gotten truly drunk or managed to sleep soundly. But Samis did neither, and he kept his sword, his whip, and his throwing knives ever handy. Along with the opium tincture, the drug he bought with some of his foul-gained treasure and shared with his hapless boys to ensnare them more fully. Lucas had carried his measure of Samis's opium, a tiny flask, in his pocket as he lay beneath the stars that night. He and Tahn shared just a bit of it and then lay dreamily staring up at the sky.

"Sometimes I pretend I can see right up to heaven," Lucas had said.

But the simple words had upset Tahn terribly. "Don't talk about that. Don't say another word."

Lucas hadn't argued. He'd never been able to argue with Tahn. Back then, Tahn had seemed fragile and yet so intense he was frightening, despite his youth. Lucas thought looking into his eyes was like seeing pictures of the nightmares that bound him, as though he could fall into the torment right along with Tahn and never really make it out. So he didn't like looking in Tahn's eyes. No one did.

But under the stars on that long-ago night, Tahn had thrashed with one of the worst nightmares Lucas could remember. He'd longed to wake him, he always did, but he knew better. Agonized screams shook the forest until Samis grew weary of hearing it and woke the boy with the lash of his whip.

It was the first of the few times Lucas had ever dared to argue with Samis. He ran and grabbed at his arm, screaming for him to stop. "No! I told you! He can't help it!"

"I see that, boy." Samis laughed and shoved Lucas away as Tahn cowered on the ground, shaking. Even in the darkness, his haunting eyes were vivid, and Lucas had been afraid.

"Leave him alone."

Lucas knew the danger if anyone touched Tahn while he still lay under the nightmare's cruel power. He would lash out like a wild animal, not even aware of what he was doing. Lucas wasn't sure he really cared if Tahn lashed out at Samis—it seemed impossible that anyone could actually hurt the brutish man—but he cared very much what Samis might do in response.

"Please don't hurt him. He's stopped. See? He's quiet."

Tahn still crouched, his deep eyes watching, his breaths coming fast like a scared beast's. Lucas knew the pain he'd dreamed. The flames licking at his skin. Tahn had told him about it after an episode in their shared room at Valhal.

"Get up," Samis commanded, but Tahn didn't move a muscle.

"He can't," Lucas had tried to explain. "Not yet. Give him just a little while. Just wait. Real quiet. Then he'll be all right again."

But Samis would not wait. He lashed out with the whip again, catching Tahn's leg. And then Tahn did something Lucas had never dreamed anyone could do. He ran at Samis, straight in the face of that whip, and leaped at his tormentor, screaming and clawing . . .

With a shudder, Lucas sat up quickly, willing away the awful memory. He glanced over at Tahn, who still lay sleeping so peacefully among the Trilett's numerous cushions. So much had changed. *Father God, bless your holy name.*

But the scene from his childhood would not so quickly leave his mind. Samis never took any insult lightly. And on that pitiful night, Lucas had thought Samis would kill Tahn for certain. He beat him off, he threw him across the dying campfire embers, he whipped at him, and at Lucas when he tried to intervene, until Tahn was nothing more than a quivering ball of sobs.

And after all that, Samis only took another long swig of his drink and solemnly declared, "You were right, Lucas. That boy's not in his right mind when he dreams. And he knows it too, don't he? A pain he knows that well, he'd do about anything to avoid."

That night was the beginning of the guilt Lucas had carried for a very long time, because he had gone to Samis only the day before. He should never have told him about Tahn's dreams, even though everyone in Valhal had already heard the screams by night plenty of times. But Samis might not have learned the things Tahn saw, the things Tahn actually dreamed, if Lucas hadn't foolishly told him all about it, hoping for some remedy. He should have known better. Samis only used Tahn's torment to twist him and snare him and turn him into a killer.

Lucas understood that the feelings stirred back then still followed them now, even with things so different. Tahn knew the salvation of God now. He had a family's love. The light of Christ had driven away so much of the darkness and torment that he was hardly the same at all. Sometimes he seemed stronger than Lucas could ever hope to be.

But still, at least tonight, Lucas could not leave Tahn alone beneath the stars, even when he seemed to sleep so peacefully. Something in his eyes since he woke that morning had been just a little like the Tahn who'd stared at him in the quiet moments after a nightmare's throes, when he'd lain so still and tried to recover himself. All of this circumstance, with

Netta's kidnapping and the torment that followed, must have been like a nightmare all over again. Perhaps Tahn was still recovering himself even now, piece by piece.

Thankfully, more peacefully than before.

With such thoughts on his mind, Lucas prayed for his friend, still thinking it strange that he'd refused to go inside. And just as strange that the Triletts, and even the healer, had been willing to yield to his wishes so completely. *Touch him tonight,* Lucas prayed. *Give him peace.*

Frogs were singing at the far side of the pond. The breeze was like a gentle whisper across his face. He had not realized his own weariness until he let himself lie down again here. The night sounds lulled him. And sleep was not far away.

***

Late in the night, Lucas stirred to the sound of an owl's call. The wind had increased across the pond, and scattered clouds had moved in, making the night darker than it had been before. He thought he heard another sound nearby, but he wasn't sure what it was.

"Tahn?"

Lucas couldn't see his friend against the hazy outline of bedding nearby, and he moved closer in dismay. *He should not be up moving about. Not alone at night when he is in pain.*

A few feet beyond the blankets, a solitary shape knelt against the stone bench overlooking the pond.

"Tahn?"

For a moment Lucas couldn't be sure it was him. He crept closer. The figure was hunched over, both arms sprawled across the seat of the bench, one of them still wrapped enough to be bulkier than the other. His head was down. His shoulders seemed to sag. Lucas moved to his side, but the old uncertainty remained in him, and he couldn't touch him without calling out again and being sure that this time he was heard.

"Tahn? Are you all right, brother?"

225

Slowly the bowed head rose just a little. "Lucas."

"Yes. Can I help you? Can I do anything?"

"Just . . . just stay."

Lucas was surprised at the answer. Concerned. "What's wrong?"

Tahn bent over the bench, his head nearly touching the weathered stone. "I can't do it, Lucas. I can't be what I need to be . . . I'm a boy running, trying to hide, and a fighter with my sword still dripping . . ."

Lucas's heart pounded. "The past is done. You know that better than anyone."

"But can I be what Netta needs? And the children?"

"You already are!"

"I thought . . . I thought . . ." He tried to turn but stopped and made the faintest sound. A tiny gasp of pain.

"You need to lie down, Tahn."

But he didn't seem to hear. "I see things . . . differently now. With heaven so close I can see how far I am from . . . from what I should be . . ."

Lucas stared at his friend, for a moment unable to answer. "Tahn, scarcely anyone feels they're all they should be. No one's asking you for perfection, just that you be the man you are."

"Sometimes . . . that's not enough."

"Then that is where God steps in, by his grace."

Lucas moved his hand to rest on Tahn's shoulder and found him suddenly quivering. His voice betrayed the continuing pain. "What's wrong with me, Lucas?"

"You're hurt. And expecting too much from yourself."

He shook his head. "That's not what I mean."

"It may be that you're nervous, Tahn. It sounds almost that way, and it's nothing to worry about. I've heard that a man *should* be nervous before he marries."

"But there's more than that."

The shaking hadn't stopped, and Tahn was still bowed as though by a heavy burden. Gently, Lucas put an arm around him and drew him close to support his weight. "Tell me. What troubles you?"

It was several moments before Tahn could speak. "I don't want . . . to disappoint anyone. Even God. But I'm afraid I will. Or I already have. You would have gone on . . . if the choice was yours. I know it of you, that there's nothing in this world that you love more than our Savior . . ."

"I'm not sure what you mean. About the choice."

Tahn breathed in carefully. "Before you got to us . . . when the angels were there . . . I felt like heaven was so close and God was ready for me . . . I felt like I could have gone with him, if it weren't for Netta. Do you think . . . does he think . . . that I love him less because I wanted to stay with her?"

Lucas shook his head. He could never have expected words like this. "No. Tahn, he surely must have wanted you to stay. To love her the way you're meant to."

"Then why? The light of heaven he showed me in the midst of everything . . . it makes me think . . . I should have died . . ."

For a moment Lucas only held him, anguished at this new struggle. What could he say? He could not pretend to know the mind of God, nor understand the things Tahn had experienced.

Father, I cannot leave such words unanswered. You love this man. You have had a purpose all along. What shall I tell him?

He could picture Tahn as they'd found him in the bandit's camp, limbs stretched apart and staked to the ground. Burle, or Lionell, whoever put him there, must have wanted him to feel utterly powerless. Suddenly he knew the words he should say.

"You let yourself be vulnerable, Tahn, going there freely. I don't believe God wanted you to die. He surely showed you what he did so that you would know he was with you and you weren't as helpless as it seemed. That *he* had the power over your life, not Lionell."

Tahn raised his eyes toward the sky. The quivering had stilled. "It was right before the arrow . . ." He bowed his head for just a moment, and when he lifted it again, it was with a laugh, a soft sound like rare music Lucas had never heard before. "I know it was a miracle. Marcus would never have made that shot without a miracle."

Lucas smiled, unspeakably relieved to find a note of lightness. "Let's not tell him that. He thinks he's quite the marksman now. He's already enjoying a reputation."

"Let him. He earned it."

"And you've earned a quiet life," Lucas added contentedly. "Wedded bliss—"

"And a friend to watch over me day and night?"

"When you need it. You won't much longer. And I'll be going back to Alastair."

Tahn pulled away a little and then stopped. "I almost wish you wouldn't."

"You know I'm needed there."

"I wish I could do more . . . for your work . . . for those children . . ."

Lucas sighed, wishing Tahn would only let himself rest. "You've done a great deal. I'm already financed by Trilett benevolence."

"It's not enough. You should have more than a tiny home for so many."

"Tahn, God does not expect you to solve every problem. You've done enough. And you may have a big day tomorrow. It's time you tried to sleep again. Your body needs it."

"My mind's been so full, I'm not sure I can."

"Try. Please."

Slowly Tahn nodded, trying to struggle to his feet.

"Let me help you."

Carefully, Lucas guided his friend back to the blankets and cushions. Tahn said nothing as Lucas eased him down, but he took up one of the cushions and pressed it carefully against his side.

"May I pray for you?" Lucas asked him.

"Yes," Tahn answered, his voice sounding strained. "Always."

The hoot owl called again.

228

You are a liar, devil, Lucas suddenly thought. *He didn't die. And he's not going to. Not till he's old and ready.*

The words of the prayer he said came out easily and flowed from him with much greater length than he'd planned. Tahn lay without the slightest movement, the breeze pushing strands of his shortened hair across his face. And it wasn't until the prayer was done that Lucas realized he was already asleep.

29

Tahn woke as the morning sun crept across his brow. The gentle breeze tossed his hair, and he brushed stray strands of it from his face, surprised at first to find it so short. Eger had the rest of it in his saddlebag somewhere. But he wasn't sure now if Eger lived or died.

He thought again about Bert asking for him yesterday. He'd not yet gotten Lucas to tell him what that was about. Nor did he know what would be done with any of the prisoners. He wondered if Benn Trilett would mind him inquiring.

The breaths seemed easier than they had in the night. Rest must have done him good. He turned his head to see Lucas kneeling in morning prayers at the pond's edge. He was a faithful man. A good friend who'd always yearned for the things of God even when they'd seemed so far out of reach.

For a time, Lucas had tried even in Samis's horrible stronghold to be like the priest he'd often watched with wonder and longing before his capture. He'd prayed as a little boy in that dark and dismal place, and Tahn would never forget those prayers, nor his own reaction to them. Fear. But more than that, a gut-wrenching envy. Because he'd wanted to feel that he also could be able to pray. He'd hoped just for the chance that God might someday care. But he'd thought it couldn't be true. He was a beast, hated by God. Worthless. Unloved and unlovable.

He'd not been able to believe differently until Netta Trilett touched his heart with the truth. God's merciful, boundless, forgiving love, free to anyone who longed for it and asked for it. He'd never known a greater miracle. He never could. And thanks be to that loving Savior, he'd been able to share the miracle with Lucas and begin to rekindle the hope that had almost been lost in him.

You've been so good to us, Lord. Faithful to deliver. Mighty to save.

Lucas turned his head away from the waters of the pond. When he saw Tahn, he smiled. "Good morning! Are you hungry yet?"

"No. Are you?"

"A bit. But I was going to offer to bring you a tray. You didn't eat much yesterday."

Tahn lifted a cushion to his side and answered him light-heartedly. "You'd have made a fine mother to someone."

"I hope you count me a fine enough friend." Lucas rose from the pond's edge and moved to sit beside Tahn's blanket. "How are you this morning?"

"A little clearer, I think. Thank you. For your patience with me."

"Tahn, the only one having trouble with patience around here is you. Sometimes you expect too much from yourself, too fast."

"I think I've heard that before."

"You'll probably hear it again if you don't let yourself rest today. Amos wants you to take a warm soak, eat at least a little, and allow yourself a soft bed after this."

"He was out here?"

"Yes. Not long ago. He didn't want to wake you."

Tahn knew that he'd have to respond to those wishes and perhaps be more cooperative than he'd been so far. But at that moment, the prayers he'd prayed and the things he'd talked about with Lucas last night filled his mind. "I think the angels are real."

"I think so too," Lucas agreed immediately. "I've believed in them most of my life, even when I figured they'd turned their backs."

"Have you ever seen them?"

"No."

"Then you have a strong faith."

Lucas glanced toward Lorne and Vari, who were rolling their blankets not far away. "I wouldn't discount your own if I were you."

"Has Netta been out?"

"Twice. Just to look at you."

"You should have roused me."

"None of us were willing to do that."

"It must not be as early morning as I thought."

"Maybe not. But it's still early." Lucas stood to his feet again. "I can bring you something to drink, even if you're not ready for breakfast yet. And Amos wanted to know when you wakened so he could spread a balm of some kind on your neck. Will you be ready soon to go in for the soak he wanted? Hildy will have a tub ready in the side kitchen."

"I'll go in. I suppose they're wondering at me shunning the house."

"Indeed, Tahn."

"I wanted to meet with God beneath his heaven." Tahn looked up at Lucas, trying to judge the response to what he said. "And perhaps I'm a little afraid of all their expectations."

"You needn't be," he answered confidently. "No one will demand more of you than you do of yourself."

"I'm not so sure about that."

Lucas lowered himself to his knees. "Why do you think it?"

"Because I'm an older brother, not only to Tiarra but to all the children. Even Lorne and Vari. Maybe more than a brother to some of their minds. And a nobleman's son-in-law soon. With Lionell's death to face."

"What do you mean by that?"

Tahn bowed his head. "They can't help but think thoughts and wonder. Benn Trilett will ask me again if I want to claim what might have been mine."

"What do you think you'll tell him?"

"That I'll not do anything to cause unrest or take anything for myself. The stars last night and the children's smiles are worth far more than Trent gold could ever be."

Lucas nodded soberly. "But sometimes, Tahn, God gives grace for the unexpected. Sometimes he rewards the just even in this world."

"I have reward. It may be possible that I wed today. If the rest of our company is here and Netta is ready."

"She will be," Lucas predicted. "But don't expect her to be able to keep herself from you all the day as the custom is."

Tahn leaned forward to lift himself from the cushions, and Lucas helped him. The light-headedness pressed at him again, but only for a moment, and the pain was not as bad. He could walk on his own, he was sure of it, but he knew Lucas would insist upon staying beside him, so Tahn let it be and accepted his help to the house.

"Until the wedding," he said. "I can let you all pamper me that long. But no longer."

Lucas only gave him a sideways glance. "I think that shall be for the healer and your wife to decide."

***

The warm soak felt wonderful. It even smelled of heaven somehow, with some sort of herb or spice applied to the water. Broth was brought while Tahn soaked, though he scarcely touched it. And when he was ready to leave the water, an attendant helped him to towel dry and gave him a blue satiny robe he'd never seen before.

"I hope Netta is being treated this well," he told the servant.

"Of course, sir."

"Please, call me Tahn. Have I told you that before?"

"Yes," the man answered with a cordial smile. "But you know me, that I forget it easily. And I'm not used to your allowing my help."

He had thought he remembered this man waiting on Lord Trilett at some time or another. He should have been far more familiar. A trusted servant who obviously was acquainted with him. *Lord, lift away any fog from my mind.*

The servant showed him to a chair in the blue room he'd been in before and soon brought a generous breakfast tray. Tahn only sipped from one of the cups, not even sure what the sweet concoction was. In only a moment, Amos stepped in with a tall bottle and a clay jar and set them on a table.

"I'll not be drinking one of those, will I?" Tahn questioned him.

Amos seemed relieved to find him light-spirited. "No. One is a liniment for your ribs and hand. The other a balm for your neck. Let me help you lie down, please. Our riders to the Trent estate have come back. You may have a wedding tonight, but you need a good bit of doctoring. I want you to relax."

Obediently, Tahn rose and moved to the bed. "How are Evan and Jarith this morning?"

"Much better. Gaining appetite."

"Good. Might they be able to attend?"

Amos met his eyes. "Not Evan. Jarith perhaps, with careful help. But in all truth, it's a bit soon even for you, Tahn."

"Why? I can stand. And I can state my will."

Amos smiled. "Perhaps further delay would be wrong, then."

"How many days ago should it have been?"

"Three."

Tahn nodded. "The time ran together. I couldn't be certain."

"I'm not surprised." Amos gently opened Tahn's robe and took a careful look at the bruises. "Has the pain changed?"

"Every time I move."

"Is it worse?"

"No. Not really."

"But not better?"

"Soon enough."

Amos nodded. "You're too used to this. But at least you're patient with me this morning."

He took some time examining Tahn's hand, which had

been left unwrapped since the soaking and now throbbed again. As he moved each finger carefully, he glanced at Tahn's face. "I know grown men who would cry when I do this. It hurts. I know it does."

"Indeed."

"I'll get a bowl in here in a few moments with an herb tincture to soak it in. We'll have to keep it set securely then, in a mudded wrap day and night. You'll not be able to use it normally for some time."

Tahn did not answer that matter. He stared up at the ceiling. In this room, even that was blue, with little patterns of gold. "How is Netta this morning?"

"Better than I expected."

Tahn almost sat up. "Why? What did you expect?"

Amos put a reassuring hand on his shoulder. "To find her faint. Terrified still. Instead, she mostly asks me about you."

"She's home where she needn't fear. What about the bruises?"

Amos seemed a little more reluctant to answer. "Hildy looked her over closely for me. No doubt she was tossed about and hit a few times. Bound hand and foot. But the bruises are not deep. Nothing broken. She'll mend quickly. But I should not be surprised if she remains wary for a long time. I thank God there were not worse things done."

Tahn nodded his head solemnly. He had thanked God too, over and over. Amos picked up the clay jar and set the lid beside Tahn on the bed.

"Try to lie very still. This may hurt a bit."

Amos dipped his finger into the jar and then touched a small amount of the oily balm carefully to Tahn's neck. Tahn closed his eyes. He had been trying to ignore this pain, to not think about the soreness at his neck, as if he could pretend that much had not happened. For reasons he didn't understand, it took his mind places he didn't want to go. Into Burle's laughter. And the dark room of the past.

Amos's touch was hard to bear. Not just the pain of the

235

touch against his wounds, but the touch itself. The hand at his throat.

"Are you doing all right?" Amos asked him. "I'm almost finished. The medicine should help, and I'd like you to keep the bandage on to cover it today."

He didn't answer. The hand stayed at his throat. The pain worsened. And Burle glared at him through darkness, speaking savage words. *"Samis isn't the only one who owns you now."*

"No!"

He felt the jarring force of his good hand striking against something solid, and he knew he'd swung out wildly, too quickly to put his thoughts together or to stop himself.

Amos very nearly hit the floor. "Tahn!"

Tahn stared, seeing only the darkness. He gasped for air, but every breath came hard. Before the shared room with Lucas, Burle had been there at night, in the fog of the early days at Valhal, a much bigger boy, climbing on him, doing things, pressing his hands against his throat with a solemn warning to never, ever tell.

He shook his head, trying to push away the picture, to bury it in his mind again. "Go. Leave me alone."

"Forgive me, Tahn," Amos spoke carefully. "I'll give you a moment. If you need me to, I can finish later, and I'll ask for Lucas to come in. He seems to understand you very well."

"Not this."

"Take a deep breath. I know it's difficult—"

"Go." He stared up at Amos and could see something in the healer's eyes change in response to the gaze.

Amos nodded, slowly, warily. "All right. I'll see you again. In a little while. Rest. Please." He left his liniment and his balm and shut the door behind him.

Tahn knew he should feel sorry. He should feel horrible to have frightened a man who tried so hard to be a help. But right then he was only glad Amos was gone. He drew both arms across his chest and shook. He felt sick to his stomach.

236

He struggled to his feet and then toward the window, striking his left hand accidentally against the back of the chair and barely squelching down a cry of pain.

No. *Must not scream. Must not give Burle the satisfaction.*

The room seemed to whirl in a haze of blue. Burle *had* made him scream, at least once. He knew that now. Burle liked screams. He'd always wanted to be the cause of them again. But it wouldn't be. If Tahn could do nothing else at all, at least he could deny him that.

He leaned against the window ledge, but the darkness still tried to close in on him, blocking away the sun.

"I'm your child," he whispered to the sky. "Redeemed by your blood . . . old things are passed away . . ."

Feeling weak, he sunk to the floor and wept, glad to be alone but thinking that at any moment someone was bound to come through that door and find him like this. He leaned his head against the wall beneath the window and closed his eyes. "Wash me, Lord," he pleaded. "Let everything be washed away."

He heard the door. He expected Lucas. He wanted to tell him to go away, but he couldn't seem to find his voice. He couldn't even look up right now. He didn't open his eyes. He didn't want to see the same familiar concern looking back at him. Someday, someday soon, he would be strong. He would not worry the people he loved like this. He would not be in pain. And he would not be strangled, tormented, and violated by people like Burle anymore.

"Tahn?"

He shook at the sound of her voice. Tiarra, his precious sister. She was all he had left to cling to of the world he'd lost. Their mother and father. Before the pain began they'd been a family—kind, loving, and safe. But his mother and father were dead long since, and it had seemed like kindness, safety, and love had all died with them.

Tiarra said nothing else, only moved to the floor to sit beside him and take him carefully in her arms. He still didn't open his eyes. He didn't want to see the pain in hers. To

237

have to feel her tremorous touch and hear the sound of her troubled tears was bad enough.

He wept, wishing he could stop. He'd never meant to be weak this way in front of her. She'd needed him to be strong, all the days he'd known her. And he'd tried to be what she needed, and never cause her pain.

Almighty God . . . of majesty high . . .

The familiar hymn circled his mind. At first it was only the one line, but as he reached toward it trying to reclaim the strength he knew was there for him somehow, more of the words came to him, chasing the darkness and dispelling the tears.

Walked on this earth . . . and came to die . . .

Tiarra put her hand upon his brow, hummed a tune he didn't know. But still the hymn continued in his head.

Such love as this . . . I cannot tell. Saved me from sin . . . released me from hell. Holy Redeemer loveth my soul . . . by his stripes healed . . . in his love made whole . . .

"Tahn." Tiarra's voice was timid. "We love you. So very much. It's all right—it's all right to cry . . ."

He breathed in deeply, feeling the softness of a forgotten dream, as though he floated again on an endless river. Tiarra still held him. He could not tell if her tears had stopped. He wasn't even sure about his own, but he thought he could feel the sunshine on his arm, his sister's long hair against his cheek. "I'm sorry," he whispered so softly he could barely hear his own words.

"Don't say that." He felt her hair brush his face again as she leaned and kissed his forehead. "You give and you give, and you try so hard. You have nothing to be sorry for."

He knew he should have found a way to regain himself for her. He should have gotten up right away and called to Amos to make sure he hadn't hurt him in swinging out with his arm the way he'd done. But he couldn't find a way to be what he wanted right then. The Dorn, unshakable, fierce, and fearless, seemed very far away.

Someone else touched him. Tiarra talked to whoever it was, and then strong arms lifted him away from the floor and put him back on the bed. He felt Tiarra's touch again, on his cheek, and then the quiet river seemed to carry him away.

※

Later—he wasn't sure how long—he felt the presence of someone else again in his room. He didn't move, hoping they would leave him. What was everyone to think now—that he would be a danger to them? That his mind was gone?

He heard the soft swish of a skirt and felt the press of the bed as someone sat beside him. Netta. He knew the pleasant scent of her perfume. Gently she eased herself down, her body against his, her hand so softly on his hair.

Angel among the trials of earth. That is the way he had always thought of her. She didn't seem to belong with the rest of the world he'd known.

"Talk to me," she whispered.

He wasn't sure he could find voice in this moment. He knew he'd wept in his sister's arms. He knew they all had worries for him. Doubts. And perhaps they should. He could not explain what had happened. He didn't think he could speak it at all.

Netta lay beside him patiently, somehow aware that he was awake. Her hand moved to the bruise on his shoulder, and he brought his good arm up carefully to enfold her.

"I love you," she whispered. "It's all right."

He took a deep breath, burdened by the things that had assaulted his mind and his own reactions to them. "I hit Amos . . . I didn't mean to . . ."

"I know."

Amos must have told them. What might he have said? What would Lord Trilett think of this incident, along with the cloud over his thinking yesterday? "Netta . . . do you think . . . your father . . . has fears for you?"

"I know he did. Until we were safely home."

He shook his head. "I mean . . . from me."

"Oh, Tahn, no! You know he trusts you. He respects you more than most men I could name—"

"But I don't know . . . Netta, what if it had been you here?" He opened his eyes to look at her, and her face was shocked and saddened.

"You would never hurt me."

"Not willingly."

"Don't fear such things! The nightmares are gone. And this is only a bitter memory of this latest trouble. You'll be all right. You're all right now! I can tell."

Words were difficult for him. He felt that he could scarcely breathe. "How can you know . . . if . . . if confusion comes on me again . . . that I wouldn't strike out even at you?"

She pressed her hand against his cheek. "Amos is a strong man. Perhaps it was just too close to the difficult memories. It would be different with me. But all that is done! It can't keep plaguing you. And you'll not hurt me except if you let these concerns turn you away."

"Amos was afraid—I saw it in him. I don't want to make people fear . . ."

"I don't fear you, Tahn. I know your heart too well for that." She kissed his cheek.

"Should you be here . . . this way?"

"Your sister is just outside. She wouldn't leave you, knowing . . . that it has been hard. My father waits with her. He wants to speak to you, but I told him I wanted to be alone with you a moment first."

"Why has he come? Amos's words?"

"Only in part. He must decide very soon whether to send the guests away."

Those words were a hard blow. Perhaps Lord Trilett was doubting whether there should be a wedding. Perhaps it was right that he should. "Netta . . ." He spoke the words painfully. "I love you."

"I know you do. And I love you too."

"I would understand . . . if you don't wish to . . . to . . . marry me now . . ."

She raised herself up so abruptly that the jarring of the bed hurt him. "Tahn—oh, it isn't that! He only thinks that maybe we should wait till some easier time, when you have had greater time to mend! I would not wish to wait for any other reason! Oh, love, don't think it, please."

He closed his eyes, drew her to him again. "You think I can be truly whole . . . and the danger is done?"

"Yes! And I want to be your wife! As soon as you can, Tahn. Just not too soon. You're hurt . . ."

He strained to lift his head and kiss her hair. "You . . . are a treasure . . . past my deserving. Can you be so sure?"

"I'm very sure. I see the strength in you even now. And it is godly strength! I have nothing to fear. God will bring you through this. And you will be a blessing as a husband, and a father. And a benefactor, wherever you go."

He moved his hand to her head and gently pulled her face toward his own. Their lips met for a brief moment, a taste, before he let her go.

"You have no fears to marry me?"

"No. None."

"Even though I've attacked my healer . . . forgotten things I've known . . . wept like a child?"

"You didn't really attack! He said—he said he was touching your neck. I think it nothing more than a natural reaction under the circumstances."

"Still—"

"You're no different than anyone might be in your place. I've wept far more than you have! Lord knows I've felt like lashing out for the things that happened to us. And I don't feel quite the same—like I've forgotten how to be entirely who I was before. But I know that will change. For both of us. We'll be all right."

The mention of her own struggles pained him, and he brushed her cheek with his hand. "Oh, Netta, I'm sorry. I should have protected you . . ."

"You did more than you should have! You've proved beyond any man's doubts that there are no bounds to your love for me. I would marry you a hundred times before all the nobles in the world and be proud to do it."

He smiled. "You make me able to believe . . . that I am not such trouble as I thought."

"You're not trouble. And you'll see—all the struggles will be gone from your mind. It's not your fault what was done to you. God's healing will be complete."

He clasped her hand. *God, I thank you for my lady. Such a gift you've given me!*

"Do you think you might be ready to see my father?"

He nodded. "We should not keep him waiting. But help me sit first. It seems not right to be lying abed."

"Oh, Tahn, he understands!"

But Tahn shook his head and strained to pull himself forward. "He is your father. If I can rise, I will rise."

30

Bennamin Trilett sat in a plump embroidered chair, study-ing the man so soon to be his son-in-law. In truth, right now he looked battered and weak. But with the Dorn, so often appearances could be deceiving. After the things he'd been told, Benn had expected the young man to be stretched out on the bed, but he had risen to his feet in respectful greeting as Lord Trilett entered, despite the evident difficulty of the gesture.

It seemed that Tahn usually managed to conduct himself with such gracious bearing, and Benn had wondered more than once how he could possibly have learned it. The young man scarcely remembered anything of his mother. And he'd known no one else even remotely likely to instruct him in the humble dignity and courtesy that he usually displayed. *It is more heart than rearing,* Benn had finally concluded. *And there is no heart quite like this one.*

Tahn sat in the opposite chair, with Netta near them, somewhat nervously, on the edge of the bed. He knew they were both anxious to resume what had been so violently interrupted. "My concerns have been deep for both of you," he told them. "But I cannot deny your right to marry as soon as you wish. If we'd had our first will, it would already be done."

Tahn bowed his head just slightly. "My lord, I feel I must know if the circumstances have changed your feelings."

"About you? Or the marriage? No. Some things are changed, yes, but you have shown me no cause to think differently of you."

243

He raised his head to meet Benn's eyes. "Then may we ask for your blessing at the earliest possible time? This night?"

Tahn's gaze was strong and certain, and yet veiled beneath the poise of the man was the weariness and hurt that could not quite be denied. "Are you sure you're ready?"

"I would not lose another day."

Benn turned to his daughter. "You feel the same? It would be no shame to wait, children. You are neither of you under any obligation to proceed to the altar in pain."

"Perhaps it is something we need," Netta said softly. "To chase the pain away. To proceed and not be stopped."

Tahn turned his eyes to her, and Benn could not quite read the look that passed between them. But he could argue it no more. "I will make the announcement. And we shall be a bustle and hurry to put all things in their place by then. But it is joyousness. I thank God for both of you. It is almost as though we are all alive from the dead."

"Thank you, Father." Netta reached her hand to clasp hold of Tahn's.

But Benn noticed the swollen redness of Tahn's other hand. The healer had not finished his ministrations. He let his eyes rest for a moment upon Tahn's neck and wondered how he could sit with such steadiness, betraying so little of the pain. *How would I feel if my neck had been bound and chafed raw?* Benn wondered. *Would I not also strike out at the hand that touched it? And who knows what else?*

"Tahn," he said with a heavy breath. "I cannot imagine what it would be like to endure what you have. I think to lesser men it would have been impossible. You shall always own my deepest gratitude that you would willingly suffer for my daughter's sake."

"My lord, sir," Tahn answered, and his voice broke. "It was duty and privilege."

"God favor you, son." For a moment he could say no more.

Tahn bowed his head again, and Netta's eyes brimmed with tears.

"He has . . . blessed me . . . immeasurably," Tahn said then. "I shall never forget his presence with us in our need."

"Almighty God, we lift our thanks," Benn spoke solemnly.

Netta added a quiet, "Amen."

Birds sang in the sunshine outside the window. Benn struggled with his thoughts. There was more, much more, that needed to be discussed. But how much of it should be brought out now? Would Tahn even want to hear talk of Trents and nobles? Jarel had been very sure that he would not, and he was probably right. But nonetheless, some of it must be said.

"Son, there is something more I must speak of. I know that you shall need to be occupied with the wedding preparations. All of us shall, and very quickly, but before the noble guests are gathered in the church tonight—"

A spark of something shone in Tahn's eyes, and Benn stopped. He could not be sure what he'd seen, only that it seemed nearly as raw as the wounds of his neck. But Tahn's voice betrayed no uncertainty. "I have known there would be things to speak of, my lord. You need not hesitate for my sake."

Benn glanced at his daughter and gave a sigh before turning his eyes back to Tahn. "Not everyone knows your heart, son. They do not all claim to understand even mine in this. The noblemen are uncertain of our intentions. Many have learned of your kinship to Trent, and they expect some announcement from us, whether you wish your noble claim formally recognized."

Netta seemed to pale, and she squeezed at Tahn's hand. "Do they want some word from us *tonight*?"

Benn sighed again. "The matter can no longer be hidden, child. Every open response we give shall allay fears that we have had any hidden motives."

"Father," Netta spoke quickly, her cheeks suddenly flushed in despair, "surely they could not fear us!"

"You know we are loved and trusted by most," he tried to assure her. But he saw the flash of emotion in Tahn's eyes and waited, saying no more.

245

"They wish me to declare whether or not I demand my rights?"

"There are far more diplomatic ways in which to phrase that, but yes, son. Some have pressed for that knowledge already. There may be an uncertain tension to the wedding if your desires are not known."

For the first time Lord Trilett saw in Tahn a remnant of the rock-hard fierceness that others had spoken of, that had once made him feared.

"You may tell them that I desire only to marry my bride! Let them have their word before the wedding that I shall demand nothing of them. Now or ever."

<hr />

Shaking inside, Netta left Tahn's room with her father after Lucas and the healer came to finish with the doctoring needs. She was thrilled with the wedding, excited for all the preparations and the realization of their hopes. But her father's words had dampened such feelings with a thread of uncertainty, despite the clarity of Tahn's stand.

They made their happy announcement of the wedding to Tiarra in the hallway, and passed the news along to Jarel, Tobas, and the servants, but Netta drew her father aside as soon as she could. "Father," she asked with quiet apprehension, "what will become of the barony?"

He opened the door to a private room. "Without a decision from the House of Trent or the council of nobles, I cannot say."

"Tahn need not press his own claim for the legitimacy to be recognized."

"I am well aware of that, daughter."

Netta's heart thundered. "But might not the House of Trent still war against such a possibility? Or even others? Remember the woman in Alastair who thought Tahn sought power for the sake of bloody revenge?"

"His refusal will go far to alleviate fears, daughter. His own manner shall be his ally."

Her father's words were little comfort until Netta went alone to her rooms and lifted her fears heavenward in prayer. *God is his greatest ally,* she concluded. *The Lord Almighty who has delivered so incredibly, so many times, shall stand with him still.*

There were a thousand things to attend to. She knew the men would help Tahn prepare for the wedding, and she would soon have attendants bustling about to help her too. This was something she'd dreamed of, to stand with Tahn in the church of her childhood, joining her life with his. Of course she remembered the husband she'd once had, for such a short time. She had loved Karll, but he would understand this, she felt sure he would, as strange as she knew that might sound to anyone else. Karll was in heaven where truth was known, where men's hearts were known. And he would understand the good in Tahn, as well as Netta's love for him now. She found great peace in that.

The excitement among the children stirred to a voluminous frenzy when they discovered that the wedding would be that very night. Every available hand would be needed to see that everyone was ready in time. Even the noble guests were in a stir as soon as the announcement was made. Everyone must get ready. And for many, that would be a lavish undertaking indeed.

Hildy and Kirka would help Netta with her dress. And with her hair, which would pose a serious challenge now with a lock of it so rudely stolen away. There was so much to think of, most of which had been put aside for days now, as though the world had simply stopped. The priest, musicians, attendants, noble ladies, all had been waiting and hopefully were still prepared to step into the grandeur of a Trilett wedding.

Perhaps the most remarkable thing about it all would be sharing it with Tahn's sister, with his friends, and with the children, all of whom had come from desperate poverty. She didn't know what her noble peers thought about the so-called commoners among the wedding party and guests, and she really didn't care. At first she'd considered that some

247

of the noble houses might even shun this wedding for that very reason, but none of them had chosen to do that, and she knew that was only because she was the Trilett lord's daughter. Except for the Trents, every noble house in the land would be represented.

And in thinking more about that, Netta smiled. The Trents were represented too. Whether they chose to see it that way or not.

Tahn had chosen Lucas for his best man, which could surprise no one who knew him. But it would be the first time Netta had ever heard of a man who was studying for priesthood standing in such a capacity. Lorne and Vari were Tahn's choices after that. A guardsman and former slave to Samis, and a teenager, former street orphan. There had never been such a wedding. There surely would never be another like it.

Netta had chosen Tiarra and the Eadon sisters to stand with her. And she had to smile thinking about how Tahn's sister, for all her ruggedness, was sure to draw gasps and admiring eyes in her stunning lace gown and pearls. Tiarra was beautiful. Not just well coifed and decorated like so many noble ladies, but truly breathtakingly beautiful. Good that the Eadon sisters were not prone to envy. They were fair enough in their own right, but they wouldn't hold a candle to Tiarra in finery.

And Tiarra would be wearing her mother's pearls. The boldness of that gesture could create a stir were it known. But it was Tiarra's right to wear them, and Netta's right to ask her to. After all, Netta would be wearing her own mother's pearls. And the Eadon sisters too would wear pearls passed down in their family. It seemed to be truly fitting.

Of course, Jarel had once suggested that Tiarra should wear the other surviving necklace that had belonged to her mother. But the open presence of that extraordinary piece would be certain to incite commotion. The Trent jewel. Once bestowed by a queen, it had been passed down through generations of Trents, an emblem of their status and power. None of the other nobles knew that Tiarra Dorn was in possession of it, that it had been given to her mother and not to Lionell's father, by Baron Klonten Trent, Tahn and Tiarra's own grandfather. The necklace had been lost, along with several other pieces of jewelry, in Alastair after Karra Loble and Sanlin Dorn were murdered. Only the two had been regained, and Netta knew how Tiarra treasured them.

She also knew how well her father understood that possession of the Trent jewel could lend valuable credence to a claim of the birthright. Tahn had a very strong case should he ever wish to press the matter. No one could truly question his parentage. Benn Trilett had quietly acquired proof of the marriage of Karra Loble to Sanlin Dorn. All the nobles knew that Klonten Trent had acknowledged Karra Loble as his daughter. And all of Alastair knew that Tahn and Tiarra were Sanlin and Karra's children. There could be no question. The House of Trent had carefully hidden for years that they were no longer in possession of their most cherished heirloom.

But such thoughts were almost dizzying. Netta knew her father had been willing all along to formally recognize Tahn and stand beside him. She now wondered how he might use his voice in the council. Surely he would do nothing without gaining Tahn's word first. Would he?

Hildy broke in upon her thoughts with an armload of linens, dressing clothes, and perfumes. "Netta, you are lovely at every moment, but you shall make the most beautiful bride that any of those people have ever seen!"

"You speak as though you won't see me too."

"You know what I mean, dear lady. All of those people assembled there in the church—"

"Hildy—be with me! I want you to attend the wedding too."

The dear older woman's face was veiled in shock. "But I have the feast to think about!"

"I know you. Many are the things prepared already. And Dreisel and Harin are well capable of seeing to the rest. You've been part of my life since I was a child. I want you to see me wed."

The woman's eyes misted with tears, and she stammered in answer. "But Netta, dear—a scullery maid at a noblewoman's wedding!"

"You are far more than that! You always have been. And what sort of wedding do you think we shall have? A celebration for nobles? Hildy, you know! My father's family now includes orphans who stole, or even killed, to survive. Our guests include a poor farm family and a wilderness tracker. There has never been such a wedding as this! Please, be there for me. Come with me in the carriage."

"In your very carriage! Lady!"

"You played with me as a child. Even scolded me, and hugged me through tears. Please, Hildy. I haven't my mother here. I need you with me at the church tonight."

Hildy sank into a chair. "Has the very world fallen sideways?"

Netta twined her arms around the robust woman. "Oh, Hildy, you know I've always loved you. I don't think of you as a servant or anything less than myself. You're family to me. You should be there."

"God bless you, child. What shall the priest and the nobles say?"

"I daresay Father Anolle shall be delighted. Of the nobles, they have enough to swallow already. It matters little if I add a harmless bit more."

"But . . . but what of the other servants?"

Netta smiled. "I'd thought of that. With my father's permission, we shall leave here only the few we must. I want the rest to join us."

"Oh, this shall be a wedding indeed!" Hildy proclaimed. "This shall be something told about when my granddaughters have granddaughters. You and your Dorn inspire love far past telling, child! I've already heard of one song written."

"A song? Really?"

"Oh yes. 'Fair-eyed Netta and Her Dark-Born Knight.'"

"For mercy! Perhaps I should hear it sometime."

"You shall. I will see to that. Your wedding shall simply add a verse! They already sing of your love and your kindness to the poor. And the evil wrought against you and your brave knight."

Netta stared in wonder. "How is Tahn called a knight? We've no king to bestow such honor."

"None but God, dear, and so it's said he's a knight in the Lord's service. It seemed not good enough to name him a common man."

Netta hugged her dear friend tightly, knowing no words to answer. Should the nobles hear such songs spread about among the people, they might become even more nervous!

31

For the sake of Netta and the wedding, it was easy for Tahn to tolerate all sorts of foolish doting. Besides the healer's attentions, a man was sent to properly retrim his hair, shave him, and offer a variety of smells from which to select. But he was rather relieved when that man left and Vari strode through his door.

"This is something. Oh, Tahn, this is the craziest way of doing things I ever heard of. It'd been so much simpler just to stand you out under the apple tree with Netta and the priest and not make all this fuss."

Tahn couldn't help but smile about that. He'd had similar thoughts several times. "But that is not the way of things when there are nobles involved. Apparently, they require some kind of fuss."

"Well, why bother with the nobles? I mean, except for the Triletts? I've wanted to ask that for a long time. Don't they just add a lot of headache? Isn't it up to you and Netta? Why couldn't you have had a wedding with just your own friends?"

"Many of the nobles *are* friends," Tahn answered more soberly. "As for the rest, I understand that it is considered a most grievous insult to withhold invitation to a wedding. And Lord Trilett has the good sense not to rile the high-born of Turis against himself."

"What a pot of old mash that is! So they're here because they'd fetch a stink if they weren't invited?"

Tahn almost laughed. "Some, perhaps. Not all."

Vari plopped onto the bed. "I won't have such a mess of

things when I marry. Nothing against Netta, but it'll be so much simpler to marry the farmer's daughter. How old do you think I need to be?"

"Old enough to know you don't need the question. Don't be in such a hurry."

"I'm glad they're here. The Wittleys, I mean. But I've barely paid them any attention at all."

"It's been no ordinary time."

Vari's expression turned sober. "Are you really all right for this? I mean, Tahn, I know you're sore and all that, but there's also going to be an awful crowd."

For a moment, Tahn looked past him, understanding very well the depth of his question. "I've had months to prepare my mind for that understanding. Wedding guests in a church are not like an angry mob stirred by the baron's lies."

"Still, I can understand how any crowd—"

"They will not bother me, Vari," he said, and then he hoped he hadn't sounded too abrupt.

Vari was quiet, his eyes resting on Tahn's bandaged hand. "Maybe you need a jeweled glove," he said finally.

"And a jeweled collar?" Tahn questioned, indicating the bandage at his throat. "Worse that this shall also show."

"Maybe it's not so bad. Maybe it shall serve to show everyone what God has brought you from."

"What I need, Vari, are boots. Can you get me a pair? The others are lost."

Vari stared with such trepidation that Tahn wondered what he could possibly have said wrong.

"Tahn, don't you remember? Netta already arranged for some kind of fancy rich-man shoes for the wedding. They go with your clothes. Hamm'll be bringing everything in for you pretty soon."

"Fine," he said with a nod of his head. "That problem's solved."

"Don't you know what happened to your boots?"

Tahn turned to the window. *Not this. Not again.* "It would be a fair wager to say that the bandits stole them. At any rate, they're lost to me."

253

Vari moved closer and faced him with concern. "How much do you remember of what happened?"

Oh, Lord, Tahn prayed. *Am I so plainly confused?* "A great deal. I think."

"What about from before? You knew about the wedding shoes. I remember when Netta showed us."

"Vari, I remember the important things. Most things. Don't be fretting, all right? It's only small matters, here and there."

Vari's expression did not change. "I wasn't belittling you. I just wanted to understand. I wish I could help—"

"You did, and when I needed you most."

"I mean now."

Tahn stared out the window to a row of flowers in the garden. How he would like to go riding alone right now, just to clear his head and spend some time again with God. But he knew he'd have limited strength for the saddle, and no one would wish him to disappear into the forest at such a time. "Vari, can you be ready early? And ask Lucas. I'd like to go to the church before the rest. I could spend some time there. In prayer."

"All right, Tahn. I think that would be all right. I think they have planned to set your steed before a carriage."

Such words were a complete surprise and made absolutely no sense to him. "Smoke will not be made to pull, Vari. He'd never accept it."

"I know," Vari answered him quietly. "Lord Trilett commissioned white steeds for the wedding party. We were going to ride ours, but . . ."

"The women shall be drawn in carriages?"

"Yes."

"And you and I . . . and Lucas . . . and Lorne. Mounted. Matching white steeds . . . I remember now."

"But it's too soon for you to ride, Tahn. We'll sit a carriage. It'll be fine."

The flowers outside were swaying in a gentle breeze. A kiss of sunlight touched his hand. "I don't know. It's a pretty vision. Four horsemen. All of white. Netta and her father wanted it so. Who am I to alter that?"

"Tahn . . ."

"It's not far to the church. A few minutes only. I'll be fine."

"Amos will have a serious qualm about that. Lucas too."

"Maybe so. But they'll accept it if I ask them. If I promise perhaps to lie abed tomorrow."

"I'm afraid you'll hurt yourself tonight! And then how will that be for Netta when her father's giving you the whole south wing until your own house is finished? You want to be all right for her."

"I'll be all right enough. No worse than right now. And maybe that's part of it. Not to change the original plan. Not to let a piece of it be stolen. She said going ahead with the wedding could even be part of the healing."

"But she'd understand!"

"Then it is a gift to her."

"Jarel is right. You're dangerous stubborn."

"Go get ready, Vari. And tell Lucas. I also want to sit with you both and have you tell me everything else that's been planned. I don't want to have forgotten anything. We'll have time, won't we? For you to tell me everything that should happen and still arrive at the church early?"

"We should have, yes." He gave Tahn a quizzical look. "You don't remember the rehearsal with the priest either, do you?"

He hesitated for a moment and then shook his head.

"Oh, Lord, Tahn. But God bless you."

***

They brought a stool from the house to make the mounting easier. Tahn in his wedding finery had to be helped to the saddle, but once there he felt steadier than he'd expected. Vari, Lucas, and Lorne, in almost identical vesture, mounted with him because the four of them were supposed to ride to the church together.

255

But before leaving, they would circle the estate with Lucas, the head of the groomsmen, blowing a silver horn. None of them really understood that gesture, but Jarel had told them it was the way of Trilett weddings, like a call to attention that the time had nearly come.

Tahn knew that Netta would be watching from her window, and that he was expected not to look her way. This was a moment for the bride, unseen, to gaze out upon her groom, and Tahn was glad he'd not denied her the tradition by accepting a carriage.

His ribs ached, his neck was throbbing against the uncomfortable bandage, but his heart swelled with a depth of satisfaction. *You couldn't stop me, Burle, Lionell, Samis . . . devil. The Lord God is greater than you all.*

He was careful not to look at any of the estate house windows, because he couldn't remember clearly which was Netta's. But he knew she'd be there, perhaps already dressed in the splendid regalia she hid from him until the moment of her revealing as she walked the church aisle. What would she be thinking as she peered out right now? He hoped it was thoughts of overwhelming joy, not concern about noble opinion or worry for him. The horse stepped lightly, and he sat tall, waving his odd hat thrice in salute. And then, with all of that fulfilled, they rode out of the gate with another sounding of the horn.

The guards at the gate cheered him. He hadn't expected that, but stranger still were the reactions of everyone they passed. Onath and its church were not far away, but they met two farmers before the border of the city, both of whom knelt and bowed low.

"Stand tall!" he called to them, at which time they gained their feet again but lifted their right arms and bowed their heads in the victor's salute.

"God's favor to you!" one of the men called with a joyous smile across his face.

"And to you both!" Tahn called in answer.

Lucas sounded the horn again as they entered the town. Tahn was not completely sure what to expect here, though Jarel had told them that the townspeople would likely come to the windows and doors, or even take to the streets to watch all parts of the wedding processional pass by. Even these earliest.

"It is the groom!" a young voice shouted.

From somewhere unseen came a sound like the pounding of pots. After seven paces, Lucas blew the horn again, and then they had only to proceed to the church. But it would be no quiet ride. From every direction, children came racing forward. Men and women were not far behind, some staying before their doors but most venturing much closer. Some bowed, some gave salute, almost everyone cheered. Through the din, Tahn turned to Lucas in bewilderment.

"They must do this for every wedding."

"I don't think so," Lucas answered solemnly. "Jarel said they love to watch the nobles in their fancy clothes pass by. He said nothing of noise."

"At least it's happy noise," Vari ventured.

Tahn looked around him at the welcoming faces, and his stomach tensed. "I think it good we left long before our noble guests."

"I think you're right," Lucas told him as someone in the crowd yelled Tahn's name.

"Blessed of God!" a woman shouted.

"One of us!" called a man farther on.

Tahn was glad when they reached the church. He had no idea what to do with the people's praise and greatly hoped he wouldn't be facing it every time he rode about. At least the people hadn't followed them. They only cheered him and remained in their places as he went by, probably hoping that the rest of the party would soon be along.

"My world has changed," he said as Lorne moved quickly from his saddle to help him.

"God give you grace," Lucas said in answer.

Two young men in blue vestments hurried toward them to be ready to receive the horses. There would be six in all to take care of the horses and carriages. Benn Trilett had sent a messenger to the priest early so that he could summon those already hired from the town for this privilege.

Dismounting was much more difficult than mounting had been, perhaps because of the ride between. As Tahn turned his body and tried to ease from the saddle, the pain was so intense that he slipped against the horse's side and nearly fell. Lorne held him carefully, supporting his weight even after he was solidly on the ground.

"All right?"

Tahn nodded, though white spots floated before his face and he knew he'd come close to passing out.

"I'm glad that when the wedding's done, you and Netta are to ride carriage together," Lorne said softly. "Too soon, Tahn."

Again he nodded. The church steps stood before him. They were not usually such a daunting challenge, but after the pain of the dismount they were an unwelcome sight.

"Can you make it?" Lorne asked in quietness.

"Let me kneel here a moment," Tahn answered. "I can begin my prayers here just as well as within."

Without thought of the sight he presented, Tahn knelt at the base of the church steps in his stunning attire, and all three of his groomsmen did the same. He would not linger here long. He wanted to be inside where he could find at least a momentary aloneness, but he was glad for his friends' loyalty, and their patience.

When the white spots left him and he began to feel steadier again, he lifted himself with a word of thanks and began to mount the steps slowly, with Vari before him, Lorne beside, and Lucas behind. He would not receive their support or their helping hands. He must mount the church steps entirely on his own power. For Netta's sake, though she was not there to witness and would make him no such requirement. But it was his own requirement. He must ride here, walk in, stand tall, and receive her with a strength far greater than pain. She deserved that. It was his gift to her.

He was almost to the top of the stairs. Vari was already opening the church door, when soft as a birdsong, music began behind him. A stirringly rich voice, resonant to carry the distance, was suddenly singing words Tahn could never have imagined.

"The Dorn, a dark-born knight, in love with the lady fair, strove for the fields of light with flowers for her hair. The darkness could not stop him, nor ever could the storm, for the love is everlasting 'tween the lady and the Dorn . . ."

With heart pounding, Tahn turned around. Who could be singing? Such a song? Was he dreaming?

The man stood not far off, with a small and appreciative crowd around him. A traveling minstrel. Tahn had seen minstrels before. With jaunty clothes and an instrument with strings, they roamed about gaining what coins they could of the common people, or if they were truly talented, far better pay from noblemen.

But why? Why would the minstrel make up such a song as that? Tahn had never seen him before. Was there some reason he was known by him? Did the people here tell the minstrel such things? Or did he simply invent the words, as minstrels were wont to do?

He knew he would not go down the steps again now. He would not sway from his mission of prayer even to ask the questions that turned around in his mind. And the minstrel, with a merry smile, seemed to understand. He pulled his feathered hat from his head and gave the sort of sweeping bow that only a practiced performer could display.

Tahn knew no response but a courteous bow of his own, and then just before he turned again to the church door the man called out, as though in fond salute, "Nobleman of the common man! One of us!"

With a careful breath and a glance heavenward, Tahn turned to the church's sanctuary, unable to respond in any other way. What could this mean? It was surely no dream! He knew there'd been talk of him from Onath to Alastair, to Merinth, Joram, and anywhere else touched by the many chapters of his difficult story. But songs? And such words as this? Why?

He could not speak of it to his friends. And they were just as speechless as he. With relief, Tahn heard the door close behind him and stood in the cavernous sanctuary of the church called Holy Redeemer. The light streamed through windows replete with color and patterns, stained glass of almost unimaginable artistry. Tahn only stood in the hush of the place for a moment, his eyes drawn forward to the play of light against the cross.

"Can you leave me?" he asked quietly.

Lorne nodded to him. "There is a room at the side designated for us tonight."

"Are you sure you're all right?" Lucas asked. "Do you wish one of us to stay at the back of the sanctuary? Or would you like to be completely alone?"

"Alone. Please."

Lucas too nodded then with a certain wonder mixed with the concern in his eyes. "Call if you need us. Or join us when you finish."

But Tahn said nothing more, only moved onward toward the cross. His friends left him, and he knelt at the altar with the colors of the light dancing over him.

"You fill me with awe, my Lord and my God. How can I find words to speak to you?"

He closed his eyes, feeling such emotion well inside him that he could not contain it. He could see the light even then, as though it had danced inside him, stirring his soul to the tears he felt. "You only are worthy of the people's shouts! Let me tell it plainly if ever I hear it again! You know me, that I am small. I am like a seed in your pocket unable to carry myself where you wish me to go. Make me what you want, Lord God. Let me grow to honor you for all of your indescribable gifts."

Leaning down upon the altar, he bowed his head and prayed for Netta and for their life together. He prayed for all of his friends, the noblemen, even the people outside. And then he prayed for Lionell's widow, and for others of the Trents, nameless, faceless people he knew almost nothing about. "I don't want them to fear me, Lord. I don't want anyone to fear me. All I want is peace."

He prayed for his sister and the children, for the children

of Lucas's mission in Alastair, and for any other children struggling and in need. He prayed for the boy who had brought the dreadful message, and for his ailing mother, and for Evan and Jarith and the families of the guardsmen who had died. And then he prayed for Benn Trilett's prisoners, for Trent soldiers, and for any of the hard-hearted bandits who might have survived.

The light around him seemed to pulse and quicken. He lifted his eyes toward the cross, and it shone red as crimson.

Victory by blood. The words were spoken into his spirit, he was not sure how.

Victory by blood—what does it mean?

"That you have redeemed me, my Lord," he whispered to the air. "That you have paid for every victory with your holy sacrifice! Your blood frees me and answers my pain and every heartache with healing. You give me hope and strength. You give me life."

The crimson of the cross faded into all the colors of the light in that great hall, and he wondered if he'd actually seen it completely bathed in red or if his unsteady eyes and mind gave him cause to question. But when he looked around, the room was filled with a cloud of light different than what poured in from the windows. It floated above him in the rafters. It lay at his feet. It filled the air around him with moistness and wonder.

"What is this, Lord? What is it you do?"

He knelt for a moment in silence, almost unable to take all of this in. "How did you know, Lord?" he whispered. "That I would need you here with me tonight so completely? It is almost as though I am reborn—to a world I don't understand. Thank you—for your light and grace."

He stayed there alone until he heard distant sounds. Lucas stepped into the sanctuary behind him and moved toward Tahn. But whatever he'd come to say seemed to be forgotten.

Tahn rose to his feet, watching the touch of light on his friend's face. He drew in a deep breath, and it was as though a river of cloud flooded inside him, easing the ache and re-

261

newing a measure of the strength he'd lacked. "Lucas—has someone come?"

"Yes, sir. Your ushers are here ready, and the first of the guests are outside."

"Why do you suddenly call me 'sir'?"

Lucas smiled. "I don't know. But—but the time is at hand."

"I think I'm ready."

Lucas nodded, his eyes suddenly brimming with tears. "I know you are."

The two men hugged, held each other, until the church door opened with a shower of unfiltered light just as Vari and Lorne joined them from the vestibule.

"God fill us," Lorne spoke softly. "And bless this union."

Ansley and Stuva, the biggest of the boys, served as ushers. And after the first guests, a slow and steady stream continued and the church pews began to fill. The priest came out from his chamber to give Tahn a happy blessing. Vari and Lorne moved to the back of the church to be ready to greet the Eadon sisters upon their arrival and to coordinate the other children to their places. But Lucas waited with Tahn until the moment he would be needed to escort Tiarra to her place at the altar.

Tahn thought joyfully of Tiarra and the changes he'd seen in her since they'd met. She'd been so embittered and wary because of the hardship of her life, and it had been Lucas to first touch her with simple human kindness and then to lead her to the Savior's love. *Perhaps,* Tahn thought, *by the time she and Lorne are ready to marry, Lucas shall be able to perform the ceremony. It would be fitting, indeed.*

"God of miracles," he spoke into the air, "you have performed a miracle in each of us."

The organ played lightly as the church filled. Tahn smiled to see a group of Trilett servants come in together and sit at the back. Soon he knew that Netta must be in the church, in the side room chosen for her, because he saw her father near the back. To his surprise, Lord Trilett swung the church doors open wide and had them propped to remain that way. Sunlight poured in like a living stream. It was Vari who moved toward the front to tell Tahn that the doors would be left open at Netta's request, so that townspeople who had followed her carriage toward the church might hear some part of the ceremony and catch a glimpse inside.

Tahn knew that was very like Netta, who loved the people of Onath as much as they loved her. But it made him a little uncomfortable anyway, because of the unpredictable air of things it created. What if that minstrel should wander in? Or if the people should take to cheering him again? He didn't know what he would do with such acclaim, let alone how the noble guests would react.

Already he knew that some of the nobles sitting here were uneasy. He could tell it in their glances and their whispers. But there were just as many who looked content and even happy to be a part of the occasion. More than one even dared to approach him with an extended hand and thank him for his part in Lady Netta's rescue.

And then the character of the organ music changed, and it was time to go to his place. The now-crowded sanctuary hushed to stillness, and Doogan and Tam in matching robes strode forward side by side, each carrying a golden candle lighter. Their faces were lit with smiles, each of them with their eyes on Tahn. He smiled in return at the boys and gave them a little wink, and Doogan seemed to have considerable trouble keeping himself from laughing.

But they managed a stately enough walk the rest of the way forward, mounted the steps at the altar, and proceeded to a candelabra resting at either side of the cross. Their timing carefully rehearsed, they lit the candles from the nearest to the outermost from the cross and then turned and stepped away at opposite sides.

Again, the music changed, and to Tahn the very air seemed charged with an unspeakable excitement. He could see Jarel waiting now to one side, but he turned his head again to the aisle. Except for the music, there was no sound in all that great hall.

Finally, Vari stepped into view holding the arm of the younger of the Eadon sisters, his smile as wide as the younger boys'. An image flashed into Tahn's mind—of Vari bound, inches from death. Tears blurred his vision for a moment. *Thank you, God, for all you've done! For this boy's life, and so much more! He would have died but for your hand. Oh, Father, thank you!*

Vari seemed suddenly as deeply touched as Tahn. Despite his smile, his eyes were moist. The lady at his side looked far different. Apprehensive, perhaps, to be in such company. But she was willing, which spoke well both of her and her family.

Vari brought the lady perfectly to her place and then clasped Tahn's hand before moving to his own. Together they turned their eyes again to the aisle to see the little girl Rae, escorted by the still smaller Jori, proceeding forward. Their hands were tight together, and both of them looked red of face. Rae carried flowers identical to those of Lady Eadon.

When they had come to the front, Lorne began forward with the second Lady Eadon. Tahn saw a small stir among the ladies of the crowd at their first generous look at Lorne, a tall, terribly handsome blond. They were followed by the second pair of children: Jeramathe in brocade and lace just like Rae's, and Rane, who seemed to struggle with nervous, unsteady steps. The two of them looked like they could be twins, though they'd been orphaned in separate towns and had never met until brought together under Benn Trilett's roof. Rane stumbled just a little as they came to the front, and Jeramathe bravely helped him before they went to their places.

All of the church grew still again, and Tahn knew that Lorne's anticipation at this moment was almost as great as his own. Tiarra would be the next in view. As the colored light danced across his eyes, Tahn saw his sister step to the aisle with Lucas, her near-priest, at her side. She looked born to such a thing. Stunning and brave. More than one gasp escaped the crowd at sight of her in exquisite lace. And pearls.

Tahn gave her a smile and touched his hand to his own throat where the collar of his coat nearly hid the bandage. Tiarra beamed with understanding. It was the first time she had ever worn her mother's necklace in public. Lorne grasped Tahn's arm and squeezed it. "Lord's mercy," he whispered but said no more.

Tiarra's smile continued all the way to the altar, and Lucas openly wept before he reached it. They both gave Tahn a cautious embrace before standing to their places, though the gesture had not been planned for them in advance.

The third pair of children came next, Duncan carrying a white velvet cushion, and Temas a large basket filled with rose petals. She strewed them merrily behind her, leaving a generous trail in her wake.

And then, as the music circled grandly about Tahn's ears, the entire congregation rose to their feet, and Netta at last came into view. He'd known she would be gorgeous. She was always gorgeous. But this vision was beyond even his expectation. Her father beside her made an imposing figure, but he could not look at Lord Trilett now. Netta's veil was light enough to see her smile behind it. She was shaking, but she let herself be guided forward steadily, her eyes never swaying from Tahn at the front.

He stood transfixed, a thousand questions racing through his mind. *Am I enough for her? How could she ever think so? What if my ignorant ways begin to wear on her over time? Will she fear our future together? How can I keep her as happy as she looks at this moment?*

He felt weak in the knees. He didn't think he faltered, but Lucas lent his arm, somehow sensing the need. Suddenly sweating, his heart racing, he extended his hand toward his love, for the first time aware that there were nearly as many eyes on him as there were upon her.

Perhaps they would judge whether the face they saw gazing upon such an angel could be sincere. But he would not let thoughts of the crowd encumber his mind. *Lord, you know my heart.*

When Netta's fingers touched his, a coolness rushed upon him, as though a mighty breeze had swept in from the doorway. But Netta's hair and lace did not sway. No one seemed to notice such a thing but him. Lord Trilett lifted his daughter's veil, and Tahn could see her sparkling eyes filled to overflowing with tears. Still she smiled, her wet cheeks glistening in the light. She touched the clumsy bandage on his left hand, and he longed to hold her. But he must wait. Wait now, until the time.

Only when she was already there beside him did he see the last of the children, Micah and Briant, dutifully guiding the incredible flowing length of train at the back of Netta's magnificent gown. The two little boys spread the train to its full glory as Lord Trilett graciously gave his daughter away with a tender kiss to her cheek.

And then it was Jarel's moment to step forward, to a lectern at the right of the altar, to share a rare moment and lift his voice in song. Jarel's voice was a gift that few had realized, for a nobleman does not often grace anyone but the closest of family with even the sacred strains. This song lifted and floated as though on heavenly wings, this hymn of grace and love. Tahn had heard it only once before, when Netta had shared with him her desire for it to be sung. But now it seemed familiar, like something that had lived in his heart already for a long time.

He stood gazing into Netta's eyes while the song continued, and she did not for a moment shift away.

"I love you," he whispered. "Always."

And her eyes danced as she told him that she loved him too.

The ceremony was a blur from there. The priest's words resounded in Tahn's heart, and his own words echoing seemed to come from somewhere far deeper than his lips alone. The moment seemed endless, perfect, a part of the heaven that visited them, until the pause that Tahn had known would come, the opportunity for any man present to raise his legitimate objection, should there be such.

Slowly, a lone nobleman stood to his feet in the center of the church, and a rustling of voices could be heard outside. Two more men rose cautiously beside their fellow, but only the first man spoke, directing his eyes to Lord Trilett at the front.

"This man's reputation has carried widely," he said. "We know that he has saved the life of your lady, twice now, it would seem. But we also know that he has killed. Many times. And it can't be denied. The statement he has issued sounds reassuring, but how can we know it is true? How can you know, your lordship, that he does not devise an evil now, that once he has married he shall overpower Trilett, claim to himself Trent, and wield the strength of both houses to our detriment?"

The tumult at the back of the church and outside was immense until Tahn lifted his hand. Lord Trilett rose to his feet and addressed the nobleman by name, but Tahn stopped him before he could say anything more.

"My lord, sir, I must myself answer the charge."

Silence loomed over the church. All eyes were upon him. Netta took his hand in hers and squeezed it. Though he trembled inside simply to stand before all of those staring eyes, he could not fail his own heart, or Netta's expectations. With his broken and bandaged arm he gestured toward the cross before them. "The Lord looks upon us. Power is his. I know what I have been, and he has redeemed me. Now I want nothing except it come from him."

The nobleman shifted his feet uncomfortably and shook his head. "What comfort is that? Oppressors the world over pretend to have divine authority! And you could claim—"

"I claim nothing," Tahn cut him off abruptly. "What do you fear? That I should war against you? I swear now by heaven I'll make no war unless defense of the innocent demands it. God witness! I care nothing for the things you speak of. I only wish to love my lady."

Lord Trilett spoke up quickly then. "You have no cause to

prevent their joining, Sebastius. You have no claim against him."

"Perhaps *you* are the one we should fear, your lordship," came a solemn answer. "If you claim he would not use you to his own ends, how can we know that you do not devise to use him, to gain through him the strength of Trent means and make yourself a ruler over us?"

Benn shook his head solemnly. "You know it is not mine to decide what shall become of Trent means. Nor who, if anyone, shall rule over us. Such things belong to the council, of which I am only a single voice. And in the council belong your questions, not in this sacred house. I can only assure you that I devise ill against no one. Your fears are ungrounded."

The man stood for a moment in dead silence and then resumed his seat; both of the men who had stood with him did the same. A brief stirring of noise followed, stilled immediately by the confident words of the priest.

"There having been found no cause to prevent this union so ordained by God before men . . ."

Netta turned her eyes to Tahn's, and he felt a tingle run through him.

"I pronounce you to be from this day forward joined by God as one flesh, to be known and accounted hereafter as man and wife. By the token of a kiss may you seal this union before all gathered here."

His heart thundering, Tahn put his arm around Netta. They kissed and then stood with their hands joined. Netta's eyes shone in the streaming light, and Tahn stood straight and tall, unable to take his eyes from her. And then came words that were somehow dizzying in their depth and magnitude.

"Lords and ladies of Turis, gentlemen and women, citizens, I present to you the estimable Master and Mistress Tahn and Netta Dorn."

32

The carriage ride. The cheering townspeople. Trumpets. All of it went by in a whirl for Netta. The feasting and toasts, followed by dancing.

But Tahn knew little of dancing and was in no shape to learn more this night. Holding her close in his arms, he danced the first dance with her, fulfilling the tradition between bride and groom. She loved every moment moving to the music, safe at his side, but she knew that he tired. They sat together in the midst of the festivities for as long as courtesy demanded, and then as the dancing continued, they took their leave and retired to the chambers that were to be theirs alone until their stately mansion house was complete enough for their presence.

Tahn had seemed to pale a little, but the smile did not leave his eyes. She insisted that he lay upon their carefully prepared bed, and she undid his shoes.

"I wish that all those who doubt you could understand the things you've done for me this day. Years from now I shall look back and wonder how you were able to ride and to dance."

"For you." He smiled. "And it is my wish that all those who doubt may be gone from your mind."

She unbuttoned his coat, and he reached his hand to loosen the bandage at his neck.

"Does it still hurt as it did?" She watched him closely, hoping that all of this had not been too much.

He took her arm and gently pulled her down beside him. "Please don't fill your mind with my pains."

"Tahn—I can't help but think of them."

"It's better. Truly. I don't want you to worry for me."

"But I don't want you doing more than you should." She kissed him, petted at his handsomely cropped hair. "You look so tired. Would it trouble you if I ask that we only lie here together tonight? We can wait . . . until you're strong . . ."

He pulled her close, and though he tried to hide it she could see the pain in his eyes. "My heart is to fulfill your wishes, my lady."

Quivering inside with a bittersweet hope, she knew only one thing to answer him. "Oh, love—I long for you. I truly do. But tonight I wish only to sleep close beside you. Don't be angry with me. I want the first time to be something we remember forever. I don't want it to hurt you."

If he was disappointed, he did not show it. She helped him off with his wedding garments and then lay her own aside and turned back the coverlets on the bed.

"You are beautiful," he told her.

But his bruised face looked almost sunken in the evening shadows. His eyes could not hide his weariness. Even his breaths were more labored again, and she knew she had told him rightly. He was sore from the day's activity, hurting more than he would admit to her. He needed only to sleep.

She snuggled beside him, and he kissed her hair. "Thank you," he whispered. "For becoming my wife."

She lay on his right shoulder, and he lifted his right arm around her. But even in their stillness, she wondered if it hurt him. One arm and hand in Amos's stiff bandage. The bruises and sores at his neck. The broken ribs! Could he be comfortable? How could she help him?

"Do you see the stars out the window?" he suddenly asked.

"Yes." Her eyes misted with tears.

"Like a thousand windows into heaven . . ."

She laid her hand against his chest, felt the movement of his breathing as he went on.

"In the daytime, God sheds his light upon us . . . and when it is cloudy, day or night, it seems even then he fills the sky

270

with his presence. We are not left without reminders that he is ever with us . . . if we know how to see him . . ."

She didn't know what to say. Such words, coming from the man who had once believed that God hated him, that there was no hope for anything better. The transformation in him was deeper than she had thought possible. And it made her feel as though this were a sacred moment.

"He asked me a question," Tahn said softly. "In the church, before the wedding. He asked me what it means that there is victory by blood."

Her heart suddenly thundered. Did he know? Had he ever had opportunity to hear the Trent motto? "What did you answer him?" she asked almost fearfully.

"That his sacrifice has won every victory." He drew a deep breath. "Perhaps he wanted me to understand aright my very foundations before I could take you to myself."

"Oh, Tahn," she whispered. "He knows you understand."

She wanted to say more, to tell him of the words that had meant so much grief to generations of Trents and those they had considered their enemies. But he was so peaceful, resting in the comfort of God, that she could not bring herself to trouble him with things he might not wish to hear.

She kissed him, and then she lay in the stillness, listening to his steady breaths, feeling the beating of his heart beneath her hand. What would the future hold for this now-gentle soul?

Father, he asks for so little. But you give more than we could hope or dream. Direct our days. Guide us in the paths you stretch before us. Help him to see all that you would have . . .

She knew when his breaths grew deeper. She lay for a long while in the quiet, looking out toward the stars that had so reminded him of God. She could not imagine feeling more blessed, despite the pain and the struggles they had come through.

"Lord, I think you have called us all along for these days . . ."

Her whispered words hung in the air, and she could say nothing more. God's presence, so near to Tahn's mind of late, now seemed to fill the room and enfold them. Perhaps it was only a dream. Perhaps she would never truly know. But as she closed her eyes to welcome the night's gentle sleep, she felt she was floating on rivers of dancing light.

33

A lion strode boldly across a field of flowers. In the dream that held him, Tahn watched in the distance as the great beast made its way steadily toward a cross upon the hill. The light in the sky was greater than the sun as the lion settled at the foot of the cross, leaning its great head upon the rough wood of the base. Little by little, the light spread over the upright post and crossbeam until the entire cross was bathed in scarlet. But then it seemed less a cross and more a canopy, spreading upward and outward, a covering from the wind. Widened and bowing in the breezes it looked almost like a clover, a scarlet trefoil, bending toward the lion laying so peacefully before it.

Yet the cross was evident still, upon the leaves and the lion, as if etched into their beings or a part of their very fibers.

The three leaves to make up one. Father, Son, and Spirit. Red, for the Savior's blood shed in love. Tahn knew these things as he watched the light of that ethereal sky burst into golden bloom behind the trefoil and the lion. But he did not know where he had seen those images before.

The ground around was rich with golden flowers, and their scent was sweeter than anything he'd known before. Music met his ears. The lilting song of a bird. He felt that he was in the Trilett mansion again, or perhaps somehow in both of these places at once.

The bird's song grew nearer, right beside the window, and he opened his eyes to the welcoming morning light. Netta had not yet risen. He felt her tender warmth beside him. Her hair, long and auburn, made him think of the lion's

273

mane, but he did not know why. Would she understand such a dream as this?

And then he remembered Lord Trilett's banner and seal. The lion. Perhaps it was the noble wedding causing him to dream such things. Or perhaps it was Netta's intoxicating nearness lending fancies to his mind.

There might have been two days more of feasting, dancing, and the company of guests. But at the midday after the wedding, Lord Trilett dismissed all, saying it was finally time for his daughter and new son-in-law to pass quiet time together in recovery from their ordeal. And then Netta was busy bidding farewells to the many noble ladies who had been with them. Only a few of the men approached Tahn, and those who did said little.

Tahn took Lucas aside at the earliest opportunity and asked him about Bert and the other prisoners.

"I don't think Lord Trilett has reached a decision yet," Lucas told him. "He asked me to pray with him concerning the matter."

"But what did Bert want of me, our first day back here, when you went in my place?"

Lucas smiled. "Tahn, he was begging for your prayers. He wanted to be brought to you, but Lord Trilett would not even consider such a thing. I prayed with him. He was shaken, but not only by capture. Your faith and confidence have worked upon his mind and awakened a fear of God in his spirit."

"Did he receive the Lord's salvation?"

"I believe that he will."

"Where are they held?"

"In the north room of the guardhouse. But Tahn, Lord Trilett does not wish that you be troubled with this. I think you should leave it to him. He shall be fair."

"What of the others? Soldiers? And a woman?"

"The woman is wife of a wounded bandit. He fares better.

She seems very satisfied with the outcome of all of this. The soldiers are young. They were there at Lionell's hire. They say they did not ever wish to hurt you."

"It is likely true, Lucas. Men bound under orders—"

"Perhaps. They plead for clemency. Both of them."

"And the bandits?"

"Bert says he does not care. He will accept the judgment due him. The woman is the same. Her husband begs more piteously to be released. He is afraid of the manner in which example may be made. The other man is silent. I've not gotten a single word from him. Nor has anyone, so far as I know."

"What is his name?"

"Judson. Tahn, please. Lord Trilett would not like that I even discuss this with you."

Tahn shook his head. "I shall have to discuss it with him. Consider the prisoners."

"What do you mean?"

"The soldiers. Young men. Why shouldn't they surrender to us? They would not wish to die because of Lionell's folly. And they could hope for clemency rightly if they turned from their orders before the guilt became their own."

Lucas bowed his head. "Tahn . . ."

"And the wounded man and his wife—had they any option but surrender? They are weaker. What chance did they have of escape from us? They have nothing left but to hope for mercy or die."

"Perhaps you're right, Tahn, though I think of the woman that there was very little to her life of her own choice. But that does not absolve the others. Nor her husband."

Tahn nodded. "What of Bert and Judson, then? Why didn't they run or fight? They had no reason to expect anything but the wrath of death after what they've done. With nothing more to lose in fighting and perhaps their freedom to gain in trying to run, why would they surrender? Did they freely?"

"Yes. Much to our surprise."

"Then it is a different matter. Perhaps a reckoning God

275

has brought them to. They find themselves fit for death, or else God may have called them to life."

"Then you think the hand of God brought about their surrender?"

"Whatever their intent, is there another manner to explain it?"

Lucas gazed across the courtyard in solemn thought. "I shall take your words to Master Jarel. What is it you want, Tahn? For all of them?"

He shook his head. "You've told me Lord Trilett would not wish me to make such a judgment. Better that you take it to the priest, friend. You and he, prayerfully. God will show you."

Not long after, the Wittleys took their leave to return to their farm near Merinth. Tobas left the estate for his home in Onath, and the Toddins made ready for their travel back to Alastair.

"Amos Lowe asked Lucas to stay a few more days," Tiarra told her brother in the courtyard. "I'm glad. I think he's good for you when you're wounded."

"I would keep him about gladly. At any time. But I know he will go."

She nodded and sat beside him in one of the weathered courtyard chairs. "He'll wait until he knows you're feeling better. Can I help you? Amos said you should be lying down."

"Soon. Netta is parting with her friends, the Eadons. I would wait for her before I go back to our chambers."

Tiarra took his hand. "I'm glad they're all going. I'm sorry to say it, but it is so much more comfortable to think of this place filled only with the familiar again."

He smiled. "I thought you were taking a liking to all the noble company."

She made a face. "I did what I could to avoid them. I don't like to be stared at."

"Tiarra, they could little help that. You should know that you're pleasant to the eye."

"Not the way I heard it! And not because I tried to listen. Some of the ladies spoke of me as though I were not even there. One thought it a horror that I should wear my hair down and loose. And another pitied that I actually am tan, like a peasant farmer."

"I've known a farmer to live a happy life."

"I know. But most of the nobles behave themselves like pampered children. I've no use for any of them except those who rode to help in the search. And perhaps Netta's maids of honor. At least *they* didn't act as though I were some pathetic little beast."

He gave her a smile. "I daresay no one who saw you at the wedding could think of you in such terms, Tiarra. You will make a captivating bride one day."

But she grew quiet. He looked out across the yard to the group assembling near the gate. Netta would be returning to him soon. And then they could be alone again.

"Tahn," Tiarra spoke more softly, "something else troubles me more than any of that. The nobles speak in front of servants as though they were deaf, or too ignorant to notice. And something Kirka told me this morning worries me."

"What?"

"She heard the Lord Batrian and his squire. I thought that all of our concerns would surely be settled after the wedding. But they fear that you might still take to high thoughts and ambitions."

He sighed.

"I'm sorry, Tahn, to tell you this. But I worry for you. They still seem to think that you shall insist upon being called Trent and demand their recognition."

He met her dark and sober eyes squarely. "I would sooner pluck out my own tongue."

"Why did they all have to be invited, anyway? All of the fuss for people who are supposed to be friends and yet don't even trust us!"

"Lord Trilett was wise to host them here graciously. Bet-

277

ter than leaving them to fret in their houses if they were not invited. He knows he has kept far more friends than enemies this way."

"But what is the matter with them? Why are they bothered by you?"

Seeing her eyes so close to tears, he sat forward and put his good arm around her. "Some will still wonder why Lord Trilett would entrust his daughter to me. Others may resent me treading where I don't seem to belong."

"You belong where God has placed you! What business is it of theirs?"

"I suppose they think all things are their business. And I can endure it if I must. Once I heard Father Anolle say that a man's fruit will show itself. Do you know what that means?"

"I think so."

"Then we can have hope in that. Why should they fear me if I show them only peace? I will ask nothing of them. And no one need call me a nobleman."

Her eyes sparkled with a scarcely hidden fury. "Don't you realize how terribly unfair that is?"

"Tiarra—"

"You almost died for a greed that's not even yours! You offered your life for the woman you love! How can they be so blind? They *owe* you something! Don't you think?"

He shook his head quickly. "No, Tiarra."

"I thought it would be different with Lionell dead. But the distrust—the talk—it's hateful. Senseless. May God in heaven take your part!"

"*There* is our peace," he said quietly. "He is with us. Please don't be afraid."

"Perhaps you can tell it in me—I am more angry than anything else! If it were *me* and not Kirka to hear the words, I would not have stepped away silent."

"Give it time, sister. They will learn."

"I think they learn nothing that they don't choose for themselves for their own prideful comfort. I thank God for Triletts, or the whole land would be sunk into darkness with such men at the head."

"Tiarra—"

"I can't help it. They've stirred the fire in me. I would fight any among them for your sake. Ignorant, heartless fools to look down upon you!"

He squeezed her hand. "Will you go do something for me?"

"What?"

"Fetch Lorne."

She gave him a quizzical look. "Why?"

"To turn your eyes to their softness again. And if not to cool the fire in you, at least to turn the heart of it in a new direction."

She smiled. "You make a good son-in-law to Benn Trilett. He would favor your smooth words of peace."

Across the courtyard, Netta was strolling toward them, her hair up in ribbons and her flowing blue dress dancing about her ankles.

"I had a dream that you were in," Tiarra said then. "You and Netta both."

The mention made Tahn think of his own dream again. "I hope it was a happy one."

"You had a son. A beautiful baby boy."

He turned his head to look at her, and the promise of it surged warm inside him. "We would like that one day."

He saw that there was something else stirring in her eyes, whether about the dream or some other matter, he didn't know. She seemed to hesitate, and then with her eyes turning toward Netta, she let the matter go.

"Perhaps I *will* get Lorne. I think that you shall wish to be alone."

Tahn leaned to give his sister a kiss on the forehead. And then he rose to his feet to meet Netta's arms. Tiarra slipped away toward the west of the house before he could say anything more. Thoughts of a baby and Netta's closeness filled his mind.

The Toddins left that night, and the next day was spent in quiet rest and time with Netta. Tahn was beginning to feel stronger, but he still could not move freely without pain. Amos visited him to apply more liniment and balm. And this time again he kept Lucas with him as he worked.

"I'm not sure what to expect of you sometimes, Dorn," Amos admitted. "I can tell when the pain is looking at me, and then you almost seem to be gone."

"I'm sorry," Tahn answered him, but Amos only shook his head.

"I know it's not something you can help. I've known you less than two years, and been called to tend you more than to most men in ten. I pray this is the end of it. You've borne up well, all things considered, but your body has taken far more than it should."

"It was my mind you spoke of a moment ago. Or something beyond my mind."

Amos nodded. "That is not so easy to address. Have you nightmares?"

"No. Strange dreams now. Beautiful sometimes. But no more of the nightmares I once had."

"Thanks be to God," Lucas added.

Amos agreed. "Then already the Almighty must work his healing within."

Someone rapped on the door, and a plumpish servant girl entered. "Pardon, sirs. I have brought Master Dorn's riding cloak now washed and pressed. Forgive the interruption. I shall lay it—"

"Miss," Tahn said quickly, "I have no riding cloak."

She looked at him as though he must surely have only forgotten it. "It is the one you had with you in the wagon . . ."

Tahn scarcely remembered the wagon now, and nothing at all about a riding cloak. But when she held it up to him, he recognized what he had seen on the shoulders of Lionell Trent. "It isn't mine. Dispose of it."

"Sir, it is a fine piece—"

"I don't care what you do with it, then. Just get rid of it."

280

"Yes, sir." She turned to the door, clearly startled, perhaps even frightened at his abruptness.

And he quickly realized. "Miss—forgive me. That you washed it, thinking it mine, I thank you."

She bowed. "Yes, sir. You're very welcome."

"You needn't call me sir. Nor bow. Please."

She nodded, much more at ease, but still she did not linger.

"Are you all right?" Lucas asked.

"Yes. Of course."

Lucas's expression was kind. "Some things are troubling to think about. Lionell, for instance."

Amos continued his careful work, spreading his strongly scented liniment across Tahn's chest and sides. He felt each of the ribs carefully with his fingertips, and Tahn closed his eyes against the pain.

"You're not much more than bone and skin here," Amos told him. "Was a good time to marry. Wives tend to put the meat on a man, and you could use some." He handed his clay jar of balm to Lucas with an awkward smile and indicated Tahn's neck. "I would yet rather *you* do this."

But Tahn reached out his hand. "Just hold the jar for me. I'll do it myself."

Lucas nodded, removed the lid, and held the balm close. "You're looking much better. Whatever this stuff is has surely helped."

"Wood sage and myrrh in badger oil," Amos informed them.

Tahn carefully spread the oily balm. In a few minutes, Netta joined them with a selection of flowers from the garden to set on the window ledge. A gentle rain began to fall outside. And Tahn drifted into sleep.

That evening, Lord Trilett went to tell Tahn that he had reached a decision regarding the prisoners he held. With a

281

prayer and a hug for his daughter, he joined them in their private chamber.

"I am within rights under the circumstances to have each of them hanged," he explained. "And yet I cannot find it in me to do that, despite what was done. At Father Anolle's suggestion, I shall commit them unto the church for a period of indentured service to the monastery at Tamask or the St. Bartholomew hermitage."

The words seemed to please Tahn. "Thank you, sir. I trust that the father has found a reasonable solution."

"Had we a king, or a court of laws where an unbiased decision could be made, I might feel differently," Benn told him. "I might have ordered an execution even a year ago without such trouble, but you have worked in my conscience to consider many things, Tahn. I hope all can agree that this is reasonable, as you say. They're not being sent off to their ease."

"But perhaps they shall be where God's hand may touch them."

With a deep breath and considerable hesitation, Lord Trilett spoke on. "I need to discuss something else with you."

Tahn sighed. "Trents?"

"Yes, son. They shall have to decide what position they shall take concerning you."

"Why? Can't they simply go on with their lives, those of them who remain, and let me go on with mine?"

"It is not so simple for them. The council is now aware of your position."

But Tahn shook his head. "It's simple enough. You may tell the council that I do not deny my mother, but I make no claim on her kin. They may say whatever they wish of me so long as they leave us alone."

"But there are more things to consider," Lord Trilett tried to explain. "Acknowledging you could become a safety to the Trents, and receiving their recognition could become a blessing."

"That doesn't seem possible. They don't want me, my lord. Why should I push myself upon them?"

282

Lord Trilett stood to his feet, paced a bit, and might have pressed the matter further. But despite the day's rest, Tahn still looked so spent that he decided to wait. "Let us speak of this tomorrow. Pray about this, please. I want you to understand."

Tahn nodded wearily. "Forgive me, my lord, if I lack the ardor you might favor in a son-in-law."

"I find no fault with you, Tahn. I know you are hard put simply to regain your strength right now. Perhaps I urge the matter too soon for you."

Benn took his leave of them then, but though he went to his own chambers, he could not rest. He had not wanted to rush Tahn. He had thought there would be plenty of time as the Trents mourned Lionell, before they would have to face the results of all this. But the matter would not leave his mind. So finally in the night he rose from his bed and knelt in prayer:

Heavenly Father, I am troubled for Tahn. I have not even told him about the message I sent. Lord, forgive me for that. The decision may come sooner than I thought, and I have not gotten him sufficiently prepared.

34

That night Tahn dreamed of a baby in his arms. The church was completely full of nobles, townspeople, and friends. And it was Lucas in priestly robes who stood at the front of the church and received the child to be blessed. In front of the altar, down the aisle, and even outside, someone had strewn hundreds of golden flowers. And a bright-eyed minstrel with a feather in his cap sang a ballad about a Bannerwood king.

Birds woke Tahn again at the morning light, but almost immediately he knew there was something different in the air.

Netta lay beside him and lifted her head at the slightest movement of his arm. "Good morning, love."

"Do you think your father shall wish to speak to me already this morning?"

"Oh no. You know him. At the earliest, he shall wait till we've breakfasted."

Tahn slid away from her to the edge of the bed and rose to the window. The sun shone bright again, and a lone guardsman crossed the courtyard from the gate. "Have we reason to expect guests?"

Netta looked up at him, clearly puzzled. "No."

"There is news from the gate."

He turned to dress but fumbled with his clothes, his left hand still thickly bandaged. Netta rose from the bed to help him. "You needn't be in any hurry. You know my father has all set in order with the guards while you recover. There's little chance they shall need your attention."

"Maybe you're right," he said softly. "But this time I don't think so." He drew her close and kissed her. "Tell me. What is a Bannerwood?"

"It is a family line, Tahn," she answered with the surprise very clear in her voice. "Once, generations back, it was a noble house in its own right, but it no longer exists separately. The only remnants of Bannerwood are mixed among the other houses."

"Have there ever been Bannerwood kings?"

"Yes—the only kings our land has ever known have been Bannerwood." She slipped on her dressing gown, still looking at him in puzzlement. "The reason we have no king now is that it is difficult for the nobles to agree which strain of Bannerwood, through which house, should have that right."

With a heavy breath he started to turn away, but she turned his face back to her again. "If you didn't know, how can you know to ask?"

He didn't like the strange uncertainty in her eyes, or the tension rising steadily inside him. "A dream."

"Of a Bannerwood king?"

"A song." He nodded. "Of a Bannerwood king. Is your father Bannerwood? Is that why Lionell's father feared his power?"

"Yes. But there is Bannerwood in Trent too, which bred in them their violent ambition."

With a deep breath, he stepped back to the window.

"Tahn? Do you want to talk about this dream?"

He stared out at the court, trying to put his thoughts together and calm the unrest in his heart. *Lord! Why show me this? Is there something more I must know?*

A sudden rap at the door interrupted his silent prayer. Netta jumped. Lord Trilett's primary attendant opened the door just a crack. "Master Dorn, Lord Bennamin requests your presence with him in his meeting hall."

"Immediately?" Netta questioned.

"As soon as possible, my lady," the man replied.

"And what about me? Does he wish my presence as well?"

"He did not say about yourself, ma'am, only that the master shall be necessary."

"I'll dress immediately," Netta said as soon as the man was gone.

"If he required you," Tahn told her pointedly, "he would have said so."

"You don't want me with you?"

Tahn took her hand. "My lady, your presence shall always be a grace to me. But your father called for me alone. I'll not supersede his judgment."

He left her quickly, heart thundering, knowing that this day, somehow, whether for the better or not, his life would change. He made his way to the meeting chamber with his heart and his ribs aching. Was there trouble at the gate? A threat of untrusting nobles? What could so urgently cause this unprecedented early morning summons?

The chamber door opened quickly as he began to push upon it, and he found Jarel holding the gilded handle on the other side. Lord Trilett stood beside his oak desk, staring at the marble floor. He looked up as Tahn entered, and his eyes were deeply troubled. "Forgive me, Tahn. Despite the wedding and your injuries, I should have taken the time to explain things to you more fully."

"What things?"

He stepped nearer. "I sent a message to Trent the day you were back to us. I explained to them their position as it now stands and the options that should be open to them. I knew they would take me seriously. But I thought their consideration would take far more time. I don't know what they will say, but the matrons of Trent stand at our gate, and I have sent to usher them in."

"Matrons?"

"Principle women. The former baron's widow, who is Lionell's mother. And Danalia Trent, your grandfather's sister."

He felt suddenly weak. "Why would they come?"

"Perhaps I pushed them to it. Perhaps they fear me. But they asked leave to see you. And difficult as it may be, they are your blood. Forgive me, but I agreed."

"I told him," Jarel said fiercely. "I told him he must consult you."

Tahn made no reply to that. "They come with soldiers?"

"An escort of four, none of whom I shall allow within the gate. Please be seated, son. I've called for Lucas and Amos, if you wish them here. You have every right, considering all—"

"No," Tahn answered, his heart thundering crazily. "I'll not need the healer's nursing or Lucas's hand."

"Son—"

"They wish to meet me. You wish it so. Tell me where you'd have me, and I will obey you."

"Tahn." Lord Trilett stepped nearer and placed one hand on his shoulder. "I did not mean to thrust this upon you so sudden."

Tahn felt the churning fire alive in him, like Tiarra's fire, an explosive flame built of pain. He saw the apprehension in Benn's eyes, the kind concern edged with caution, and he tried to still the tumult inside him. He lifted his eyes and prayed again for peace.

"Please," Benn Trilett repeated. "Be seated, son." He indicated a well-cushioned divan beneath the Trilett crest. "I do not mind that they should know what their son has done to you, or that I treat you with the greatest respect."

"What do you want from them?" Tahn asked with a new suspicion. "Are things such that you can make demands?"

He shook his head. "Their decision is their own. And I know not all the matter. But I do want justice for you. I've wanted that all along." He glanced at his nephew. "Jarel and I will stay to receive their audience. But I'm glad you've not brought Netta, though they are women. I am not that much at ease with their visit."

Tahn sat as he was bidden, leaning back against the cushions in an effort to ease the throbbing pain in his midsection. Jarel passed another cushion to him, and he pressed it against his side.

Lord Trilett bowed his head and prayed. And then they could hear in the hallway the noise of their guests being ushered forward. The doors were soon thrust open, and two of Benn Trilett's hired men escorted to the chamber the Trent matrons. They were both gray and wrinkled and dressed in incredible finery. *Two weak old women,* Tahn thought, *trying to look like princesses.*

Each of the ladies gave Lord Trilett a respectful bow and then stood waiting. One turned her cold eyes upon Tahn, the other looked away toward Benn Trilett's tapestry.

Benn did not greet them with any customary cordiality nor show them a seat. "Speak freely," he told them. "Tell us what you have come to say."

One woman continued gazing off in silence, but the one who had stared at Tahn now spoke. "Your lordship, sir, the first thing we must express is our gratitude for the release of bodies to us. We understand that there is no provision that would have required it of you."

"It was my nephew's decision," Benn answered. "And the most charitable one."

The woman turned her head and bowed graciously in Jarel's direction. Her eyes filled with tears. "Your Lordship Trilett, you know it is a time of grieving."

"Yes, Anaya," Benn answered bluntly. "Your son's misguided zeal cost the lives of many good men and unspeakably endangered my daughter."

Shaken, the woman bowed again and then placed her hand at the back of a nearby chair to steady herself. For a moment, she could not seem to speak.

"His choice was his alone, Lordship; he did not seek our council. We would not have agreed—"

"I much appreciate your telling me that," Lord Trilett said more kindly. "Claim the chair if you wish it. Perhaps the journey has tired you."

"The anticipation of your response to us far more than the journey, Lord. You have not been the only man to inquire after our intentions. It has become very clear that we must accept a proper stand before the council in order to survive."

Tahn had listened quietly until hearing such words. "Who would threaten you?"

288

The woman, most surely Lionell's mother, turned her eyes his way. "Oh, there are more threats than with blood or sword. How painful to see our wealth and title, the very house of our fathers, simply torn away."

Tahn did not even try to answer her.

"How fares Lady Elane?" Lord Trilett asked abruptly.

That he should change the subject so drastically seemed strange indeed, until Tahn saw the uneasy reaction of both women. The one whom Lord Trilett had described as his grandfather's sister lowered herself to a chair, her cheeks flushed red. Lionell's mother stayed on her feet, but the muscles of her jaw worked and tightened.

"That is one part of the matter for which we have come," she said with an added strain to her voice. "We cannot withhold the announcement that Lady Elane's child has been born a healthy girl."

This time it was Jarel who sunk to a chair and stared at Tahn. But it seemed not news large enough for such a reaction. These were strangers, after all.

"Congratulations," Benn Trilett said immediately, but neither of the women greeted his gesture with anything resembling a smile.

"You know why we should come to tell you this news personally," Lionell's mother said gravely. "You've driven us to it."

"I did nothing but point out to you the way the matter shall rest with the council, which you yourself should know. You must vouchsafe the next baron, by agreement of your house."

"And we are subject to the judgment of the council upon the matter of legitimacy!" the woman wailed. "You know what you have done, Benn Trilett! You know you leave us no option! We have no man to meet your threatened challenge! You've stolen us!"

Tahn sat forward, not understanding her emotional words.

But Lord Trilett was calm, and perhaps more sharply

calculating than Tahn had ever seen him. "Then I am not the man you should be speaking to."

The grandfather's sister trembled. Lionell's mother was visibly angry. She stood in silence for a moment but then swallowed down hard and turned to Tahn again with her fiery eyes somehow afraid.

"Sir—Mr. Dorn, sir," she stammered. "I assume you understand the import to us that my son's babe was not born a boy."

The grandfather's sister rose to her feet again, approached the other woman, and took hold of her arm.

How many are the Trents now? Tahn wondered. *Are they all women that she should say they have no man? And what challenge?* He could not picture Lord Trilett, even in his anger over what happened, threatening these women. "Not fully," he answered, turning his glance for a moment toward Benn.

"I'm sorry," Lord Trilett told him. "This is what I meant to explain to you today."

Lionell's mother looked at Benn with uncertainty. "He is not himself behind your plot?"

Lord Trilett sighed. "No, Anaya. And it is more a disclosure of truth than any plot. You cannot deny."

With her eyes still fiery, still afraid, she turned to Tahn again and drew a steadying breath. "By royal decree, the baron must be descended from a baron unless sovereignly appointed. And if the condition is not met, the barony itself goes into the authority of the council."

She paused, looking for some reaction. He gave her none, though his gut tensed and his head was now pounding.

She went on slowly, as though the words were a heavy weight upon her tongue. "We have no more males qualifying in direct lineage. Only cousins and those with marital tie. But you . . ." Her voice quaked. "You are the son of the daughter of Klonten Trent, ninth baron of our line. You are the only blood grandson."

He shook his head. This was far too much to take in, and not at all what he wanted. "No."

Anaya Trent crossed her arms in sudden indignation. "Perhaps you don't understand what that means! By right of your mother's birth—as extraordinary and appalling as it seems—you are become the lord of all things Trent, master of a significant fortune. We have no choice. By necessity we must bestow upon you the title! You are the baron. And our . . . our head!"

For a long moment Tahn was quiet. No one else spoke. They only waited, eyes on him. But he shook his head again, addressing the woman carefully. "If you would not choose it, then it need not be so. I have no desire to be lord or master over anyone. I don't want your fortune. And I am sure you do not want nor need me as your head. Let us only agree to part in peace and go on with our lives."

But the words Tahn thought would relieve her only seemed to inflame her more.

"Do you toy with me by design?" she demanded. "Haven't you understood what I'm saying? We have no choice! It *must* be you! Or we stand at risk of losing all that we are accustomed to, our lands, our homes, everything. The council could reduce us to nothing. The House of Trent has nothing without a head."

He turned to Lord Trilett in shock. "The council of nobles—surely they'd not . . ."

"Tahn," Benn said slowly, "a long injustice has come to their attention. And the royal mandate will not be set aside. I should have explained everything as soon as I realized this could happen. But now nothing can change what is. I believe they *shall* confirm you to the title of baron, son, and I shall gladly support the move with all my ability. As Lady Trent has pointed out to you, there is no other true option left to us."

Tahn sat stone still, a tremble coursing inside him.

"You *are* Baron Trent," Lord Trilett said on, "by what remains of our law and tradition, whether or not you ever use the title or anything that comes with it."

35

A lion romped in the morning sun and rolled with joyous abandon in the field of flowers. Across its shoulders rested a mantle of scarlet, woven of leaves, its trefoil pattern repeated endlessly. And upon the lion's head there sat a wreath of golden flowers, gold as the sun, and as the border of Benn Trilett's Bannerwood tapestry.

But the dream fled from his mind as Tahn rolled upon his blanket, the voices of children mingling with a bird's song and stirring him awake. The little boy named Doogan plopped to the blanket beside him. "We had a messenger at the gate. Lord Trilett told me I could come and tell you that the matter is confirmed without dissension."

Tahn stared up at the bright clouds above him, his heart strangely peaceful with news he hadn't thought he'd be able to accept.

"What does that mean?" Doogan asked.

He glanced across the courtyard at Netta in a circle of children, and then at Tiarra along with Lorne picking berries with one of the servants. "I suppose it means that we are very rich."

Doogan scrunched his brow. "We're already rich."

Tahn smiled. "Yes. Indeed we are."

On his back on the blanket, he looked upward to the sky again. The clouds seemed to swirl and dance like live things. He thought of the many angels' wings in the heavenly sky he'd seen, or dreamed, or perhaps been visited by. *God of heaven, you are the one who gave me my life when all was lost. What would you have me do with this now?*

Doogan glanced up at the clouds, shook his head, and turned to Tahn again. "Do you think there are still boys stealing from the fruit vendor in Tamask like I used to do? I'd like to go back there someday. We've got an awful lot of food around here. We could bring them a feast!"

Tahn sat up, his eyes on the boy but far beyond him. "You're right."

"Does that mean you want to go too? Vari says you shouldn't ride again yet. What you did for the wedding was past sensible an' just about put you in the bed for days—"

"Vari said that?"

"Yes, but he was just worried for you. Everybody was. You feel better now, don't you?"

"Better."

"Well, if we're going to Tamask, I should tell Netta. Is she coming too? Will she like this? She's not too keen sometimes on you going anywhere."

Tahn looked her way again with a smile. "I think she'll not need to fear so greatly. But I never said we were going to Tamask."

"But you liked the idea! Of taking them a feast!"

"Indeed. And I thank you, Doogan, for letting the heart of God speak through you."

The boy looked confused. "What?"

"Help me up. Do you mind?"

Doogan took hold of Tahn's arm as he maneuvered his still-sore body upright. "Was Lord Trilett in his chamber, child?"

"No. In the blue parlor with Jarel. He said he'd have reckoning for you, whatever that means."

"Perhaps I should go and see."

———

The House of Trent owned four grand estate houses and vast holdings of land, including the entirety of Alastair. The treasury contained a sum so large that Tahn could not even understand its meaning.

"Your desire shall command it," Lord Trilett told him. "As you wish with the entire fortune."

Tahn sat in a chair and shook his head. "Then I'm bidden of God to a thousand tasks. Are there tenant farmers?"

"Many."

"They should own the ground they work."

Lord Trilett stood in silence for a moment and then smiled. "You shall give this people conscience, Tahn."

He bowed his head. "Then beyond the gift that Netta is to me, I learn to understand the reason I was spared alive. I want to finance a mission in each of the cities, like the one Lucas serves in Alastair. To give shelter to the street children. How many of the properties are now occupied by Lionell's relatives?"

"*Your* relatives, son. You shall have to come to terms with them. Or perhaps, better said, they with you."

Jarel looked up at them both with a smile.

"Their principle residence is the Alatrid, the oldest of the estate houses. Except for Lionell's mother and his wife who resided with him at his most favored mansion, which is the nearest to Alastair. But I was supposed to tell you—his wife seeks leave to return to her father's house."

"Seeks leave? Of me?"

"Yes, Tahn. Her child is a Trent. You have the right to command."

"But I'll not! She may go where she pleases. Are all the noble houses ruled by such stiff-necked absurdity? Why would I want to keep her from her kin?"

Jarel laughed. "Ah, you shall be a merry vexation! I can see it now."

Benn Trilett suppressed his smile. "It is customary for the head of the family to have the final voice in all significant decisions. You can well understand how the rigidity, or the absurdity, of that particular custom could vary widely depending on the disposition of the individual leaders."

Tahn shook his head. "Thank God for *your* common measure of sense."

Benn laid a genial hand on his shoulder. "I'll accept that as a gracious compliment."

———

Tahn decided to leave the estate house called Alatrid and its surrounding land in the hands of his Trent relatives and immediately give his choice of the other properties to Lucas to be used for benevolence. He set aside a generous fund for the families of the guardsmen who had died, and a separate amount for Jarith and Evan and their families. Lord Trilett helped him produce the written decree releasing all Trent land occupied and farmed by tenants into the hands of the families thereon. Then followed a similar decree releasing the homes of Alastair to their occupants.

He dismissed all Trent soldiers including those who served the family at Alatrid and began hiring new, accepting the former back to their places only after rigid examination. He gave significant gifts to the churches at Onath and Alastair, as well as the monastery at Tamask and St. Bartholomew's hermitage.

And he bought boots. The first he could ever remember that were not bestowed by Lord Trilett, issued by Samis, or stolen on the streets.

A ring for Netta. Three pairs of shoes for Tiarra, who had once so despised going barefoot.

"But enough frivolity," he told Lucas. "I can no more be too free with this money than I could with Benn Trilett's. It belongs to God. And I must use it wisely."

———

In a year was born a comely baby boy, and Benn Trilett was there to hold him and display his joy when Lucas, as a newly instated priest, offered a blessing. Fear of the Trent name faded as Tahn repeatedly shied from the recognition of nobles and the increasing acclaim of the common people. He never personally used the title of baron, or the name Trent instead of Dorn.

As the people began to call for a king again, the council of nobles traced with careful consideration the Bannerwood line, with an eye to a truly stable and unified governance. Tahn paid no attention to any of that business. His life was full. A precious wife, a beautiful son. The many adopted children. And the affairs of his house, the fortune he continued to use in honor of the Savior he served.

People spoke of him throughout Turis. People repeated again and again the tale of the tortured child, the enslaved killer, who had offered his life for love and become a benefactor to them all.

And the lion and the scarlet trefoil began to appear in the work of craftsmen and weavers, as well as in the songs of the minstrels who roamed about the land:

"The lion wears a mantle of scarlet, woven in trefoil leaf, for the dark-born knight and the lady have birthed the union of peace. Give us your clear-eyed baby, oh lion and trinity foil, for the noble threads of Bannerwood draw together in heart and in soul . . ."

L. A. Kelly is a busy Illinois writer who is active in the ministries of her church. She works at home and enjoys spending time with her husband and two beautiful children.

CAN TAHN UNRAVEL THE MYSTERY

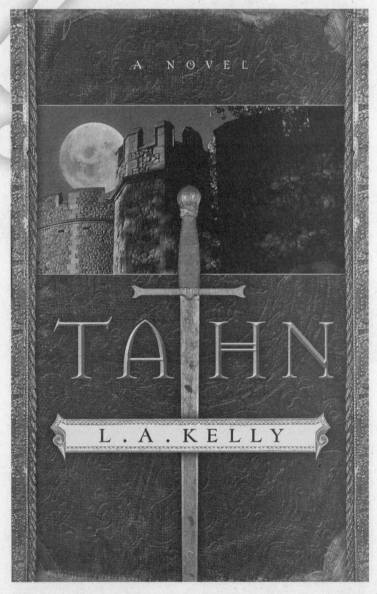

A NOVEL

TAHN

L.A. KELLY

Don't miss the beginning of

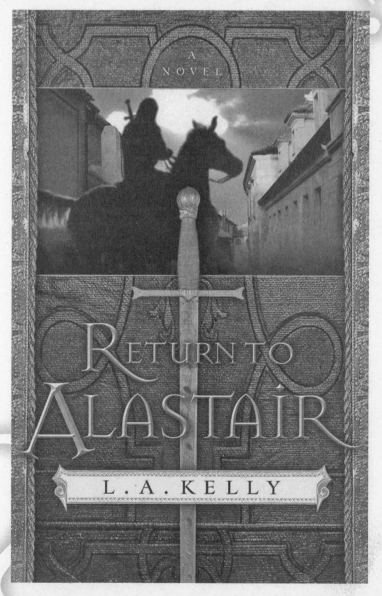